BY TERRY BROOKS

SHANNARA
First King of Shannara
The Sword of Shannara
The Elfstones of Shannara
The Wishsong of Shannara

THE HERITAGE OF SHANNARA
The Scions of Shannara
The Druid of Shannara
The Elf Queen of Shannara
The Talismans of Shannara

THE VOYAGE OF THE *JERLE SHANNARA*
Ilse Witch
Antrax
Morgawr

HIGH DRUID OF SHANNARA
Jarka Ruus
Tanequil
Straken

GENESIS OF SHANNARA
Armageddon's Children
The Elves of Cintra
The Gypsy Morph

The World of Shannara

THE MAGIC KINGDOM OF LANDOVER
Magic Kingdom for Sale—Sold!
The Black Unicorn
Wizard at Large
The Tangle Box
Witches' Brew

THE WORD AND THE VOID
Running with the Demon
A Knight of the Word
Angel Fire East

Sometimes the Magic Works: Lessons from a Writing Life

THE WORLD OF SHANNARA

THE WORLD OF SHANNARA

Terry Brooks
&
Teresa Patterson

Illustrated by
David Cherry and Rob Alexander
Maps by Ann Burgess and
James Clouse

BALLANTINE BOOKS • NEW YORK

To my children, Kira Shands and Kasi Cherry,
whose love is the magic in my life.
—David Cherry

To Terry Brooks, for taking me there in the
first place, and to David Cherry, for timely
introductions and advice.
—Rob Alexander

Copyright © 2001, 2009 by Bill Fawcett and Associates

All rights reserved.

Published in the United States by Del Rey, an imprint of The Random House Publishing Group, a division of Random House, Inc., New York.

DEL REY is a registered trademark and the Del Rey colophon is a trademark of Random House, Inc.

The first edition of this work was published by Del Rey, an imprint of The Random House Publishing Group, a division of Random House, Inc., New York, in 2001.

ISBN 978-0-345-48068-2

Printed in China

www.delreybooks.com

9 8 7 6 5 4 3 2 1

Second Edition

Contents

Foreword

Seven years ago, in response to repeated reader requests, Del Rey Books decided to compile and publish a companion book to the *Shannara* series. This volume would explore in detail the history of the world, provide detailed character studies with accompanying drawings, and offer in-depth examinations of creatures, places, talismans, and the like. It was a project that had been discussed many times over the years, but which had always been placed on the back burner. Finally, it was decided that it should go forward.

There were good reasons for this to happen, not the least of which was the aforementioned level of reader interest. The thing about writing fantasy is that creating imaginary worlds and characters fuels an interest in readers for more details, more explanation, and just plain *more*. While it would be a good thing if I could give them all this, the reality is that it takes all the energy I can muster just to do a book a year or maybe two once in a blue moon. Trying to fill in all those gaps between books or even to expand on the existing story arc tires me out just thinking about it. A companion book, I knew, might go a long way toward resolving the problem.

Besides, I believe that writers should listen to their readers. If readers want something badly enough, a writer has to consider giving it to them. I couldn't do that easily with the material that made up the primary stories because the ideas for those stories were generated and fueled by the things that interested me at the time. Once those times are gone by, it is hard to recapture them. But someone else could manage it, if there was someone out there with sufficient interest in and talent for doing so. Someone else could provide readers with the maps, drawings, prehistories, and all the rest that they were so anxious to have.

Couldn't they? Please?

Shelly Shapiro, Del Rey's editorial director, stepped in to spearhead the project from the publishing end. Shelly and I had worked together at Del Rey for the better part of twenty-five years, and I could trust her to do the job in a way that would satisfy everyone. Like myself, she grew up in the company under the whiplash—oops, excuse me, *guidance*—of Lester and Judy-Lynn del Rey. I was more than pleased to have her acting as editor for the project.

Bill Fawcett was chosen to be the book packager. I know, his job title sounds like something out of Hollywood, but what he does is find the right writer and the artist for the book and then act as liaison with the publisher and myself. He must also shepherd the project along so that it doesn't stall out or miss its deadlines. Bill has served in this capacity before, notably with companion volumes for Anne McCaffrey's *Pern* and Robert Jordan's *Wheel of Time* series. Bill is a sharp guy, and he knows what he is doing.

Teresa Patterson agreed to do the writing and David Cherry, the art. I hadn't met either before, but I knew of their work. Together with Bill, they made a pilgrimage to my Seattle home to spend a few days picking my brain about the world of *Shannara*. Because I possess a small and shallow brain, I wasn't much help. They would ask me questions about characters, places, creatures, and events, hoping for additional insights and direction. I would reply to these questions mostly with something along the line of, "What do *you* think?" I was telling them that this was going to be their baby, and I was counting on their creativity to carry the day.

To their credit, they didn't throw up their hands and decamp. I know now that they appreciated the artistic freedom. I was pretty sure Teresa and David knew the books better than I did—the same way all my readers seem to know them—so it seemed foolish not to let them use that knowledge. I've always believed that once I finish a book and turn it in for publication, it no longer belongs to me; it belongs to the readers. Teresa and David were smart and creative enough to figure out what was needed. The best thing I could do was to stay out of the way.

Now, these seven years later, we are offering an updated version with fresh material and a fresh perspective. In that time, I have written six new sequels to the original series and three books in a prequel that chronicles the events surrounding the Great Wars that ended the Old World and gave rise to what would become the new world of *Shannara*.

With Shelly busy on other projects, Betsy Mitchell has stepped in as editor, but Bill, Teresa, and David are back. As well, we have the very able and talented assistance of artist Rob Alexander to add to the mix. Every part of this new, expanded edition is infused with elements of their hard work and creative effort. As I said the last time out, whatever you like about this book, you can thank them for providing. I cannot imagine anyone doing it better.

All the best,
TERRY BROOKS
February 2008

Introduction:
The Lost Legacy

ince the near annihilation of the world during the Great Wars, a fragmented humanity has endured more than three thousand years of struggle in the attempt to rebuild civilization. The world today is far different from the Old World. It is a place where magic has been reborn, where legend and reality often merge, and where the balance between good and evil is dangerously precarious.

The Druids were formed to protect that balance and assist our crawl out of barbarism. They collected lost knowledge to protect it for future generations. In most cases, however, that information has been jealously guarded and dispersed to only a select few. Up until now, the diverse people of the Four Lands have known little about each other, and less of the history and complexity of the world at large.

In an attempt to redress that, I have opened a portion of the Druid Histories to the authors, that they might create the first comprehensive work of information for the common man. All the Races deserve to know their history and that of their neighbors. All the Races must know of the world if we are to have a chance to unite against the constantly growing threat of evil. The Druid credo is "Through knowledge, power." In this case, it may well be the power to prevent our world from sliding into darkness.

—*WALKER BOH, HIGH DRUID OF PARANOR*

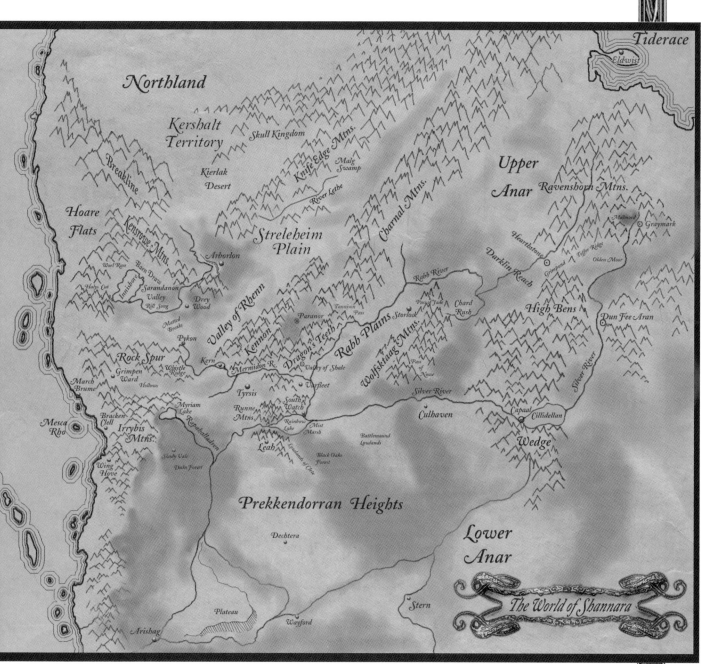

Tiderace

Eldwist

Northland

Kershalt
Territory

Skull Kingdom

Breakline

Knife Edge Mtns.

Kierlak
Desert

Malg
Swamp

Upper
Anar

Ravenshorn Mtns.

River Lethe

Charnal Mtns.

Hoare
Flats

Kensrowe Mtns.

Streleheim
Plain

Heartbcone

Malmord   Graymark

Darklin Reach

Grimpond

Taffer Ridge

Arborlon

Worl Run

Baen Draw

Halys Cut

Sarandanon
Valley

Innisbore

Drey
Wood

Rill Song

Rabb River

Olden Moor

Mattel
Breaks

Valley of Rhenn

Paranor

Tannison
Pass

Pauper Jake

Chard
Rush

High Bens

Dun Fee Aran

Pykon

Kennon

Dragon's Teeth

Storlock

Rock Spur

Kern

Mermidon R.

Valley of Shale

Rabb Plains

Wolfsktaag Mtns.

Pass
of
Noose

Silver River

Grimpen
Ward

Whistle
Ridge

Hollenn

Capaal

Cillidellan

March
Brume

Tyrsis

South
Watch

Varfleet

Silver River

Culhaven

Mesca
Rho

Bracken
Clell

Irrybis
Mtns.

Myriam
Lake

Runne
Mtns.

Rainbow
Lake

Mist
Marsh

Wedge

Rappahalladran

Leah

Battlemound
Lowlands

Shady Vale

Duln Forest

Black Oaks
Forest

Wing
Hove

Prekkendorran Heights

Lower
Anar

Dechtera

Stern

Plateau

Wayford

The World of Shannara

Arishag

Descent into Darkness: The Old World and the Great Wars

While Man worked all those years to discover the secrets of life, he never managed to escape his overpowering fascination with death. —Allanon, Druid

*I*magine a world of machines, filled with glass and metal buildings reaching for the sky. A world in which there was only one known Race—that of Man. His cities covered most of the face of the earth; his dominion reached beyond the world into the great void of space. This was the world before the Great Wars. Man ruled the earth with machines that he had built from science of a level that is unimaginable today. He had used those machines to probe and explore everything from the outer reaches of the sky to the inner reaches of the sea floor. He could travel across the width and breadth of the world in only hours, using machines to transport him faster than any airship can fly.

The people of the Old World knew nothing of magic. They did not need it. Theirs was the magic created of their technologies, magic they knew and could document to the innermost levels of creation. Every child was trained to understand the basic rules of science; every child knew how to use machines. There appeared to be no problem or challenge that could not be conquered using science and a little hard work. Their discoveries enabled them to conquer disease and repair impossibly damaging injuries. They all but eradicated

Eldwist

Far to the north where the Eastland ends, a tiny isthmus connects the land to a peninsula jutting into the Tiderace. On that peninsula stands a huge stone dome, the last remnant of an Old World city known as Eldwist. Before the age of the Federation and the coming of the Shadowen, Eldwist loomed above the waves of the Tiderace. For centuries, its towers and walkways were almost perfectly preserved in stone by a creature of Faerie, a last reminder of the shape and scope of Old World architecture. Those few hardy souls who dared journey to the Tiderace were greeted by buildings built so tall they seemed to threaten the sky. They stood in row upon row, like towering soldiers above a gridwork of perfectly straight streets. Tunnels built for underground carriages burrowed beneath the impossibly tall buildings. Huge open squares were filled with statuary and fountains frozen in stone.

The city was destroyed almost eighty years ago; the land was reclaimed by nature. All that remains is the fossilized dome that once stood at its center, the lone monument to all the thousands of souls who once lived, worked, and died there.

Eldwist, ruins of a city dating from the Old World before the Great Wars.

the normal process of aging, slowing it so that the average person lived 100 to 150 years or more. They were close to conquering death itself and might have eventually done so in a few more years if their civilization had survived.

Unfortunately, Man's fascination with the science of life was equaled by his involvement with that of destruction and death. Science itself is neither good nor bad and can be used for either purpose, but Man's need to be all-powerful, to control all aspects of giving and ending life, proved to be his undoing. Weapons of unimaginable potency were created, thousands of weapons that could wipe out a

city—or a world—with a single push of a button. The people of that time swore that such weapons were created only to prevent conflict and were never intended for use—but they were built nonetheless. The "enemy" might make deployment necessary.

For despite the fact that Man was the only known Race, he still managed to find differences between himself and his brothers and sisters—differences of the coloration of their skin, of the location of their homeland, of the nature of their politics—and Man distrusted anything that was different.

Conflicts were common during this

time, though they were usually confined to small areas and affected only small groups of people. But these conflicts began to occur more often, growing in

Creepers

The creatures known as creepers were originally created by Old World technology. A weapon of war that survived the holocaust, they were originally designed as armored carriages to carry men who controlled them and used them as protective armor as well as offensive weapons. Later versions no longer needed human contact to operate and could function while being directed from a distance. The final version, probably used in the Great Wars, was completely autonomous, able to carry out commands and complete missions of destruction with no human intervention at all. These machines were made in a wide variety of designs, large and small, and could travel over any surface, surmount almost any obstacle. Many of them contained weapons with awesome firepower and were made of materials impervious to most types of attack. Some of these original machines are believed to have survived the Great Wars and may still be in working order in remote parts of the world.

A creeper, used as a weapon in the Great Wars.

number and severity. The limited disputes ignited, inflaming basic hatreds. Disputes escalated into battles and began to spread and grow, becoming wars. Inexorably more and more countries were pulled into these wars. Like a fire started from a few embers in dry grass, it began to consume the world. Then one afternoon the flames reached flash point, and the doomsday weapons—never intended to be used—were unleashed on the world in a series of massive retaliatory strikes. Explosive devices of unimaginable power wiped out entire regions in great firestorms. Deadly engineered plagues killed the populations of entire cities, rotting them from the inside. All the advances of the science of killing were unleashed on the world. The last battle of the Great Wars lasted only a few moments, but the results were the eradication of thousands of years of advanced civilization and the extermination of most of the life on the planet.

As if the destructive vehemence of the weapons was not enough, the massive energy released during the final exchange triggered a cataclysm within the earth. The planet violently rebelled against such abuse and reacted with earthquakes and volcanoes, writhing as the pressures reshaped large areas of her surface. Mountain ranges fell and sea floors rose. Floods smashed down upon the coasts as glaciers melted, and cities sank into the sea. Infernos raged in the forests. The sky was black in mourning from the smoke and ash as the world cried out her pain.

Nothing should have survived, but somehow—by some miracle of the Word, perhaps—there were survivors. A few vestiges of humanity managed to live through the horror only to be faced with an all-but-uninhabitable world. For the next thousand years, these survivors of the holocaust struggled to endure its aftermath.

Many were irrevocably changed by the struggle. Some survivors lived by escaping into large underground caverns. They fed on the animals that lived underground, crawling and climbing through their harsh, dark environment. Over time, their bodies began to change, as survival favored shorter, stockier bodies, more powerful musculature, and eyes that could see well in the darkness of the dimly lit caves. By the time they emerged to live above ground, hundreds of years later, they had become very different from Men, a separate Race, and had evolved their own language and culture. They became known as Dwarves, after a mythical creature with similar attributes.

Many people did not manage to find underground shelter. Most died, but a few unusually strong individuals managed to survive the poisoned air and the mutated land. They escaped to the northern mountains, evolving into a fierce tribal culture of nomads. Only the largest and strongest were able to procreate. The few children who survived were forever marked by the poisons their parents had endured. After a thousand years, their offspring evolved into huge, muscular people with barklike skin, bearing almost no resemblance to their Old World ancestors. These people became known as Trolls.

Some people fled to the forests and hills, finding what shelter they could, but not enough to protect them entirely from the holocaust and its aftermath. Only those who were small, quick, and cunning survived. But they had only slight protection from the toxins. Their bodies were changed by it, until they too no longer appeared quite human. Their offspring, like those of the Trolls, carried the legacy of their exposure as well as their survival

Demonic Influences

The official causes of the Great Wars did not survive them, but there is now reason to suspect that there may have been demonic influences involved. Although Man did not believe in magic and certainly did not use it, magic, and the demons that have been a plague to the world since the time of Faerie, were always present. There is no question that the destruction of this otherwise powerful civilization would have been to the demons' advantage. This cannot be proven, but if true, it explains the sudden escalation of the global conflict from such innocuous beginnings.

traits. Some believe that their minds were damaged as well, though that has yet to be proven. They became known as the Gnomes.

A small number of the survivors were virtually untouched by the worst of the devastation, primarily by virtue of living in remote or protected areas. Lacking direct exposure to the damaging influences that created the Trolls and Gnomes or the conditions that caused the Dwarves to evolve, they emerged physically unchanged. Their civilization, however, was completely destroyed, and they also reverted to a life little above that of animals. They were the Race of Man.

When Man emerged from barbarism to begin to rebuild a semblance of civilization, he discovered four other Races, and named them to fit their attributes: Dwarves, Trolls, Gnomes, and Elves. Though the Elves were not descended from Man, they emerged to rejoin the survivors and were accepted among them. The differences that had kept them apart from Man throughout most of his history were no longer as apparent with the mutations of the new Races. They were accepted as also having descended from

Man, and for many years they kept the facts of their true heritage a secret from the other Races.

With the death of the Old World, something even older than Man was reborn into the new world: magic, all but dormant since the age of Faerie. Even Druid scholars are unsure whether the cataclysm triggered the reawakening of magic or whether it was always there but became more potent once the technological world was gone. Perhaps the combination of the man-made poisons and the latent magic was responsible for the powerful arcane forces that arose within the earth. The only certainty is that magic appeared within the land as a force that could be tapped for both good and evil. Creatures born of magic populated the remote areas of the lands. Technology and physical science had been all but wiped from the world, but magic promised the same Pandora's box and could save or seduce and destroy just as certainly as the weapons of science had done in the last age. In many ways, the Races would face the same deadly choices that had undone their ancestors, only this time they could not hope to understand the power inherent in the forces they faced within the magic.

Paranor:
The Druid's Keep

Within the walls we are a community, a family . . . engaged in a single course of action—to gain knowledge of our world and its workings. —Athabasca, High Druid of Paranor

Throughout the ages, a legend has survived among bards and story-tellers, a story of a massive magical citadel built as a crown atop a great volcanic cliff within the heart of the Four Lands. According to the tales, this keep housed the ancient magicians known as Druids. From within its impregnable walls, they controlled all learning and all magic. The castle was called Paranor, and it was said that at the height of the Druids' power it was the central repository of knowledge within the Four Lands. But for three hundred years those few intrepid souls who journeyed to the site of the legendary keep, intent on proving the tales, found only a spruce forest, an empty stone bluff, and a few stone blocks remaining of what might have been outbuildings but could just as easily have been the remains of a herder's holding. The legends were accepted as fanciful stories and the Druids themselves as little more.

Then, sometime in the last century, Paranor reappeared. The Rovers who first spotted its return found it standing in silence atop its cliff base, as if it had never been gone. It was an unreachable enigma, closed off to outsiders. Those who ventured too close told of being stalked by a ghost beast, a spectral moor cat that appeared long enough to warn off trespassers.

For eighty years after its discovery, the Druid's Keep stood solid but out of reach, a stone specter. Then, within the last few years, something changed, and the keep was opened to approved visitors. Some of its vast libraries and artifacts were made available to scholars. With this new knowl-

edge, the legends were given substance, and the truth of Paranor and its mysterious designers was at last revealed.

To understand the Druid's Keep, it is first necessary to understand the history of the Druids themselves. After the Great Wars, civilization no longer existed. The remnants of Men lived as animals for almost two thousand years. Books and advanced knowledge were sacrificed to

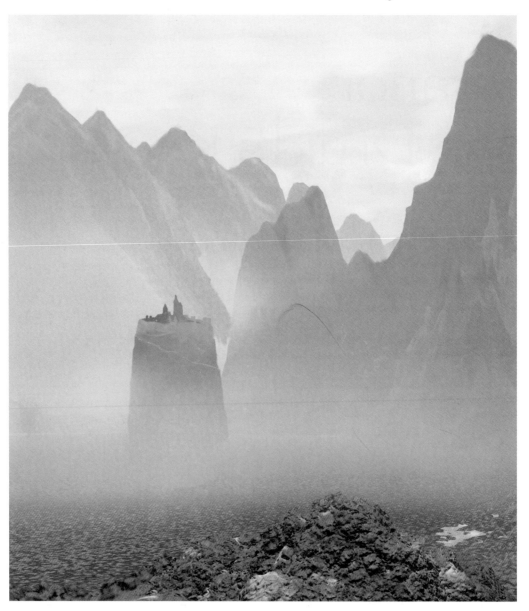

Paranor, fortress of the Druids.

Galaphile,
FIRST HIGH DRUID,
FATHER OF THE DRUID COUNCIL

Built to be both a revered cultural center and an impregnable fortress, Paranor was the result of the work of craftsmen and scholars from all the Races. Elves, Gnomes, Trolls, and Men all had a part in her building. But she was the inspiration of one man, a brilliant Elven philosopher and historian known only as Galaphile.

The actual dates and circumstances of Galaphile's birth have been lost to history, but it is almost certain that he discovered or was entrusted with knowledge from the Old World at an early age. What is known is that Galaphile saw the emerging Races struggling toward a semblance of civilization, only to lose that struggle as they began to focus more on conflict with each other than on growth or progress. He realized that the bits and pieces of knowledge that had survived the wars were the key to regaining any semblance of a civilized society, and that those fragments of information were at risk of being completely lost if the barbarism continued among the Races. His solution was to collect the wisest men and women from all the Races into one place where they could gather and protect the remains of the knowledge of the past while seeking solutions for the future. In honor of an Old World term for learned men, he named these men and women Druids. Their council became known as the Druid Council, and Galaphile was named as the first High Druid.

Galaphile, Father of the Druids.

the more immediate needs of survival. What little of the Old World that had not been destroyed by the wars or the cataclysms that followed gradually succumbed to ignorance and neglect. Only a few survivors recognized the need for safeguarding knowledge in hopes of rebuilding some of what had been lost. These few were also mindful of the need to keep such knowledge from any who might be drawn to re-create the mistakes that had led to the catastrophe. They safeguarded the knowledge, often with their lives, and secretly passed it on to their descendants in what became a family tradition.

The priceless information was sometimes written in ancient books or fragments of text, but more often, to keep it from the wrong hands, it was passed via a verbal tradition, subject to the gradual discrepancies of memory. At this time, there was no central place where the knowledge could be collected. Most toiled in their sacred task completely unaware of others who were doing the same. Some small, isolated groups attempted to gather their fragmentary knowledge and even to begin to write it down, but the growing distrust between the Races made even such small attempts at consolidation impossible.

Many small libraries full of priceless knowledge were painstakingly collected only to be lost to a raid or burned during battle. By the time the Elf Galaphile began collecting his own library, untold thousands of artifacts from the Old World had been irredeemably lost.

Galaphile realized that only a concerted effort from all the Races could save what remained. He dreamed of a place where those who were entrusted with the legacy of the past could share their burden or work to further their knowledge. He set about creating a council that would be focused on gathering and protecting the relics of the past while working for the betterment of all the Races. He sent a summons out to all the lands and was gratified to find that many answered. The best and brightest of all the Races were willing to join with him to form a council that would promise a path out of the stifling darkness of ignorance and hate that was threatening to suffocate the world.

But Galaphile needed more than a council; he needed a place to house them while they worked. And that house would have to provide protection for the priceless artifacts and defense of the people who lived and worked there. He needed a place that would be impregnable to attack, since most in the lands did not share a dream of uniting the Races. It also had to be a structure that would create awe among any who looked upon it. It had to stand alone as an example of the grandeur that the combined talents of the Races could achieve.

Galaphile gathered his followers, the first Council of Druids, in the caldera of a dormant volcano near the Kennon Pass. Within the outer caldera was a large central cone forming a cliff of volcanic rock and obsidian that rose above the first. This was to be the site for the keep he would

call Paranor. There are no clear records to tell how long Galaphile searched for the site for his keep. Some writings suggest that he may have found the site as a boy, and that it was the image of the massive up-thrusting stone standing defiant above the forest floor that helped him to conceive the idea for his council.

However he discovered it, the choice was carefully made. The large outer calderas formed a gentle crater, probably created during an earlier eruption around the time of the Great Wars, possibly even caused by the pressures of that cataclysm. The main vent had obviously remained active, building a cone of magma and ash in the center of the larger outer crater. That younger cone had also erupted at some point in its past, as the cone was topped by a smaller caldera, measuring some three hundred feet across. The volcano's upthrust stone heart created a naturally impregnable base, while the caldera at its top was ample enough to hold the main fortress and all its outbuildings as well as a defensive wall. There were three fissures opening to the surface; one was apparently inactive, but the other was an active vent reaching to the magma far below that allowed a method for heating the building. A natural artesian spring, forced up through a third lava vent, ensured an uninterrupted supply of fresh water. In addition, natural lava flumes within the mountain, created when venting lava escaped during a partial eruption, left a maze of easily traveled natural passages. This allowed several levels to be built below ground with relatively easy access as well as providing for a method for venting lava if the volcano became active once again.

Those first Druids and the assembled craftsmen must have felt daunted looking upon the smooth stone of the volcanic

The Druid's Well

Galaphile may have had more than natural defense in mind when he chose the Paranor Mountain for the home of his new council. At one point, there are indications that he banned all the workers from the mountain and sequestered himself with his most senior Druids for a week. When the workers returned, the mysterious fissure known as the Druid's Well and the tower that covers it were complete. The actual contents of the Druid's Well have remained a secret known only to the Druids themselves, though there is no doubt that magic of some type lurks there. Some say it is something that has been there since the time of Faerie, one of the few doorways that connects the worlds of life and afterlife. Some say it is a shaft that channels magic from realms no living soul has ever visited, containing power that no creature would dare to challenge—perhaps even a channel to the dead.

Whatever the source, its power is immense, as it is undoubtedly this magic that allowed the entire fortress to vanish from the world for so many years. Within those parts of the Druid records that have come to light, it is clear that only a few of those within the Druid order knew anything of the nature of the well. Whether intended for defense or to power more arcane studies, the magic within the well served to save the keep on at least one occasion, when it was used to destroy dark forces that had infiltrated Paranor during the time of the Druid Allanon. It apparently cannot be completely controlled, however, as it did not protect the keep from falling to the renegade Druid Brona at the outset of the Second War of the Races.

The well itself appears to be a bottomless shaft cut or burned through the heart of the mountain. Its depths are cloaked in impenetrable blackness. The tower built above it rises several hundred feet above the ground level to become the highest point in the keep and is constructed of large blocks of masonry six to eight feet thick. The stairway within ascends to the sanctuary, a small round room at the top protected by various traps. This chamber probably served the builders as a retreat, or lab, but it has remained empty for many centuries.

Those who have been to the Druid's Well and survived to tell of it report that the darkness below seems to move. Some report hearing a sound like the scrape of scales on stone; others have heard harsh, unintelligible voices. There are tales that tell of how it was used over the years and of the terrible things it has swallowed. One recently discovered manuscript believed to have been penned by the Druid Bremen claims that the well was used to contain all the Druids' arcane discards:. "...Magic and science, the living and the dead, mortal and immortal have gone into its depths."

All who have walked within Paranor agree that the keep is alive. If so, its soul is deep within the Druid's Well.

cone rising over a hundred feet above their heads. It would make a fabulous fortress, but it would also be the greatest engineering challenge since before the fall of the world. The few surviving records are in conflict about how many years it actually took to build Paranor. But they agree on the fact that it took the combined army of the council's best masons, carpenters, architects, sappers, and craftsmen at least ten years to build the main body of the keep. This accomplishment is all the more amazing when it is realized that they first had to rediscover or invent the skills and sciences needed to complete the work.

During the construction, Galaphile and

Elit Druin

The crest of the Druids, used to represent their order and all they stood for, was the image of a hand holding forth the torch of knowledge. Their credo was "Through knowledge, power" ("elit druin" in the Elven tongue). It also translates as "Through truth, power." Early in the first days of the Druid Council, Galaphile was gifted with a medallion molded in the form of the hand and torch to wear as a badge of office. It was called the Elit Druin, possibly in homage to his Elven heritage and the fact that the Elves were the dominant Race involved with the creation of the Druids.

The Elit Druin was forged of gold strengthened with some small amount of alloys and laced with silver trappings. According to legend, it was imbued with magic during its forging. It was passed down from each High Druid to his successor until the fall of Paranor during Athabasca's tenure as High Druid. The outcast Druid Bremen managed to rescue the medallion before it could be captured. He used it to forge the legendary Sword of Shannara. The hand and torch can still be seen on the pommel of the sword.

When the second Druid Council returned to Paranor, a new medallion of office was made in the hope that Allanon, who had re-formed the order, would accept it. He never did. The new medallion never had the beauty or the magical properties of the original. Ironically, the original medallion did eventually return to Paranor. As part of the Sword of Shannara, it was on display in the Vault Room for many years.

"Through truth, power": The Elit Druin medallion, a magic talisman worn by the High Druid as the symbol of Druid power.

the rest of the Druid Council lived in a makeshift village near the site until the actual living quarters were complete. It was during this time that the work of compiling the Druid Histories was begun. As soon as the living quarters of the central keep were livable, Galaphile moved the council and its retainers into the greater safety of the protected site. Paranor officially opened its doors to the world almost exactly one thousand years after the Great Wars had ended. With pennants from the Races who had shared in its construction flying from its glowing white battlements, and the banner of the hand and torch, symbol of the Druid Council, flying from the top of the Druid's Tower, the new fortress greeted those who made the journey through the Kennon Pass with the promise of an age of enlightenment.

At first, it appeared the promise would be fulfilled. Paranor became the center of knowledge and learning for the world. The people looked to the Druids for guidance. The success of the council helped the emergent world gain confidence in its own abilities. The Druids were a very powerful force—probably the most powerful single force in the world at that time. Their goal, which was to re-create the best of the Old World while avoiding their ancestors' mistakes, appeared to be a certain achievement. But the sciences they sought to master eluded them. Too often crucial keys to particular disciplines were missing. Or the information conflicted, and the Druids lacked the necessary experience to re-create what had been lost. Some within the walls began to look to other paths to achieve their goals. Many of them blamed the failure of the old sciences for the destruction of the world. They turned to the mystic arts for the power that had been denied them through the study of hard science.

These rebels believed they were destined to shape the future of the world. Among them were some of the most brilliant of the Druid minds. For many years, they worked within Paranor's walls, possibly in secret. Their work eventually caused a schism in the ranks of the Druid Council. The resulting conflict between those who sought answers in science and those who sought arcane solutions ended in a break in the council. The mystics were forced to leave Paranor.

For 150 years, the Druid Council successfully provided guidance for the Races. Then a small sector of the Race of Man revolted against the teachings of the council. In an impossibly short time, they amassed a highly trained army and set forth to subjugate the rest of Man, and from there, the other Races. The revolt grew into full-scale war before it was crushed by the combined might of the Druids, Elves, Trolls, and Gnomes. During the war, Paranor served as the strategic

Druid Guard

The building of Paranor was a time of great discovery and great risk, for until the fortress was finished, the council and all it stood to achieve were vulnerable to attack. A multinational force was created to protect against outside threats. These became known as the Druid Guard. When Paranor was completed, the members of this elite unit continued their service as the guardians of the keep and the fighting force of Paranor. Their gray uniforms, with the distinctive red torch emblem embroidered on the left breast, became synonymous with the power of the Druids in the age before the Second War of the Races. Their prestige and power failed along with that of the Druids after the partitioning of the Four Lands, and they ceased to exist altogether after the fall of Paranor during the Second War of the Races. The last Captain of the Guard was the Elf Caerid Lock, who served for more than fifteen years. One legend tells that Caerid was given advance knowledge of the coming attack so that he could escape, but he chose to stand and fight with his men even though he knew it was hopeless. Such courage and dedication were the hallmark of the Guard.

A member of the Druid Guard, the elite fighting force of Paranor.

and political seat of the alliance. The Druids provided the tactical leadership from Paranor's walls, unaware that it was one of their own who was ultimately responsible for the revolt. The mastermind of the war, known only as Brona (which means "master" in the archaic Gnome tongue), was believed at the time to have been a mythic figurehead. It is now known that he was very real and was the leader of the exiled Druids.

After the war, in an attempt to prevent another conflict between the Races, the Druids and their allies partitioned the known world into four lands, one for each of the Races, with Paranor and the Druids at its crux. It was believed that such extreme segregation would prevent any one Race from ever trying to control the others. Paranor's central location put the Druids in a geographical position that mirrored their political supremacy. Because of the damage done by magic during the war, the Druids all but outlawed the study of the arcane arts. Science and philosophy, they insisted, were the only true paths to the future.

For the next three hundred years, the Four Lands existed in peace. Lacking an exterior threat, the Druids turned their attention inward, abandoning their worldly role as teachers and benefactors in favor of the more secular pursuits of pure research and meditation. Paranor's massive parapets, designed to repel invaders, served instead to keep the Druids isolated from the lands they had originally sworn to serve.

That isolation proved to be their downfall. Three hundred and fifty years after the First War of the Races, an army of Trolls came down out of the Northland intent upon taking the Druid's Keep. The Druids were totally unprepared for an attack. Despite the surprise, the keep would probably have withstood even a prolonged siege if not for the fact that several within the Druid order had been suborned. Betrayed from within, Paranor fell to the Northland army of the Warlock Lord in a matter of hours. A handful of Druids managed to escape before the attack to join with the outcast mystic Bremen, but most did not. The majority of the order were either buried alive within the lower levels of the keep or transformed into creatures of dark magic in service to the Warlock Lord. It is said the souls of the ones who died now reside within the Druid's Well. The fall of Paranor heralded the beginning of the Second War of the Races.

Though the fortress would have made an impregnable base for the Warlock Lord, he abandoned it and took his Skull Bearers and his armies north, leaving the Druid's Keep empty for the rest of the war. There are some indications that Brona feared the latent magic of the keep itself.

At the conclusion of the war, Paranor once again became home to the Druids. The Druid Bremen and his heir, Allanon, held residence there for a time. Then, three years after the end of the war, Paranor disappeared. There was no battle, no victorious army. The entire keep just vanished. But like a ghost determined to haunt the world of the living, it was seen to reappear at unusual intervals—sometimes at darkest night, sometimes at brightest noon. It is probable that Druid magic, linked to the power of the Druid's Well, was responsible for this and subsequent disappearances.

After a mysterious ghostly existence lasting some sixty years, Paranor returned to the land of mortals. It is assumed that Allanon, the only surviving Druid, was responsible for its return. The Druid order was re-formed, though with far fewer members than its previous incarnation. For the next five hundred years the raw

The Sword of Shannara, on display in the Vault Room at Paranor

beginnings of a second Druid Council and a cadre of guards lived within Paranor's walls. There is no record of whether or not the Druid Allanon lived at Paranor during these years, though it is likely that he was in residence at least part of the time. Very little is known about this second council of Druids. Their primary purpose seems to have been to hold Paranor ready for an unnamed future conflict. Some surviving records indicate that Allanon and the other Druids knew of and expected the return of the Warlock Lord.

A few years after King Jerle Shannara's death, his heir brought the legendary Sword of Shannara to the fortress for safekeeping, probably at Allanon's request. The large room known as the Vault Room, off the Great Hall, was remodeled at this time to hold the sword in state in a large square block of mirror-finished Tre-Stone.

The sword remained there for almost five hundred years, until a division of Gnome Hunters, under the command of the Warlock Lord, took Paranor and captured the sword. For the second time in its history, the walls of the Druid's Keep were witness to the massacre of all its defenders and residents. There was some internal damage to the keep, especially in the furnace room, but the doors and gates were untouched, leaving historians to believe that, like the previous fall, the takeover was engineered with help from the inside.

Paranor was not recovered until the Warlock Lord was defeated. Again it was repopulated with a tiny group of guardians, though none of these residents, save Allanon himself, dared call themselves Druids. The keep did not see action again until almost sixty years later, when the Mord Wraiths took Paranor in an attempt to capture the Druid Histories hidden there. For the third time, all defenders within the walls were executed. For the second time, the High Druid Allanon, only remaining survivor of the order, had to accept the loss of the Druid's Keep and the deaths of those he had set to watch it.

In a bold stroke, undoubtedly knowing that Paranor could not be retaken by conventional means, Allanon decided to allow the keep to defend itself. The surviving fragments of Brin Ohmsford's diary record that Allanon unleashed Paranor's own magic, the spirit within the Druid's Well, much as Bremen had done before. This defense, though an integral part of the castle since its creation, had never been used. While it would destroy any who were caught inside the walls, it also effectively eliminated the objective by removing Paranor itself. "This marks the end of all that has been. The age closes, and Paranor must pass from the land," Brin's diary quotes Allanon. "In my lifetime and yours—in the lifetime of your children and perhaps your children's children—no man shall set foot within the walls of the Druid's Keep after this night." Allanon himself, last of his order, died only a short time later.

True to the prophecy, Paranor and its Druid masters faded from the world of men and into the mists of legend for over three centuries, returning only with the rebirth of the Druids through the man known as Walker Boh, now known as the heir to Allanon's legacy.

Within the Walls:
A TOUR OF PARANOR

When Paranor was new, the Druid Guard warded the surrounding spruce forest. In the time of the Warlock Lord, huge wolves roamed the paths. In later years, impervious walls of thorns and deep thickets of brambles replaced the wolves. Today the ancient trees of the forest are the only surviving witnesses to Paranor's many trials. They stand as towering sentinels, giving mute support to the castle rising above them in broken splendor.

The rutted, overgrown paths leading to the four gates of the keep show the wear of several hundred years of use, and several hundred more of neglect. All that remains of the ramped drawbridge at the south entrance are a few rotted timbers lying in the bottom of the ravine. The gates themselves, stone portals sealed by massive wooden and iron doors, bear no marks to show the battles fought within, though the windows in the towers above seem to stare out across the land like

blinded eyes, bearing silent testimony to all those who died within the cold stone walls. Of the hidden entrances known to exist within the cliff's face, there is no sign; they are as enigmatic and mysterious as the men who built them.

Inside the curtain wall, the ravages of past battles have left large portions of the keep in ruin. The barracks and other outbuildings are stone skeletons, their roofs and much of their wood interiors burned away. Throughout the large courtyard complex and in many portions of the inner keep, blackened and cracked slabs of masonry and melted flagstones mark the locations of heated battles and, often, deaths. In most cases, each damaged area

Symbol	Meaning
●●●●	Fence
[●●●]	Portcullis
→	Up from level
⇒	Down from level
▭▭	Window
▭▭▭	Crenalation

Paranor

Road built up to meet gate
North Gate
Smooth volcanic rock
Labs
Chickens & doves
Slopes
Guard barracks 1 level under, 3 levels above
Well House
Labs
Barn (Hay in loft)
Pen
Tunnel
Tower workshops
Corral
Stalls for 96 horses w/grooms quarters, hay and grain storage above
30' wide 40' long
Barn (Hay in loft)
Grainery
3 stories ↑
1 story ⇓
West Gate
10' hill on this side
Druid's Tower
Slopes
Quarters for
Support People
East Gate
Artesian fed water fall
Meditation Garden
Apartments
Class
Fire pit
Fire pit metal catwalk with periodic stairs or rung ladders to access equipment
Class
Assembly
Class Main Hall
Rooms
Rooms
Guard barracks 80' X 120'
3 stories ↑
1 story ⇓
3rd floor connects to hall in wall
Ground floor shown. Hall is on 2nd floor
Great Hall
Class Rooms
Garden of Beauty
Druid quarters
Druid quarters
Druid Well
Ground floor shown. Assembly & Main Hall on 2nd floor
Falcon Cote
Stables for 60 horses
Healing herb garden
Towers at corners 40' wide X 40' tall
Rocky incline
House of Healing 2 stories ↑
1 story ⇓
18' area with 6' walls
Glass Pots
Hayloft over stables 84' X 120'
Horse Corral
Each tower interlocks with wall
Forge
South Gate
Guards
Guards
Stair grade 2 wide X 1 tall
Steep, ravine-like Crevass 12' X 20' deep here
Drawbridge catch
Curtain wall 20' thick, 20' high 1st & 2nd floor then has 6' walls with 8' halls between
20' X 30' Drawbridge
Road

Secret Passages

Outside the grand rooms of Paranor's public areas lies an all but unknown maze of halls and tunnels—the secret passages of the Druid's Keep. Some are well documented, such as the narrow corridors that honeycomb the upper levels. Built into the walls, they were designed to allow servants unobtrusive access to those they served, or to hide the presence of secret visitors. Other passages, such as those within the outer wall, were designed for defense. Hidden doors, fifty yards apart, were built into alcoves along the curtain wall. These doors are all but invisible from the outside, but easily seen on the inside. During the years of the Council, these doors were always guarded at night.

Below ground is a web of passages for which there exists no complete map. Most of these tunnels were unknown even to the majority of the Druids. They were often built along existing lava flumes—tunnels cut through the softer portions of the mountain by escaping molten rock. The lava created smooth-sided, winding tunnels, some of which were large enough for an armed man, or even an entire wagon. By using these natural formations the builders had only to cut stairs and corridors into any flumes that traveled in the right direction. The result is a maze of tunnels winding throughout the mountain. Some provide secret access to the outside, with their outer portals cleverly concealed and guarded by hidden doors. In most cases, they are concealed by magic as well.

The largest of the flumes is not a passage meant for people, but for molten rock. Cut through the mountain from the main vent shaft to the outer edges of the cliff, it was once a lava flume opened during an ancient eruption long before Paranor was built. When the keep was built, workers cleared all but the outer end of this flume to allow a passage for pressurized lava. In the event of an eruption, the magma from the vent will force its way through the existing flume to the outside rather than pushing upwards to destroy the keep above. The outer end remains sealed by rock to prevent any use of the passage by invaders, but any lava flow will easily dislodge the rock.

Paranor Cross Section

Lava vents were used as the basis for many secret passages beneath the Druid's Keep.

Paranor Level 1

Paranor Level 2

is the only monument to the defenders who tried, and failed, to repel demonic invaders.

Within the keep, the massive double doors leading to the Assembly are little but twisted metal hinges and splinters of broken wood, shattered during the battle with the Warlock Lord, but the great room beyond still retains hints of its former glory. Most of the tapestries that once hung here are gone—burned away or rotted—but the great arched ceiling still stands proud above the scarred marble floor. Some of the ancient paintings still hang high on the walls, their forgotten subjects looking down upon the few remaining pieces of armor and statuary within the niches along the length of the

room. It is still possible to imagine this great meeting place filled with scores of Druids debating the knowledge of the known world.

Across the keep, the wooden walls of the Great Hall are also damaged, though most of the scars are cuts by edged weapons rather than the more destructive fires. Despite the damage, the wood still gleams through the dust from centuries of careful polishing. Paintings line the walls, though most are torn or slashed. Faded places on the wood mark where still others once hung. A few priceless pieces of statuary rest upon lavish mosaic pedestals. Larger statues exquisitely sculpted of iron and stone stand a silent vigil next to carved wooden doors along the hall. These

Druid Histories

The library at Paranor contained the few books found since the destruction of the Old World as well as many books compiled from information and records the Druid Council had written down over the years, but its most valuable collection was the priceless Druid Histories, the chronicles of and by the Druids themselves. These hundreds of huge volumes, bound in burnished leather and etched with elaborately gilded script, contained the results of the council's efforts to recover lost knowledge of both science and magic, the details of the Druids' attempts at uncovering the secrets of the Old World's greatest advancements, and considerations of all possibilities, however remote, concerning devices and formulas, talismans and conjuring, reasoning and deductions that might one day find understanding. Some of the knowledge within the pages of the Histories dated from the time of Faerie. These books, and the knowledge they contained, were the true power of the Druid Council, both the by-product of their existence and the reason for it.

In order to protect this, the treasure of Paranor, from misuse, the Histories were stored in a secret room behind a locking shelf in the main library. Such precautions would have been enough to stop an ordinary man, but not another Druid or a creature of magic. Shortly before the fall of Paranor during the Second War of the Races, the last Druid librarian, Kahle Rese, resorted to magic to protect the Histories. Though magic and the study of mystic arts was forbidden in the council at that time, he had been given a magic dust by the outcast mystic Bremen, to be used on just such an occasion. The dust created a granite wall, exactly matching all the other walls in the hidden room, that sealed the Histories away. Only one who was given the key to the spell and the power to use it could unlock the Histories from their protective tomb. Kahle managed to save the Histories, many of which had been transcribed by his own hand, but at the cost of his life.

Today, each volume of the Histories is also protected by magic. If attacked, the book, and anyone who is in physical contact with it, returns to the vault within the library at Paranor.

surviving statues from a forgotten era long before Paranor's birth guard empty corridors and lonely rooms that are themselves largely forgotten. The tapestries that once lined the hall hang in tatters. Pieces of broken pedestals litter the hall, the treasure they once held lost during a battle long ago. One huge pillar stands untouched in an alcove, supporting a graceful urn inset with jade and onyx. The matching alcove across the hall lies empty except for shards of pottery and broken pieces of the same rare stones.

At the end of the Great Hall, the tall carved doors leading to the Vault have been torn from their hinges. The ruins of a large stone pillar lie within the large double doorway, amid the remains of the broken doors. The room beyond, however, is largely untouched. The Vault is possibly the best preserved of all the major rooms of Paranor. Light from the many tall windows built high into the walls illuminates the marble below, making it easy to pick out the slight discoloration at the center of the room. This is the spot where the Sword of Shannara, enshrined in a block of Tre-Stone, rested for almost five hundred years. Here, alone of all the great rooms, the tapestries have survived, flowing in faded glory from the high ceiling to the polished marble of the floor. Even the masterly paintings on the walls are untouched. A few ornate furniture groupings occupy the perimeter of the room, facing the center point as if in tribute to the missing sword.

While the Assembly, the Great Hall, and the Vault are undoubtedly the three most lavish areas of Paranor, its three towers are its most widely recognized physical features. Their spires rise more than a hundred feet above the keep's ground level, making them visible from the Kennon Pass.

One of the towers was built over the active volcanic vent and houses the most technically innovative construct of the building—its heating system. Designed using limited Old World technology combined with the natural properties of the volcano, the tower protects the machinery of the great furnace, venting the excess heat and smoke through its chimney top. The furnace itself lies several hundred feet below ground level. The heat from the magma below is drawn upwards and pumped through vents and shafts into all the main rooms and corridors of the keep. Wherever possible, the designers used existing lava flumes as the heart of the vent system below ground, and they built vents into the walls of the keep above.

A catwalk platform system built onto the walls of the main pit allows access to the furnace from the underground corridors of the keep. Even here, in the depths of its stone heart, Paranor has suffered the ravages of battle. The catwalk has been severely damaged. Scorch marks from fire hotter than that within the furnace has scarred the walls around the walk in several places. Below the catwalk, metal rungs of an access ladder descend to the depths of the furnace and its fires. These rungs are useable only when the furnace is idle and the fires are only those natural to the volcanic vent.

The second tower, more elevated than the first, was built to house the High Druid, so that he could easily survey his realm. It contains offices for support staff on the lower levels and the Druid's Retreat on the upper floors.

The third and tallest tower is rarely mentioned in old texts outside the Druid Histories. Below its heights lies the bottomless pit known only as the Druid's Well. The doors that access this tower are usually kept locked and chained with heavy chains. Even at the height of the Druids' power, this tower was kept locked away, an embarrassment, built by Galaphile and used by those the order wished to forget. At the top of the tower, accessible only by a precarious stairway built into the tower's inner walls and lined with traps, lies a single chamber. Unlike the High Druid's rooms, the windows of the Well Tower room are smaller, high up in the room, and covered with bars. The room's original purpose is unknown, but it bears age and disuse like a shroud.

Well below the tower level and away from the grandeur of the Assembly lies the single most important asset of Paranor— its library. Located at the end of a second-floor corridor—with no massive carved doors or statuary to mark its location—the room is the same as any one of a hundred others, as if the designers thought it unimportant. Despite its innocuous appearance, this room once held all the combined knowledge gathered by the Druids since the fall of the Old World.

Though small when compared to the scale of the rest of the keep, Paranor's library is large enough to hold several thousand books. At the height of the Druid Council, the shelves lining the walls overflowed with thousands of books, artifacts, and parchments. Most of the tabletops

A volume of the priceless Druid Histories, the chronicles of the Druids and their magic.

were stacked several feet deep. Today, however, there are only a thousand works remaining in the main room. Large numbers of irreplaceable records were stolen or destroyed during the keep's turbulent past. Murders and battles have damaged the shelves and their contents. Unlike some of the other areas of the building, however, the Druids carefully restored the library to order each time the keep was regained.

The reason for such extraordinary care lies behind a hidden door built into one of the large bookcases. The hidden door reveals a secret room, previously known only to the Druids themselves. But the room itself seems nothing special. Here, to any but a trained Druid, there are only barren granite walls with a single table and chair. Magic hides the true treasure—the Druid Histories. Here, since the time of Bremen, they have remained safe through all the ravages the keep has suffered, protected from all who would destroy or pervert the knowledge they contain. These volumes are the true treasure of Paranor and, perhaps, the key to the world's future as well as its past.

The Druids:
Legacy of Mystery

The Druids are the land's conscience. They seek out what troubles the land and her people, and they help to put it right again. —Walker Boh, Druid

Galaphile created the Druids to be the wise men and educators of the land. He believed it was the first step toward his ultimate goal. He was determined to re-create the Old World that had been lost, while avoiding the corruptions of power that had led to its destruction. The Druids were to be the guardians who would keep the dangerous knowledge controlled.

Unfortunately, the wonders of the Old World were not easily reconstructed, especially after having been lost for two thousand years. It was complicated by the fact that the world had changed drastically

from what it had been. Magic and magical creatures were an integral part of the new world. The Histories reveal that the early Druids attempted to explore the magic, to determine whether it indeed could be used along with science to rebuild the world. They discovered very quickly that the use of magic was insidious and addicting. It had no easily definable rules, and the power it promised often had unforeseen consequences.

Some of the Druids were completely seduced by its easy power and addictive character. They believed that magic should be used exclusively, instead of science. After discovering the insidious promise of the darker magics, they advocated that the power granted by magic should give the Druids the right to control the Races, rather than just educate and protect them.

The majority of the order were alarmed by the dangerous nature of magic. They were appalled at the concept of becoming rulers rather than educators. The Druids favoring magic use rebelled and were banished from the order, only to return during the First War of the Races, corrupting the Race of Man as their pawns and using the might of their magic against the other Races. Though the Druids and the other Races prevailed, the dark magic used during that war caused a backlash within the Druid order. Magic was much too dangerous, volatile, and unpredictable to be used in any meaningful way. The order as a whole abandoned it as a serious subject for study. The goal of the order became tightly focused on the use of science alone to accomplish the rebirth, and the focus shifted so strongly to rediscovering the sciences that the leadership role of the Druids was almost lost entirely. In time, this short-sighted withdrawal led to the destruction of most of the order. After the Second War of the Races, only one man was left to carry on the tradition of the Druids.

The history of the Druids since that time is the history of the few dedicated men who shouldered the mantle of the Druids as lone representatives of an otherwise extinct order.

Bremen: FIRST MYSTIC DRUID

The first Druid to actually succeed in promoting the combination of the study of magic with other disciplines was the

Bremen, mystic Druid.

Druid Bremen. Unfortunately, he succeeded primarily because he and his followers were the only Druids to survive Paranor's fall during the Second War of the Races. Bremen is best known for his role in creating the legendary Sword of Shannara, a magic-imbued weapon he designed to defeat the Warlock Lord.

Abandoned by his parents shortly after birth, Bremen was raised by his grandfather, a skilled metalworker, who was probably responsible for both the boy's understanding of metallurgy and his dedication. Always searching for knowledge, Bremen was a student of history and ancient tongues, disciplines that made him an ideal candidate for the Druid Council.

He joined the council as a young man and became active in assisting in the evolution and development of the Races. Over time, he watched as the Druid Council began to pull back from the rest of the

Druid Sleep

The most obvious difference that sets the Druids apart from others is their apparent immortality. Some have lived five hundred years or more, with legends claiming that at least one may have survived for almost a thousand. This is possible through the art known as the Druid Sleep, first officially used by the Druid Bremen, who rediscovered and refined the art, which he later passed down to his successor.

Druid Sleep is an extended regeneration, almost like a type of hibernation, that allows the trained practitioner to use magic to rejuvenate the body and restore what it loses to normal aging. It is unrelated to natural sleep and may last months, years, or even decades, depending on the need and the skill of the practitioner. For each day of waking and for each extreme physical or magical expenditure, a debt is owed that must be paid. Only complete immersion in Druid Sleep can restore the balance. If Druid Sleep is done correctly by a skilled practitioner, aging will slow to a point that the person will appear to have stopped growing older altogether. In cases where the damage is too great because the practitioner has seriously overextended himself or herself, aging can occur very suddenly. In such cases, even Druid Sleep will not repair all the damage. The sudden signs of aging brought on by such stresses are permanent. The Druid Sleep cannot restore youth. It can only delay aging.

The art requires extensive training, great discipline, and sacrifice to ensure that body, soul, and mind are preserved intact. It is possible, however, to create the impression of immortality without the extreme sacrifices necessary for the Druid Sleep. Certain types of dark magic can provide apparent immortality with little or no effort, save immersion within the magic itself. Brona is known to have used such a shortcut to achieve his immortality and invincibility. But such immortality is an illusion, for the body and soul do not join the mind. The magic takes a heavy toll, eventually consuming the practitioner entirely. Though far more easily mastered than the more difficult Druid art, the ultimate price, as Brona discovered, is the humanity of the practitioner.

world, disillusioned by its failure to re-create the old sciences.

Frustrated by the setbacks, Bremen began to look to magic as a possible alternative. In his early journal entries, now part of the Druid Histories, Bremen wrote: "Magic could provide a more manageable and durable form of power than that found through science. It has untapped potential beyond that of the sciences, even at the levels of scientific advancement found in the Old World."

At that time, the study of the arcane arts was permissible but discouraged. Magic was to be treated as a curiosity only, not a serious discipline. One group of Druids had already been exiled for their insistence on the use of magic as a tool to make the Druids the masters of all the Races. Bremen was warned against traversing the same path. The fact that magic had been used in the First War of the Races to ill effect did nothing to help his cause. He wrote, "It is quite unnatural to me to discard a possibility simply because it has once failed. Do we discard science because we have failed to re-create the wonders of the Old World? Of course not. Why then discard magic just because it was once blatantly misused? If we discard every possibility that is not immediately successful, we are left with no possibilities at all."

He believed that magic could be harnessed and controlled with enough discipline and training.

A few of his fellows apparently agreed with him, but they were in the minority. Unwilling to risk censure, they backed away from the matter. Bremen did not. Eventually his insistence on considering magic a valid and serious alternative to science earned him banishment from the council.

After his banishment, Bremen traveled to the Westland to study with the Elves, where he lived for many years. He believed the Elven libraries, which had the greatest collection of ancient writings in lost Elven dialects, held the secret to understanding the old magic from the time of Faerie. The Elves embraced Bremen and his search, since they too were interested in rediscovering abilities that had been lost. Certain magics, such as some degree of the Druid Sleep, were skills Bremen already practiced. But with his knowledge of ancient tongues, he was able to uncover treasures of magical lore and decipher otherwise discarded texts that increased his knowledge and abilities far beyond what he would have gained at Paranor.

Inspired from his years of success with the Elves, Bremen left them to travel to other lands, seeking whatever lost bits of magic he could find, in much the same way as the early Druids had searched out the texts and lore related to the Old World sciences. According to his journals, he found an amazing amount of lost magic, though none as greatly concentrated or as highly developed as that within the Westland. In many cases, the magic he found was completely foreign to those who used it.

At some point in his travels, probably while in the Southland, Bremen began to suspect that the First War of the Races had not actually been organized by the Race of Men who appeared to have started it. He found evidence that the leader—referred to only as Brona, which means "master" in Gnome dialect—who had long been thought by the Druids of his order to be a mythic figurehead, was in fact a real being. Bremen suspected he was the leader of the Druids who had broken from the council and renounced their brotherhood over the question of magic many years before. He also found evidence that Brona was still alive, despite the impossible number of years that had passed, and was planning another assault on the Four Lands.

Unlike the rest of the Druids, Bremen had no trouble believing Brona could still be alive, because his own life had been lengthened beyond a natural span by his use of the Druid Sleep. But he knew he would have to have proof before the council would believe him.

He spent the next several years tracking the elusive Brona, going so far as to travel to the Skull Kingdom. Upon his return to Paranor, both Bremen and his information were rejected by the council. He left with only the few who believed his warning of impending attack. Shortly after his visit, Paranor fell to the armies of the Warlock Lord, betrayed from within. Bremen and those who left with him—the Dwarf Warrior Druid Risca, the Elf Tay Trefenwyd, and the apprentice Mareth—were the only survivors of the order.

Before he left, Bremen provided the magic that saved the Druid Histories from the invaders. The opened portion of the Druid Histories also credits him for preventing a long-term occupation by the Warlock Lord by triggering the magic of the Druid's Well.

By default, the death of the Druids left Bremen as the acting High Druid. But while he did rescue the Elit Druin after Paranor's fall, he never formally accepted the title. He used the medallion in the forging of the Sword of Shannara, the magical weapon used to end the Second War of the Races and the War of the Warlock Lord.

Of the Druids who followed Bremen from Paranor, only Mareth survived the war. She declined to complete her training as a Druid, leaving Bremen as the last of the Druids, even as he was the first to successfully balance magic with the good of the Races. He adopted a young man known only as Allanon, whom he had befriended during the war, and took him as apprentice, heir, and eventually son.

Paranor vanished only a few years after the war, and some scholars now believe that Bremen, with his knowledge of magics, was responsible for that disappearance.

While many consider Bremen to have died approximately three years after the end of the Second War of the Races, Allanon's journal records that he did not die, but instead "doomed himself to an existence of half-life that may not end for all eternity" by entering the mysterious Hadeshorn. This interpretation is also found within the diaries of Brin Ohmsford, where she records seeing an apparition that was identified as Bremen while at the Chard Rush, decades after Bremen's supposed death.

Allanon: PROTECTOR OF THE FOUR LANDS

For over half a century, the enigmatic teacher known only as Allanon moved among the people of the Four Lands, leaving a legacy of magic and mystery. Wise men knew him as a scholar and philosopher without equal. The common people knew him as a stranger who often paid his way with good advice. Others knew him as a widely traveled historian. Only a few

were aware that the mysterious man in the flowing black robe was a practitioner of the mystic arts and the sole heir to the Druid tradition of Paranor.

Allanon and his magic were an integral part of the history of the Four Lands. At over seven feet in height, the lean, dark-haired Druid had a commanding presence that kings and commoners alike found compelling. It was he who found the Shannara heir and enabled him to slay the Warlock Lord, ending the Northland War. His was the guidance that enabled the Ellcrys to be reborn and the Forbidding to be restored. His was the unseen hand that guided the quest to destroy the Ildatch.

Born in the Borderland village of Varfleet, Allanon became an orphan during the Second War of the Races when the Northland army razed the village to the ground. The sole survivor of that massacre, he seldom spoke of his early years, and never revealed his family name. The legendary Druid Bremen found him in the ruins of Varfleet and was drawn to the intense boy with strange eyes. Together, outcast Druid and orphan boy were a formidable team during the last battles of the war. Eventually the boy was apprenticed and then adopted by the old mystic. Allanon claimed that a magical bond had been made between them, stronger than any blood tie could ever be—a bond that lasted even beyond the grave.

After the Second War of the Races, Allanon studied the Druidic arts with Bremen within the walls of Paranor, becoming a Druid in only three years. He followed in the tradition Bremen had begun, concentrating on the magical arts— learning how to control and use them for the good of the Four Lands. His magical abilities and control soon surpassed those of his father. After three years, Bremen, who was failing from the dual weight of

Allanon, Master Druid.

old age and battle scars, walked out of the world and into the Hadeshorn. Allanon was left to carry on the tradition of the Druids as the sole heir to their legacy. It is clear that Bremen felt that the Druids, and ultimately he, as last survivor, were responsible for the creation of the Warlock Lord. He had focused all of his later life on eradicating Brona from the world. The Warlock Lord's survival and his own failing health forced him to realize that he could not fulfill his pledge, and he was obliged to pass the responsibility for Brona's final destruction on to his adopted son.

Allanon has written in the Histories that his father did not die; driven by the guilt of his order as well as his own, he made a greater sacrifice for the good of the land. "He bound his spirit to the world in which his body could not stay, so he could reach beyond life's end to see the fulfillment of the pledge he had made . . . exiled in a world of dark where past and future joined, where summons could be had when the need was there. Never to be freed until it was done, until both of us have passed." Allanon took his father's pledge very seriously, dedicating his life to the final destruction of the Warlock Lord. His father's guilt became his own heavy mantle.

After Bremen's death, Allanon spent nearly five hundred years waiting for the chance to make good on his pledge. During that time, he perfected the discipline that had given his father longevity, the Druid Sleep, taking the art to a new level. He traveled the lands, gathering and sharing knowledge, single-handedly continuing the traditions the Druids had originally been created to fulfill. He brought Paranor back into the world, probably in preparation for the task of rebuilding the Druid order, and placing the Sword of Shannara, key to the Warlock Lord's defeat, safely within its walls under guard. He did not know that this would prove to be an almost disastrous mistake.

Upon the Warlock Lord's return, Allanon discovered that his adversary was cunning and quick. The Druid barely managed to save the last Shannara heir, Shea Ohmsford, before Brona's minions could find him.

The Druid became a driven man, determined to see the Warlock Lord destroyed despite the advantages he had lost. He became secretive, intent on personally controlling the rest of the campaign. The journals of those who traveled and fought with him are full of accounts of Allanon's refusal to share information or give trust, though he demanded both from his companions. Fortunately, the champion left to him, Shea Ohmsford, proved able and brave. The young man managed to destroy the Warlock Lord, despite Allanon's inability to be with him at the final moment.

With the death of Brona and his sworn debt discharged, Allanon disappeared from the Four Lands to sleep. Shea Ohmsford was the last known person to speak to him for many years, though there were claims that the tall Druid had been seen in other lands.

Allanon reappeared in the Westland fifty years later, showing no signs of the years that had passed, to warn the Elves of the collapse of the Forbidding and the death of the Ellcrys. Once again, he was in the forefront of battle, helping to unite the Elves, the Dwarves, the Gnomes, and even the Trolls against their common enemy, the demons that had escaped their prison. It was the first time the Elves, Trolls, Dwarves, and Gnomes had ever fought together on the same side.

After the War of the Forbidden, Allanon once again disappeared. It was almost twenty years before he was seen again, drawn out of seclusion by the discovery that the evil he had thought eliminated was still within the Four Lands.

Though the Warlock Lord had been killed, the dark magic that had twisted him still remained active within the book known as the Ildatch. If Allanon was ever to discharge his father's sworn oath and find peace from the guilt that haunted them both, he had to see the Ildatch destroyed. Together with Brin Ohmsford and Rone, the Prince of Leah, Allanon set out to find and destroy the ancient tome of evil. It was a quest that he would never complete.

While passing through the Wolfsktaag Mountains, at the waterfall known as the Chard Rush, the party was attacked by a Jachyra, an almost invincible creature from the time of Faerie. Knowing he was the only one who could possibly be a match for such a beast, Allanon engaged and fought the creature. Using every bit of magic lore and power at his disposal, he eventually managed to destroy the Jachyra, but not before receiving mortal wounds to body and spirit.

According to Brin Ohmsford's diaries, Allanon may have known in advance that he would not survive. He spoke to her of a vision that told him, "When I go from the Four Lands this time, I shall not come again." Before he died, Allanon marked Brin, telling her he had chosen her line to carry on the Druid tradition.

But death did not end the debt. After Brin and her brother, Jair, succeeded in destroying the Ildatch, they returned to the Chard Rush and were greeted by Allanon's spirit, "almost as if he were still alive." He told them that because of their victory, he and his father were released from their vows and able to find peace.

But was Allanon at peace? It seems that the Druid was not willing to succumb to final oblivion. There were further sightings of the Druid three hundred years later, both haunting the dreams of the Ohmsford descendants and rising as an apparition from the Hadeshorn. It has even been suggested that it is his spirit come again in Walker Boh to take up the mantle of the Druids. If so, Allanon may be the first true immortal.

Walker Boh: DARK UNCLE

Known as the "Dark Uncle," Walker Boh was the only reluctant Druid to be initiated into the order. A direct descendant of

Brin Ohmsford through his father, Kenner Ohmsford, and of Kimber Boh through his mother, Risse Boh, he grew up resenting the Druids and all they had done to his ancestors. He resented his Ohmsford lineage, which left him with the distinctly Elvish features common in the Ohmsfords, though he also had the pale skin of the Bohs. Walker was the first of Brin's descendants to manifest innate magical ability past childhood.

As a child, Walker did not know he was different. He grew up with his parents in Hearthstone, the Bohs' ancestral lands. With all of the wilds of Darklin Reach as his playground, Walker had plenty of room to explore his gifts. He discovered he could sense thoughts and feelings in other people. He could sense things from most animals and even plants. Sometimes he could make himself disappear. His parents supported him in his explorations. Though his mother told him that he was different from other children, he did not understand what that meant. A year later, she died of fever.

When Walker was twelve, Kenner Ohmsford, realizing that his son was not going to grow out of the magic, as he had done, told him the story of Brin and Allanon. Walker did not like the idea that his abilities were tied to a dying Druid's curse, but he was unwilling to stop using the magic. At the age of thirteen, he discovered that the magic could be destructive. When angry, he could summon blue fire or break things without touching them. Gradually a void grew between father and son as the differences between them became more obvious. There is some evidence that Kenner feared his son, though he tried to prevent Walker from noticing.

Despite Kenner's personal fears that the magic would eventually overwhelm Walker, Kenner refused to suppress the boy's abilities, insisting that his son's talents were a gift with a special purpose. He also encouraged Walker's appetite for knowledge, maintaining a sizable library so that Walker could indulge his insatiable curiosity. From the first day he could read, the boy devoured texts on mathematics, science, and history. He understood almost everything he read and developed a passion for history.

When Kenner developed a wasting illness, they were forced to move to Shady Vale to live with Jaralan and Mirianna Ohmsford and their sons, Par and Coll. It was there that he learned that he was different and that magic, especially when combined with Elvish blood, was something that most people feared and resented. As a young man, he was outcast and alone. He became known as the "Dark Uncle." His father's death a year after their arrival in Shady Vale only cemented his isolation. The magic, Allanon's legacy, had become a curse.

His only close ties were with young Par Ohmsford, who had begun to manifest innate magical abilities. Walker became his protector and mentor, knowing that he was the only one who could possibly understand what Par was facing. He stayed in Shady Vale for seven years, then left to return to his birthplace in Darklin Reach, leaving civilization and all its prejudices behind. He abandoned the Ohmsford name, calling himself Walker Boh, after his mother's family—perhaps in the hope that a change of name would also spare him from the Ohmsford legacy. He even tried to escape the magic by avoiding its use. But the magic would not be avoided. After a year spent without using any magic, it began to manifest in new and frightening ways, threatening to overwhelm Walker's tenuous control.

Fortunately, Cogline, Kimber Boh's grandfather and a student of the Druid arts, arrived in time to help the young man. The old man began to train him in the use and control of his magic. He also gifted him with a moor cat named Rumor, who became his constant companion. For three years, Walker studied the Druid arts and lore, until he gained mastery over the magic and himself. But Cogline was not content to teach only magic. He went beyond the usual Druid teachings of Allanon's time and began to teach the young man the mysteries of the Old World sciences as well. Walker was an apt pupil, soon going beyond Cogline's teachings to experiment with combinations of magic and Old World science with surprising success. He was the first to ever attempt such combinations.

Sometime near the end of his third year of study, something changed for Walker. He refused to allow Cogline to teach him more, claiming the old man's attempts to continue were Druid manipulation. Whether his refusal to continue his education was based on his fear of the Druids who had manipulated his ancestors or whether he feared the limits of his own control is unknown. Cogline left Hearthstone, returning as an occasional guest but not as a teacher.

For six years, Walker lived a solitary life within Darklin Reach, content to leave the rest of the world to fend for itself. He was drawn out only when Par Ohmsford came to him and challenged him to face Allanon, with the other Ohmsford descendants, at the Hadeshorn. His close ties with the boy forced him to face the dead Druid, despite his belief that Allanon was responsible for the magic that plagued him. Allanon's shade charged him to find the Black Elfstone and bring back Paranor and the Druids. He finally decided to

Walker Boh, called the "Dark Uncle," a reluctant Druid.

attempt the search, but lost his arm, and very nearly his life, on a misguided search for the Elfstone in the Hall of Kings. He sacrificed his arm to free himself, but even with Cogline's aid could find no cure for the poison. The struggle forced him to come to terms with himself and reconcile with his mentor. He was forced to accept the fact that Allanon's spirit had helped keep him alive so that he could complete his charge.

It took the magic of the elemental girl Quickening to save him. He joined with

Druid Rite of Passage

The path to becoming a Druid has changed even as the Druids themselves have evolved and changed. In the early days of the Druid Council, the order was open to students from all the Races, though it was initially dominated by the Elves. Novices were required to study the Histories and assist in deciphering old texts. They served as apprentices until their mentors felt they were worthy to become full Druids. Mastery of at least one branch of knowledge was required to achieve Druid status. Magical abilities, while not required, were welcomed and encouraged. When ready, novices underwent a ritual ordination, including the use of magic, to welcome them to the Druid mysteries.

In the aftermath of the First War of the Races, magic use was dropped from the list of viable subjects for study and from the initiation process. Druids were initiated based primarily on academic abilities. Some novices even hid their innate magical abilities.

After the Second War of the Races, only one Druid survived: Bremen. His heir, Allanon, was initiated on a starlit night at the edge of the Hadeshorn after three years of learning the Druid mysteries of history and magic. He became a Druid as he watched his adopted father carried into the water of the Hadeshorn. While all Druids who use Druid magic are changed by it, no one can say how greatly it changed Allanon, since he became a Druid at such a young age.

For the newest Druid, Walker Boh, there was no living Druid to initiate him. He was forced to undergo a rite created by Allanon centuries before. He had to use the Black Elfstone to absorb the essence of all the Druid Spirits into himself. The ordeal was more intense and dangerous than any initiation before, but it was the only way for the necessary knowledge to be passed successfully. Walker Boh came away from his initiation carrying the knowledge and the combined abilities of all who had gone before.

He also came away physically changed. The magic increased his size and strength. Those who met him soon after the transformation could see Allanon in his face. Some say that Allanon, who cheated death at the Chard Rush, now lives on in Walker Boh. Ironically, the man who swore he would remain his own person was the one Druid who ended up bringing the spirits of all the Druids together within himself.

her on her quest to stop the Faerie creature Uhl Belk and succeeded in discovering both the Black Elfstone and himself.

Once armed with the Elfstone, and with new confidence in his abilities, Walker used the stone to enter Paranor where it existed within limbo. He found that Cogline and Rumor, whom he thought killed, had survived but had been transported to the keep by the magic within the Druid Histories. He discovered that the only way to save them and return them to the real world was to become the thing he hated most—a Druid.

With Cogline's aid, he studied the Druid Histories and deciphered the secrets of the rite of passage—different for each Druid. Walker managed to survive the ordeal, with Cogline's assistance, to become the newest Druid and master of Paranor. He returned Paranor to the world and began life as a Druid with a vow that he would not be the same type of manipulator his predecessors had been.

Walker Boh went beyond Allanon's accomplishments to become the first of a new type of Druid—one who combined the magic of the new world with the science of the Old. Ironically, by accepting the heavy mantle that Allanon had left for him, the once reluctant Druid had accepted a charge to protect the very Races he had tried so hard to escape.

Cogline: THE LAPSED DRUID

No history of the great Druids would be complete without mention of the man known only as Cogline. Though he was never ordained or initiated, he studied with the Druids long enough to learn their lore, and he surpassed many of them in the use of Old World science and some of the arcane arts. Cogline lived for almost a thousand years with the aid of the Druid Sleep, a record no ordained Druid has ever matched.

He was born fifty years after the First War of the Races, into a time when the Druids were at the zenith of their power. As a boy, he had an inexhaustible thirst for knowledge and a desire to understand how the world worked. His search led him inevitably to the Druid Council, where he enthusiastically joined in the search for Old World knowledge. He began his studies at a time when the council was focused more on the exploration of magic than on science. Cogline loved the reliability of science, the simple beauty of mathematics, and the creative power of chemistry. To him, magic was unpredictable and dangerous. He often compared it to a wild animal that was as likely to turn on its user as obey commands. But magic was part and parcel of what Druids were, so the novice resentfully studied the Druid arcane disciplines.

As he neared the completion of his novice training, Cogline began to avoid magic altogether. Instead, he concentrated his research on rediscovering the most powerful of the Old World sciences. He learned the secret recipes for corrosive potions that could burn through metals, explosive powders, and chemical reactions that could shatter stone. Here was a form of power that could be controlled by anyone who understood it.

Unfortunately, the Druid Council felt that these sciences were related to the very things that had helped to destroy the world during the Great Wars. They forbade Cogline from continuing his research. He was to focus on benign sciences—and magic. Unwilling to give up his work, Cogline chose to leave the Druids, forsaking all he had struggled to achieve within the order.

Once he left Paranor, Cogline disappeared from known records for almost seven hundred years. Ironically, only a few decades after he left them, the Druids changed their focus and began to concentrate on Old World science rather than magic—until eventually magic was studied only in private, as a curiosity. It is certain that Cogline knew of the change, but he never returned to the Druids, probably knowing that his type of science would never be completely acceptable. Bremen, a young man at the time, was the only Druid Cogline maintained as a friend, possibly because neither of them fit into the Druid hierarchy. It was Cogline to whom Bremen turned when he needed the formula for making steel suitable for the Sword of Shannara. Only Cogline had maintained such detailed technical knowledge from the Old World science.

Cogline had rejected the Druid path but not all the Druid skills. He used magic to keep himself alive, constantly working to perfect those skills he deemed valuable, such as spirit projection and the Druid Sleep. The Sleep allowed him to have many lives, but he kept his history secret. No one close to him knew he had studied

Cogline, adept of science and magic.

with the Druids—had, in fact, been one in all but name. They knew only that he had a knack for working with potions and powders, and that he preferred a life of solitude.

He found that solitude at Hearthstone, in Darklin Reach, which became his personal refuge for many years. He loved the wild land and seemed to have an amazing rapport with the animals there. It was said that wherever he went, there was certain to be one of the huge moor cats nearby. When one cat died, another would take its place. Anyone who came too near discovered how fiercely protective the cat could be.

He built a home at Hearthstone and eventually adopted a girl by the name of Kimber Boh, who called him Grandfather, though it is unlikely that she knew his age. He was almost seven hundred years old at the time, but treasured Kimber as if she were his own granddaughter. By the time Kimber was a young woman, Cogline had become senile. Those who met him, such as Brin Ohmsford and Rone Leah, assumed it was because of his advanced age. It is now suspected that his mental eccentricities were caused by something that had gone wrong with the magic while he was in the Druid Sleep. He did recover his mental faculties, but not until after Kimber had married and left to live with her husband's family.

Despite his isolation in both time and geography, Cogline discovered he could not avoid the Druids. It is believed that he met Allanon while the Druid still lived, and that Allanon knew who he was and what he had been. Cogline respected Allanon, though they were never close friends. It is likely that Allanon made use of that respect when he warned Cogline that his descendant, who was also Brin's, would be the heir to his legacy. The Druid may have even used his power from beyond the grave to make certain that Cogline would live long enough to act in his stead, ensuring the safety of the man who was, in many ways, heir to them both.

Cogline acted on Allanon's warning and became Walker Boh's mentor, saving him from his innate magic before it could consume him. He also made a point of teaching Walker his own special knowledge of science and explosives. But to him, it was much more than a task Allanon had given him. In many ways, he saw Walker as his son, not just part of his bloodline. He knew that Walker would have to take the path that he himself had rejected. Despite his misgivings, he did all he could to make that path easier. He even entered Paranor, with Allanon's protection, within the limbo of the netherworld, just to recover a volume of the Druid Histories. The book was necessary to give Walker Boh the incentive he needed to complete his charge. To get it, Cogline had to face the keep he had known so well while he floated "within a realm of yesterdays filled with gray haze and death." His writings from the time prove that his regard for Walker and his respect for Allanon's visions of doom were all that drove him to face such horror.

The same book later saved his life during a Shadowen attack. Instead of being killed, he and his moor cat were transported by its protective magic to Paranor.

Unfortunately, Paranor still lay in limbo. Cogline was trapped within the halls of green mist he had braved months before. His only chance for salvation was linked to Walker's destiny. If Walker became a Druid, Cogline would be free. Otherwise, he would fade into the mist of the lost keep.

This may have been part of Allanon's plan, for it is unlikely that Walker would have braved the ordeal required to become a Druid if Cogline's life had not depended on it. Fortunately, he did survive the ordeal and returned the keep, and all within it, to the world. No doubt, when Cogline found himself facing the awesome sight of his student as a newly made Druid, he wondered if he had chosen the right path.

Less than a year later, Cogline returned the favor by rescuing Walker from a Shadowen. He was mortally wounded but succeeded in tipping the balance so that Walker could destroy the creature. Because of the prophecy, he had known he was living on borrowed time for Walker's sake, and he was willing to die so that Walker could live and carry on the Druid tradition.

Though he had never been an ordained Druid, he had lived longer and done more for the order than most who had held the title. He was buried in the woods below Paranor, a prodigal son come home at last.

Realms of
the Dead

I have studied the magic that wards the netherworld and its portals into our own, and I have traveled such roads as exist between the two and returned alive. —Bremen, Druid

Is there life after death? This question has dominated much of human thought since Man was capable of reason. Both the Druids and the earliest rulers of the Four Lands believed in the afterlife. The ancient kings believed they could reach it through death ritual and protected burial in sacred ground. The Druids believed they could breach the barrier between the living and the dead through the use of magic. The rulers built the Hall of Kings to protect their bodies as they awaited passage to the next life. The Druids used the mysterious lake known as the Hadeshorn as a portal to the netherworld.

The Hadeshorn

For thousands of years the influence of the Druids shaped the course of history within the Four Lands, yet their lives have always been mysterious and shrouded in secrecy, hidden behind the walls of Paranor and the cloak of their magic. Their deaths are no less mysterious. Druids such as Bremen and Allanon influenced events in the world long after their mortal bodies died. Some scholars believe that the Druids have conquered death entirely. In actuality, they have not defeated the reaper, but rather have found a way to reach beyond the grave through a portal to the netherworld known as the Hadeshorn.

Located two days' travel from the walls of Paranor, the Hadeshorn lies within a hidden valley, known as the Valley of Shale, just beyond the edge of the Dragon's Teeth mountain range. The Dragon's Teeth surround most of the region around Paranor like a protective wall, rugged and uncrossable save for a few passes. To reach the valley from the Druids' Keep, it is necessary to cross the mountains through the Kennon Pass, a channel nature cut through the heart of the mountains when they were yet young. The Kennon Pass leads to a trail that skirts the southern edge of the Dragon's Teeth, above the Mermidon River. Here a poorly marked and seldom-used trail leads back up into the foothills of the southern edge of the Dragon's Teeth. Just beyond the foothills, this trail narrows, becoming rugged with broken rock and clusters of fallen boulders. Thousands of years ago, these boulders were part of the core of a mountain destroyed by a great cataclysm—a mountain that once may have stood where the Valley of Shale now lies.

Beyond the final ridge of broken boulders, the trail suddenly opens onto a great barren bowl that appears to be made of glittering black glass. This is the Valley of Shale, the doorstep to the Hall of Kings and home to the spirits of the ages. Its

Calling the spirits of the dead, at the Hadeshorn in the Valley of Shale.

name comes from the crushed shards of glistening, razor-edged shale that cover its surface. The slippery rock makes footing treacherous. Within the valley, there are no trees, plants, or life of any other kind— only the crushed black rock that seems to both reflect and absorb all light. An oppressive silence blankets the entire valley, as if it were cut off from the outside world. Even the Druids come here only when the need is great, and then only at night.

In the exact center of the valley lies the Hadeshorn. Broad and opaque, it is not really a lake in the traditional sense at all. Its waters pulse with a deep green inner light, as if the entire lake were alive. In the darkness of a moonless night, the green glow from the lake is the only illumination, reflected by the mirror-bright shale in eerie chorus. Like a living thing, the lake has been said to have moods. In the strongest wind, its waters may lie perfectly still, a sheet of unblemished glass, yet on the most still of nights it may swirl and writhe as if driven by an unseen storm. When awakened, the waters pulse and mutter with voices just beyond understanding.

No mortal can touch these waters and live. Indeed, the whole of the valley is a place of death, forbidden to all, the waters deadly poisonous. The Druids claim it is a portal, a breach between the mortal world and the netherworld—a joining between past, present, and future. Some of the ancient writings indicate that it is a passageway that leads to the afterlife. Allanon's writings of Bremen indicate that it is a gate into the void between life and death, the same limbo to which Paranor itself was consigned for so many years—a void where souls may eternally linger between death and final peace. The lake itself is believed to be only a single portal

into this void. The Druid's Well is almost certainly another. There may well be many others that are as yet undiscovered.

It is said that all the spirits of the ages are consigned here, but only the Druids are strong enough to answer a summoning and reach through the portal to communicate with the living. There are no records of any non-Druid spirits being summoned, so it is unknown if someone who lacked magic in life could return through the portal in death. It is known that Druids have an unusual affinity with the lake. Bremen was able to walk into its embrace before death to enter a state between life and death. The Druid Allanon, near death at the Chard Rush, was able to cause the waters of the Rush to alter their behavior to mirror that of the Hadeshorn, despite the fact that the Chard Rush was many miles from the Valley of Shale. Since then, Allanon's spirit has appeared at both the Chard Rush and the Hadeshorn, indicating that the physical laws of this world may have no bearing on the lake or those who have passed beyond.

While it may not be the only portal to the realm of the dead, the Hadeshorn is the only place where the spirits of the dead can be summoned to communicate with the living. Such a summoning can be done only by a Druid trained in the arts, and even then, only at the hour before dawn. A summoning is very dangerous, even for the trained adept.

Bremen was the first Druid who was recorded as having summoned the spirits of the Hadeshorn. He claimed to have learned the art from the ancient texts of the Elves. It is probable that Galaphile, an Elf, also knew of the art, as did some of the earliest Druids, but if so, their knowledge was never recorded in the Druid Histories. The ability was lost until Bremen recovered the knowledge and used it to reach

Summoning the Dead

THE FOLLOWING EXCERPT WAS TAKEN WITH PERMISSION FROM THE DRUID HISTORIES. THE ACTUAL MAGIC AND RITUAL WORDS HAVE BEEN OMITTED TO PROTECT THE UNTRAINED.

Calling the dead requires extreme strength of purpose and single-minded determination. It must not be done lightly, for there is always a price for daring to know that which is forbidden. The need must be great enough to justify the risk.

A summoning can be done only at the Hadeshorn in the hour before dawn, and the spirits summoned must return to the waters at dawn. The adept must approach the water's edge at the appropriate time, being careful not to touch the waters themselves. The waters may begin to stir at the approach of a living being. The adept must then find within himself perfect stillness and firmness of purpose as well as the belief that what he will see and hear cannot touch him or shake his resolve, for he will be sorely tested by those he dares to wake from eternal sleep. Once the ritual begins, even the slightest hesitation or distraction can be deadly.

The summoning ritual must be performed slowly and carefully. This ritual will be slightly different for each adept, as it must be tailored to the skills and needs of the one who calls. It is necessary to speak the name of the summoner, and to speak of the history and need. If the spirits are willing to respond, the lake will suddenly churn and boil as they fight to break free of their bondage. The adept must stand fast despite the horrific nature of the cries from the souls the lake holds within.

Once the summoning has begun, the summoner will be encompassed in a realm that is not entirely part of either world, neither living nor dead. Only the dead and the one who calls will be allowed within this vacuum. Those outside may be able to see through its barriers, but they will hear nothing. The summoner will hear anguished cries without words and feel fear that demands escape. To survive, the adept must remain fixed on his purpose and stand fast.

When the called spirit appears, the summoner must speak its name. A spirit cannot remain unless it is recognized and named by the summoner. Once named, the spirit may choose to answer questions. These answers are most often in the form of visions. These visions are of the truth of the future as seen by those from the past. But the visions are often incomplete and out of context. Though the visions show truth, the spirits are of a realm beyond ours and have an imperfect understanding of the world they have lost. Care must be taken to avoid assumptions. It is best simply to memorize every detail for later analysis.

The spirits may remain only until dawn and will return to the lake at first light. The adept must not attempt to hold a spirit even if the answers are incomplete. A spirit cannot be held past its time; to try to do so can have disastrous consequences.

The Hadeshorn will reclaim its dead with vehemence equal to their release, but the dead will not return to their bondage easily. As a price for their disturbance, they always take something of the living with them. The summoner will pay for his knowledge with some part of his life force. If the summoner lacks sufficient strength, he may not survive the ordeal at all.

Galaphile's spirit. Since that time, the Druids have passed the knowledge to each successor, that he might have the knowledge to learn secrets hidden from the living. To ensure that Allanon would be able to reach him, Bremen is said to have passed into the deadly waters before his time, so that his spirit would be available for his son and heir at need. Because of this, summonings were not as difficult for Allanon as for his father.

Allanon himself seems to have transcended the normal rules of the afterlife, in that he alone of all the dead managed to appear to nonadepts at a place outside the Hadeshorn. He also was said to have manipulated dreams from beyond death and to have appeared to those in need without being summoned by name. Perhaps Allanon, believed to be the greatest of the old Druids, found a way to use his formidable skills to eternally link himself with the world of the living in a way no other spirit had ever managed. Even so, his shade was reported to have said that he lacked "the power in death that I possessed in life. I am permitted to see only bits and pieces of the world that was or the future that will be. Death limits both time and being. I am the past."

While most who dared the Hadeshorn came seeking guidance, some came looking for assistance that was more tangible. At least twice the power of the lake was used to enhance weapons. The first time was to empower a talisman already forged from both magic and steel. It is said that the Sword of Shannara gained its formidable magic for truth from the spirits of the Druid dead who consecrated it. The second time was to enhance a weapon of iron and make it something more.

No one knows exactly when the Hadeshorn was formed. Some scholars speculate that the lake must have been created by the earliest Druids while they experimented with passages to other dimensions; others suggest that it was created during the Great Wars in the aftermath of the terrible forces that changed the entire world. Still others insist that it was always here, though veiled from any who did not have eyes to see, and was revealed only as the presence of magic in the land grew stronger with the demise of technology. All that is certain is that the Hadeshorn, whether eternal or created, provides a chilling look into the future that none living can escape.

Hall of Kings

Beyond the Valley of Shale lies the only path to a place even more fearsome and forbidding than the Hadeshorn. It is the Hall of Kings, ancient tomb of the royal dead. But where the Hadeshorn has often served as a portal to allow contact between the spirits of the dead and the living, the primary purpose of the Hall of Kings was to keep them eternally apart.

The path between the valley and the tomb is an arduous half-day's trek, rising northwards through the upper reaches of the Dragon's Teeth mountains, where snow blankets the peaks year round and temperatures seldom rise above freezing. The footing is treacherous. Loose rocks underfoot, avalanches overhead, and hidden crevices present constant danger to even skilled Trackers. It is hard to imagine the heavily laden funeral parties of the ancient kings bearing their dead and their treasures over such terrain, but there is no other path to the hall's entrance.

Once through the heights, the trail begins a slow descent toward an impenetrable cliff wall. Just when the traveler feels certain that there is no way out, the path dips sharply down into a canyon cut

Death of a King: Ancient Burial

In the first centuries after the Great Wars, organized civilizations of any kind were rare. The few rulers who managed to create a semblance of order were valued by their people and hated by their enemies. When one of these kings died, in order to insure his safe passage to the afterlife he was taken to the priests at the Hall of Kings to be given over to the Gods of the Dead. It was believed that a dead person could only have an afterlife if his physical body were protected from harm.

When a ruler died, his body was carefully anointed with scented oils and wrapped in fine linens in preparation for the journey to the Hall of Kings. The dead king's attendants gathered his most prized possessions so he would have use of them in the next life. Then the king, his treasure, his mourners, family, and attendants made the arduous journey through the Dragon's Teeth Mountains to the entrance to the Hall of Kings. There, under the watchful gaze of the fearsome stone warriors towering over the shadowed cavern, the final public funerary services were held, formally passing the ruler and his possessions from the land of the living to that of the dead. It is likely that favored animals, servants, and concubines were sacrificed at this time to join their dead ruler.

The priests took the bodies and the treasure deep into the caverns, leaving the funeral party outside the doors. Only the dead and their priests could pass the portal. Any other living creature that entered would soon join the dead; the creatures that guarded the passages allowed their masters and their royal burden to pass unmolested, but were alert for any other who dared to follow. Upon reaching the Tomb of Kings, the royal treasure was placed beneath the great coiled-serpent altar, where it would be treated with poisons to protect it from grave robbers. A ritual consecrating the treasure was probably performed at this time, as was the internment of the sacrificed servants and concubines.

The king himself was carried through the far doors of the Tomb, to the Assembly, where his body was placed on the stone altar, the Pyre of the Dead, before the reflecting pool. The priests performed the necessary rituals, then left the body to be guarded by the great serpent of the pool, Valg. The king's body would lie in state on this stone altar for a certain number of days, the number determined by his rank and station. During this time, his soul would be judged. If the soul was found worthy, the spirit would free itself of its mortal shell to journey on to the afterlife and the body was preserved so that the spirit might make use of it in the next life. If the soul was unworthy, the dragon Valg devoured the body so the soul would never be free. The spirit was then dammed to eternity in the land of the lost.

At the end of the required period of mourning the body of one found worthy would be interred in the Tomb of Kings in a vault set into the rotunda wall, which was carved with the ruler's name and a song of his deeds. A statue prepared by artisans during the period of mourning would be placed before the vault, facing the center of the great rotunda. The statue may have served as a second home for the spirit in the afterlife. The treasures and possessions of the ruler, now deadly to living tissue, were placed at the foot of the statue so that the deceased could have access to his most prized personal possessions in the afterlife. In their time, the ruler's family would be interred near him, though only those who were themselves kings would have a statue to mark their graves.

It was believed that so long as his body and treasures were protected on this plane, the king and his family would have full use of them in the afterlife. He was expected to continue his reign among the subjects of the netherworld.

deep within the mountains, to wind through a narrow mist-covered passage between two cliffs. After several hundred yards, the trail widens and the mist fades to reveal a cavernous opening in the cliff face. Like the Hadeshorn, the place is unnaturally still, deathly silent. Two huge stone warriors measuring at least a hundred feet in height stand guard on either side of the shadowed opening. Despite the silence, the warriors seem almost alive, looming expectantly, their stone eyes appearing to follow every movement. They guard the entrance to the Hall of Kings, tomb of the ancient rulers of the Four Lands. The sole adornments on the opening itself are three words carved into the stone above the entrance. The words are undecipherable, written in a lost language, but the warning they give is clear: Only the dead and their priests are meant to cross beyond this portal.

The Druid historians believe the hall was built sometime between the Great Wars and the First War of the Races, probably during the first thousand years. At that time, the magic unleashed during the final cataclysms was still strong in the land. Civilization was sparse and consisted primarily of many small warring kingdoms. The priests who built the Hall of Kings and controlled it served a pantheon of ancient gods of death. The names of those gods have been lost along with those of the kingdoms whose royalty was interred here. But the magical creatures they unleashed to protect the tomb, ancient and powerful creatures from the time of Faerie, survived their masters and are still very much alive. Because the priests were able to harness these creatures, it has been suggested that they may have been early Druids, or at least men who had the use of the magic in a fashion similar to that of the first Druids. Whoever

they were, very little remains except their temple and the deadly guardians within.

Built within an existing series of ancient caverns, the hall was designed to make use of the naturally winding pathways of the caverns to protect the dead and confuse the living. The largest rooms were utilized for the tomb itself, and to house the creatures that guarded the dead. The original system of caverns is the largest cavern known to exist within the Four Lands. While no one is certain of the exact size of the complex, it probably covers at least fifteen square miles, and it is suspected to contain over fifty miles of passageways on various levels.

To ensure that the dead would travel safely to the afterlife with all their possessions intact, the builders placed their magical creatures along the passageways in a series of deadly traps designed to kill anything that entered. These ancient priests wanted to be certain that the world of the living and that of the dead stayed clearly separated. Since the time of the War of the Races, only a few have dared venture within. The survivors are alive only because they were protected by strong Druid magic. For anyone else, to enter the Hall of Kings is to embrace certain death. Even for the Druids, it presents a severe test of strength and will.

The Druids discovered the existence of the hall sometime during the period in which the first Druid Council was in place, and they attempted to explore and map it. There is no record of how many lives were lost during that first expedition, but the numbers were high enough to cause the Druids to bar their own order from further explorations. After the ban, only those with great strength of will and magic ever dared to pass into the cavern. At least one of those early Druids survived long enough to learn of the dangers and create a few rudimentary maps. These maps are kept hidden within the pages of the Druid Histories to prevent casual discovery.

The great Druid Allanon survived the passage at least twice, though only the latter expedition has been documented. The only non-Druids known to have survived passage through the caverns were the five men who were part of that famous expedition. They were there not to explore the hall or partake of the treasure, but simply to find safe passage through the mountains that were otherwise blocked by the Warlock Lord's armies. Since that time, only one other man is known to have survived a journey to the Hall of Kings: Walker Boh, who later became a Druid. He did not survive unscathed, however, paying for his passage with the loss of his arm.

The entrance to the hall leads to a maze of winding passageways and chambers. The purpose of most of these chambers has never been discerned. It is likely that many of them are living quarters for the priests and their retinues. Due to the dangers involved, even the Druids are unwilling to study them for further clues.

Most of the walls are of rough stone carved out over millennia by water seepage, but the floors have been smoothed of all irregularities by human hands. In some cases, the floors appear to have been covered with a coating of sand or fine stone dust.

Approximately a half-mile or so along one of the passageways lies the first major room of the cavern, the Cave of the Sphinxes, and the first major hazard, the Sphinxes themselves. There are no accurate descriptions of the Cave or the amazing living statues that inhabit it. Any who have looked upon its denizens have been turned to stone by the mere sight. As a result, scholars have had to depend on other clues provided by blindfolded survivors or the visions provided by Druid magic to determine the details of the room. The chamber is known to be quite large, as it generates substantial echoes, and measures at least 150 yards across at the point where the pathway passes through it.

According to Druid records, the Sphinxes within the room are creatures that predate the Great Wars, and they may even predate human existence on this world. They do not have the attributes of living beings at all, but appear to be carved from solid stone, much like the warriors that stand as sentries at the cavern entrance. The Sphinxes are huge, probably in excess of a hundred feet tall, with great beastly bodies topped by human heads and faces. Still as the stone of which they are carved, they do not kill by physically attacking their victim. They do not move at all, but instead compel their victims to look upon them by the sheer overwhelming force of their will. This force is great enough that men of strong purpose, even Druids, have admitted that the compulsion completely superseded all rational thought. Those who were prevented from looking up by blindfolds or who were protected by magic reported that the images sent into their minds were as vivid as reality.

Walker Boh wrote of his own near-fatal journey: "My eyes were well covered, but within my mind I could see the great Sphinxes towering over me, wondrous in their terrible beauty—older than time and all powerful. I could feel their burning red gaze boring into me, as if my eyes were open and my spells were for naught. Their voices called out to me, demanding that I pay homage to their glory with an insistence that was almost physical—I who was a mere mortal and unworthy of their presence."

The power of the compulsion is only a lure for the real power of the Sphinx: its deadly gaze. If a victim glances up at them, even for an instant, he or she is immediately turned to stone. The Druids claim that there are at least a hundred unfortunate statues standing along the path, lured by tales of the treasures that were buried here, only to be frozen in stone, forever paying homage to the glory of the Sphinx.

Beyond the cave, the passageway narrows, twisting and turning back on itself as it winds downwards into the rock. Some sections of the tunnel are natural, while others appear to have been hollowed out with tools. The rough stone walls of this tunnel emit a greenish phosphorescence, possibly caused by bioluminous animals, or by residual magic. The glow is bright enough to allow passage over the smooth floor without torches, though not enough to make out detail. This phenomenon may be a recurring natural effect, and is found throughout the cavern system. The eerie luminescence

Asphinx

Believed to be the most deadly snake in the world, the Asphinx is not really a snake at all, but a creature from the age of Faerie. It has the body and outward appearance of an asp, but it is more closely related to its cousins, the Sphinxes. Like the asp, it hides, tightly coiled, in small hidden spaces until disturbed, and then it uses its considerable speed to strike at its victim and bury its fangs within the victim's flesh. Like the Sphinx, its weapon is its ability to turn its victims to stone.

The Sphinx is unaffected by the use of its magic, but the Asphinx can strike only once—the release of venom turns both the snake and its victim to stone. For the snake, the transformation is instantaneous; for the victim, it is a slow and painful process that can take anywhere from a few hours to several days, depending upon the strength of the victim. The horror is compounded by the fact that the Asphinx fuses its body to both the victim and its resting place at the moment of transformation, effectively trapping the victim in place while the poison works. The victim suffers fever and chills, nausea, and extreme pain while watching his or her body slowly change to stone. Mercifully, the victim usually lapses into unconsciousness and then dies long before the entire body transforms.

The poison cannot be countered by most known forms of medicine or magic. Amputation of the affected limb may slow the process and allow the victim to gain freedom, but it will not stop the process. The poison infiltrates the entire body on contact. Druid magic or medicinal compounds also serve only to postpone the inevitable. Walker Boh is the sole person known to have survived the bite of an Asphinx, but only through both amputation and the intervention of a powerful Faerie elemental. The remains of his arm still lie within the Tomb of Kings, locked within the embrace of the Asphinx.

It is believed that the Stone King placed the snake that bit Walker within the hidden recess in an attempt to cover the fact that he had stolen the Black Elfstone originally placed there by the Druids for safekeeping. The priests of the death gods probably used the deadly creatures as guardians in other areas of the hall from which this one was transplanted. Unlike mortal snakes, the Asphinx does not require food or water, and it is content to remain within the area it is set to guard until something disturbs it and triggers its deadly attack.

continues within the corridor for a little over a mile, then abruptly fades at a bend in the passage. At this point, the tunnel walls and ceiling recede into uninterrupted darkness, heralding the next major room in the cavern system, the Corridor of the Winds. Within this chamber, the darkness is so encompassing that the brightest of torches cannot reach either walls or ceiling. All accounts of the room reported that torches are always extinguished soon after entering the vast room by sudden winds that scream out of nowhere, wailing with the voices of lost and tortured souls. In each case, the travelers were left in oppressive darkness. Shea Ohmsford wrote: "As with the Sphinxes' domain, only the floor was real and certain. But this darkness was all the more terrifying because this time my eyes were wide open and straining, and the winds seemed to tear at me as if they were alive."

These winds are the corridor's namesake, but they are much more than wind—they are the voices of the Banshees, invisible creatures named after the legendary harbingers of death. They cry of damnation and torturous death until those who cannot escape their screams are driven insane. The Banshees' only weapon is their voices, but the danger is quite deadly, for once driven mad, the victim becomes lost in the darkness and is then easy prey for the many other deadly creatures within the caverns. Some have written that the voices were accompanied by crazed flashes of colored lightning that blinded, but which illuminated nothing. Some have said that the cavern itself rumbled and shivered with the sound as if from a quake.

The Corridor of Winds is not really a corridor at all, but a huge room. Even the Druids do not know its true size. Some suspect that it may even be partially within another dimension—that of the tortured dead themselves. If true, the feeling of being lost in an infinity of darkness may be an accurate representation of reality, and the screams may well be the voices of the dead crying out their agony at feeling the living so close at hand. Others believe that the room is probably of fairly standard size, but that the magic of the Banshees so affects the minds of those within its influence that they cannot perceive anything save what is presented by the magic. In either case, the effect is limited to the area within the corridor.

Beyond the corridor, the winds and the cries fade to silence as the cavern narrows into a smooth passageway approximately forty to fifty feet in diameter. The green phosphorescence seen in the earlier passage is also evident on these walls, though this passage is believed to have been carved out of the rock by the builders of the hall, as it is smooth and shows none of the natural edges and formations of some of the higher areas. This cave is the anteroom to the Tomb of Kings, ending at two huge stone doors, the height of the cave.

These doors are one of the only two sets of actual doors known to exist within the caverns, both of which mark the main burial chamber. The first set marks the entrance to the royal crypt; the other, the passage from the crypt to the final room in the system, the Assembly.

The doors are intricately carved with runes in the same ancient language as those above the cavern's main entrance. The runes are said to glow as red as fire, as if the magic burns like embers within each line and curve. The red glow is doubtless quite striking against the green of the walls. Iron bindings and hinges support the huge stone slabs. Despite the tremendous weight of the stone, the doors are balanced so perfectly that even after thousands of years, they open at the lightest touch, swinging easily on their hinges. Whether this is accomplished by a lost feat of engineering or by magic, no one is certain. There is no lock upon the doors. Perhaps magic originally warded the doors and that magic has faded, or perhaps the ancient priests believed that no one would be able to pass the earlier obstacles unless they had a right to enter the tomb.

The tomb itself consists of a very large circular chamber with recessed crypts built into its smooth walls, each one sealed by a slab of stone carefully fitted into the opening. At first glance it appears to be more a conference chamber than a tomb, for life-like statues of dead rulers stand at regal attention around the perimeter of the rotunda, each in front of the crypt that bears his or her remains, each facing the altar at the center of the room as if deeply considering some news or philosophy that only the statues can hear. The favored treasures of their lifetime—jewels, furs, weapons, scrolls, and precious metals—lie piled carelessly at their feet, all partially hidden by a thick coating of dust. But though the treasure appears unprotected, it is quite deadly. The priests coated each item with a poison that is lethal to all living things. The potency was probably enhanced by magic. Even now, the slightest touch will cause any would-be thief or admirer to die within a few minutes.

Behind each statue, the crypts containing the ruler's remains and those of the ruler's family and retainers bear inscriptions giving the names and deeds of those within. Above the ruler's crypt, his or her name is inscribed with the song of deeds below it, listing all the great victories and actions of that ruler, including the manner of death. Scholars believe that the tomb was in use for well over five hundred years. The majority of the inscriptions are written in languages long forgotten, but some are in dialects that are more recent. Most of the rulers depicted have been forgotten outside of this tomb, their names and their nations lost in the long night before the first Druid Council.

A large stone altar carved in the form of a coiled serpent, an asp with fangs bared, dominates the center of the chamber. The altar is believed to be a representation of the God of Death and Judgment in his animal form. To many ancient cultures, the serpent was also a symbol of the divine sovereignty of the ruler. The last of the many funeral rites was carried out on this altar at the time of final interment of the body.

All the earliest recorded descriptions of this room indicate that the ceiling was left in its natural state, containing quartz formations and stalactites. The same green glowing phosphorescence that illuminates the majority of the passageways also illuminated the ceiling within the tomb. A battle during Allanon's expedition damaged the ceiling, which is now shrouded in darkness. Broken fragments of stone loosened during that battle litter the rotunda floor. The only remaining light now emanates from the upper edge of the walls and the inscriptions on the massive doors at either side of the chamber.

Only a few yards from the altar, a more recent relic stands as a reminder of the hidden dangers of this place. Protruding from a recessed pocket within the floor is what appears to be the stone sculpture of a man's arm held in the grip of a coiled snake. But this arm, like the unfortunate statues in the Cave of the Sphinxes, was once flesh and blood. It was within this chamber that Walker Boh sought the Black Elfstone, only to find the Asphinx and very nearly his death. He

Valg

Since the dawn of the Four Lands, there have always been legends of dragons. Each of the Races has at least one story of a great serpentlike creature that brought destruction to any who disturbed him. Most people believe these tales were just flights of fancy, but they are in fact remnants of stories about the one the Gnomes called Valg, whose name means "death." The Druids claim that Valg is older than humanity, having been created in the time of Faerie, before the dawn of the first mortal civilizations. His power is that of the ancient magic, and his loyalty is to unknown masters who long ago abandoned him to his lair beneath the Hall of Kings.

The legends tell of a massive fire-breathing creature with deadly venomous jaws, but those who have seen Valg insist that the legends fall far short of the truth. His exact size is unknown, but he is believed to be at least seventy-five feet in length, with a head large enough to crush a wagon. His body is serpentine, with massive fore and hind limbs armed with razor-sharp hooked claws suitable for disemboweling prey. His large, misshapen head is capable of disgorging sheets of fire that can incinerate a man in seconds. The venom itself will burn any living thing it touches, making a bite from the knife-edged teeth, each the size of a dagger, the least of the dangers of a confrontation with this beast.

Allanon is the only man known to have survived a direct confrontation with Valg, and even then he survived only because of his Druid magic and the aid of the brave warriors with him. It was during his tumultuous battle with the dragon that the Assembly and the tomb were damaged. Valg himself cracked the walls and shattered most of the stalactites with his body. Some believe that the dragon was killed during that battle, but most scholars believe he still lives, as creatures of such powerful magic are almost impossible to kill. To date, no one has been willing to return to the Assembly to find out the truth.

Beyond the Assembly the tunnel leads to the only other known exit from the caverns, a doorway that brings one to a cliffside trail called the Dragon's Crease, which twists and turns its way down past the falls to the Rabb Plains. The trail has been damaged by quakes and rockfalls over the years, so very little of it remains passable.

Valg protects the Assembly from trespassers in the Hall of Kings.

escaped, but his arm remains as a grisly reminder of the price of arrogance.

Before the bodies of royalty could be interred, the spirit had to be freed from the body. This was done within the Assembly on the Pyre of the Dead, which lay beyond the second set of stone doors. The Assembly is the last large room known to exist within the cavern system. When originally discovered, it appeared to have suffered very little from the passage of time. The builders left the majority of the room in its natural state. Allanon wrote during his first visit: "The high ceiling dripped with the long spear shapes of ancient stalactites, formed over thousands of years from water seeping through the layers of sediment above. Rough walls laced with green phosphorescence formed a large hall around a long rectangular pool of glass-smooth water. The pool must have been at least a hundred yards in length. In the dim green glow the mirrored surface of the pool reflected the canopy of stalactites into an infinity of stalagmites that seem to create an enchanted city of spires."

The reflecting pool is fed by an underground spring, but the actual depth of the water has never been measured. Some of the ancient texts claim that the waters are bottomless and actually connect with the realm of the netherworld as one of the great doorways to the realm of the dead. There is no doubt that the priests who built this hall believed that to be true.

The doors to the tomb open onto a high stone platform, then to a broad alcove overlooking the room. From the alcove, wide steps were carved into the stone, leading down to a tall stone altar set at the head of the long pool. On either side of the pool, narrow stone walkways originally led to the far end of the chamber and the only other known passageway out of the mountain.

The altar, known as the Pyre of the Dead, was built out of slabs of heavy stone. A single word was carved into the surface of the altar: *Valg*. The word was both the ancient Gnome word for death and the name of the creature who lived within the deceptively calm waters of the pool—a great dragon who was old before the Races were born. It has been said that the Gnomes may have taken their word for death from the legends of the Dragon of Death.

The Hall of Kings is extraordinary not only for the amazing networks of caverns it contains, but for the sheer power and number of ancient creatures it houses. The Banshees, the Sphinxes, and Valg are all believed to be beings created during the time before Man was born—the time when the creatures of Faerie were dominant—with the power of ancient magic inherent in their being. What manner of men must those early priests have been, to have been able to command and control such creatures? Were their death gods so powerful that they were able to grant these priests control over these creatures of the ancient world? Or was it the creatures themselves who were the real gods, and the priests merely their servants? The truth is forever hidden beneath the murky depths of the altar pool.

The Southland:
History of the Federation

The Race of Man lives almost solely in the confines of the Southland. It knows nothing at all of the Northland and its peoples, and little of the Eastland and Westland. A pity that Men have developed into such a shortsighted people, for once they were the most visionary of the Races. —Allanon

The Southland has been touted as the most hospitable of the Four Lands. With its temperate climate, green rolling fields, and abundance of resources, it is hard to believe that its boundaries were established as a land of exile for a defeated people. To appreciate the Southland, it is necessary to understand the history of those who live there: the Race of Man.

History of the Southland
Once there was only one known Race—that of Man. In the lost age before the Great Wars, he dominated the planet and believed himself to be alone in the world. Elves and Faerie creatures were considered nothing more than myth. Man thought himself the heir to the secrets of the universe, and was even close to cracking the mysteries of life and death. But he had not outgrown his own basic human nature, with its inherent petty jealousies and territorial imperatives. He had not outgrown the need to kill. He had simply improved the technologies for doing it.

History records that it was Man who was responsible, in his arrogance, for the Great Wars that destroyed civilization and reshaped the world. In the aftermath, many of the survivors fled south. The temperate climate and protected conditions there allowed them to survive without suffering physical mutations. From one generation to the next they remained predominantly unchanged from the stock of their prewar ancestors. Upon discovering the other groups of survivors, such as Dwarves and Trolls, whose survival had been more dearly won, they realized that they were the only group to retain their ancestral purity. They declared each new group a separate Race, naming them after creatures in mythology.

It is unclear why the other Races were willing to accept such naming—which left the title of Man only to those who had not been mutated by the conditions of their survival—but accept it they did, eventually taking pride in those names. Only the Elves were labeled truly, though the Men who named them were unaware of their true nature, assuming at the time that they were also mutated humans.

Some historians believe it was this basic arrogance that led Man to move out of the south and attempt to assert himself as the dominant Race. Others point out that several of the other Races attempted the same domination at various times, but with less lofty goals. The resulting conflicts undermined all attempts at restoring civilization. The Druid Council was formed to end the strife and create an environment in which all the Races would learn to work together to rebuild a new civilization. Their influence curbed the battles between the Races, and for a time it heralded a period of peace.

The peace did not last, however. And Man was the tool used to destroy it. The rebel Druid Brona found in the Race of Man the perfect fodder for his quest for power. He fueled the belief that Man had a moral right to subjugate the other Races, a

belief that some Men had never lost. After all, Man was still unchanged from the original nature of his ancestors, the only "pure" Race. Many were also drawn in by the promise of power within Brona's magic, a magic he said only Man was destined to control—through him.

At first only a small number were drawn to Brona's message and his magic. They began to organize into loyal groups and coerce others. Those within the Race who opposed it—who realized it was a path of prejudice and oppression—attempted to discredit and then defeat Brona's followers.

The resulting civil war spread throughout the Race of Man. But Brona had the might of his magic and the lure of great power on his side. The opposition had only their convictions and their strength of arms. In a little over a year, Brona's followers controlled the Race of Man. Man then turned on the other Races. The result was the First War of the Races, a bloody conflict made all the more horrific by the unchecked usage of dark magic by Brona's generals.

Up to this point, no one had ever seen widespread usage of magic, much less its use as an offensive weapon. Before the war, technology and science had been anathema, feared for their role in the Great Wars. But Brona and his army of Men and creatures of magic created an awareness of magic as a new and equally destructive force.

It took the combined might of the Druid Council, then at the height of its power, and the armies of the other Races to stop Man's push for domination. At the time Brona was believed to be simply a mythic figurehead, rather than the primary instigator that he is now known to have been. The blame for the aggression was placed squarely on the Race of Man alone. He was driven from the field and forced to flee to the deep south in humiliated defeat.

In the aftermath of the war, the Druid Council partitioned the land into four parts, each assigned to one of the major Races. It was hoped that such segregation would lessen the potential for more racial conflicts. The southern region was allocated to Man and was named simply the Southland.

When dividing the lands, the Druids found it expedient to assign each land according to the racial majority already living within it. Thus, the Race of Man received the Southland because most of its survivors had fled or were already living there. The major change in population of the region at the time of the council's decree was the exodus out of the South by members of the other Races. While law never mandated complete segregation, it was encouraged and, in the case of Man, enthusiastically embraced by all sides. Only the Men of the Borderlands retained their connection to the other Races.

The seven centuries that followed are known as the Southland's isolationist period. They rebuilt their towns and major cities far south to avoid contact with the other Races. The Borderlands became a buffer between the majority of the Race of Man and the other Races until it began to be seen as a separate land. This seclusion succeeded so well that most Men outside of the Borderlands did not even know of the Second War of the Races until long after it was over. Man was the only Race not involved in that conflict. He believed himself persecuted by the other Races, fighting to keep his dignity and honor and protect what he saw as the tiny parcel of land that was left to him.

The Southlanders extended their doctrine of isolationism to include each other,

establishing themselves in small, decentralized communities, each with its own autonomous government. Since there was no one authority, there was also no one style of government. A wide variety of systems arose, from small monarchies such as the Highlands of Leah to villages such as Shady Vale, governed by councils of elders.

Trade created what links there were between the communities, though there were initially no official alliances. Trade for goods produced outside the Southland was rare and was done through the Borderlands, so that the South itself never had to trade directly with the other Races.

Over time, several of the Southland towns grew into cities large enough that intercity trade agreements were needed. About a century before the War of the Warlock Lord, a few of these cities began to band together to form a loose confederation primarily geared toward smoothing the flow of goods from one city to another. The confederation was governed by a body of representatives from each city, known as the Coalition Council.

After the War of the Warlock Lord, the southern cities belatedly realized the danger the Warlock Lord had posed to their essentially unprotected region. They realized that a stronger form of protection and government was needed, and they began to combine under the Coalition Council. The new alliance became known as the Federation. Ironically, the Southland did not officially participate in the War of the Warlock Lord either, despite the fact that three of that conflict's bravest heroes—the Ohmsford brothers Shea and Flick, and Menion, the Prince of Leah—were Southlanders.

Ten years after the War of the Warlock Lord, the Federation had grown to encompass the cities of Arishaig, Dechtera,

The Seekers: Federation Secret Police

Formed during the expansion period, the Seekers were charged with seeking out and eradicating dangerous magic from the Federation. Dressed in black from head to toe, except for the emblem of a white wolf's head worn on breast and shoulders, the Seekers' very appearance was calculated to strike terror into the hearts of the population, especially those who dared to practice magic. Armed with short swords, daggers, and truncheons, the Seekers were skilled fighters and deadly Trackers. Most people in the Southland feared the magic, but they feared the Seekers more. Almost all of the people arrested by the Seekers disappeared, never to return.

The Seekers also worked as part of the Federation army, in command roles, in intelligence, and as an elite fighting cadre. In battle, the Seekers were responsible for handling the massive creepers, as well as for defending against any magical attacks.

The most famous of the Seekers was Rimmer Dall, who served as both a member of the Coalition Council and head of the Seekers. A large, powerfully built man who came to his seat on the council at a young age, Rimmer Dall was known to be a ruthless politician as well as a fearsome fighter. Recognizable by his coarse reddish beard and the black glove he always wore on his left hand, he was the guiding force behind the Federation expansion, the invasion of the Eastland, and the building of Southwatch.

It is now known that the Seekers, including Rimmer Dall, were slaves to the very magic they were charged to eradicate. They were the Shadowen. This fact was known to only a few until the fall of Southwatch, at which point all the Seekers, as well as several council members, vanished or were burned to ashes.

The people arrested by the Seekers for practicing magic were either drained of their magic and their souls, turned to Shadowen themselves, or driven mad by the magic and dumped in the Pit in Tyrsis to rot. Coll and Par Ohmsford are the only captives known to have escaped that fate.

Wayford, and Stern, as well as their surrounding lands and townships. Arishaig was made the capital and was considered the center of power for the Southland, even though monarchies such as Leah still existed within the Southland's borders.

Approximately sixty-five years later, the Federation seemed to lose interest entirely in the regulation of trade and began to focus only on politics and control. Ironically, this was just after news of the death of the last of the Druids reached Arishaig. Around this same time, rumors of dangerous creatures of old magic known as Shadowen arose. Sightings and strange deaths began to terrify the population. These creatures were said to use magic power to steal a person's body and devour the soul. The Federation's Coalition Council claimed that such creatures did exist, created from the use of old magic, and that they alone could protect the people of the Southland from danger. To prove it, they formed a band of secret police, known as the Seekers, whose charge was to purge the population of deadly magic and capture those who used it.

The Federation had begun to combine city militias into a standing army after the War of the Warlock Lord, but it was a slow process. The Shadowen threat created the impetus to speed the process and to recruit more soldiers under the Federation's banner. At the same time, the power within the council shifted to favor the military, which the Prime Minister supported. The instigator of this shift was believed to be the youngest and most influential council member, Rimmer Dall, head of the Seekers and main advisor to the Federation military commander. The coalition, now dominated by the military, used the newly formed army to spearhead a rapid expansion that claimed the entire Southland for the Federation. It was presented as a consensual alliance, but most areas were given no choice when the consent was coerced by the power of the army. Even the long-standing Monarchy of Leah eventually submitted to Federation rule.

All that remained was the Borderlands, originally part of the Southland but by this time clearly established as a separate and sovereign region. Callahorn had resisted the unification for many years. The Federation insisted that the Borderlands were theirs by right, since they were primarily populated by Man. With the rest of the Southland under their control and their separate militias absorbed into the Federation army, they invaded Callahorn.

The Borderlands, which once boasted both strong monarchical leadership and the most skilled fighting force in the Four Lands, had become indecisive and weak. The Legion was no longer the elite fighting unit it had been during the time of the battle for Tyrsis, and Callahorn lacked the strong leadership it had known during its years as a monarchy. Less than a year after the initial invasion, the divided and feuding Borderlands agreed to become a protectorate of the Federation. The last buffer between the now greedy Federation and the rest of the known world crumbled.

Shortly after Federation consolidation of the Southland, the Elves disappeared, leaving the Westland largely unpopulated. This disappearance made it a simple matter for the Federation Council to claim the

Rimmer Dall, head of the Federation Seekers, who was secretly a Shadowen.

Westland as a protectorate, for there was no one to challenge them but a few traveling bands of Rovers. The council justified its takeover by claiming that the Elves created the dark magic that threatened the land, and that the results of that magic had caused them to vanish. It was the Federation's duty, they claimed, to cleanse the entire Westland of the lingering effects of the misbegotten Elven magic. They emphasized their position by forbidding the practice of magic, even street magic, in any form within the Southland or the pro-

Federation Army

The Coalition Council created the Federation army by combining the separate militias of member cities and towns into a single standing army. The consolidation was inspired by the War of the Warlock Lord but did not gain momentum until the threat of the Shadowen loomed over the Southland. In only a few years, it went from a ragtag group of regional militias to the largest and best-trained army in the Four Lands. It was the first and only army to have uniforms, all in silver and black, for all of its soldiers, as well as a strict policy of discipline and decorum.

The regular Federation army marched under a banner with a red stripe and a white stripe across a field of black. Its ranks included infantry, cavalry, and siege divisions. The infantry included archers and swordsmen, both drilled to fight in formation, both armed with short swords, shields, daggers, and in some cases spears. The cavalry was divided into heavy cavalry and light cavalry. Both infantry and cavalry wore mail armor under their uniform surcoats. The smallest unit in the army was a patrol, which became part of a squad, and that part of a company.

The Seekers, no longer in existence, marched with the army, but under their own banner, which displayed a white wolf's head. They were the special forces, controlling creepers and other specialized offensive weapons.

The first job of the Federation army was to enforce the consolidation of the Southland by encouraging the Borderlands to become a protectorate. But the first real test of the army was the invasion of the Eastland. Though well drilled and equipped, the army faced a determined foe in the Dwarves, one who used unorthodox methods and utilized the rugged nature of the Eastern wilderness to great advantage. The poorly equipped and outnumbered Dwarves held the Federation army at bay for five years. In the end, it was the Seekers with their creepers, not the might of the finest army in the lands, that broke the Dwarves' resistance and ended the Federation-Dwarf war.

The army was almost victorious in its campaign against the badly outnumbered Westland Elves, until the Shadowen that made up a large part of its officer corps were burned where they stood on the field of battle. Demoralized, the army broke and left the field. The war ended soon after.

In the last century, new divisions have been added to the regular army with the development of the airship. Airship crews are considered part of the regular army but follow a different set of protocols than do those soldiers who fight on the ground. Airships that are crewed or commanded by Rover mercenaries fight as part of the Federation army but do not follow its standards of protocol or wear its uniform.

The new branch of the army has increased its fighting potential, but for the first time, the army is facing an enemy of nearly equal numbers and similar skills.

tectorates. Ironically, the council never actually attempted to occupy the Westland, possibly because they knew that there was no dangerous magic in the West and that their subjects would never know the difference.

Once certain that Federation rule was unquestioned in the South and West, the council turned their attention to the Dwarves and the Eastland. They claimed the Dwarves had aided the Borderlands

Shadowen Creepers

During the Federation Wars of expansion, a new twist on an Old World war machine wreaked havoc among the Federation's enemies. Called creepers, they resembled the huge war machines used in the Great Wars with one major difference—they were alive.

Morgan Leah wrote of his first sight of a creeper: "It was an apparition composed of the worst bits and pieces of things scavengers might have left. There were jagged ends and shiny surfaces, iron grafted onto flesh, and flesh grown into iron. It had the look of a monstrous, misshapen crustacean or worm, but was neither."

The creepers were a combination of Old World technology and Shadowen magic. Some of the original creepers are believed to have survived the Great Wars, rebuilding themselves with spare parts and, occasionally, living tissue. The Shadowen knew of the creepers, possibly through covert contact with the creeper at Eldwist. They managed to locate a few that were still functional and enhanced them with grafted flesh and Shadowen magic. The resulting creatures combined the most fearsome aspects of machine and monster. The magic gave them life and made them almost invulnerable. By the time of the invasion of the Westland, the Shadowen apparently learned how to make creepers from scratch, ending their reliance on Old World machinery. It is now suspected that the creatures were made and housed at Southwatch.

The new magic-enhanced creepers were huge creatures, sometimes over thirty feet tall, who could scale almost any surface or penetrate almost any defense. Most had clawed feet and pincers or mandibles. They killed by tearing their victims apart. The last known creepers within the Four Lands disappeared after the Shadowen War.

during their resistance and deserved to be punished. The charges were ludicrous, but there was no one to help the Dwarves challenge them. The Elves were gone. There were no Druids. Even Paranor was gone. The paltry remains of the Border Legion were now a part of the Federation, save those few hardy souls who joined the Dwarves, believing more in justice than in survival.

The outcome was a foregone conclusion. The Dwarves had no standing army, while the Federation army was the largest and best-trained in the known world. The Dwarves were forced into a purely defensive war as the Federation juggernaut rolled almost unchallenged over the towns and cities of the Eastland. Entire populations were taken prisoner and sent to the mines in the South. Escaping Dwarves abandoned their cities for the rugged terrain of the high country. They discarded standard military tactics in favor of guerrilla actions. The Federation, though far superior in numbers and armament, was unprepared for a war of this type, and it paid a heavy toll for control of Dwarf land. In the end the Federation needed five bloody years to defeat the Dwarves and drag them down from the mountains. It took the use of creepers, unstoppable monstrous creatures of machine and living flesh combined, to totally destroy the Dwarf nation. The few Dwarves who managed to escape fled to the North, where they, along with some Gnomes and a handful of dissenting Men, established an ongoing resistance movement.

Dwarf prisoners of war as well as any related malcontents were sent to work camps in the South as mine laborers. Few survived. It was a terrible chapter in the

250 —

200 —

150 —

100 —

Secret passage spirals up
counterclockwise to avoid windows.
Has interior peep holes.
Entrances on stair landings.

50 — * Col →

Base square for
G - 3rd otherwise
tower is octagonal └ G

-50 —

River

Bedrock

Bedrock

-100 —

Solid rock

Rainbow Lake

Solid
rock

-150 —

Southwatch

0 10 20 30 40 50

-200 —

View cutaway through the
gate from the south

-250 —

history of the Southland, yet most Southlanders had no idea that such work camps existed.

The Gnomes, who had watched the Federation's ruthless campaign against the Dwarves, surrendered their territories without a fight. With the last serious threat to their authority in the East removed, the Federation claimed the Eastland as a willing protectorate. Their control officially extended everywhere in the Four Lands except the Northland. They even claimed the valley of Paranor, since Paranor itself was no longer there.

The Northland remained unaffected only because the Federation command realized that facing the might of the Trolls on their own forbidding turf would be far more costly than the Dwarf campaign,

with nothing of value to be gained. The Trolls were willing to ignore the Federation so long as the Federation returned the favor. The council, still recovering from its surprise at the strength of the Dwarves' resistance, was not difficult to convince. As far as they were concerned, Federation control now extended to all of the known world that mattered. The Four Lands were now two: the Federation and the northern wilderness.

To mark the unification of the greater portion of the Four Lands under Federation rule and to honor those who had fought so hard to achieve it, the Federation constructed a great tower fortress on the northern edge of the Rainbow Lake. The great black monolith was named Southwatch.

"This fortress will forever reassure the people of the world of the benevolent protection of the Federation and of the strength of the Race of Man," the Coalition Council leader announced at its completion. To most of the citizens who saw it, however, the looming black tower was anything but reassuring.

Over the next sixty years, the Federation tightened its grip on the lands until the strength of that grip began to crush the people. The thriving trade the Federation had originally promised diminished to the lowest levels ever recorded. Taxation increased until many families and townships lost their homes and lands to the council's tax collectors. Within the protectorates, poverty was commonplace. Life was especially hard in the Eastland, where the Federation government seemed determined to wipe out the remains of the Dwarf Race.

Even the land itself seemed to sicken. Plagues and failing crops became commonplace. It seemed that only the council and the Federation army remained strong.

Southwatch

0 10 20 30 40 50

N
W — E
S

→ Up
⇒ Down
-S- Secret door or passage

River

Grasslands

Main Tower

Courtyard

High, steep, rocky bluff

Rainbow Lake

Grasslands

6' wall thickness
4' colonade
2' arches support 2nd,
arched windows
support 3rd floor

Inner side of curtain wall

3rd
2nd
1st

Gate House North Tower

Office of the Officer on duty

Office of the Guard Captain

Barracks for guards in gate house towers

Barracks for other soldiers in towers

Gate House South Tower

The sole threat to complete Federation domination came from the members of the still-active resistance movement, now calling themselves the Free Born, who were hiding in the mountains to the north. The council knew that the Free Born themselves were not strong enough to contest Federation rule, but they were in negotiations with the Rock Trolls, who could be a serious threat if they decided to abandon their neutrality.

The council's position was complicated further when, almost exactly a hundred years after the Federation claimed the abandoned Westland, word came that their claim was contested. The hated Elves had returned. The Federation army, which had been focused on eradicating the resistance, now mobilized its might to destroy the Elves.

The resulting war lasted only months, but its brutality was unmatched since the Second War of the Races. As before, the result seemed preordained. The Elves, led by a daughter of Shannara, were joined at the end by the Free Born and the Rock Trolls, but the Federation had Seekers with strange powers, and their invincible creepers.

Unknown to most of the combatants, the war had a hidden front, for the Shadowen the Federation had warned about did indeed exist—within the Coalition Council itself. Southwatch was the source of their power, not the Elven Westland. The Seekers, who were charged with protecting the people of the Southland from old magic, were themselves Shadowen creatures who were slaves to that magic.

The assault on Southwatch, led by the Druid Walker, eradicated all Shadowen

Southwatch

On the north bank of the Rainbow Lake, where the waters of the Mermidon poured through the edge of the Runne Mountains, a monolithic fortress was erected to celebrate the unification of the Three Lands under Federation rule. Christened Southwatch, the looming black tower became the symbol of Federation domination and oppression. Its name, as well as its placement, seemed intended as a reminder that the people of the land were under the eye of the Federation.

The construction of Southwatch was legislated by Rimmer Dall, then the most powerful man in the Coalition Council. Dwarf labor gangs performed the actual work, and Dwarf blood colored the mortar. The keep was built of black granite so skillfully joined and polished that it had the look of obsidian. When complete, the main tower rose malevolently over two hundred feet above the surrounding countryside. The tallest single building in the Four Lands, it could be seen from many miles distant, thrusting into the sky like a blackened stake. Even stonemasons and engineers marveled at its height. They said it was too tall to stand, especially given the narrow base and the limitations of the materials. But stand it did, for almost a century. One local stonemason claimed it was growing still taller. He spent years measuring and observing the tower from a distance, and claimed he had proof that the tower had increased significantly in size despite the fact that construction had ceased decades before. The man disappeared a few weeks later.

Used primarily as the official headquarters for the Seekers, Southwatch also housed a staff of workers, a full garrison of Federation soldiers, as well as an unknown number of creepers, yet to casual observers the keep appeared nearly deserted. Most of the activity was hidden behind the high walls of the courtyard. The upper levels of the Tower were used as quarters and offices for the Head Seeker and his men, as well as the occasional important guest—or prisoner. The apex of the tower contained a series of small irregular chambers, only ten to fifteen feet across, set into a maze-like configuration. These rooms had no actual doors, only entranceways, and were forbidden to any but the Seekers. The rooms at floor level and just above were larger and were primarily used to house the men in the garrison and the staff.

As tall as it was above the ground, the building burrowed equally far into the earth below, extending downward to end in a large pre-existing cavern that groundwater had hollowed out of the stone. The lower levels contained lairs for the creepers, storage areas, and a dungeon with cells for prisoners. The lowest level was usually heavily guarded.

Even before it was completed, the local inhabitants noticed disturbing changes in the land around the fortress. Previously fertile farmland refused to yield crops. The usually bountiful waters of the Rainbow Lake were devoid of fish. Even the hardy plains grasses began to shrivel.

Morgan Leah wrote of Southwatch, "It loomed over us, immutable and fixed, the blackest dream that sleep had ever conjured, a thing of such evil that the act of viewing it was enough to poison the soul. I could feel it breathing and watching and listening. I could feel its life."

In actual fact, we now know that Southwatch was alive, and was draining the life magic of the land to feed the Shadowen. Morgan Leah was among the small force led by Walker Boh that breached the Tower's defenses to confront the Shadowen and free the magic. They were the only survivors of the battle that ended with the violent destruction of Southwatch. The resulting pillar of fire and ash was seen as far away as Tyrsis and Varfleet.

On the site where Southwatch once stood, there is now only scarred rock and earth. The rubble smoldered for days, but when the last embers went out, there was nothing left of the great black tower, or of the Shadowen who had controlled it and the Southland for almost a century.

and Shadowen-spawned creatures from the land in a terrible conflagration. The effects reached far enough to decimate the Southland army in the field at the Valley of Rhenn. It destroyed all those touched with stolen magic, including the creepers. The remaining soldiers fled the field leaving the day and the battle to the Elves and their allies.

The war with the Federation did not end despite their defeat at the Rhenn, but without the power of Southwatch and the Shadowen involvement, the Southlanders were no longer the impervious force they had been. After a few more pitched battles that ended in defeat for the Federation, the Southlanders withdrew. Several members of the Coalition Council itself had also died horribly at the moment of Southwatch's destruction. They had been the members most intent on pursuing the war. Lacking their influence, the council questioned the wisdom of continuing the war. They finally decided to call the army back to the Southland and leave the Westland to the Elves.

The Borderlands, which had chafed under Federation rule, used the Southland's defeat in the West as a call to arms. Padishar Creel, leader of the Free Born resistance, instigated and led a revolt that drove the Federation from the Borderlands.

The Dwarf resistance also found new vitality, rising against their disillusioned Federation masters. Both these uprisings, coming as they did on the heels of such costly losses in the Westland, created a growing dissatisfaction in the South with the whole program of expansion. After a few months of token resistance, the Federation abandoned the outlying land completely.

It is unclear if the Men of the Southland ever realized that they had been used as pawns for the second time in their history against their fellow Races. There is no doubt that the aftermath marked all the Races for generations.

Unfortunately, the Federation never completely gave up its desire to expand. For several generations there was peace. But Southlanders, especially those who ruled the council, still spoke of the Borderlands as a lost protectorate that must one day be reclaimed. Eventually the plan became more than talk, and almost one hundred years after they had been driven back to the Southland, the Coalition Council again attempted to take over Callahorn, declaring war when Callahorn refused.

The Borderlands, home of the Free Born, had not forgotten the harsh lessons learned under Federation rule. The Free Born met the attempted invasion head on, their ferocity against the greater numbers of the Federation force a testament to the courage of the Borderlands people. They still might have failed, faced with the Federation's ability to field large numbers of troops, but they were joined by the Dwarves and Elves, who were equally determined to keep history from repeating itself. The Dwarves had especially bitter memories of the Federation under the Shadowen, for their Race had been decimated. Together they formed the Southland Coalition.

After eight years of harsh fighting, the Free Born and their allies managed to halt the Federation advance below the Duln. For several years the two armies have mercilessly pounded each other across a stalemated front along the broad expanse of the Prekkendorran Heights—neither side gaining ground, both paying an alarming price in men and equipment.

Of all the conflicts fought since the Great Wars, including this latest

Federation–Free Born War, the South-landers officially participated in only three. In all three they were the aggressors, though they were proven to be pawns of other forces in the First War of the Races and the Shadowen War. But if there is something within the Race of Man that makes him predisposed to domination and manipulation, there is also something inherently noble that often reveals itself in the most unlikely places.

Many great heroes throughout history were Southlanders. Names such as Ohmsford and Leah were involved on the side of truth in almost every conflict since the Second War of the Races. The Druids Bremen, Allanon, and Walker Boh were all born within the South. Many other Southlanders whose names have been lost fought and died to stop the aggression of their brothers. Their sacrifices are as much a part of the Southland's history as any of the tales of Federation oppression. Theirs is often believed to be the true spirit of the Southland.

The Southland:
Cities of the Southland

The survivors of the Race of Man fled south after the war, rebuilding the homes and cities that were lost, trying to create life, rather than destroy it. —Shea Ohmsford

The Southland's isolationist stance would not have been possible if not for the fact that the territory encompassed within the Southland contains both fertile farmland and areas rich in metal ores. The quality of farmland in the South is unsurpassed, save by that of the Sarandanon in the West, and the quality of its metal ores are matched only by those in the mines of the far North. The combination allowed the Southland to provide both food and industrial goods for its people without resorting to trade with the other Races.

Arishaig

Arishaig, the capital of the Federation, is also the Southland's youngest and most modern city. Called the "Jewel of the Federation," it sits far to the southwest, below the older, more industrialized cities of Wayford and Stern. Boasting a population of almost one hundred thousand people, the city lies on the west bank of the Rappahalladran River. Built over the town of the same name, Arishaig was rebuilt and modernized in the aftermath of the War of the Warlock Lord. The newly created Federation needed a capital, and none of the older cities would do. Tax monies raised by the new government were used to transform the sleepy town into a city fit to house the Federation control center. Arishaig, alone of all the Southland cities, was rebuilt to a master plan. It alone has roads paved with brick, flagstones, and cobblestones instead of the normal dirt and gravel. Because Arishaig's focus is on governmental business and trade, most manufactured and farm goods are shipped from the other Southland cities into Arishaig for use by its residents. Specialized craftsmen and tradesmen thrive within her borders.

At the center of Arishaig is the Governmental Compound, dominated by the large, ornately carved stone capitol at its heart. Towering over the other state buildings, the capitol's gracefully carved and ornamented upper archways, adorned with intricate stained-glass windows, overlook the ministry buildings to either side. Though smaller, these buildings—the Ministry of Defense, Ministry of Agriculture, Ministry of Labor, and Ministry of Trade—are all the work of a skilled designer. Adorned with fluted columns, frescoes, stained-glass windows, and elegant statuary, the entire administrative complex is designed to create a sense of awe in anyone entering the main gate of the walled compound. A broad walkway cuts through immaculately kept gardens toward the capitol, where it joins an esplanade passing before each of the ministry buildings. Grand staircases front each building, adding to the sense of authority exuded by the area. Clustered nearby are other, smaller edifices that house governmental offices or serve as residences for governmental officials and their staffs. A walled park with guarded gates and sentry posts to prevent uninvited visitors from gaining access to the grounds surrounds the entire complex. Only those with documentation or an invitation are allowed entry. It is ironic that the Federation, the government of the people, has more protection around its capitol than any of the monarchies of the Four Lands—old or new—ever required around their palaces.

Within the heart of the capitol, past the massive entrance rotunda, is the great round theater where the Coalition Council sits when it is in session. The room, known as the Council Room, contains a lower circle of seats for the main body of the council, centered on a raised dais. There is an upper balcony for seating invited guests during open sessions. The perimeter of the room is decorated with murals depicting Man's heroic struggle for survival in the aftermath of the Great Wars, as well as some of his greatest victories since that time. The mural depicting Southwatch was removed after the Shadowen War.

The Prime Minister and his staff use the west wing of the building. It contains day apartments and offices, as well as various smaller council rooms and briefing areas. The east wing is used by the council members and their staffs and is similarly designed, but with more rooms on a slightly smaller scale.

A dedicated cadre of elite Federation soldiers guards the complex as well as the politicians within it. There are no unguarded corridors within the public areas of the governmental complex. Each of the ministers also has a household private guard. When outside their residences, they are always accompanied by at least two of their personal guards.

To further ensure both the safety and the secrecy of the government, a series of concealed underground tunnels was built connecting the Council Room and the Prime Minister's chambers to the various ministries. No politician ever has to be seen making deals with another. It is doubtful if most of the people of the Federation, or of Arishaig, know these tunnels exist.

The rest of the city is designed to radiate outwards from the glory of the central complex. Outside of the Governmental Compound's high stone walls, a series of small open parks extends for about fifty yards beyond the walls. From the capitol area, wide paved roads radiate toward the outer edge of the city like spokes on a wheel. Other roads cross and crisscross these main thoroughfares in a pattern that tightens toward the outskirts of the city.

Nearest to the governmental compound are the large walled estates belonging to various diplomats and council members. These estates often consist of several buildings set amid manicured grounds, centered on great manor houses. A series of well-maintained gardens separates the estates and larger houses. Open to the public, these parks all contain grand fountains and statuary carved by the finest artisans in the Southland.

Farther out are the homes and businesses of tradesman, craftsmen, and merchants. This area also contains shops and eating and drinking establishments of all types as well as the better class of brothel. On the riverfront side of the city, this area contains the docks for river trade boats and warehouses for goods sent from the other cities as well as various riverfront shops and taverns.

On the north and west sides, beyond the trade district and toward the outer edge of the city, are the less affluent areas, which include hovels for the poorer workers and the less reputable brothels and taverns. Beyond the poverty areas, the city gradually flattens into farmland and forest areas.

From her clean, carefully ordered city center, with its modern buildings, artfully controlled gardens, and paved streets, to its secret passageways, Arishaig is designed for power. Control, order, power, and secrecy—the qualities that are the spirit of the Federation are embodied in the bedrock of Arishaig.

Wayford and Stern

Believed to have originally existed as townships in the age before the First War of the Races, Wayford and Stern were the first settlements reestablished after that war. Both were built deep in the southern plains near river routes and farming country, but far away from the other Races. At this time, the South was mostly made up of tiny farming communities, which relied on the larger towns for trading their crops and procuring manufactured goods. Wayford and Stern grew from villages into industrialized cities and trade centers supporting the farming communities around them. They were each governed by a council and protected by an armed militia made up of citizens and local farmers.

Now, as part of the Federation, they are under the control of the Coalition Council, represented by their elected council members, and protected by a garrison of the Federation army. Federation rule brought with it efficiency of government and a renewed emphasis on manufacturing that led to greater growth and employment. They increased the number and quality of roads between cities to allow faster wagon traffic, but the roads within both Wayford and Stern are still primarily dirt and mud, except for those near the garrison and the governmental offices, which have been covered with gravel.

According to official Federation records, the population of each city hovers between eight hundred thousand and one million. Most of the people within

Wayford and Stern are tradesmen, general laborers, or shopkeepers. The only way to become a tradesman is through the apprentice system. Most shops, regardless of the product, are controlled by a master craftsman who employs journeymen and apprentices beneath him, each hoping to eventually earn the master rating and a shop of their own. Unskilled laborers not looking to apprentice can find work in the larger warehouses or serving municipal needs. These days, though, anyone not employed by a guildsman is likely to be conscripted for the Federation army. Dying is considered unskilled labor.

Each city is built around a central plaza, once the village green, with governmental offices nearby. The rest of the city is divided, rather haphazardly, into warehouse and storage districts, shops and manufacturing districts, the tavern district (which also contains inns and brothels), and the residential district. Many people live where they work, in quarters built over or near their shops. Only the more well-to-do citizens have separate homes within the residential areas. The poor either live in the back rooms of the shops that employ them or in rooming houses in the tavern district. The very poor live on the streets, though any that are able-bodied are certain to be snatched up for the war effort.

Dechtera

If Arishaig is the "Jewel of the Federation," Dechtera is its grime-encrusted workhorse. Located north of all the other major Federation cities, Dechtera sprawls across the arid central plains that run south of the Prekkendorran Heights. The largest city in the Four Lands, Dechtera is also the least attractive. By day, the smoke belching from its thousands of foundries can be seen for miles over the southern plains. By night, its furnaces glow red like the fires of the underworld.

Almost as old as Wayford and Stern, Dechtera was originally established as a mining town, located between the ore-rich deposits of the southern hills and the great western forest. During the First War of the Races, the need for weapons and military equipment spurred its growth into a premier manufacturing center, home of the finest metal-smiths in the Southland. It was here, during the Second War of the Races, that the legendary Sword of Shannara was made by the master smith Uprox Screl.

The forest is long gone, sacrificed to the voracious hunger of the insatiable furnaces, but the mines have grown ever larger and deeper. By the time of the War of the Warlock Lord, most of the surface ores were depleted and the shafts were extended deeper into the earth, increasing the dangers involved in mining the needed ores. Tunnel collapses and subterranean gas leaks were regular occurrences. It became more difficult to find workers willing to risk their lives for the small amount of pay allocated to mine workers. During the years of Federation expansion, the mines of Dechtera were infamous for consuming lives almost as fast as its furnaces consumed coal. The Federation began conscripting prisoners of war as slave labor to work the mines. This solved both the labor problem and the question of how to eliminate the prisoners. Killing them outright might have alarmed the population, but everyone knew that miners died all the time.

In the aftermath of the Federation-Dwarf War, almost a third of the Dwarf nation met their deaths in the mines. While a few of the labor camps have been converted and modernized for use by

Uprox Screl

Uprox Screl, Master Smith, was the embodiment of the heart and soul of Dechtera. Arguably the finest swordsmith in the Four Lands, he almost refused to cast the blade that became the Sword of Shannara.

A powerfully built but gentle man, Uprox was honored for both his skill and his hard work. Born near Dechtera, he moved to the city to learn the smithing trade, working his way up from apprentice to master in less time than most. His craftsmanship was highly prized. By the time he was thirty he perfected the art of making fine blades as strong as iron, yet light as tin. When word of his skill spread, buyers flocked to buy his pieces. Soon the sale of his work enabled him to build his own smithy and buy a home outside of town, away from the smoke and soot, in which to raise his family.

But one day a buyer returned to tell him of the marvelous carnage his blade had wrought. The warrior was delighted, but Uprox was heartsick. Uprox was an artist, who loved shaping steel—he had never really thought about the pain his creations could inflict. He began to realize that his beautiful lightweight blades were being used as terribly efficient weapons of death. The more weapons he made, the more it ate at his soul, until he could no longer find joy in his work. He tried to make other things, but all anyone wanted were his famous blades. By the time the Druid Bremen found him, he had given up metal work for woodcarving.

The Druid convinced the smith to cast one more very special blade, a weapon that would have no equal—one that would save lives rather than end them. A sword forged with magic.

It took three days of preparation and one long night of casting to make the great sword. Legends are still told throughout Dechtera of the night when green magic burned in Uprox Screl's forge, spirits danced in tune with his hammer, and a hand with a burning torch rose out of the fires to embrace the molten blade.

By dawn, Druid and smith together had forged the last and greatest weapon Uprox Screl would ever make, and the only one that was destined to save lives: The Sword of Shannara. Uprox was the first and only smith to forge a sword with magic in the history of the Four Lands. But as it does with all things, the magic changed him. Within a month, he took his wife, children, and grandchildren, and left Dechtera forever.

He settled in the Borderlands, in a village above the Rainbow Lake. Changing his name to Uprox Creel, he lived out his life in peace, never guessing that his heroic descendants, Panamon Creel and Padishar Creel, would both become part of the history of the sword that was his best and last creation.

*U*prox Screl, master smith who forged the Sword of Shannara.

Federation convicts, some of the original sheds used to house prisoners during the Dwarf War still stand on the plains outside the city. They are grim reminders of the atrocities committed in the name of human domination, for while it was the Shadowen who instituted the program that nearly destroyed the Dwarf Race, it was often Men who carried it out.

The mines are still active, supplying the ores needed for the ongoing war effort, but now the majority of the laborers are Men, usually prisoners, who serve out their sentences in the dark depths of the mines. Conditions have improved in that fewer workers die from the labor than during the Shadowen period, and adequate food and shelter are provided to ensure the survival of all but the weakest, but the work is still arduous, the conditions still hostile, and death still a constant threat.

While the mines may seem like a passageway to the underworld, the city itself often resembles artists' images of the nether regions. The fires of the great foundry furnaces burn night and day, belching out clouds of smoke and soot. The combination of the fires and the heat-retaining smoke cause the temperatures inside the city to remain several degrees above that of the surrounding plain. The resulting soot and ash coat everything with a dark gray pall. Those who can afford it live in the suburban and rural areas on the outskirts of the city to avoid the soot and the heat.

Unlike Arishaig, or even Wayford and Stern, Dechtera was built to no set plan. It has simply grown as needed. Foundries and shops, warehouses and brothels stand side by side along the dirt and gravel streets of the huge city. Open areas are often piled high with scrap metal or raw ore. Alehouses and taverns dominate the central area of the city, but even there, the

occasional small blacksmith shop can still be found. The clang of the hammers and the roar of the furnace can be heard day and night. The larger foundries and smithies run two shifts to avoid having to cool the furnaces or bank the fires. The fuel to feed the fires, hard coal and wood, is brought in from mines and forests on the Eastland borders.

As dirty as the city appears, the creations of the artisans and craftsmen who live there have no equal in the Southland. From simple tools to fine weapons and complex machinery, all are made here. Unlike the conscripted miners outside the city, the people who live and work in Dechtera do so because they choose to. Most of them are craftsmen who have found their own type of magic in the science of metallurgy or in the joy of shaping and honing a fine piece. From the lowest apprentice to the most highly skilled master smith, all take pride in their work. Even the shopkeepers and tavern owners take pride in the work Dechtera produces, for they know the Federation cannot find its way to the future without them.

Highlands of Leah

Balanced between the Southland and the Borderlands, the Highlands of Leah are a community separate from either, yet claimed by both. While technically part of the Southland, Leah's isolated location has allowed it to retain its individual identity for most of its history

The aftermath of the First War of the Races left much of the Race of Man discouraged and seeking new homes within the South. Most men fled deep into the South, in an attempt to put as much distance as possible between themselves and the memory of their bitter defeat. But a small group of hardy individuals, led by a man named Tamlin Leah, stopped running when they discovered the wild beauty of an isolated upland just south of the Rainbow Lake. The land was heavily forested and full of game, yet protected on all sides by natural barriers that would discourage visitors. The land eventually took on the name of its first family and became known as the Highlands of Leah.

It is easy to imagine how these settlers, worn and travel-weary from the escape to the South, had been caught up by the rugged splendor of the lands as they rose above the surrounding forests and marshlands. Some legends claim that Tamlin Leah was a warrior who wanted a safe place away from the rest of Man because he and his small band of friends had been among those who opposed their Race's push for world domination. Others say that he was a skilled hunter who found in the Highlands a land, plentiful with game, that he and his family could love and protect.

In either case, Tamlin and his family and friends found their new home, far from any existing towns, on a high plain that overlooked the lowlands and forests around them. There they built a village. The isolated location was no hardship. Between its game-filled forests and fertile soil, Leah was completely self-sufficient. The village prospered and, in time, grew into a city. That city in turn spawned its own outlying hamlets.

By the Second War of the Races, men from Leah were fighting side by side with those of the fledgling border outposts in an effort to stop the southward advance of the Northland army. Their battle cry, "Leah! Leah!" was heard often on those bloody battlefields. Many towns and villages fell under the assault, but the Northlanders were stopped well short of the Rainbow Lake and Leah. The legacy of the fighting sons of Leah began with their

Menion Leah, hero of Kern.

battles against the Trolls in that war. Once the war was over, the people of the Highlands proclaimed the elder Leah as King, thereby becoming the first monarchy south of the Dragon's Teeth.

The new king created a standing army, headed by the survivors of the War with the Warlock Lord, which was dedicated to the protection of the people of Leah and of their rural neighbors. He built the city into a walled fortress large enough to protect all the citizens of his land. "So long as there were Leahs on the throne," he vowed, "there would always be warriors ready to defend the Kingdom."

For the next six hundred years, the Leah family ruled in an unbroken line of succession, beloved by the people as benevolent caretakers and lauded for their attention to the well-being of their people and their land. The Leahs were the only government the tiny kingdom had ever

The Sword of Leah

Almost as well known as the Sword of Shannara, the Sword of Leah was originally forged as the Sword of State for the Kingdom of Leah. Bearing the royal markings and colors of Leah, it eventually became part of the royal regalia for the Crown Prince of Leah, to be handed down to the new heir at his coming of age. Beautifully wrought and balanced, the sword was worn across the back in the Highlander fashion in a scabbard of fine leather also bearing the royal seal. It was considered one of the finest weapons in the Southland despite the fact that, for many years, it rarely saw usage outside of ceremonial events.

But the Sword proved itself to be a valuable weapon in the hands of Prince Menion, who wielded it skillfully in many skirmishes against foes, both mortal and not, in the War of the Warlock Lord. He proudly handed his honored blade down to his son and heir, Owain.

Owain Leah retired the honored blade, now battered from hard use, and commissioned a new sword for his heir. But the Sword of Leah was not content to remain in retirement. Rone Leah, Menion's great grandson, was drawn to the old blade despite its worn and battered hilt and scabbard. The blade was still serviceable, having been given expert care over the years. Rone's father noticed his admiration of the weapon, and gifted Rone with the sword as a small symbol of his standing as the youngest Prince of Leah. Rone needed a way to protect his friend Brin Ohmsford on her quest to destroy the Ildatch, a quest given her by the Druid Allanon. But Rone and his cold iron blade were no match for the eldritch creatures they had to face. To be her protector he needed magical help. Allanon gave him that help at the shores of the Hadeshorn.

Rone Leah later wrote: "The Druid bade me dip the Sword of Leah into the deadly waters of the Lake. I did not know what to expect. I carefully lowered the blade into the swirling waters until it was completely submerged, being careful to keep my hands clear. As the metal touched the lake, the waters boiled and hissed about the blade as though they were alive. After a moment, the boiling stopped, and Allanon bade me remove the sword from the water. When I did, the polished silver sheen of the blade was gone; it had turned black, covered with the waters of the Hadeshorn, which clung to it, swirling as if alive. I almost dropped the sword to see it move so. But Allanon was not done. Blue druid fire flared from his fingertips along the length of the sword. He said he was fusing the water and metal into one. When he was done, the blade was clean and its edges true. Its surface was a black mirror with murky green pools of light swirling lazily just below the surface. I knew it was magic! But the magic was not just in the blade. I could feel the sword's power, as I had never done when it was merely iron. It was now a part of me in a way I did not understand until much later, both a wondrous gift and a magical curse."

The Sword of Leah

The transformation allowed the Sword of Leah to cut and parry magic as well as physical attacks. Rone discovered the sword could now destroy even Mord Wraiths, whose magic made them immune to conventional weapons. A direct cut from the sword turned most magical creatures to piles of black ash. But, as with all magic, it was both light and dark. Its magic created a dependency on the sword that grew with every use.

Rone Leah was the first to taste the magic of the sword. His addiction to it nearly cost Brin Ohmsford her life. He managed to come to terms with his need for the magic in time to aid Brin in the Battle at the Maelmord.

After the campaign against the Ildatch, Rone realized how powerful and dangerous the sword could be, and retired it rather than pass it to his children. It remained in a place of honor in the Palace of Leah, and was one of the artifacts carefully removed before the Federation confiscated the Palace. The magic inherent of the sword became a legend told to the sons of Leah to remind them of the days of their kingdom's greatness.

Three hundred years later, Morgan Leah requested the old sword. No one else was interested in the ancient relic in its battered scabbard. His father gave it to him, having never used it himself. By this time, the tales of its magic were considered nothing more than a way to explain the strange black finish on the blade that never dulled. Its scabbard had been replaced many times, and the hilt half as many, but the blade was still sharp and true. Morgan simply wanted a good blade; preferably, one that would remind him of the legacy his family had lost to the Federation. He was doubtless surprised, during his first battle with a Shadowen, to discover that the magic was real. But Morgan also discovered the dark side of the sword's power. The magic's use drained him during long battles, and bonded him, body and soul, to the sword. He later wrote: "The sword seemed to be using me even as I was using it. I thought it was killing me, but I could not stop."

The sword's power was not invincible, however. In a desperate battle against the Shadowen in their Pit in Tyrsis, he shattered the blade while escaping. The remnant of the magic saved him in a battle with a Shadowen Spy at the Free-Born Stronghold at the Jut. The sword remained broken until the elemental Quickening restored it upon her death as a reward to Morgan for his love and bravery.

Morgan went on to use the restored sword's magic against the Shadowen in the battle of Southwatch. He also carried it during the battles to liberate the Eastland, though its magic was not needed, merely its steel.

After the Federation was driven from the East and the Borderlands, the Sword was again retired and put on display in the Leah manor house as an honored part of the Leah heritage. It remained there for nearly a century, until Corran Leah gave it to his oldest son Quentin to use on his voyage on the Jerle Shannara with the Druid Walker Boh.

The magic of the sword has kept the blade in mint condition for hundreds of years. It is a magic that responds only to the threat of other magic. It cannot be activated by will or for simple curiosity. As a weapon of both metal and magic, the Sword of Leah has served the need of the brave sons of Leah, even as they have served the need of the Four Lands in battles against dark magic.

known or wanted. Under their guidance the Highlands flourished.

By the time of the War of the Warlock Lord, Leah was the oldest kingdom in the Southland. The Crown Prince, Menion Leah, acquitted himself with honor during the war and is credited with saving the people of Kern and helping to defend Tyrsis during the final battle with the Warlock Lord's forces. After that war, Leah formed an official alliance with Callahorn and the Borderlands. Menion cemented that commitment by marrying a daughter of the former kings of Kern.

Protected by their isolated location, the Highlands were never attacked directly, yet the Leahs continued to pass the knowledge of battle and hunting from father to son so that skills honed in the wars would not be lost. Though they never had to defend their own borders, the warrior princes of Leah and their descendants carved a path of honor through most of the major conflicts within the Four Lands.

Unfortunately, their courage and fighting skills proved useless against the enemy that finally took their kingdom. Nine hundred years after Leah was established, the oldest monarchy in the South fell without a battle, devoured by the Federation. Overpowered and outnumbered by the Federation war machine, the King of Leah gave up his throne without a fight rather than endanger his people in what would have been a useless massacre. In exchange, the family members were allowed to keep their freedom and most of their lands. The Federation made Leah a protectorate, abolishing the monarchy and installing a provisional governor and cabinet. They disbanded the army of Leah and stationed a garrison of soldiers to maintain order. Though Leah was a small kingdom, the Federation believed that its army, and the independent nature of its people, posed a threat to Federation rule. It was also seen as a stepping-stone to control of the Borderlands.

Controlling Leah was difficult for the Federation. Though the people showed no outward signs of disobedience, small terrorist actions, many of them masterminded by sons of Leah, plagued the occupation force and the provisional governors. At one point the Palace was even burned to the ground. It had been commandeered for use as the governor's mansion, a use that many within Leah found distasteful, though none would say so publicly. The Governor and his family escaped but never managed to find the arsonist. Sixty years after the Shadowen War, the Federation was driven out of the Borderlands. A few years later it was no surprise to anyone that the most recent provisional governor seemed eager—almost grateful—to finally relinquish Federation control of Leah and escape back to Arishaig.

Rather than reinstate the monarchy, a council of elders was formed, with the head of the Leah family given a seat on the council. There are rumors that the senior Leah was offered a crown and refused it, only reluctantly taking a seat on the council. It is his son, Coran Leah, who now sits as First Minister, leading the people much as his ancestors did, despite the change of title. His sons, Quentin and Bek, have already proven that they too are part of the legacy of the courageous sons of Leah.

The City of Leah

Thick gray stone walls surround the perimeter of Leah, the capital of—and only city in—the Highlands. Gates and gatehouses are set into the wall at the four points of the compass, though the majority of the traffic travels through the main entryway at the West Gate. Though it never had to repel an attacking foe, the city was built to be a fortress haven for the people of the region.

Smaller than Tyrsis or the great cities of the deep South, Leah is a sizable metropolis in comparison to the tiny hamlets and sparse population of the surrounding rural region. It is the only Southland city of any size north of the Prekkendorran. Within the walls, homes, shops, and taverns are nestled among trees, ponds, and flowering gardens. The main thoroughfare, a well-packed dirt road wide enough for two wagons abreast, enters the city proper at the West Gate. The road is lined with small shops and markets until it reaches the inner city, where it opens onto parks and residences.

In the days of the monarchy, the road led to the Palace, a grand two-story mansion set into a grove of hickory trees amid an estate of manicured lawns and fragrant gardens, screened from the street by high shrubs and vine-covered iron gates. The Palace, though quite tiny if compared to the Palace of Tyrsis, was comfortably spacious, built of stone and hardwoods with a sizeable Great Hall, boasting the largest stone fireplace in the Highlands. Its many rooms were large and decorated with tapestries and hunting trophies. The kitchens contained large fireplaces suitable for roasting wild boar or venison, and even the servants' quarters were warmed by individual fireplaces. Most of the furnishings were made from hand-carved wood or bone and upholstered in leather or furs. The workmanship was unequaled in all the Southland.

After the Palace was burned, the provisional governor was forced to abandon the estate. The land was left empty for forty years, with only the crushed-rock walkways and burned foundation stones to mark where the Palace had once stood.

Though officially still Federation property, Leah family retainers tended the gardens. For over 250 years, the Leahs lived outside the city walls on their country estate, where they raised cattle. But fifty years ago, when the Federation finally left the Highlands, Coran Leah's father reclaimed the land confiscated by the Federation government, and built a new two-story home on the site of the old Palace.

The new manor house is much simpler than the Palace of Leah, with far less housing for servants and armsmen. Yet it is still the largest home in the city. Multiple eaves and dormers set off its long rooflines and deep alcoves, though the hickories that used to add such charm to the original building have never completely recovered from the fire. Each of the major rooms has a stone fireplace for warmth in the winter, though none are as large as the one originally built in the Palace's Great Hall. In place of the Great Hall, the manor house has a spacious dining hall and several large comfortable drawing rooms, which are often used for council business. The decor is still primarily wood, bone, and leather, though increased trade had added to the variety of materials used by the craftsmen who furnished the house. Unfortunately, many of the original furnishings confiscated by the Federation were lost in the fire or confiscated by the Federation and sent to Arishaig.

Across from the old Palace grounds, on the opposite side of the main street, is the city park. Covering approximately fifteen acres, the park is graced with a small central pond, with many paths and seating areas placed among flowering shrubs, trees, and gardens. Beyond the park, narrow streets of hard-packed dirt spread outwards to the city walls. Most of these streets are lined with all manner of shops, markets, taverns, and a few inns. The number of inns has increased over the last century, as more travelers have come to Leah. In the early years, visitors were rare, and most of the city's residences were located within the protection of the thick walls. Now the outer city sprawls away from the walls, and homesteads and farms blanket most of the once-open high plain. As one travels away from the city, homes and small residences gradually give way to large estates, sheep, cattle, and horse farms, and eventually large cooperatives maintained by the citizens.

To the north, the hillside rises to meet the highland forest that extends over much of Leah. Woodsmen's cottages and a few homesteads have been established within these woods, but most of the small hamlets and villages of Leah are situated in open meadows or upper plains hidden within the hills, though a few habitations and cattle farms have been established on the grasslands to the west.

The majority of the land belongs to the Leah family and has been left as wilderness, with an occasional hunting lodge or trapper's cottage hidden in the trees. The finest of these lodges was built in the days of the monarchy for the use of the royal family and guests. Hidden in a stand of pine at the edge of the Highlands, it was unknown to most outside of Leah, especially the Federation, who cared little for venturing outside the walls of the city unless forced. Built to be a base for hunting and fishing in the mist lakes, the lodge became a favored refuge for the sons of Leah during the years of the Federation occupation.

Built to last, the lodge was constructed of timber and stone, with stone floors and walkways and a large open central room with a high vaulted ceiling framed with pine timbers. The lodge looks much as it did when built, with a well-stocked ale bar to one side and a huge stone fireplace dominating the rest of the room. Most of the original leather and wood furniture remains, though many of the pieces have been repaired or refinished over the years, and the kitchen is still well supplied with staples and equipped for handling game and fish. Hunting trophies have been added to the walls, changing and multiplying as each Leah has adjusted the decor to match his personal tastes.

One of the most luxurious features of the lodge is located outside its walls. Approximately a hundred yards to the rear of the lodge are several small clear blue spring-fed pools, used as bathing pools. The pools provided a refreshing end to the most exhausting hunting expedition. For those who craved something even more exotic, mud baths were located about a mile away from the main lodge. They were not used as often as the pools but were very popular on hot summer days.

Beyond the Highlands

The land surrounding Leah has always been its first line of defense. To the west, beyond a border of shrub-covered grasslands, lies the Duln, a thick-forested wilderness, and the swift Rappahalladran River. To the north, a mass of cliffs overlooks the great pool of the Rainbow Lake. The south and east are well protected by the dead wasteland known as the Lowlands of Clete, and beyond that, the dense mass of the Black Oaks and the impenetrable Mist Marsh.

In the years of the monarchy, travelers from outside the region rarely visited the Highlands. Travel from the west was possible only by those who knew the trails or who had excellent Tracking skills. There were no established trails. The local villagers who regularly traveled to Leah used their knowledge of the area to follow existing deer trails through the forest of the Duln wilderness.

The southern and eastern approaches to Leah were guarded by the Lowlands of Clete, a dismal, treacherous bog that, on the east, connected the Highlands to the Black Oaks, an ancient forest of giant oaks that stretched for over a hundred miles south from the marsh at the edge of the Rainbow Lake.

The nearly impenetrable wood was over twenty miles wide in most areas. Considered the most dangerous forest in the Southland, it stood like a wall between Leah and the Lower Anar. The great oaks were so numerous and their branches so thick that it was impossible to see the sky from the ground. The citizens of Leah, who were born in the forests of the highlands and grew up traversing the Duln, avoided the Black Oaks whenever possible. They believed the forest was alive with ancient magic trapped there since the Great Wars or before. But the greatest danger was the unnaturally huge wolves that ruled its dark domain, preying on the unwary. Over the years, more than a hundred people fell victim to the wood. Most died as a result of mishap, starvation, or the wolves, but some died from unknown causes.

During the age of Federation occupation, roads were built through Clete and the Black Oaks. Hundreds of man-hours were spent clearing the huge trees and filling the bog with gravel so that the Federation could move its wagons and men more easily to Leah and on to the Borderlands. Once the roads were complete, the wolves were no longer seen in the forest, apparently moving to deeper and safer territory. Travelers discovered Leah and the beauty of the Highlands.

Once the Federation left, there was no one to maintain the roads. The Lowlands of Clete began to reclaim her own. Many roads are now overgrown by brambles or have subsided into the quicksand. The roads in the Black Oaks are overgrown as well, though still useable by carts and larger wagons.

But even the Federation could not build roads through the Mist Marsh. Located between the northern edge of the Black Oaks and the Rainbow Lake, the Mist Marsh blocks the most direct route from Leah to Varfleet. Unchanged for centuries, slime-covered water hides the treacherous bottomless mud of the marsh. The green grasslike covering has lured many creatures to a slow death by suffocation. Thick mist constantly shrouds the marsh, making it impossible to tell location or even time of day. But the bog is not the only danger. Predators such as the Mist Wraiths prey on those who become confused in the constant twilight and wander too close to the swamp. Wolves from the Black Oaks may even feed on victims waiting to die in the unrelenting grasp of the marsh mud. Most wise travelers take the long route to the north and avoid the marsh at all costs.

Though Leah is no longer as isolated as in pre-Federation days, its people still prefer the wilds of the Highlands and their own company to that of the more advanced cities of the south. While they welcome the travelers that have come with the roads, and make use of those roads themselves to see the world, it seems clear that most within Leah would not regret a return to the age of isolation, when the men of Leah could choose their battles and fight for the one thing they never lost—Highlands pride.

Shady Vale

Though not a city, Shady Vale is typical in many ways of the many villages and hamlets that make up much of the rural

Mist Wraiths and Log Dwellers

Within the Mist Marsh, the fog and the murky waters hide a danger much greater than grasping mud, for powerful creatures of ancient magic lurk beneath the slime. Two such are the creatures known as Mist Wraiths and Log Dwellers. Born of ancient magic and the horrors unleashed during the Great Wars, both lie beneath the waters, buried in the mud of the marsh as they await their prey.

Log Dwellers are so named because they often appear to be partially submerged trees. When disturbed, they erupt from the water to attack with great jaws full of razor-sharp teeth and forelegs with sharp, grasping claws.

The Mist Wraith has an affinity for slime, blending into the marsh with its mottled greenish skin. It attacks using its many powerful tentacles to grasp its prey and drag it into the waters to be devoured. Though none have ever been captured, survivors have estimated its average body size to range between fifteen and twenty feet in length, and eight to ten feet in height, with tentacles as much as twice that long. It appears to have a large tearing beak within the center of its tentacles, which it uses to crush and consume its meal.

Despite the size of both creatures, they are tremendously quick and can kill a full-grown man in minutes.

A Log Dweller, one of the deadly creatures native to the Mist Marsh.

population of the Southland. Located a day's walk west of Leah, beyond the Rappahalladran and the Duln, Shady Vale sits nestled into one end of a valley ringed by the Duln forest. Its remote location has allowed it to escape most of the battles and difficulties faced by other areas. It was only occupied once, during the Shadowen War. For the most part the farming village has managed to continue almost unchanged through the centuries.

Within the town, single-story houses sit in tidy array along a dirt road that meanders through the valley. It is common to see farm animals wandering among the neatly trimmed hedges and carefully maintained cottages. The valley wall pro-

tects the village from the worst of the weather as well as unwanted attention.

The largest building in the Vale is the Inn, built by Curzad Ohmsford twenty years before the War of the Warlock Lord. Constructed of huge logs interlocked over a stone foundation and boasting one of the earliest shingle roofs in the Vale, the Inn consists of a main building and a lounging porch, with two long wings extending out and back on either side. The large lounging room contains benches, high-backed chairs, and several long wooden tables but is dominated by a fireplace on the opposite wall and a bar running down the length of the center wall. Sleeping rooms for the guests were located in the two wings, while the family lived in several rooms in the east wing. The Inn has been partially renovated over the years, though the basic construction remains sound. The Ohmsfords still own the Inn, though they now live in a cottage at the edge of the tree line and allow a friend of the family to run the Inn.

Most of the people who live within Shady Vale make their living by farming. The community is self-sufficient and considers itself large enough to give aid and support to the smaller farming communities and isolated homesteads within the area. Those willing to share their skills often travel to other hamlets and towns to give assistance. Payment is usually made in goods and hospitality. Simple values and a simple way of life are the focus for the people of the Vale.

But unlike other hamlets within the Southland, Shady Vale is more than a sleepy farming village. It is also home to the Ohmsfords, a family whose heroism has been proven in every conflict within the Four Lands since the Second War of the Races.

Two Families:
A Legacy of Courage

We are the children of Jerle Shannara, heirs to the magic of the Elven house of Shannara, keepers of a trust. —Walker Boh

ince the Second War of the Races, the house of Shannara and its Southland children have been at the fore of every major victory over the forces of darkness. Bound by their blood, they have been supported in almost all these conflicts by the children of the equally noble house of Leah.

A tiny kingdom and an isolated farming village seem unlikely places to find heroes, much less entire families of them. Yet the hamlet of Shady Vale is home to the Ohmsfords, heirs of Shannara. The neighboring Highlands of Leah are home to the Leahs, who for as many generations have stood with the Ohmsfords—at their side or guarding their back—in almost every conflict, proving the nobility of the line that once ruled that tiny highland kingdom. Only the Druids have made as great a continuing contribution to the protection of the Four Lands—though it must be noted that the last of the Druids still living is himself an Ohmsford.

Of course, the Druids, by the very nature of their order, assume a role as guardians of the land when they are ordained into the order. The Ohmsfords and the Leahs made no such vow. They

The Blue Elfstones

During the Age of Faerie, when magic was commonplace and man was yet unborn, the Elves created a variety of talismans designed to contain and work with Elven magic. Among these were the jewel-like stones of power known as Elfstones. Originally there were many different kinds of Elfstones, each designed for different purposes and each identifiable by its color. Over the ages all were lost but three kinds: the Blue Elfstones, the Black Elfstone, and the Loden.

The Blue Elfstones, so named for their brilliant blue color, are "seeking stones" that can be used to find anything that is lost or hidden once the user wills it to be so. The three small stones represent the heart, the mind, and the body. They can only be used together, and only when the user has joined his or her heart, mind, and body toward one purpose. The power of their magic is directly proportional to the strength of the man or woman wielding them.

All Elfstones also contain secondary defensive capabilities. They can be used for protection against other forms of magic or to defend against creatures made from magic or sorcery. Since they were made with Elven magic, only those with Elven blood can use the Blue Elfstones. They will also only work for one to whom they are freely given. If they are stolen or taken by force, they will not serve the bearer.

The Elves gave the stones to the Druid Allanon, and he in turn gave them to Shea Ohmsford to use on his quest for the Sword of Shannara. The stones allowed Shea to reach the Skull Kingdom during his search for the sword. It was the Elfstones that brought innate magic to the Ohmsford line. When Shea's grandson Wil forced the stones to work despite his diluted Elven blood, the magic irrevocably changed him, becoming a part of his blood, to be passed to his children and from generation to generation. It is the Elfstones that began the heritage of Ohmsford magic.

The Ohmsfords secretly gave the stones back to the Elves, once their Elven blood was too diluted to make use of them. The Elves kept the stones for many years, but they were lost on an Elven expedition across the Blue Divide.

The Blue Elfstones, "seeking stones" made with Elven magic.

were simple people who answered a call to defend the land. They were not born soldiers. Only the Leahs were even trained to fight. Yet if not for them, the history of the Four Lands would be far different. The world would almost certainly be shrouded in the power of dark magic and ruled by the beings who are enslaved by it.

But how did a family of innkeepers and Healers become defenders of the land? Curzad Ohmsford, an innkeeper who had been recently widowed, discovered a young woman and a half-Elven baby at the door to his inn. The woman was a distant cousin who had been born in Shady Vale. All her other relatives were gone. She was also very ill. Curzad took her in and cared for her, glad to have someone besides his own small son to look after. Unfortunately, there were few skilled

The Sword of Shannara

When the Warlock Lord and his armies swept out of the North, they appeared to be unstoppable. Weapons of iron or magic could not harm the Warlock himself. The Druid Council, which might have been able to stand against him, was gone, destroyed by his conquest of Paranor. Only a small handful of Druids escaped, but they did not have the means to defeat their foe. They needed a weapon that was unlike any other, a weapon that could breach the rebel Druid's mystic defenses and destroy him. They needed a weapon of greater magic.

Bremen first saw the answer in a vision given to him by Galaphile's spirit at the Hadeshorn. It was a sword of metal stronger than iron and magic greater than Brona's. Bremen was the grandson of a smith, but he did not have the knowledge or the skill it would take to forge such a sword. He went to Cogline, who still kept the knowledge of the old world sciences of metallurgy. Cogline gave the Druid the formula for a metal that would be tremendously strong and impossibly light.

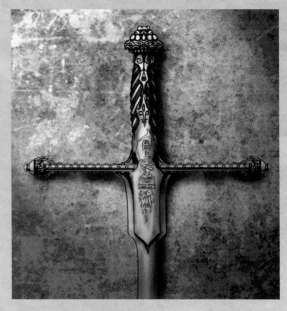

To forge the sword, he sought out the finest smith in all the Southland—Uprox Screl. Together they combined Cogline's science with Bremen's magic and added the magic of the Elit Druin, talisman of the Druids—the talisman of truth. The resulting blade was the finest sword Uprox had ever made. Its burnished hilt bore the hand of the Druids holding forth the burning torch with the flame racing toward the tip of the blade. The blade was bright and sharp and of an unusual length and size, but was lighter and stronger than any other sword in existence. It could not be shattered in battle, whether struck by iron or magic. It was built to withstand any test.

The Sword of Shannara.

Bremen took the finished sword to the Hadeshorn to present it to Galaphile's shade. He writes in the Druid Histories: "I expected only Gallaphile to appear from the waterspout, but a line of dark forms began to emerge. I realized that they were the ghosts of all those Druids who had gone before, larger in death than they had ever been living. Despite their lack of substance, they radiated a terrible presence that struck fear in my heart. I held the sword out to them, and each one in turn touched the Elit Druin upon its hilt. Then Gallaphile spoke. 'We have given what part of us we can. Our lives have passed away. Our teachings have been lost. Our magic has dissipated in the wane of time. Only our truth remains, all that belongs to us in our lives, in our teachings, in our magic, stark and hard-edged and killing strong.'"

The magic of the sword was truth, the one thing the Warlock Lord could not face, as his existence was based on illusion. Its magic drew its strength from the minds of those who wielded it—the power of the sword was their own desire to remain free, to give up even their lives to keep that freedom.

Bremen chose Jerle Shannara, King of the Elves as the rightful wielder of the sword. It was then that the sword received its name and became the Sword of Shannara. Bremen expected that Jerle would either succeed in destroying Brona, or he would fail and the lands would fall to the power of the Northland army. In fact, Jerle did engage the Warlock Lord in the climactic last battle of the Second War of the Races. The Sword's magic of truth was effective, but the Elven King faltered at the last. Only Bremen knew the truth—the one event he had not considered had occurred: Brona was driven from the field, but not destroyed. The sword would be needed again.

Jerle Shannara carried the sword until his death, and then passed it to his heir, Alyten, who carried it for many years. When Allanon reinstated the Druids at Paranor, Alyten had the sword set in a block of Tre-Stone and sent to Paranor. It remained in the vault room of Paranor for five hundred years. The inscription on the base read: "To be held against the coming of the darkness. When the Warlock Lord rises again from out of the Northland, a son of Shannara shall come forth to take up this sword against him." The Elven people saw the sword as a promise that they would never have to fear the creatures from the spirit world. The legend alone was a powerful amulet against the darkness.

Bremen had not realized at the time that by giving the sword to the Elven house of Shannara, he had insured that only those descended from Jerle's blood could invoke its power. The Warlock Lord did realize the mistake, and when he had regained strength enough to return to the lands, he eradicated the entire line of Shannara Elves. He then attempted to capture the sword itself. His forces were intercepted by Elven forces, led by King Eventine Elessedil. In the resulting battle, the sword was lost. It reappeared in the hands of a maddened gnome deserter named Orl Fane who carried the sword all the way to the Skull Kingdom, where he was captured by the Warlock's Trolls. They considered the sword a harmless trinket and left it locked in the hands of the raving prisoner. Shea Ohmsford and his party tracked and recovered the Sword in the dungeons of the Skull Kingdom.

It was there, in the very heart of the rebel Druid's domain that Shea drew the sword for the first time. "At first, nothing happened. Then abruptly the pommel grew warm, releasing a pulsating wave of heat that coursed from the dark iron into my hands. I tried to release it, but my hands were frozen to the hilt. The blade began to glow with a blinding white light. I felt myself drawn inward, forced to face my innermost truth and confront the illusions that made up my life. It was the most terrifying and exhilarating moment I have ever known." Moments later, the young valeman faced the Warlock Lord, armed only with the sword and its truth, and destroyed him.

After the War Shea left the Sword of Shannara with the border people of Callahorn, at Tyrsis. He felt that no one had a better right to be entrusted with its care and preservation than the people who had held the line against the might of the Northland Army. The legendary sword was implanted blade downward in a block of red marble and placed in a vault in the center of the gardens of the People's Park.

Hundreds of years later the sword's magic protected the Ohmsford bothers Par and Coll from the Shadowen lies that threatened to trap each of them in turn. Once the Shadowen were defeated, Walker Boh took control of the sword, returning it to Paranor. It remained within Paranor for over a century before the Druid removed it. It was last seen on board the Jerle Shannara.

The Sword of Shannara, a weapon that was built for the single purpose of defeating the Warlock Lord almost a thousand years ago, is still in service, and will remain in service so long as any live who can wield it, because the need for the power of truth is eternal.

Healers in those days, and the woman quickly worsened and died. She never spoke of the baby's father other than to say that he was dead. It is now known that minions of the Warlock Lord, who never knew that he had fathered a son with a human woman, killed him.

Curzad felt the loss of the young woman keenly, even though he barely knew her, and adopted her baby as his own. Over the years the boy, Shea Ohmsford, matured and grew strong. When he was nearly grown, the armies of the Warlock Lord swept out of the north in a campaign of terror designed to subjugate the lands. At the time, no one but the Druid Allanon knew that Shea was actually the last of the heirs of Shannara, descendant of one of the greatest Elven kings in history, Jerle Shannara. As the last living descendant of the Shannara line, he was also the only person who could wield the legendary Sword of Shannara, the one weapon that could destroy the Warlock Lord.

All other blood descendants of the Elven royal house had been killed by the Warlock Lord. In the Second War of the Races, Jerle Shannara had used the sword to defeat the Warlock Lord but had failed to destroy his enemy. Five centuries later, the enemy was back. Though barely more than a boy, Shea Ohmsford was asked to finish the task his illustrious ancestor had begun. He joined the Druid Allanon on a quest to find the Sword of Shannara and destroy the Warlock Lord once and for all.

While Shea's participation was mandated by his lineage, that of his adoptive brother, Flick, and his older friend Menion Leah, Crown Prince of Leah, was not. Yet both insisted on joining the dangerous quest to protect their friend. Each of the young men involved became a hero

Flick Ohmsford, reluctant hero.

in his own right. Flick Ohmsford rescued the King of the Elves, Eventine Elessedil, from the midst of the Troll army, thus ensuring the involvement of the Elves in the final crucial battle of the war. Menion Leah is credited with creating and implementing the plan that enabled the people of Kern to escape from their besieged city. He also fought valiantly at the battle for Tyrsis, where the Border Legion held the line against the advancing Northland army until Shea and the Sword of Shannara could destroy the Warlock Lord and break the magic that held his army together.

Though just a valeman, Shea Ohmsford endured many hardships, including separation from his companions, before he found the Sword of Shannara. In the end he faced his fears to triumph over the Warlock Lord as his royal ancestor had not. It was the first of a series of quests and battles involving the heirs of Shannara and the sons of Leah that would span almost five hundred years.

The Ohmsfords

SHEA AND FLICK

Shea and Flick Ohmsford grew up quietly, with country values and simple tastes. Shea was only five years old when his dying mother brought him to Shady Vale. The people of the vale, who had known his mother and were all friends of his adoptive father, Curzad, accepted Shea's half-Elven appearance. Shea made friends easily, while Flick, as the older brother, was much more cynical and reserved. Their closest friend outside the vale was the Prince of Leah, Menion.

Flick was a hard worker who loved his younger brother dearly and was desperate to protect him. As a young man, he was one of the few people in Shady Vale who enjoyed traveling beyond the safety of the valley to bring goods and services to people living in remote areas. Flick never considered himself a hero, just a practical man.

Shea, Flick, and Menion joined the Druid Allanon and his party of Elves, Dwarves, and Bordermen on the quest for the Sword of Shannara, despite the fact that neither valeman knew anything about wars or the outside world. Their only protection was a bag of Blue Elfstones, given to Shea by Allanon. Only Shea could use the Stones, an Elven talisman, but their magic provided protection and guidance that helped them survive.

Though Flick had vowed to protect his brother, fate intervened, separating the party when Shea fell from a high cliff into the swift waters of a river. Flick was unconscious at the time but could not forgive himself for being unable to aid his

brother. That feeling of guilt drove him throughout the remainder of the war and is probably responsible for his courageous performance when he and his companions fought to stay one step ahead of the Gnomes and Trolls. When it was discovered that the Northlanders held the Elven king prisoner, it was Flick who, despite his terror of Gnomes and Trolls, masqueraded as a Gnome, infiltrating into the very heart of the camp of the Northland army to rescue Eventine Elessedil.

Shea survived his fall and was captured by Gnomes. He ended up in the Northland, where he found the Sword of Shannara and faced the Warlock Lord in his own domain, aided only by a brave Troll and an honorable thief. His own courage was severely tested as he faced the sword's magic and the Warlock Lord's power, but he prevailed.

After the war, Shea and Flick returned to the vale. Though they could claim credit for turning the tide of the war and saving the lands, they were content to have anonymity in the peace of their little village.

The experience gave Flick an abiding hatred for most Gnomes, which he never overcame. Shea and Flick both married, but Flick's wife died childless. Shea had a son and a grandson, but both his son and daughter-in-law died from a fever when their son was very small. His wife died several years later, leaving Shea and Flick to raise Shea's grandson, Wil.

WIL OHMSFORD

Wil Ohmsford inherited the steadfast nature of his grandfather, as well as his courage and Elvish appearance. The death of his parents left him determined to be a Healer. He was disillusioned with the skills of the Southland Healers, who had been unable to save his family. He was determined to be trained by the best Healers in all the lands—the Stors. He journeyed to Storlock and asked to be trained. The Stors had never accepted anyone outside their own village and rejected the valeman. Wil learned their language and applied again. They rejected him again. For over a month Wil applied once a week and was rejected every time until, finally, with no explanation, he was accepted. Wil Ohmsford became the first outsider ever allowed to study at Storlock.

That might have been legacy enough but for the fact that the Druid Allanon needed another hero. Demons were invading the lands, escaping the barrier between their prison and the world. The Elven Ellcrys tree, which held the magic barrier in place, was dying. Amberle was the last of the Chosen and the only one who could save the Ellcrys. He turned again to the Ohmsfords, asking Wil to aid him by protecting the Elven girl on her quest to find the legendary Bloodfire so that she might restore the tree and the barrier known as the Forbidding. Wil was a Healer, not a warrior, but he agreed despite Flick's objections.

He was armed with nothing but his Healer's skills and the Elfstones, which had been given to him by his grandfather. Wil braved unscrupulous Rovers, Demons, the witch sisters of the Hollows, and the Reaper to complete his quest to bring Amberle to the Bloodfire. With the help of a young Wing Rider, they made it back to Arborlon before the Westland was overrun by the Demons, but the price was high. Wil had fallen in love with the Elven girl only to lose her to the greater need of the lands. She sacrificed herself to become the Ellcrys and restore the Forbidding.

But Wil's greatest legacy was not his protection of the Chosen, but the magic that he brought into the Ohmsford family. No Ohmsfords before Wil had had magic of their own. The magic that became a part of the Ohmsfords began when Wil used his grandfather's Elfstones to save the lives of the two women he loved. Wil's Elven blood was too thin to use the Stones safely, but his great need drove him to use force of willpower to activate the Stones. The Elfstones responded, but Wil was irrevocably altered in the process. The magic was absorbed by his body, becoming part of him, possibly to compensate for the resistance of his human blood. He knew he had been changed, though he did not know how until his children were born.

During the quest for the Bloodfire, Wil met a Rover girl, Eretria, who saved his life. Beautiful and brave, she became his friend and companion on the quest. He took her back to Shady Vale to be his wife. She joined him as a Healer, and together they were responsible for bringing the superior healing methods of the Stors to the Southland. They had two children, a girl, Brin, and a boy, Jair. Both children commanded innate magic. They had but to sing to bring it to life. Wil's use of the Elfstones had created within the Ohmsford line a magic even greater than that of the Elves—in the case of his daughter, Brin, possibly the most powerful innate magic ever seen in the Four Lands.

BRIN AND JAIR

To Brin and Jair, however, the magic was simply a curiosity—a game. Brin named their magic the "wishsong." In her writings, she explains, "We had but to wish for something, then sing while thinking of the wish, and the magic would do the rest. I would just start to sing. The words and the music were never planned or rehearsed; it just flowed out of me. It seemed the most natural thing in the world." The name *wishsong* is still used to refer to the magic legacy of the Ohmsfords.

Brin's and Jair's abilities manifested using the same technique, but the effects were very different. Jair could create illusions that seemed very real. But Brin's magic could actually affect the behavior of anything that lived. She was initially unaware of the significance of such magic, but the Druid Allanon needed a power greater than his own to destroy a dark magic, the Ildatch, that was slowly corrupting the land. He turned again to the Ohmsfords, and to Brin, believing her wishsong was strong enough to subvert even living darkness.

Brin agreed to aid the Druid, though the full extent of her magic was still unknown to her. Rone Leah insisted that he be her companion and protector, as his ancestor before him had been for Shea. There is reason to believe that the Prince of Leah did not fully trust the Druid, though Allanon apparently trusted Rone enough to transform the ordinary Sword of Leah into a weapon of magic—a weapon the Prince used valiantly to protect both Brin and the Druid from attacks by the Mord Wraiths.

While the Druid had no use for Jair because of his youth and the limited nature of his magic, the King of the Silver River did. The Silver River was being fouled by dark magic—the same dark magic the Ildatch had spawned. The King of the Silver River needed a champion who could carry his magic dust to the river's source at Heaven's Well and cleanse it. As a result, both Brin and Jair were sent, separately, deep into the Eastland to Graymark to fulfill their charges.

Before Brin's party ever reached the Eastland, they were attacked by a Jachyra.

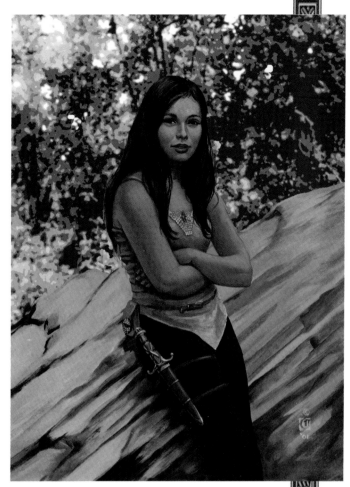

Brin Ohmsford, wielder of the power of the wishsong.

Allanon was mortally wounded, and Rone Leah was badly injured. The young woman found herself suddenly without any guidance or protection other than her own, though, even on the verge of death, Allanon apparently believed that was enough. His last living act was to mark Brin with his blood, passing to her the legacy of his magic and telling her that she would bear his trust through her descendants. Whether it was the strength of Allanon's faith in her or her own steadfast courage that enabled Brin to continue her journey, Brin finally managed to get Rone to a place of safety. The poison from the Jachyra's claws was killing him. She saved him by using the wishsong as a healing force. It was the first time she had managed to use her magic for significant good.

She could not heal Rone's dependence on the magic of his sword, however. The sword had been lost in the waters of the Chard Rush during the battle. He felt that they were helpless without his sword.

The pair traveled to Hearthstone, where they met Cogline and his adopted granddaughter, Kimber Boh. Brin and Kimber became fast friends.

With Allanon's death, Brin had lost all guidance, and so she sought whatever advice Cogline or Kimber could give. From them, she learned of the Grimpond, a creature that could give true answers, though always twisted and couched in riddles so that they did the querist more harm than good.

With no one else to turn to for help, she sought out the Grimpond, despite the fact that she was warned that the creature would attempt to mislead her. But Brin had something the Grimpond had never encountered—the wishsong. She used her magic to force the Grimpond to give her the answers she sought, thus becoming the only person known to have gained true, honest answers from the ancient creature. Under duress, it told her how to access the Maelmord, where the Ildatch lay, and where to recover the missing Sword of Leah. The Grimpond never forgave her and is known to have nurtured a hatred of Brin and all her descendants ever after.

Brin had asked about the sword because she realized that Rone needed his sword's magic, but while helping him recover it from the Spider Gnomes, she discovered a terrible truth about her own magic. She became lost in the Olden Moor, near the Spider Gnomes' camp. When Gnomes attacked her, she panicked and turned her magic on her attacker, brutally killing one of the Gnomes. Brin writes: "It was then I realized what Allanon had been trying to show me—that the wishsong could destroy and kill as easily, or more easily, than it could heal. I had not meant to kill anyone, but I could not deny the shredded body that lay dead by my will. It brought me face-to-face with the darker nature of my magic, and myself."

It was doubtless this discovery that led her to later mislead Rone, Cogline, and Kimber, so that she could leave them behind and enter the Maelmord alone. She wanted to protect them from her magic. The decision nearly cost her soul. Her doubts left her vulnerable to the power of the Ildatch, which hungered to consume her and use her magic. Had it succeeded, Brin would have been a greater force for evil than even the Dark Lord, Brona. It was only the timely intervention of her brother that saved her. He was nearby, at Heaven's Well, cleansing the Silver River, at the moment when she faced the Ildatch in the Maelmord. Later he said that it was a gift from the King of the Silver River that enabled him to use his magic to travel to her side, face his sister's magic with his own, and bring her back to herself before she was lost to the darkness of the Ildatch. He used his illusions to show her the truth of her life, her loves, and her home. He gave her the balance to find her own and destroy the Ildatch.

The King of the Silver River had given Jair the things he needed to save his sister, but it was Jair's own courage and that of his companions that made it possible. Though just a boy, Jair witnessed the fall of Capaal and endured capture and imprisonment before he was rescued by his friends and allowed to reach Heaven's Well. It was while protecting Jair that the great warrior Garet Jax fought his last and greatest battle.

Once the Ildatch was destroyed and the Silver River restored, Brin, Jair, and Rone Leah returned to Shady Vale. Brin and Rone had always been close, but their adventures and the connection to magic that both now shared brought them even closer. Brin and the youngest Prince of Leah eventually married and had children, cementing the bond between their two families that had begun years before.

Brin and Rone maintained their friendship with Kimber Boh, a friendship that continued through their children and grandchildren, with both families eventually intermarrying. Jair also married and had children. His descendants spread as far as the Westland, where they intermarried into the royal house of the Elves.

PAR AND COLL

By the time of Federation expansion, the Ohmsfords of Shady Vale included Jair's descendants, Jaralan and Mirianna, their children Par and Coll, their cousin Wren, and Brin's descendant, Walker Boh. Wren and Walker had both lost their parents, but Jaralan and Mirianna were happy to be parents to all. They did not always understand the problems Walker or Par faced with the magic within them, but they knew it was all part of the Ohmsford legacy, and did their best to understand and support all their "children," never guessing that each and every one of them would become a hero in the war against the Shadowen.

As young men, Par and Coll Ohmsford became bards. Par had inherited the wishsong from Jair and used it initially to bring their stories to life for their audiences. The Ohmsfords had been storytellers since before the days of Curzad Ohmsford, though at that time the stories were told primarily for the entertainment of customers at the family's inn. Wil had

Jaralan Ohmsford and his son Coll. The Ohmsfords were a tightly knit family.

been the first to take the stories beyond the vale in his travels as a Healer. It was Jair who had begun using the wishsong to bring the stories to life, but always with the purpose of spreading the stories of the past so that the people of the lands would never forget their history.

Unfortunately, Par and Coll discovered that the Federation did not welcome magic, even such apparently innocuous magic as the wishsong. Both boys were hunted by the Federation, for practicing magic, and by the Shadowen, who wanted Par's magic for themselves. Perhaps the Shadowen knew even then that Par's magic had the potential to surpass even Brin's.

Wren Ohmsford left Jaralan and Mirianna at the age of five to be trained by Rovers, according to her mother's wish.

Walker Boh left them to find himself and come to terms with his magic in his mother's ancestral home of Hearthstone.

All the Ohmsford children were reunited and drawn into the war against the Shadowen when the dead Druid Allanon called select members of the family. He required them to fulfill specific charges lest the world fall to darkness. Par was to find the Sword of Shannara, Walker was to find the Black Elfstone and bring back the Druids, and Wren was to find and restore the missing Elf nation. Though not called directly, Morgan Leah stood with them as a companion and protector, in the tradition of his family.

In the following year, the Ohmsfords were responsible for uncovering the Shadowen control of the Federation and defeating the Shadowen menace as well as returning Paranor, the Druid order, and the Elves to the land. Morgan Leah stood with them through the worst of their battles and was there at the final moment of triumph. No other family contributed so much during that dark time.

Wren became Queen of the Elves. Walker became the Druid of Paranor. Par married Damson Rhee, the daughter of rebel leader Padishar Creel, and with Coll continued to spread the tales of the history of the land.

BEK OHMSFORD

But all that was long ago. Today there are no Ohmsfords left, at least none that bear that name. In fact, however, it is another Ohmsford, Par's great-great-grandson Bek, who joined with Walker to combat the darkness of this age. Adopted by the Leahs, Bek has the family magic and the ability to use the Sword of Shannara. At his side is his brother and friend, Quentin Leah. Together they continue the legacy begun almost a thousand years ago by the Elven king Jerle Shannara—sailing into adventure on a ship bearing his name.

The Leahs
MENION LEAH

As a young man, Menion Leah seemed completely unfit for his responsibilities as Crown Prince. Menion's mother had died when he was twelve, with Menion as the only son and heir, but he was a cocky idler who cared more for hunting in the highland forests than for the welfare of his people. His skills as a hunter were unmatched in all the Southland, but his father despaired of ever teaching him his role as a ruler.

It was undoubtedly his thirst for adventure that led him to join his friends Shea and Flick Ohmsford on their quest for the Sword of Shannara. His skill with sword and bow served him well, saving the lives of himself and his companions on many occasions during their quest. Menion was the first to carry the famous Sword of Leah in service to the Druids and the house of Shannara.

The War of the Warlock Lord changed Menion. The irresponsible youth became the man who is credited with saving the entire population of Kern from the Northland army. It was his plan that enabled the people of Kern to evacuate their city before the Northland army could burn it to the ground. He met his wife, Shirl Ravenlock, while rescuing her from kidnappers. He also rescued Balinor Buckhannah from imprisonment by his brother, the Mad Prince of Callahorn. In the final days of the war Menion stood side by side with the legendary Balinor Buckhannah at the battle for Tyrsis, holding back the Northland army from the rest of the Southland until his friend Shea Ohmsford could destroy the Warlock Lord.

After the war, Menion married the beautiful woman he had rescued, Shirl Ravenlock, daughter of the kings of Kern. As King and Queen of Leah, they became the best-loved of the rulers of Leah. The irresponsible youth became the finest ruler Leah had known since its creation.

RONE LEAH

Menion's great-grandson Rone Leah was the youngest son of King Owain Leah. As the youngest prince, he had few royal responsibilities, spending most of his time in Shady Vale with Brin and Jair Ohmsford. They considered him part of the family, despite his rank. When the Druid Allanon called Brin, Rone joined the quest as her protector. Like all the men in his family, he had superior fighting skills, but even his skills were no match for the Mord Wraiths.

Rone's determination to protect Brin undoubtedly led to Allanon's decision to

Prince Rone Leah, first to wield the transformed Sword of Leah.

transform the Sword of Leah into a magical weapon. Rone was the first Leah to carry the transformed sword and to feel the effects, both good and ill, of its magic. He used the sword to protect both Brin and Allanon, battling Mord Wraiths and Demons with fierce abandon.

The sword seemed to make Rone invincible, until he met the Jachyra. He lost his sword and very nearly lost his life to the creature that killed Allanon. Brin managed to heal him, but the loss of the magic he had known for such a short time threatened to undo him. Rone became a driven man, desperate to regain the magic. When the sword was found, he was so focused on it that he forgot about Brin and left her behind in the dangerous Olden Moor. By the time he recovered himself, she had been attacked by Spider Gnomes and had been forced to use her own magic to defend herself because he was not there.

Rone never let the magic control him again, though the experience probably helped him understand at least in part what Brin was facing with the wishsong magic. He could not follow her into the Maelmord, but he fought valiantly against the Mord Wraiths to protect her pathway back out. When she came out of the Maelmord, he was there, waiting for her. He had discovered something more important to him than the magic of the sword.

MORGAN LEAH

Morgan Leah, the eldest son of Kyle Leah, resented the Federation and all that it stood for. If he had lived two centuries earlier, he would have been Prince of Leah. But his family had been forced to turn their country over to the Federation. They had relinquished their titles and been driven from their palace. Morgan still carried the skills and pride of his royal ancestors, however. In many ways, he was the embodiment of the free spirit and strong sense of justice that were the heart and soul of the Highlands. He often cast himself as the hand of retribution. Though he never officially confirmed it, Morgan is believed responsible for the constant mishaps and embarrassments that plagued the Federation officials during their occupation of Leah, including burning the Palace of Leah to the ground. He could not fight the Federation openly without risking reprisals for himself and his people, but he could make them uncomfortable. If the other citizens of Leah knew of his activities, they carefully avoided telling of it.

While fishing he had suffered a boating accident and been rescued by a Dwarf, Steff. He became friends with the Dwarf and traveled to Culhaven. As much as he hated what the Federation had done to

Leah, he hated even more what they had done to the Dwarves. The Federation seemed bent on exterminating their entire Race. Morgan was frustrated by the fact that he could do little to help. He was a man of action, but there was not much a single man could do against the entire Federation, regardless of his willingness to fight.

When the chance came to join his friends Par and Coll Ohmsford on a quest for the Druid Allanon, Morgan joined in enthusiastically. At least as their protector, he could make a difference. So much the better if they managed to do damage to the Federation along the way.

Within Leah, he had only been able to harass the Federation, but with Par, Coll, and Walker Boh, he found himself caught up in a war against both the Federation and the dark Shadowen magic that threatened the entire land. His own heirloom, the magical Sword of Leah, became an important weapon against an almost invincible foe. It was the only sword capable of destroying Shadowen, whose magic made them impervious to most weapons.

He used the sword to protect Par and Coll from the Shadowen as they sought the Sword of Shannara, and to aid the cause of Padishar Creel and his Free Born outlaws. But he discovered there were limits to the power of his sword. While escaping the Pit of Tyrsis with Padishar Creel, the sword shattered. Its magic shattered with it, damaging Morgan, who had been bound to the weapon by the use of its magic. After the loss of the sword, the Highlander seemed a broken man. He kept the remains of the blade close at hand but seemed to have forgotten how to use it or any weapon. At the Battle of the Jut, Morgan withdrew from the fighting. Witnesses believed he had lost his courage.

Morgan's loss may have hindered his

Morgan Leah, freedom fighter.

Ohmsford Family Tree

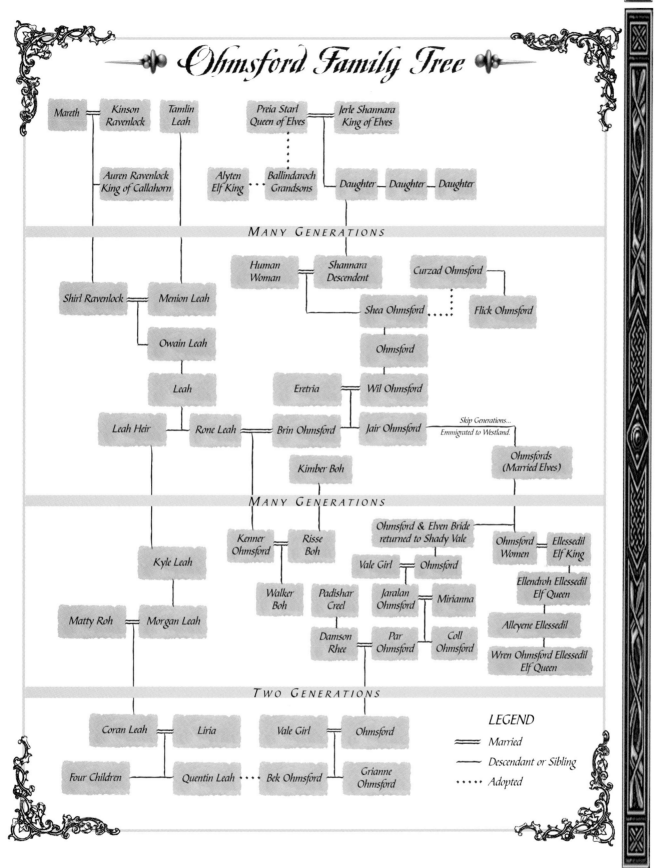

MANY GENERATIONS

MANY GENERATIONS

TWO GENERATIONS

LEGEND

═══ Married

─── Descendant or Sibling

····· Adopted

ability to fight, but it did not steal his mind or his courage completely. Even without his sword, he revealed a Shadowen spy that had infiltrated the Free Born. In a fierce hand-to-hand battle, Morgan succeeded in killing the Shadowen and saving Padishar and the rebels. In the process, he discovered that some small amount of magic still remained in the broken blade.

The spy had been using the body of a Dwarf. Morgan realized that all his Dwarf friends had been compromised. With only his determination and the limited magic of the broken sword, he traveled to Culhaven to free his friends. It was there that he met Quickening, the elemental daughter of the King of the Silver River. She recruited him to join her in her quest to destroy the Stone King, Uhl Belk. To gain his participation, she promised to restore his broken sword.

Morgan found himself far from his original task of aiding Par and Coll, on a quest with the beautiful elemental that teamed him with a Federation assassin, a Tracker, and Walker Boh. They traveled to the land of Eldwist. During the Quest, Morgan fell in love with Quickening. He used all his skills and the little magic that remained to him to aid Quickening in her task. In the final battle with Uhl Belk, he found his courage. But Morgan discovered that the triumph was bittersweet. With vic-

tory, Quickening was able to use her magic to undo the damage to the earth the Stone King had done, and restore the Sword of Leah as promised, but only at the cost of her own life.

Morgan returned from Eldwist with a whole blade and a broken heart. He threw himself back into the war, rejoining the Free Born. He met Matty Roh, a Free Born spy, at the Whistledown tavern in Varfleet. He was drawn to the fierce young woman and in time grew to love her despite his pain over Quickening's loss.

It was Morgan who rescued his friend Wren, now Queen of the Elves, from the Shadowen. He and Matty Roh were also part of the team that joined Walker Boh in the victorious Battle of Southwatch.

After the Shadowen were destroyed, Morgan and Matty returned to the Eastland, where they fought for the liberation of the Dwarves. Morgan's courage and tactics were considered key factors in the final expulsion of the Federation from the Eastland. Morgan and Matty married and split their time between Culhaven and the Highlands of Leah. Once the Federation was finally driven from Leah as well, Morgan and Matty returned to assist in the governing of the land that Morgan still loved best—his Highlands.

The Borderlands: Crossroads of the Four Lands

The Borderlands will never be part of any one land because it's been part of all Four Lands for as long as anyone can remember. —Panax, Dwarf

The Southland, as established by the Druid Council during the partitioning, was bordered in the north by the Dragon's Teeth Mountains and the Mermidon River, but the majority of the Race of Man abandoned everything north of the Rainbow Lake, preferring more distance between themselves and the other Races. They settled in a smaller region bordered by the Rainbow Lake and the northwestern branch of the Rappahalladran River on the north, the Irrybis Mountains on the northwest, and the Battlemound Lowlands on the northeast. This left a large unpopulated territory all along the northern border, in effect a separate country, which came to be known as the Borderlands. The people remaining in this sparsely settled area called their land Callahorn.

The Borderlands were initially populated by a few hardy souls who refused to follow the mass exodus of their Race to the larger southern cities. These men and women were a breed of rugged individualists who did not agree with the prevailing human sentiment against the other Races. Most of them felt that each man should be accepted for what he was, regardless of his Race, and treated accordingly. Unlike the rest of the Southland,

The battle for Tyrsis in the War of the Warlock Lord.

which prided itself on its isolationism, the Borderlands became a crossroads for the Four Lands, open to members of all Races and all nations.

Immediately after the partitioning, civilization in the border areas consisted primarily of small towns and outposts, some of which dated from before the First War of the Races. The majority of the border people lived in small hamlets or remote farms. There was no standing army, only a small militia of fighting men quartered in the fortified town of Tyrsis. Then around three hundred years after the Four Lands were established, the Northland army swept out of the Eastland and blew west across the Borderlands, wiping out everything in their path as they bore down upon the Westland Elves. Within the Borderlands, only the fortified town of Tyrsis survived. It is unknown whether the city escaped because the Northland commanders did not want to expend the effort needed to take the town, or if it simply was bypassed through the expediency of routing the huge army by way of the Mermidon River. In either case, Tyrsis only faced small skirmishes with outlying units of the Northland army, none of which possessed the strength to take the walled town.

The Borderlands were the only part of the Southland affected by the Warlock Lord's march to the west. They alone felt the might of his armies. Most Southlanders did not even know of the war until long after it was over. That experience set the people of Callahorn even farther apart from the rest of the Race of Man as they realized that they would always be the first to feel the brunt of any attack. Any foe, whether aimed at invading the Southland or moving from East to West, would come through Callahorn first.

Over the next few decades, fallen towns were rebuilt, and the outpost of Kern was founded. Trade with the Eastland and Westland was reestablished, helping the outposts of Kern, Tyrsis, and Varfleet to grow into city-states, each with its own small volunteer militia. Each crowned its own king to rule over and protect the surrounding farmlands and villages. But the fear of another invasion remained a very real concern.

The Borderlands people knew their separate tiny kingdoms could not survive alone, spread out as they were across the lands between the Mermidon and the Rainbow Lake. Raiders from the north and east, drawn by the lucrative caravans of goods traveling in and out of Callahorn, constantly bedeviled the poorly protected lands. Eventually the separate city-states joined all their communities together under the rule of one charismatic leader to form the largest kingdom in the Southland. The first king of Callahorn was Auren Ravenlock of Kern. His father was Kinson Ravenlock, hero of the Second War of the Races and founder of Kern. Auren knew that only a serious fighting force could provide security and safety for his land, so he founded the Border Legion, a standing professional army capable of facing even a foe such as the Warlock Lord.

The Kingdom of Callahorn was established as an enlightened monarchy. The King technically ruled, but his rule was assisted by a parliamentary body of representatives from each community who participated in the government, especially in the creation of laws and policies. It was the first monarchy in the Southland to make use of a representational form of government.

Four hundred years after the Second War of the Races, the crown was passed to the Buckhannah family, and the capital of Callahorn was moved from Kern to Tyrsis, already the headquarters for the Legion. It

Padishar Creel, rebel leader of the Free Born.

was the beginning of the golden age of Callahorn. Under the Buckhannahs' rule, Callahorn thrived and grew strong. The undefeated Border Legion, now under the personal command of the King, became a legend among the Four Lands, protecting the weak wherever they were needed. Tyrsis became a crossroads for the nations, a place known for the tolerance of its people toward men of all Races. The people of Callahorn believed that they were the first of a new age of Man, the beginning of a

future where the separation of the Races was no longer needed. They were among the first to refute old prejudices, looking instead for common ground and ways to build bonds between the Races. The three major cities of the Borderlands grew and thrived, as Callahorn became the center of trade for the Four Lands.

Callahorn still considered itself a part of the Southland and took its role as the Southland's first line of defense very seriously. But its inhabitants did so believing that any sacrifice on their part would be to buy time for the rest of the Southland to prepare for battle, perhaps in time to come to their aid. Less than five hundred years after the kingdom was formed, that assumption was put to the test when the Warlock Lord's armies once again swept out from the north, intent on destroying all of Callahorn on their way to domination of the Southland.

The Northland army came very close to success. An infiltrator within the royal household almost managed to destroy the Buckhannahs, knowing that without them, Callahorn would fall. This infiltrator killed King Ruhl Buckhannah and was responsible for the brief reign of the Mad Prince, Palance Buckhannah, who disbanded the Border Legion and left Callahorn vulnerable to the Warlock Lord's armies. When the Northland army descended on Kern and Varfleet, the Legion, which had been undefeated for so many years while protecting the rest of the lands, was unable to protect its own. Only the timely ascension of Balinor Buckhannah to his father's throne through an almost bloodless uprising allowed the Legion to re-form in time to save Tyrsis.

Balinor and his understrength Border Legion were all that stood between the combined armies of the Warlock Lord and the rest of the Southland. The Legion fought valiantly to hold the line, taking heavy casualties. Kern was destroyed, and Varfleet was overrun. Tyrsis was breached and had regressed to fighting in the streets, with a last line of defenders holding the line at the Bridge of Sendic, before the Palace gates.

Relief, when it came, was not from the

Padishar Creel, Father of the Free Born

A direct descendant of Panamon Creel, Padishar Creel was the son of a thief from a family of honorable thieves, yet without him, Callahorn would not be free. Though his full life history is still not completely known, Padishar Creel, enigmatic son of "Baron Creel," is best known for uniting the Free Born and liberating Callahorn from Federation Rule. Though he did not create the Movement, it was his leadership that made it effective. His silver hawk ring, originally used as a signet to prove his will, became the symbol of the Free Born Movement.

Though the tales of his origin are as varied as his moods, he claimed his father was "Baron Creel," the beneficiary of family wealth accumulated from Panamon's activities as a thief. The Federation took his family's lands and wealth and, when his father objected, left him an orphan. He grew up fast, learning the skills of the street to survive. He joined the Movement, working as a forger of weapons for the outlaws. There is reason to suspect that he was also active in the black market, especially where it would hurt the Federation most and provide gain for himself. He married, fathering a son and two daughters.

Within the fledgling Movement, Padishar recognized a fatal lack of organization. Knowing the leaders would never accept the changes he knew were necessary, he formed his own company, focused on the icon of the silver hawk ring he had inherited from his father rather than his name. Under his leadership, the cry "Free Born" became a common rally cry.

The other leaders saw Padishar's company as a threat to their control of the Movement. They arranged to have him eliminated by giving him up to the Federation Seekers. The Seekers attacked his home in the early hours of the morning, burning it to the ground. Only Padishar and his youngest daughter, Damson, escaped the flames. The men who betrayed him disappeared, one by one. Their bodies turned up in the sewers of Tyrsis, badly mangled.

Once Damson was grown, he refused to publicly acknowledge her as his daughter, creating a separate identity for her and swearing her to secrecy so that no one could ever use his family against him.

Under his leadership, the Free Born movement gained momentum among the people of Callahorn. Padishar spread his people throughout the cities of Tyrsis and Varfleet and established a series of secret strongholds and redoubts within the wilds of the Dragon's Teeth range. His careful planning allowed the Free Born to constantly stay one jump ahead of the Federation. His bold leadership helped the Movement to grow, gaining popularity with the common people of the land even as he unified the splintered groups within the Movement, eliminating their leaders where necessary. He used old family ties to the Rock Trolls, possibly from Panamon's day, to open relationships with the Trolls and convince them to ally with the Free Born against the Federation.

Once the Federation was defeated at the Rhenn, Padishar took his message to the people of Callahorn, sparking an uprising that drove the Federation from the Borderlands. The Free Born movement survives, now encompassing all of Callahorn and beyond. But it is Padishar Creel and the image of the silver hawk that supplied the momentum.

Southland they defended, but from the Elves of the Westland. The cities of the deep South never stirred to send armies or aid. They never even called up their own militias, expecting the Border Legion to protect them, as it always had before. They did not wish to be involved and refused to believe the gravity of their danger. Callahorn spent years recovering from the damage done during the War of the Warlock Lord, but the wedge of distrust driven between the border people and the Southlanders never completely healed.

Over a half century later, it was that distrust that prevented Callahorn from sending more than two regiments of the Legion to the defense of the Westland during the War of the Forbidding. The Southland Federation had belatedly realized the need for military strength and cohesion and was attempting to unify all of the Southland under its control. Callahorn no longer considered itself part of the Southland and declined the invitation to join the Federation, only to discover that the Southlanders were still advancing on their borders. Balinor Buckhannah's son had died without issue, leaving the throne to a distant cousin, Quincellen Nall. A weak and cautious man, he was afraid that sending military aid to the Westland would leave Callahorn vulnerable. The Borderlands acknowledged their debt to the Elves for their aid during the siege of Tyrsis, but they felt that sending more of the Legion to the Westland would be an open invitation to their southern "allies" to invade. Undefended, Callahorn would be forced to accept Federation rule.

The two regiments were only a token force, but they were the Legion's best, the Free Corps, under the command of Stee "Iron Man" Jans, and later, the Old Guard. In the ensuing battle, the Free Corps and the Guard were all but annihilated, but the

Bordermen made the difference that allowed the Elves to hold Arborlon until the Forbidding was restored.

During Quincellen's reign, the combined councils of the cities controlled most of the government. By the time his son held the throne, the king was little more than a figurehead. When the Buckhannah line finally died out, the monarchy was abolished. Control of Callahorn passed to the Council of Cities, a governing body made up of the representative leaders of Tyrsis, Varfleet, and Kern. Unfortunately, each group was focused only on the agenda of its particular city. Without a single unifying leader, there was no one on the council to look out for the best interests of Callahorn as a whole. The council devolved into feuding factions. The increasing pressure from the Federation intensified the divisions within the council. Preying upon the weaknesses of the factions, the Federation leaders frightened the council into becoming a protectorate of the Federation.

Though all records of that time were destroyed, it is believed that the council was assured that they would retain control of Callahorn. They were promised an alliance that would add the strengths of the Federation to the Borderlands in a situation that could only benefit both. They promised increased trade and military assistance. In truth, regardless of the promises, the council had little choice. By the time the papers were signed, the Federation army had already invaded Callahorn with only minimal resistance. Such a bold move would not have been possible during the heyday of the Border Legion, but the Legion, though still in existence, was a pale shadow of its former glory. In earlier times the Legion could have made such an invasion very costly for any enemy, but it had been thinned and weakened by a government that could not agree on anything, including proper management and support of its army. For years the funds normally reserved to pay and outfit the Legion had been gradually siphoned away to pay for more immediately gratifying programs. Historians who believe that Callahorn should have taken the field against the Southlanders forget that the Legion, as it stood, was so far understrength that any defense it mounted would have served only to anger the Federation, resulting in the complete destruction of the Legion as well as severe repercussions for the populace.

So it was that almost 150 years after they had first declined Federation rule, Callahorn, the last free country within the Southland territories, fell to the Federation without a battle. Immediately after the papers were signed, the Council of Cities and the Border Legion were disbanded. Any former councilors who complained too loudly simply disappeared. The country that had proudly served to protect the Southland from all invaders, the country that had never been occupied by any enemy, was itself invaded and occupied by the very people it had so diligently protected. The people of Callahorn found themselves outsiders in their own land as governors from the deep South took power.

The Borderlands did not fare well under Federation rule. Its farmlands sickened, its cities fell into disrepair, and its people were treated as second-class citizens of an occupied territory rather than respected allies. The tolerance toward other Races that had been the cornerstone of Borderlands philosophy was outlawed. Neither Elves nor Dwarves were welcome within Borderlands cities except as prisoners. As a result, Callahorn's once thriving trade with the other lands evaporated. The

combination of the loss of trade and the diseased farmlands led to a major decline in prosperity. Within the cities, the numbers of poor and destitute grew exponentially. Federation coffers were the only certain source of income, so the Federation became the main employer. In Tyrsis alone, there were five thousand Federation soldiers. Providing for their needs—food, weapons, clothing, and entertainment— became the largest single industry within the city. In Varfleet and Kern, locals were even recruited to provide the manpower to fill the garrisons. It meant a uniform and steady pay but required they accept and enforce Federation policy against their own neighbors.

Many in the Borderlands resented the occupation. They especially resented the loss of the basic freedoms that had been an integral part of life in Callahorn. Almost immediately after the Federation took power, pockets of underground opposition began to form. Their ultimate goal was to drive the Federation from the Borderlands. At the very least, they were determined to wreak as much damage as possible to make their occupation difficult. They called themselves the Free Born. The Federation called them outlaws.

At first the Movement, as the resistance was commonly known, was fragmented and ineffective, doing little real damage to the Federation. But then a charismatic man named Padishar Creel took control of the largest cell within the Movement. He began to consolidate the separate groups into a well-organized force with specific goals. The more effective Movement became a serious problem for the Federation; its elimination became a top priority. The Seekers used every weapon at their disposal to eradicate the Free Born. Using information gained through a spy, they brought them to bay at their stronghold atop the Jut in the Parma Keys. Federation propaganda claimed the battle a clear victory, ending in the destruction of the Movement and the death of their leader.

In fact, the Free Born survived reports of their demise, escaping the Jut with very few casualties. They returned, allied with several thousand Northland Rock Trolls, to join the Westland Elves in their fight to stop the Federation invasion of the Westland. The resulting battle for the Rhenn Valley became the definitive battle of the Federation War, though it was the destruction of the Seekers and other Shadowen that actually turned the tide, rather than the arrival of the Bordermen. The Free Born and their Troll allies did make it possible for the Elves to hold the line long enough to rout the Federation army once their morale was broken by the violent demise of the Seekers and their creatures.

Victory at the Rhenn marked the beginning of liberation for the Borderlands. Heartened by the defeat of the Federation in the West, the people of Callahorn followed Padishar Creel and his Free Born in a revolt that drove the Federation from Callahorn. It marked the end of an era; from that time forward Callahorn would never again consider itself part of the Southland, and its people would never again give up their freedom without a fight.

Almost a century later, their descendants were forced to prove the strength of that vow. Recalling the courage of their ancestors and the legendary Border Legion, they met the Federation's second invasion with an army of Free Born determined to live free or die. With the help of the Elves and Dwarves, the courageous Bordermen drove the Federation back to the South, where the Federation–Free Born war still

rages. Though the war remains undecided, the Free Born have already won an important victory: Callahorn stands free.

The Border Legion of Callahorn

The spirit of freedom inherent in the people of the Borderlands was epitomized by the warriors who defended that freedom for centuries—the Border Legion of Callahorn. A precision fighting machine, it was famous throughout the Four Lands for the skill and ferocity of its fighters. The Free Born of today owe most of their traditions to the men of the Legion.

Originally formed by the first King of Callahorn, the Legion was the first professional standing army assembled within the Southland. Memories of the devastation caused by the Northland army during the Second War of the Races were still fresh in the minds of the survivors and their children. If Callahorn was to stand against such a foe, it had to have protection provided by an army that was both skilled and courageous enough to face even Trolls. The Legion became that force. In the 650 years of its existence, it was never defeated in battle, though its troops sometimes fought to the last man to claim that victory.

Unlike the militias that had formed its core—and that still protected the Southland cities—the Legion had to do more than defend a single city. It had to protect the entirety of the Borderlands as well as provide the first line of defense against any assault directed at the Race of Man and the rest of the Southland. The Legion achieved all that and more. In times of need, units of the Legion often traveled to other lands to drive out raiders or bolster existing defenses. No foe ever survived

The Free Corps of the Border Legion

The Free Corps is probably the most famous single unit in the entire history of the renowned Border Legion. It was also the most controversial. The regiment only survived for thirty years, but in that time it established a reputation for valor that has never been matched. With their distinctive gray and crimson uniforms set off by the wide-brimmed hats with a single crimson feather that became their trademark, the Free Corps stood apart from every other regiment. It has been said that the courage of the Corps was matched only by their arrogance, but if this is true, it was an arrogance earned with blood.

At full strength, the Free Corps numbered between six or seven hundred men, but unlike other units of the Legion, there was no rotation. Soldiers of the Corps had no other home and no other occupation. From the moment they joined until the day they died, the Free Corps was their life. The name came from the promise made to every man who joined: Once within its ranks, they were free of their pasts. Within the Corps, there were no questions, no recriminations, and no need for explanations for anything that had come before in their lives. Murderers, cutthroats, and thieves, cheats and soldiers broken from other armies, those high born and low, men with honor and men who had none, all came together with one thing in common—the need to escape their pasts and begin again. Only service with the Corps could give them that. As a member of the Free Corps, each was created anew as a free man, dedicated to protecting the lives and freedom of others.

Life within the unit was usually short. The Free Corps were the shock troops of the Legion. It was they who were always first into battle, and first to die. They were considered expendable and had the highest casualty rate of any unit within the Legion. But to the men of the Corps, death was the only certainty of their existence. What mattered most was to meet it with honor, in glorious battle, covered with the blood of the enemy.

The soldiers received rigorous training in an unusually wide variety of weapons. It was an inside joke that a member of the Corps would sooner sleep with his sword than with a woman, since he was certainly able to trust the sword more. The men of the Corps were said to be the finest fighters on horses in the Four Lands. Most of them had mastery of at least five different weapons.

Time and time again, the Free Corps survived seeming suicide missions, facing odds and forces that would have destroyed any other unit. They pulled victory from defeat so often it became expected. When the Elves called on Callahorn for aid against the Demons of the Forbidding, initially only one token unit was sent: the Free Corps, under the command of the legendary Iron Man, Stee Jans. They were later assisted by a second unit.

The Free Corps fought valiantly at the Battle of Halys Cut, and again at Baen Draw, always in the vanguard, always covering the retreat with their lives.

A proud member of the Free Corps of the Border Legion.

The Mystery of the Iron Man

They called him the Iron Man. His name was Stee Jans, and he commanded the Free Corps of the Borderland Legion during the War of the Forbidding. As with most members of the Free Corps, nothing was known of the fire-haired warrior before he joined the Legion as a young man. He rose quickly through the ranks, a difficult task in a unit where death was more certain than promotion.

Stee quickly gained a reputation for being a skilled fighter, a brilliant tactician, and above all, a survivor. When he was only a corporal with seven months in the Corps, his patrol stumbled on a large force of Gnome Raiders in the village of Rybeck. Despite the vastly superior numbers of raiders, they held for three hours. Of the twenty-two men in the patrol, only Stee Jans lived to fight again. It was the beginning of the legend of the Iron Man.

From that time forward, it seemed that Stee was incapable of dying. His men took heart from his invincibility and followed him wherever he led. Stee was equally devoted to his men. Even after he gained command of the Free Corps, he insisted on sleeping where his soldiers slept and eating what his soldiers ate. He accepted no privileges from his rank, but always met his responsibilities head-on. No matter where the Corps was sent, Stee always scouted the area personally. He claimed that he wanted to know everything about the place where he might die.

The battle for Arborlon was the last for the Free Corps, but not for Stee Jans. He was offered a command by the Elves, and was offered another regiment by the Legion. He refused both, preferring to work as a freelance instructor. Many said he had outlived too many of his men and was looking for death; others claimed that he was just too good to be held back by the limitations of a formal command.

He did return to Arborlon to train a special unit of the Home Guard for Ander Elessedil, and to the Legion, but only to instruct special units. But after his work with the Legion, the Iron Man disappeared from all records.

A few years later, a mercenary known only as the Weapons Master became the bane of the Gnomes in the Border Wars of the Eastland. The Dwarves he trained became the first of a crack unit of fighters who turned the tide of the Wars and drove the Gnomes back from the Dwarf territories. The man, calling himself Garet Jax, had no equal in hand-to-hand combat and was said to be skilled with every weapon ever developed in the Four Lands.

Some time after the end of the Eastland border wards, he reappeared in the South, fighting in the civil wars then raging between member states of the Federation. Occasionally fighting as a mercenary warrior, occasionally as an assassin, he always achieved his goal, whether it was the defeat of an army or the defeat of a single foe. He never lost a fight. His mounting death toll soon made him unwelcome in the Southland.

Garet Jax befriended Jair Ohmsford, rescuing him from Gnome captors and joining his quest to cleanse the Silver River, He told Jair that he believed the boy would lead him to the most important battle of his

contact with the Legion to reach the Southland. They faced invasions from tribes of fierce Northland Rock Trolls intent on plundering cities and villages, roving bands of Gnome Raiders, and of course, the return of the Northland army. They pre-

vailed or held the line in every case.

Only two defeats mar the history of the Legion: the fall of Kern, and the defeat by the Federation. In both cases the Legion was prevented from taking the field— though in the case of the former, it was that

Garet Jax, the Weapons Master, may also have been known as the Iron Man in his youth.

life. Jair later wrote: "He was looking for the one opponent that would be a match for him, the one battle that would test the full measure of his skills. He told me there was no point in being a Weapons Master but to test the skills the name implied. I wonder if he meant to die."

It seemed to Jair that nothing could defeat Garet. He faced the might of the Kraken at the fall of Capaal and was pulled into the chill waters of the Cillidellan by the great beast—only to emerge virtually unscathed. There was no sign of the beast.

But at Heaven's Well, Garet Jax finally found his match. A Jachyra, identical to the one that had killed the Druid Allanon, guarded the Well. No mortal had ever slain a Jachyra without the use of magic. The Weapons Master faced the deadly creature in a pitched battle while Jair completed his task. There were no witnesses. When Jair reemerged from the Well, Garet Jax lay dead. The Jachyra was nowhere to be found.

The Croag, the pathway leading to the spire at Heaven's Well collapsed before Garet's body could be removed. He still lies at the site of his last battle with his greatest foe. Jair wrote, "Perhaps it was best that the Weapons Master be left where no other mortal could follow."

He died as he lived—a man of mystery.

No one can be certain that Stee Jans and Garet Jax were names for the same man, and no one but Garet knows if he actually won his last battle. But perhaps there is no question after all—for he finally won his death, on his terms.

city's Legionnaires who provided the necessary diversion to allow Kern's evacuation.

The secret of the Legion's success lay in its organization. Unlike the volunteer militias that had previously guarded most cities, the Legion was a true professional army. Its soldiers were paid for their time and were drilled and trained to be the finest fighters in the Southland. At full strength, the Legion consisted of five divisions of approximately one thousand men each. During normal conditions, at least one-third of this force was on duty at any given time, spread out throughout the duty stations within the kingdom, while the other two-thirds rotated out to their homes and secondary occupations. In times of war, the entire force could be called to duty within a matter of days.

Service with the Legion was not required, but most men within the kingdom made it a point of pride to serve in the Legion. During the reign of the Buckhannahs, the height of the Legion's glory days, over 80 percent of the adult men within Callahorn were either serving in the Legion or had done so in the past. Those who did not usually had extreme obligations or were infirm. To the people of Callahorn, it was an honor to be a part of the force that kept them free.

Each of the regiments within the Legion had its own crest, traditions, and motto. During the monarchy, the First Regiment was traditionally under the command of the Crown Prince, and its soldiers bore his personal insignia as their crest. During the reign of Ruhl Buckhannah, Prince Balinor commanded the First, one of the most famous regiments of the battle for Tyrsis. Their crest was Balinor's crouched leopard. In later years, it was the regiment known as the Free Corps, which became the crack unit within the Legion.

The Legion's fighting force consisted of cavalry, usually armed with long hooked pikes and swords; infantry, armed with short swords, spears, and square shields; archers; spearmen; and sappers. The professional nature of the Legion allowed for a level of training and drill that had been impossible with the old militia system. Its effectiveness was enhanced by the tactical skills of its commanders. Great captains such as Ruhl Buckhannah, Balinor Buckhannah, and Stee Jans often pulled victory from the jaws of defeat with daring plans that depended on the skill and courage of the Legionnaires under their command for success.

When the council abolished the monarchy, it was the beginning of a slow demise for the Legion. It dwindled as its numbers and funds were cut. By the time the Federation officially disbanded the Legion, it was anticlimactic. The Legion had already been defeated by the apathy of its rulers.

The Borderlands: Fortresses of Trade

It was Tyrsis' barbaric walls of stone that had given the South a chance to develop. The security of those walls allowed Callahorn to become a place where Man was accepted for what he was and treated accordingly. —Prince Balinor Buckhannah

Winding from the vast emptiness of the Streleheim Plains in the west through the heart of Callahorn to end in the vast Rainbow Lake, the broad Mermidon River is the lifeblood of the Borderlands. Its waters nurture the rich black farmland of the region as well as provide the primary corridor for transportation. Spaced along its length from west to east, the three fortified cities of Kern, Tyrsis, and Varfleet stand as they have stood for centuries, the first line of defense for the Race of Man.

The treasure they protect cannot be measured in terms of mere gold and silver, for their true treasure is freedom. Callahorn's location and the freedom it provides have enabled its cities to become the major trading centers for the Four Lands. Only within the border cities do members of all Races come together to trade freely. Furs from the North, fine metalwork from the East, grain from the West, and manufactured goods from the South all meet in Callahorn. It is the gateway to trade with the Southland as well as the main thoroughfare for trade between East and West. In many ways, it has become the cultural center the Druids sought to create with Paranor, though it lacks the Druids' focus on knowledge.

Tyrsis

The oldest of the border cities, Tyrsis actually dates from before the First War of the Races. It is believed that the first settlement established on the site was an outpost built before the Druid Council was ever formed. In that uneasy time of warring nations and raiders, only an outpost built on an easily defensible site could survive for long. The first settlers chose a high plateau, three miles across at its widest point, situated on the north end of a small mountain range. The plateau was backed by a steep, smooth cliff, where the northernmost mountain, which they named Mount Sendic, had shattered, leaving only a bluff with a sheer stone wall and the plateau below.

The high plateau prevented easy access from the north, east, or west, and the steep cliff made the southern approach completely inaccessible. The site provided a natural defense from both raiders and war. Underground streams flowing down from the mountains through the plateau provided a source of water, as well as a few underground caves that could be used as caches or hiding places. The plateau overlooked a grassy plain that stretched all the way to the Mermidon River, ten miles to the north, allowing an almost unobstructed view of any approaching danger. The river itself provided a means of easy transport to other settlements as well as good fishing. Able to survive the raids and battles that bedeviled most other small communities, Tyrsis grew into a trading village and finally into a fairly sizable town.

Unfortunately, her natural protection was not enough. The original settlement was destroyed during the First War of the Races. Populated primarily by Men who had been among those swayed by Brona's

cause, it was overrun and burned to the ground by the Druids and their allies. Today nothing remains of that first settlement but a few ancient support timbers.

Tyrsis was rebuilt after the war, but using masonry instead of timber. It was expanded to include the beginnings of the current massive outer wall, fortifications along the edge of the plateau, and removable iron and wood rampways leading from the plateau to the plains beyond. Tunnels were begun, and eventually they were expanded to allow the entire population the safety of an underground bolt-hole—an escape route—should the city ever again be overrun. At the time, Tyrsis was the only fortress in the lands built by Man, and the only real city within the entire South.

During the Second War of the Races, Tyrsis was the only border settlement to survive the Northland army's march to the west. This was partially due to the fact that the bulk of the Northland army passed along the Mermidon, ten miles away, but only partially—distance did not save any of the other border towns. Scattered enemy patrols made attempts to take the city, but the defenses held despite damage to the fortifications and the destruction of the wooden rampways. Since Tyrsis was not directly in the path of the main army and posed no threat to their purpose, the Northlanders never committed the entire army to the assault. It is doubtful that the city could have survived a concerted effort by the Northland army, given the existing fortifications and the lack of a serious defense force. As the lone remaining settlement in Callahorn, Tyrsis became a haven for refugees fleeing the destruction of their homes. Many of them remained after the war, increasing the population to make it one of the largest cities in the Southland.

After the war, Tyrsis was completely

renovated. The rampways were rebuilt out of iron and stone, with removable pins to allow them to be collapsed but not burned. The outer wall was strengthened, enlarged to a height of one hundred feet, and topped with ramparts complete with niches for concealed bowmen. A massive iron gateway with locking bolts and a drop bar was added to the outer wall, and an inner wall was constructed. A professional fighting force was formed to create an active defense—a force that would become the Border Legion—and housed in long barracks between the outer and the inner walls. A grand palace was constructed at the southern apex of the city, against Mount Sendic's steep face, with a high-arching bridge passing over the low greenbelt area to connect it to the main thoroughfare of the city. It became the palace of the kings of Tyrsis. The bridge was called the Bridge of Sendic, due to the fact that it appeared to connect the city directly to the mountain.

For almost five hundred years, the city proudly weathered all attempts by tribes of Trolls or Gnome Raiders to breach its defenses, but none ever managed to get beyond the outer wall before being driven back and defeated by the Legion. None was ever a serious test for the city—until the Warlock Lord's armies once again descended from the North.

This time the Northland army was intent on invading the Southland, thereby dividing the Westland from the Eastland. Separated, each land would be an easy target. Only one thing stood in their way—Tyrsis. This time Tyrsis would not be overlooked. This time the Northland army pitted their full might against the people of the Borderlands, determined to reach the fatted land of the deep South and guarantee the fall of the rest of the Four Lands. It was the greatest test

the defenses of the fortified city would ever face.

In the resulting battle for Tyrsis, an understrength garrison and the great walls and bulwarks stood against over a hundred thousand Trolls, Gnomes, and Skull Bearers. The battle lasted for three days. By its end the ramps were down, the iron gates on the outer wall were broken—their locking bolts jammed open by spies inside the city—and the inner wall had been breached. The Legion had managed to hold majority of the enemy outside the inner wall, but a small patrol of Trolls made it almost all the way to the Palace, to be held by a thin defensive line at the Bridge of Sendic. Only the destruction of the Warlock Lord in the Northland saved Tyrsis from falling. The Bridge of Sendic itself was cracked in the cataclysmic storm that followed the Warlock Lord's defeat.

How could an impregnable city come so close to disaster? The defenders had forgotten the tunnels placed beneath the city. This time, instead of protecting the people of Tyrsis, the tunnels almost resulted in their destruction, as enemy forces used the tunnels to gain access to the city. Tyrsis' defenses, and the courage of her Legion, were severely tested, but they held long enough to allow the Warlock Lord to be defeated.

The damaged city was rebuilt over the next decade. A vault was erected beneath the Bridge of Sendic as the resting place for the Sword of Shannara, the weapon that had ended the Warlock Lord's reign—and saved Tyrsis.

Approximately two hundred years later, when Callahorn became a protectorate of the Federation, Tyrsis became the capital of the Protectorate of Callahorn. Under Federation rule, the city deteriorated. The Palace, taken over by the Seekers, fell into disrepair. The beautiful Bridge of

Sendic collapsed into ruin. The People's Park became a dangerous wilderness. Only the outer defenses were maintained, but this time they were designed as much to keep people in as to keep enemies out.

With the end of the War with the Federation, Tyrsis was repatriated to the control of the people of Callahorn. They gradually restored the proud city, attempting to recapture the grandeur of her past.

Tyrsis now stands much as she did during the age of the Buckhannahs, though some of her battle scars remain. Fertile farmland and homesteads stretch before her north and west across the open plains between the plateau and the Mermidon and east to the forest of Callahorn. Today almost as many people live outside the city in the rural land surrounding it as live within the walls. The plateau still rises high above the plains, accessible only by a massive iron-and-stone rampway and—to those foolish enough to attempt it—through the hidden tunnels.

Atop the bluff, the fortress of Tyrsis is still unequaled by anything within the Southland, her towering walls and jagged ramparts reminders of a more barbaric age. Along the very edge of the plateau, a few large stones mark the location of the hastily erected bulwark put in place against the Northland invasion. Above her ramparts, the tall, rugged outline of the great cliff rises hundreds of feet above her southern edge, the ageless guardian of the lady nestled in its arms below.

Beginning at the cliff on the western side and ringing the city in a semicircle to the eastern edge of the same cliff, the enormous outer wall is dwarfed only by nature's wall to the south. The wall stands two hundred yards from the edge of the plateau, its great blocks of stone rising nearly one hundred feet above the bluff,

carefully smoothed to allow no possible handhold for enemies. Atop the wall the ramparts, archers' nooks, and towers are protected by crenellations in the stone. Great iron gates in the wall stand open above the rampway, replaced after the original gates were destroyed during the War of the Warlock Lord. Within the gates, between the outer wall and a smaller inner wall, are the long barracks, parade grounds, stables, and storage buildings once used to house the Border Legion. Today a garrison of Free Born soldiers makes its home within the barracks buildings. Built to house five thousand, they are usually only half full.

Within the protective embrace of the second wall, the city itself stretches across the bluff, sprawling from the wall to the southern cliff in a series of winding streets lined with neat homes and businesses. The main thoroughfare, a broad stone-paved avenue called the Tyrsian Way, runs from the main gates through the center of the city to a large park and a low third wall that once marked the beginning of the government sector of the city. Beyond the wall, across a ravine, is a low-lying greensward that runs the width of the plateau, approximately two miles at this point. Within the greensward, across from the Tyrsian Way, lie the ruins of the Palace of the Buckhannahs.

The ravine and greensward stand on the site of the original People's Park. Once the Tyrsian Way ended at the Bridge of Sendic, which arched over the gardens of the People's Park to connect the courtyard at the Palace gates with the Tyrsian Way. Today only the ruins of the supports for the original Bridge of Sendic still stand within the remains of the gardens, as does the vault where the Sword of Shannara was once interred.

The sword is gone, though the vault

Balinor Buckhannah

Balinor Buckhannah, the eldest son of Ruhl Buckhannah, was a brave warrior as well as a hero of the quest for the Sword of Shannara. He is also considered the greatest of Callahorn's rulers. Balinor ascended the throne upon the death of his father and brother at the hands of a traitor while his capital city was under attack. His reign began with the battle for Tyrsis, and very nearly ended during that three-day siege. After the war, he dedicated his reign to securing Callahorn's defenses and improving trade routes. A warrior at heart, he followed in his father's footsteps, insisting on personally leading the Legion in any conflict. His only son, Ceran, was a skilled fighter, much like Balinor, and also campaigned with the Legion. It is probable that Balinor never seriously considered the consequences of having his son and heir ride with his regiment, since he had always done the same. He believed that a true ruler must lead into battle, not from the throne room.

But one day Ceran and several members of the Legion did not return from a journey to Culhaven. They disappeared while crossing through the Wolfsktaag Mountains. Balinor immediately took his regiment of the Legion and rode out to find his son. He returned, wounded, with his son's body and only half his men. He would not speak of what they had found, saying only that the threat to Callahorn was gone. The Legion commander said privately that Ceran was a hero. Balinor took to his bed and died a few days later, despite the Healer's best efforts. The Healer's official statement was that there had been poison in whatever had attacked the king.

Balinor's greatest fear during the battle for Tyrsis was that he would be the last of the Buckhannahs. Over thirty years later, his fears became reality.

and its inscription have been left as a source of inspiration to the people. The Bridge of Sendic was rebuilt as a decorative span over the new park during the Federation occupation. Some within the city want to restore both the palace and the bridge to their former glory; others want to leave them as ruins, to remind the Free Born of all that they nearly lost those many years ago when Shadowen roamed freely in Tyrsis.

Only the ruins of the bridge pilings and the harsh black scars on the stone of the abandoned palace remain to tell of the horrors of the Pit, the travesty visited on the parkland by the Shadowen. The Pit was a place of decay and rot where dark Shadowen magic abounded. Those who dared to enter rarely left alive. With the fall of the Shadowen, the Pit was transformed back into a forested meadow filled with wildflowers, though the ravine remained.

During the time of the Buckhannahs, the palace was set amid lushly beautiful grounds, carefully landscaped and open to the people of Tyrsis for their enjoyment. At the time, it was the only parkland within the city, and covered most of the area between the city proper and the cliff for most of the width of the bluff. The government sector actually contained several buildings: a public forum and the Hall of Parliament, as well as the royal Palace.

The Palace is a magnificent columned building with large ornate doors and high windows set with decorative stone facings. At its height, it had a splendor unmatched in all the Southland. The colorful murals lining the main halls have faded, but the paintings and crests from generations of rulers still hang along the corridors and the walls of the Great Hall.

Balinor Buckhannah, greatest of the kings of Callahorn.

Fine wood trim still glows through the dust, the centuries of polish showing through the decades of disuse. Most of the original furnishings were elegant masterworks crafted in the Eastland out of the finest woods and metals. Very few pieces survived looting by the Federation. The West Wing, which was used primarily as living quarters, suffered the least damage.

Ironically, the library, possibly the greatest treasure of the royal house of Tyrsis, stands untouched. The collection, protected and increased by each king to rule the land and to a smaller degree by

the later Council of Cities, represents the collected works of some of the greatest minds of the Four Lands. It also contains the personal journals of many of the kings of Callahorn. Even in the time of the Buckhannahs, such collections of actual books were rare. Only three such collections are known to exist. The greatest collection, of course, resides within Paranor; the second is in the palace at Arborlon in the Westland; and the third is here in the Palace at Tyrsis. Though it is not a deliberate secret, most of the people of Tyrsis have no idea that the library exists, or of the value of its treasure.

The other great secret of Tyrsis is the network of tunnels below the palace. Beneath the wine cellars and storage areas are the ancient dungeons. Below the dungeons, and connected to them, are the tunnels—secret subterranean byways that wind below the city in a tangled maze of wells, sewers, caves, and waterways.

By the War of the Warlock Lord, the tunnels had fallen into disuse, sealed when a young Ruhl Buckhannah closed the dungeons shortly after his coronation. Most had forgotten their existence—an oversight that very nearly caused the downfall of the city. The Northland army learned of the passages from a spy planted in the royal entourage. They attempted to invade the city through the tunnel that connected the plains to the dungeons beneath the castle. The plot was discovered in time to stop the invasion and save the city. After the war, they were sealed again and then, over time, nearly forgotten again. They were rediscovered and put to use by the Free Born resistance movement during the Federation War. This time, instead of an invading army, it was the city's liberators who made use of the dark passages.

Though rarely used, the tunnels still

exist, winding throughout underground Tyrsis in a tangled multilevel maze that runs from the cliff and the dungeons beneath the palace to the plains below the bluff. Through a myriad of connections, the tunnels are accessible to most major streets and buildings throughout the city. Storage rooms and living quarters lie below old wine cellars and sewer drains. Altogether, the tunnels extend for over a hundred miles throughout the rock of the plateau. Many layers deep, the tunnels can be deadly to one unfamiliar with their twists and turnings. There is no one now living who knows the location of all of them, and few are willing to brave the darkness to explore.

Aboveground, far removed from the gloom of the subterranean world of underground Tyrsis, the parks district is usually filled with sunlight and the bright, cheerful gaiety of children. The district consists of a number of small parks and markets sprinkled with residential estates. A favored location for a family outing, the parks contain numerous markets shaded with colorful canopies as well as several pavilions where families may spread their picnics without fear of sun or rain. Large shade trees line the roads, gracefully lifting over the brightly ribboned carriages passing below. The parks are usually crowded with vendors specializing in sweets, fruits, ices, and banners, as well as all manner of entertainers. Here the children of Tyrsis, and some of the adults, are delighted by mimes and musicians, jugglers and magicians, dancers and drummers, and even animal acts such as the ever-popular dancing monkeys.

The Mole

The only person to have completely mapped the tunnels and passages beneath Tyrsis was a man known only as the Mole. A strange, squat, fur-covered man who strongly resembled his namesake, the Mole made his home in the subterranean chambers within the plateau beneath Tyrsis. Nothing is known of his life before leaving the surface, or what trauma drove him to live forever in the twilight and darkness of the tunnels, though there is little doubt that the Federation occupation of the city may have been a factor.

The Mole lived alone, his only family a collection of stuffed animals rescued from the refuse of surface dwellers. They, like him, were outcasts of a society that had lost the ability to see beyond the surface of a toy—or a man. His home was any of a dozen underground chambers, furnished with castoffs scrounged from the surface. Yet as unlikely as it seems, this eccentric little man became a hero of the Free Born. It was the Mole who was largely responsible for the Movement's success in liberating Tyrsis from the Federation. With the Mole as a guide, the Free Born were able to enter and leave the city undetected, as well as make use of the boltholes built into the city's sewers centuries before as hideouts. His willingness to share his knowledge of underground Tyrsis with the Movement played a crucial role in the Shadowen War.

With his aid, Tyrsis eventually became free, but despite his success, the Mole never returned to the surface. Though his friends encouraged him to join them above, especially in later years, when the cold and the damp of his chosen home affected his health, he refused, living in his subterranean refuge until his death two decades after Tyrsis was liberated. His "children"—the stuffed animals, which numbered over a hundred by the time of his death—were "adopted" by his friends and given a special room in the palace as a monument to his courage.

Glowstones

Torches are often cumbersome and impractical for those who explore the tunnels below Tyrsis. During times of siege, their light and smoke could easily reveal boltholes and passageways to the enemy. Instead, glowstones were used to provide the illumination needed to navigate the tunnels.

Found only in the mountains of the Borderlands, glowstones are considered street magic, because they appear to use magic but in fact utilize natural phosphorescence within the rock. When cold, the stones appear to be simple white rocks streaked with silver, but when warmed, the rocks glow with a dim silver light that can be reactivated by additional warming. Body heat, from holding them tightly in the hands or by pressing them to the body for a few moments, is enough to activate them. The glow is actually caused by luminescent particles that are dormant until heated. Warmth excites the particles, causing them to give off energy, which appears as light.

The stones were heavily used during the early centuries of Tyrsis' existence, when a run into the tunnels for safety during an attack was a common occurrence. As the people turned away from the tunnels, the stones became more of a curiosity. They had a brief resurgence of popularity during the Free Born infiltration of the city, but by that time there were few of the stones still in existence, and the location of their origin had been lost.

Glowstones are used to light the way in the tunnels of Tyrsis.

Not far from the parks district, set right off the Tyrsian Way, is the heart and soul of modern Tyrsis, the Open Market. Here goods from all over the Four Lands fill open-air stalls as well as the larger brokerage centers in buildings beyond them. Trade, the true lifeblood of the Borderlands, is exemplified within this, the largest of the Borderlands markets. Only in the Borderlands markets can people of all Races vie for the finest goods from the four corners of the lands. Almost anything can be found in the market—for a price. Trolls and Elves barter with Gnomes and Dwarves. Caravans loaded with goods from other lands enter and leave daily.

While the other lands all have markets, and all but the Southland encourage trade with other Races, only the Borderlands connects all four of the lands. Southland-manufactured goods and Borderlands wines are only available through the Border markets. Teamsters for the South transport goods to and from Tyrsian markets, but never further. There is no doubt that the Federation would prefer to trade directly with the other lands, but few are foolish enough or brave enough to deal directly with the Federation, especially given its historic hatred of other Races.

Trade is not the only asset Tyrsis has to offer, for the Borderlands are also home to the largest distilleries in the Four Lands. Over 80 percent of the wines and ales within the Four Lands is produced in breweries and distilleries in Tyrsis and Varfleet. Grapes from the vineyards around the Rainbow Lake, as well as some from the Westland vineyards, are transported to the border cities, where they are transformed into the finest wines and ales in all the Four Lands. Only within the taverns and alehouses of the Borderlands can a true gourmet sample all the varieties of wines and ales produced within her breweries. Spirits make up the single largest export item shipped from Callahorn.

Varfleet

From Tyrsis, the Mermidon winds east through the edge of the Forest of Callahorn before it turns south across the grasslands, breadbasket of the Borderlands, and finally through the Runne Mountains to the Rainbow Lake. The city of Varfleet guards the only sizable passage through the Runne Mountains. Situated on the edge of the Mermidon in the grasslands at the southern end of the Rabb plains, Varfleet lies at the eastern edge of the Borderlands, a place where the seasons are both harsh and beautiful. The farms in the area grow grain and raise cattle, which are marketed within the city.

The people of Varfleet understand what it means to live at the edge of civilization. Varfleet is always the first to feel the brunt from any northern or eastern attack, the first to fall, and the first to overcome its losses and rebuild.

Varfleet was first founded as a frontier outpost sometime after the First War of the Races on the site of an earlier town whose name has been lost. The settlement's location on the northeastern edge of the Southland made it a home for rugged frontiersmen.

The Northland army razed the original town of Varfleet during the Second War of the Races. It was an attack no one expected. At that time, Varfleet had no wall and no fortifications. All of its people were killed or driven off, except one—a

boy called Allanon. The Druid Bremen wrote of the carnage: "People and animals lay dead at every turn, sprawled in grotesque, careless heaps amid the rubble. The attack had happened at night; most of the dead appeared to have been caught sleeping. There were few spent weapons. It was hard to believe that this charnel house had ever been a thriving town."

The city was rebuilt thirty years later, with a stone wall for protection. It became the bastion of civilization in the East; its garrison of Legionnaires were often called to defend the outlying villages against raiders from the North and East.

During the War of the Warlock Lord, the wall and the city's garrison managed to keep the city from being overrun, but only because the Northland army focused its energies against Tyrsis once Varfleet was rendered helpless. Communications were blocked between Varfleet and Tyrsis, forcing the defenders of Varfleet to simply fight a holding action while their city was under siege and hope that Tyrsis could prevail to come to their aid.

After the war, the proud city rebuilt once again, strengthening the outer walls and ramparts with stone but constructing most of the interior buildings of slat wood. Years later, as with Tyrsis, the wall did little good against the Federation. Unlike Tyrsis, Varfleet was so far from the centers of Federation rule that they rarely bothered to enforce their laws. As a result, the city became a haven for the lawless and refugees. Most of the soldiers that made up Varfleet's Federation garrison were recruited from local talent; they were understandably reticent to bring the full power of the Federation to bear upon their neighbors. Most of them simply needed a steady job. The city became known as an outlaw city just barely within Federation rule, where anything was possible if one was bold enough. Even magic was still tolerated—an open secret almost defying intervention from the Federation. For the most part, the Federation ignored its outlying possession, content to drain its resources and leave its people to their own inventions.

During the Federation years, the city became squalid and run-down. The poor built makeshift shelters along the outer edge of the city wall and begged in the streets. As the once fertile farmlands around the city failed, destitute people crowded into Varfleet. But the Free Born Movement thrived. There were too few trained Federation officers to cause them trouble and large numbers of dissatisfied people who were eager to become part of a revolution.

Once the Shadowen fell, Varfleet was the first of the border cities to rid itself of its Federation masters. Once it was free, the city served as a support base for those who fought with the Dwarves against the Federation.

Now Varfleet is once again a proud border city, despite the fact that she is not so beautiful as either of her sisters. Supported by farming, fishing, and of course trade, it is a thriving metropolis only slightly smaller than its sister city of Tyrsis. Its location on the Mermidon gives Varfleet access to trade routes from both east and west, as well as easy access to goods from Tyrsis and Kern. Sprawled across a series of low hills, the city appears from a distance to be a maze of stone walls and winding streets. Most of the buildings inside the walls are built of wood, with pitch-sealed roofs, although the more affluent estates are constructed of stone.

Like Tyrsis, the outer edge of the city contains the barracks and parade grounds originally used by the Border Legion. Unlike her sister, Varfleet's poorer residents also live near the wall and outside it.

Reaver's End is one such poor section, filled with warehouses, poorer tenements, forges, and manufacturing areas as well as taverns and entertainment for the workers.

The wall surrounds the city except where it touches the banks of the Mermidon to the north and east. There the piers and boathouses jut into the river, always busy with fishing boats, barges, and the occasional riverboat. Taverns and hostels serving the dockworkers line the shore along with fishmongers' stalls and all manner of warehouses for the goods sent by river to be stored for market.

Within the city proper, the streets are all named, and merchants and tradesmen hang neatly painted signs outside their shops to advertise their wares. In the center of the city, the main road, Wyvern Split, leads to the principal square, a paved commons ringed by taverns, inns, and pleasure houses. Most of the buildings are slat-boarded houses that share a wall with the buildings on either side. As space is limited within the city, most buildings rise two or three stories, with living quarters on the second and third floors and shops or working quarters on the ground floor.

Despite the unattractive outer shell, many of Varfleet's homes and shops are quite attractive inside. Its people tend to prefer focusing their attentions within their walls, leaving the outside as plain as is practical.

Most of the more affluent homes are located in the southern part of the city, near the Council Hall, a great stone edifice that was originally built to house the King of Varfleet during the brief city-state period before Callahorn united under one ruler. Most of the few parks within Varfleet are clustered in this district, between the manor houses of the councilmen and the merchants.

Kern

West of Tyrsis, on an island in the center of the Mermidon, lies the youngest and smallest of Callahorn's cities, Kern. Though the city was not founded until after the Second War of the Races, it was the birthplace of the first dynasty of the kings of Callahorn. Founded by Kinson Ravenlock and his wife, Mareth, both heroes of the war, Kern was a protected haven for traders from the Westland and Northland.

The Ravenlocks, searching for a place to settle after the trauma of the war, fell in love with the wooded island in the shadow of the Dragon's Teeth Mountains. The broad Mermidon ran full almost year round, its waters deep and swift, making the island easily defensible while providing a water highway for traders from the Westland and easy access to Tyrsis and Varfleet downriver. Kinson and Mareth established a trading post on the island and were soon joined by others from the Borderlands who had lost their homes in the war. The island town became a symbol of rebirth, growing into a thriving community and then, in only a few decades, a city.

As did Tyrsis and Varfleet, Kern declared itself a separate monarchy, choosing for their king the enigmatic son of

The Evacuation of Kern

Almost five centuries ago, the people of Kern found themselves facing annihilation from the Northland army. Over forty thousand people were trapped on the island by the mass of the Warlock Lord's army, over a hundred thousand strong, gathering on the banks. Only the raging fury of the Mermidon, swollen from rain, held them back. The Border Legion had been disbanded, save the small local garrison, leaving no hope of rescue for the trapped city.

Menion Leah, who had also been trapped in the city, designed a bold plan to use the river highway to evacuate the people. Boats of all types and sizes were commandeered and cobbled together to carry the people of the besieged city to the landing north of Tyrsis. Rafts, cargo barges, skiffs, and ferries were gathered at the dock along with craft concocted from old furniture, pallets, and anything else that would float. A small garrison of two hundred seasoned soldiers under the command of Lieutenant Commander Janus Senpre crossed the river to strike at the flank of the massing army, making them pull in the sentries that watched the city. The men landed at Spinn Barr on the north bank. Leaving a small contingent, including the Prince of Leah, to guard their retreat, they attacked the Northland army where it slept. Menion later wrote: "The few men of Senpre's command so disrupted the camp that all the sentries left their posts, believing they had been flanked by another army. Even four hours after the strike, the enemy camp was still confused and disorganized."

As soon as the enemy sentries were gone, the mismatched armada took to the water, carrying forty thousand people, including the survivors of the attack, to safety downriver under the noses of the Northland army.

Only hours after the last boat left the docks, the Northland army invaded the island city. In their fury upon finding Kern deserted, they put her to the torch, leaving nothing but charred earth where the city of the Ravenlocks had once stood.

Senpre survived the attack and the evacuation and, for his bravery, was promoted to full commander and given command of the city defenses of Tyrsis days later, during the battle for the city.

Kinson and Mareth, Auren Ravenlock, the man who eventually united the Borderlands under one rule as the first king of the Borderlands of Callahorn. The capital remained at Kern until the Buckhannahs of Tyrsis came to power, when it was moved to Tyrsis. After that time the Palace of Kern stayed within the Ravenlock family. They referred to it as Ravenlock Manor, though most within the city still called it the Palace. Its vaulting archways and elegant courtyards were said to be more beautiful than the Palace at Tyrsis.

Unfortunately, nothing remains of the Palace or the original city of Kern. It was destroyed by the Northland army during the War of the Warlock Lord. But though the city was lost, the people were not. In one of the more amazing acts of courage of the war, the people of Kern were evacuated downriver to Tyrsis before the Northland army attacked.

It took fifty years for Kern to be rebuilt. Many believe that the newer city lacks the beauty of the old. There is no doubt that the second incarnation of Kern is different in many ways from the first, but she is still an elegant city. The Palace was never rebuilt, since there were no longer any kings, but the Council Hall and most of the major trade centers were improved. Fortunately, most of that elegance remains, since Kern did not suffer as badly during Federation occupation as did Tyrsis and Varfleet.

The city has no walls, save that provided by the rushing Mermidon. The only access to the island is via ferry or private boat, though there is a period of about a month during the dry season when the waters are calm enough to allow access by swimming. Most of the buildings on the island are stone—possibly to make it more difficult for an enemy to burn the town again—and are built several stories tall.

Limited land area has forced its citizens to build vertically wherever possible.

The existing Council Hall is believed to be a close replica of the one destroyed in the burning, with arched windows laced with metal latticework, covered walkways, carved wooden doors, and graceful columns along the exterior. The original council table, a masterpiece of burnished wood, was lost. The new one is elegant, with a more modern styling of flutework on the legs and edges.

Today the city of Kern is one of the primary trading centers for goods moving from the Westland to points east and south. Warehouses and craft halls line its streets, and its docks are active year round with fishing and trade. The forests of the original city are long gone, but a number of parks have been cultivated with shrubs and trees native to the area, enhanced by the addition of flowering bushes and colorful gardens.

Beyond the Cities

Northwest of Kern lies the Tirfing, a land of woodlands and small lakes. The area is a haven for Rovers journeying to and from the grasslands of the Westland. North of the Tirfing, at the farthest reaches of Callahorn's borders, are the flats below the valley of the Rhenn, where the climactic battle between the Elves and the Federation was begun. The alliance that faced the Federation included Padishar Creel's Free Born as well as five thousand Rock Trolls.

The participation of the Free Born in that crucial battle was only possible because of their success eluding the Federation long enough to build a fighting force and ally with the Trolls. They evaded the Federation by using secret strongholds built within the wilderness of the Dragon's Teeth Mountains.

PARMA KEY AND THE JUT

Located north of the Mermidon's north-south juncture at the edge of the Dragon's Teeth are miles of unending ravines and defiles cutting all the way back to the bedrock of the mountains. Set amid a thick blanket of misty forest and almost impenetrable scrub, these deep ravines and sharp ridges, known as the Parma Key, hide the all-but-invisible trails that were the highways for the Free Born during the occupation. Anyone who dared enter the Parma Key without a guide was doomed to become hopelessly lost soon after entering. Even today, few dare to journey far within its range without at least carefully marking the trail. It was deep within this rugged land, atop a rock outcropping known as the Jut, that the Free Born established their primary stronghold.

Padishar Creel's hawk signet ring, the symbol of the Free Born Movement

The sheer wall of the Jut rises above the lands of the Parma Key for hundreds of feet. It is a natural stronghold capable of resisting even a sizable army. Midway up the cliff is a grassy bluff, approximately three hundred yards deep, ending in series of caves and tunnels. During its use as a Free Born outpost, the bluff was accessed via a series of lifts. These gated lifts were large enough to hold up to a half dozen people and were lifted by large winches set into rock ledges. It took three different lifts to reach the top ledge from the ground. Each lift was guarded. An enemy would have to take all three to gain access to the bluff.

A waterfall spilling from the mountains above to a pool on the bluff provided fresh water. The largest of the caves on the bluff, over two hundred feet across inside its main central chamber, opened into dozens of smaller chambers, which were used as storage areas and training rooms, as well as sleeping quarters during inclement weather. The Jut was home to between two hundred and five hundred men at any given time.

The deepest of these storage caves leads to a tunnel, disguised with a false front, which bores through the mountain to come out above Parma Key just south of the Dragon's Teeth. Crevices split the path at several points along the tunnel. Some of the remnants of the rope-and-wood bridges used to span the crevices are still in place. The largest of these crevices is located a mile into the mountain. It cuts a deep channel, over fifty feet wide edge to edge, through the largest chamber known to exist within the mountain. The iron drawbridge, which was designed to be raised and lowered from the Jut side of the crevice, still stands across the yawning crack, though its gears and levers have been jammed, locking the bridge in place. Beyond the bridge, the tunnel winds for miles over similar terrain before emerging from the mountain.

Several other caves on the Jut lead to tunnels as well. Some of them also lead to the outside, but most simply lead into a maze of underground passages that dead-end deep within the mountain. Most of the Free Born knew better than to attempt a tunnel passage without their leaders. Anyone who chose the wrong passage was hopelessly lost before he or she realized the mistake.

Fortifications were built along the edge of the cliff and around the cave mouths to protect against arrows or spears. Defenses were mounted in the cliff walls above the bluff within the splits in the rocky face. Some of the remains of these fortifications can still be seen today.

FIRERIM REACH

The second largest stronghold used by the Free Born was located at Firerim Reach, so named because of the breathtakingly brilliant crimson sunsets visible through the mountain mist. At sunset, the whole mountain range appeared to be burning.

Firerim Reach is located in the rugged slopes of the Dragon's Teeth Mountains, northwest of the Rabb. It can only be accessed by a narrow trail that passed through the cliffs to a secret entrance within a cliff wall, though there are rumors of a second secret entrance that may not be revealed to those outside the Free Born. At many points, the trail appears to disappear into boulders or cliffs. Only those who know the way can find it. Climbing ever higher, the trail narrows at several points to the width of one man. Many of these splits are open to the sky, providing a point of attack if an enemy ever found the path.

The Reach itself is a large plateau with a spectacular view of the mountains to the west. To the east, a ridge overgrown with cedar and spruce protects the plateau. During the occupation, the Free Born built their makeshift cabins and tents within the shelter of these trees. Some of the stone-lined pits used for cooking fires are still visible.

The northern and western edges of the plateau dropped away over a steep cliff above a mass of canyons and jagged fissures. If anyone ever found a way to access the area near the Reach, he or she would never be able to climb the sheer walls to reach the redoubt.

Firerim Reach was used primarily as a fallback fortress for the Free Born. The Reach, even if it were revealed, could never be taken, but it was too far from the cities to provide active support for groups working within the cities. It was here, at Firerim, that Padishar Creel consolidated his forces before moving on to support the Elves at the Battle of the Rhenn during the Shadowen War.

The Northland: Land of Trolls and Warlocks

I only feel truly alive within the vast wilderness of the Northland, for it is only when I am lost within her unforgiving embrace that I find true serenity. —Horner Dees, Tracker

The Northland is a barren and inhospitable place where survival must be earned anew each day. It is also ruggedly beautiful, with snow-capped mountains crowning wild forests that open onto vast tundra. It is home to the fierce Koden, sure-footed Mountain Sheep, and large herds of Northern Deer as well as Trolls, Urdas, and a few Gnomes.

Bounded by the Upper Anar on the east and the Breakline Mountains on the west, the Northland extends from the Dragon's Teeth Mountains around Paranor in the south to the vast waters of the Tiderace in the far north. The land between contains some of the most beautiful and deadly country in the known world.

The Charnals, the largest mountain range in the Four Lands, run from the Jannison Pass at the edge of the Dragon's Teeth northeast to the Tiderace. The spine of the Northland, they form a forbidding barrier between the Eastland and the Northland that can only be traversed by experienced Trackers—or lucky fools. Their snow-covered peaks and vast forested valleys are home to a wide variety of life, as well as the majority of the population of the Northland. Tribes of Trolls and Urdas are scattered throughout the valleys and uplands of the range, dominated by a few larger Troll "cities," such as Norbane, in the far north.

Beyond the Charnals to the west and extending northward to the Knife Edge Mountains lie the Streleheim Plains, a vast, lonely expanse of grassy tundra broken occasionally by tufts of dense brush and a few bushes. Herds of Northern Deer frequent these grasslands during the spring and summer months.

West of the plainland is the forbidding Kershalt Territory. Within a wild and dangerous land, the Kershalt is considered the most dangerous section. It is country that even the natives avoid. Bracketed by the Malg Swamp and the river Lethe on the

The Warlock Lord

The Spirit Lord, as the Trolls knew him, was not always evil. The ruler of the Skull Kingdom was originally one of the very Druids sworn to aid the lands. As a Druid, Brona had accepted the charge to reclaim what had been lost during the Great Wars. He was a brilliant and ambitious man, but he was also impatient, and soon realized that the process of recreating an entire civilization from shards of lost knowledge would be painstakingly slow, if not impossible.

Brona discovered a shortcut within a book of ancient magic hidden in Paranor. This book, the Ildatch, led him to discover powers far beyond anything the Druids had thus far managed to re-create. He began to experiment with magic and determined that it would provide the answer the Druids sought. The council attempted to dissuade him, realizing the danger of his approach, but he was reckless in his haste and was seduced by the power of the book.

In the end, Brona and his followers broke with the Druid Council and left Paranor, taking the Ildatch and its promise of limitless power. The council believed him dead. In fact, he and his followers had hidden away in the Northland. They were gradually subverted by the dark magic, which connected with the evil within them. Pawns of the book, though they did not know it, they sought world domination. In the First War of the Races, Brona managed to incite the Race of Man to attack the other Races. Man was eventually defeated, but Brona escaped to the Northland.

Brona became obsessed with the magic. It granted him power, but took away his humanity. He discovered the Druid Sleep, but used it without care to become immortal. It took away his heart and soul until in the end he had nothing but his will and the demands of the magic that sustained him. The mortal man Brona died, consumed by the dark magic. The magic reached through him, tainting the land and transforming the Skull Kingdom into a barren wasteland fit only for the dead. As Brona's strength grew, so did the reach of the magic and its taint.

From this stronghold in the Northland, the Warlock Lord and his followers began anew their campaign for domination. They were more powerful, having taken centuries to learn more of the dark secrets of the Ildatch. This time Brona first destroyed the Druids at Paranor, so that they could not stop him again. He then conquered the Trolls and Gnomes of the Northland. They were gathered into a massive army, augmented by creatures he had conjured with the magic, and sent boring down upon the Eastland, across the Borderlands, and into the Westland. The campaign ended there when he ran up against the courage of the Westland Elves, a few Druids, and a King named Jerle Shannara who wielded a sword made from Old World steel and Druid magic.

The Sword of Shannara almost destroyed the Warlock Lord, but he managed to break the warrior king's concentration long enough to escape to the North. His spirit hid within the Skull east and the Kierlak Desert on the west, the Kershalt is a land of death. It was a fitting place for the Warlock Lord and his undead minions.

After the First War of the Races, the Druid Council assigned the Northland to the Trolls. They were the only Race that could easily survive its harsh climate and difficult terrain. Many of the tribes already made their homes among the rugged peaks and valleys of the Charnal Mountains.

Unfortunately, the man secretly responsible for that war also decided to make his home within the Northland's wilds. He guessed—correctly—that no one but Trolls would notice his kingdom in the barren Kershalt Territory. He knew the

Mountain until he could once again begin his work. Those of his original followers that had survived rejoined him. It took five hundred years, but they gradually regained their strength and began again to build an army. It was easier to gain control of the Trolls this time, since he could prove that he was beyond the reach of mortals, a creature of the gods. His power had increased so that he no longer needed to command his armies in person, but could send his trusted Skull Bearers in his place and control all from his scrying basin. He first killed all the Elven heirs of Shannara, so that there would be no one to wield the Sword that so nearly killed him. He ordered the Sword of Shannara brought from its hiding place in Paranor, and began his campaign. The Northland Armies were sent against the Southland to drive a wedge between the more powerful armies of East and West, preventing an alliance that might defeat him again.

The last heir of Shannara, a valiant Troll, an honest thief, and the courage of the Borderland people combined to destroy his plan. The sword ended up within his dungeon, though not as he had planned. The heir to Shannara found it before Brona realized it was there. The Warlock Lord confronted him, and was destroyed within the dungeon of his own stronghold. Of course, Brona had actually died centuries before; it just took the power of the sword to make him realize the truth.

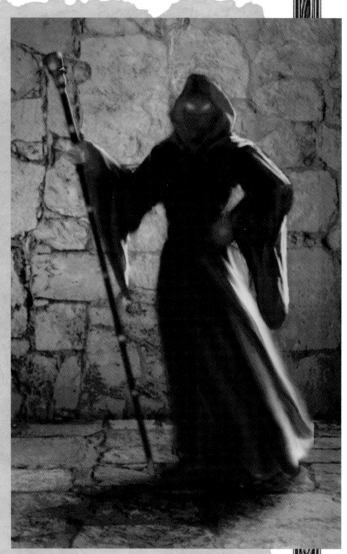

The Warlock Lord, known to the Trolls as the Spirit Lord, was originally a Druid named Brona.

A Skull Bearer, one of the Warlock Lord's servants.

Druids, who barely suspected his existence, would never look there. The Trolls who noticed were recruited—or killed.

Brona became known as the Spirit Lord. His kingdom, centered in the dying, broken peak called Skull Mountain, became the center of dark magic, the Skull Kingdom. The lands it encompassed slowly died and rotted. The Spirit Lord gradually subjugated the Trolls, tribe by tribe, until he had created an army. The Trolls were impressed by his magic and by his power. Many joined willingly, for promise of victory and the spoils of war. Those who refused were convinced by the power of his magic. Gnomes living in the Northern Anar quickly joined as well, realizing that they were no match for any power that could subjugate the Trolls. Together they formed the bulk of the Northland army. Almost three hundred years after the Trolls were given their own homeland, they swept out of the North on a campaign designed to capture the Four Lands for the Spirit Lord, their master.

Skull Bearers

When the Druid Brona left Paranor, a number of his followers left with him. For many years, no one knew what had happened to those people. We now know that they became his dread captains, the Skull Bearers, so named because of the silver skull pendant each wore upon his breast. The pendant was the mark of their service to the dark lord. It became their badge of rank.

Like Brona, these Druids were drawn to the magic and consumed by it until it changed them. They became corrupted creatures infused with the power of dark magic. Their shape twisted to match their souls until they no longer resembled men and were instead hunched creatures with leathery wings and claws skulking within black cloaks. Terror emanated from their bodies, affecting any mortal creature that came near them.

Usually hidden in shadows during the day, they hunted by night, feeding off the living, though they no longer needed to eat. The magic sustained them. They were in service to the Warlock Lord, sworn to him and to the magic that used him. They became his generals. Some could transform at will into the likeness of a human, to pretend to be all they had given up for the magic. Some could even sire children, though those children often carried a part of the magic within them. Most preferred the shape they had earned.

Normal weapons could not harm them; only powerful magic could kill them. When the Warlock Lord was destroyed, they faded into smoke and dust. With his death, their connection to the magic was broken. It was only the magic that sustained their lives.

The Skull Kingdom

The Warlock Lord chose Skull Mountain as his stronghold because of its remote, protected location, though the appearance of the mountain may have also appealed to him. The ancient peak had been worn by time and the elements until the southern face resembled a huge, menacing human skull stripped of flesh. Gaping openings to internal caverns resembled eyeholes, and the smooth top of the mountain was rounded much like a human head. The mountain itself may have been shaped by one of the cataclysms during the Great Wars, its shape worn by wind and water driven by explosive forces. It is believed that the Warlock Lord used his magic to enhance its malevolent appearance, as well as to strengthen the ancient rock to keep it from breaking further.

The interior of Skull Mountain was riddled with hundreds of caverns and winding tunnels, some bored by nature, others by magic. The caverns and tunnels extended from well below ground level, where they were primarily used for dungeons, to the single large chamber at the mountain's apex. That chamber, the largest within the mountain, was open to the north, where a large chunk of the mountain's exterior had cracked and fallen away long before.

The Druid Bremen, the only man known to have infiltrated the audience chamber and survived, wrote that the room was the location for one of the Warlock's most powerful tools: his scrying basin. "In the center of the cavernous room, upon a large stone pedestal, I saw a dark basin of murky water. As I hid, cloaked with magic so that I would appear to be one with the mindless, pitiful minions that crawled through the shadows, I saw him appear,

Mutens, Servants of the Darkness

Mutens were originally created by the Warlock Lord to serve his empire. The Trolls who were forced to serve with them named them Mutens. Large, misshapen, nearly mindless creatures, they were vaguely man-shaped with great drab bodies and nearly featureless faces. Their skin had the texture of chalky putty and was rubbery to the touch. They stood upright on two legs but moved with a lumbering shuffle. They could speak, though their voices were raspy, as if they no longer worked correctly. Some legends claim they were once human but were transformed by dark magic to be servants. Others say that they were created from earth and clay and animated by magic. They served as the watchdogs for the Spirit Lord's domain, though they did not die out immediately when he was destroyed.

coalescing out of the mist. There was nothing left of the mortal who had been Brona. Only his darkest essence remained. The robes that outlined his form were filled with nothing but a green, malevolent mist. The hood revealed no face, just the burning red sparks where eyes should have been. He gestured to the basin—just a touch of his magic, and it cleared to reveal to him a window upon the world. He could see all within his domain—and possibly beyond—without ever leaving the protection of his mountain."

The Skull Bearers and the small, black, broken creatures that Brona had enslaved to be his servants used the rest of the upper chambers. At ground level were chambers for the Mutens, the watchdogs of the kingdom. Belowground were the rows and rows of cells carved into the rock and sealed with windowless iron doors. The only entrance from the ground to the interior of the mountain was through a fissure in the side of the skull several hundred feet tall. The opening led to the tangle of caverns within the mountain. Trolls serving at the Skull usually preferred to make camp outside the mountain rather than accept a billet within the cold, dank rock.

Skull Mountain lifted out of a wide depression of barren dirt, the surface of which was broken only by a scattering of rocky hillocks and dry riverbeds. It was protected on all sides by formidable natural barriers. To the west was the Kierlak Desert, a vast wasteland, over fifty miles of sand-covered plains made deadly by the poisonous vapor from the river Lethe, which wound into its interior from the south. The invisible vapor hung over large parts of the desert, killing any creature that happened to breathe it. The furnace of the desert and the volatile vapors caused even the dead to decay in a matter of hours.

The impervious Razor Mountains protected the northern approach. Beginning five miles north of the Kierlak and continuing in an unbroken line to the edge of the Malg Swamp on the east, the craggy Razors had no passes. These jutting slabs of rock were neither the tallest nor the most rugged of the Northland mountain ranges, they were, however the most deadly. Hidden among the mountains' cracks and crevasses lived thousands of tiny spiders, the only indigenous creature to survive the creation of the Warlock Lord's kingdom. They nested by the thousands within the cracks in the otherwise barren rock. These Razor Mountains spiders are believed to be the most deadly spider in the known world. Their venom kills in minutes. The bare rocks of the Razors are littered with piles of bleached bones—all that remains of the tiny spiders' victims.

To the east, the Razors end abruptly at the fetid bog of the Malg Swamp. The Malg was a poisonous sinkhole that could not be crossed by living creatures. Its shallow waters covered acres of mud and quicksand. Animals foolish enough to attempt to drink from its depths were soon trapped, though the vapors often killed them before the quicksand pulled them under.

The Malg stretched for miles to the south, eventually feeding into the river Lethe, which passed below the Knife Edge Mountains, meandering westward through the Kierlak Desert to empty into a small lake within the desert.

Beyond the Malg, the south of the Skull Kingdom was warded by the towering bulk of the Knife Edge Mountains. Jutting out of the bedrock like huge spear points thrust up from the depths, they were the tallest mountains in the entirety of the known world. Lancing thousands of feet into the Northland sky, they loomed over the rest of the kingdom, their icy

Panamon Creel

Panamon Creel was a flamboyant highwayman and a scoundrel. He was also one of the heroes of the War of the Warlock Lord. Born in the deep Southland, Panamon was a wild youth who preferred adventure to work. He lost his hand in an accident while still a young man, only to find that decent-paying work was particularly hard to find for a one-handed man but finding trouble was easy. Eventually he discovered he had a flair for a particular job—that of robber. He replaced his missing hand with a deadly pike tip, began dressing all in scarlet, and discovered he was too good as a highwayman to quit. After a few years, he included the lower Northland in his territories, having discovered that robbing Gnome patrols was particularly satisfying, since they usually gained their loot from raids or battle. He was a fierce and deadly fighter who could read a man's worth in his face and took honor very seriously.

He rescued a wounded Troll named Keltset, who became his partner in crime. Together they were an unbeatable combination. They rescued Shea Ohmsford from Gnomes and ended up joining his quest to find the Sword of Shannara and destroy the Warlock Lord.

After the Warlock Lord's defeat, Panamon was believed killed when he remained behind to protect Shea's escape from the Skull Kingdom. Amazingly, he turned up months later, alive, on Shea's doorstep.

Panamon Creel, thief and hero.

It is doubtful that he ever knew that it was his ancestor, Uprox Creel, who had originally forged the legendary Sword of Shannara. But the forging would have been for naught if Panamon had not made it possible for the heir of Shannara to find and use the sword as it was intended.

The Northland Army

In the Second War of the Races, the Northland army was primarily built around the might of conscripted Rock Trolls. The total roster included lesser Trolls and Gnomes and was filled out by creatures summoned from the netherworld by the Warlock Lord. The generals were Skull Bearers, who commanded the Troll Maturens and the Gnome Sedts.

In the War of the Warlock Lord, the makeup of the army was similar, except that there were fewer creatures of magic and more Trolls and Gnomes. In that campaign, the main army camp covered a little over one square mile.

Brona's captains were called Skull Bearers because of the skull pendant they wore to signify their pact with the Warlock Lord.

The Rock Trolls, considered the finest hand-to-hand fighters in the known world, wore body armor, carried shields, and tended to fight in formation to make optimal use of their numbers. Only serving as infantry units, their weapons of choice were pikes, great swords, broadswords, axes, and large maces. When in phalanx or box formation, they were nearly unstoppable, and had even been seen attacking their own troops to reach an enemy objective.

The Trolls did not use projectile weapons, but they often threw their pikes, maces, and axes with deadly accuracy. No other unit could stand against an equal unit of Rock Trolls. When the Troll war horns sounded the call to battle, an honorable death in battle was all that would stop a Troll.

The rest of the army lacked the skill and training of the Trolls but made up for that lack with the sheer weight of numbers. Gnomes served in units of archers and slingers, used to soften an enemy as well as destroy cavalry. They also served as cavalry, though they were poor horsemen, lacking the equestrian mastery evinced by the Border Legion or the Elves. Gnomes also served as Trackers (their forte), sappers, and infantry. The Gnomes within the infantry were little more than arrow fodder to fill out the lines. They fought, but with little skill and less determination. It was only fear that kept them in the lines.

Most units were completely Troll or Gnome and were commanded by a Maturen or Sedt, who answered to the Skull Bearers. There were some mixed units, especially of lesser Trolls and Gnomes, but they were almost always infantry units attached to another command.

The Gnomes also supplied the drummers. In both wars, the booming percussion of Gnome war drums served to inflame the Gnomes and intimidate the people they faced.

summits seeming to reach beyond the sky. The only path through the Knife Edge was through a narrow, twisting canyon that led from the banks of the Lethe to the foothills at the edge of Skull Mountain. The toxic river ran along the base of the Knife Edge all the way to the Kierlak. The only way across it was by raft, though no normal raft could stand the corrosive waters of the river. The Spirit Lord's ferryman captained a wide-bodied raft of rotted wood and rusted iron, probably reinforced with dark magic. The ferryman himself was probably a Mwellret, with scales where skin should have been.

The only other passage into the Skull Kingdom was through the few miles of foothills where the Razors gradually dropped into the Kierlak. The area was open, but it was also a trapdoor, always under guard by Trolls and Mutens ready to close the ring behind anyone foolish enough to venture into the Spirit Lord's domain.

During Brona's reign, the entire region, already sparsely populated, became blighted and barren because of the dark magic concentrated at Skull Mountain. All living things within the region died or were driven away—except for those who were captured and perverted for the Spirit Lord's pleasure. During the year of his campaign against the Borderlands, a deadly wall of mist appeared, forming another barrier around the kingdom. However, unlike the other, natural barriers, the wall of mist expanded as the Warlock Lord's power grew. Before the fall of the Skull Kingdom, the black wall of mist reached almost to the Dragon's Teeth at the southern edge of the Northland.

Driven by magic, the wall of mist became a shroud of darkness, clinging to all living things that passed within its influence, lulling them into a stuporous, eternal sleep from which most never awakened. Even plants withered and died from the smothering touch of the mist. It rolled slowly southward, consuming the land even as the Northland army sent before conquered it.

When the Warlock Lord was finally destroyed, the dark magic dissipated as well, causing cataclysmic reactions as the land shook off the darkness that had held it prisoner for so many centuries. The resulting quake destroyed Skull Mountain and shattered the Knife Edge Mountains, its fury reverberating all the way to distant Tyrsis, where it cracked the Bridge of Sendic.

Today the Skull Kingdom is only a name within the Kershalt Territory. The kingdom is broken. The sharp tips of the Knife Edge Mountains are now blunted,

Rock Trolls are the finest fighters in the Four Lands.

the pass between them sealed with boulders and rubble from the once-towering peaks. The Lethe River has changed course to bear around the boulders that litter the foot of the mountains, but the river no longer reeks of poison. The Kierlak is still dangerous, but desert creatures and plant life have returned. The land surrounding the Skull Kingdom is now filled with life. Hills that once were barren now bloom with hardy grasses and a few small trees. All that remains of Skull Mountain is a pile of rubble, from which the rock of one broken eye socket cants forlornly skyward. It is the only memorial for all who died within the depths of the Warlock Lord's mountain.

The damage the Warlock inflicted on the Northland went far beyond the corruption of the Kershalt Territory. The Troll Nation was conquered and subjugated to become the backbone of his army in both the Second War of the Races and the War of the Warlock Lord. As a result, most living outside the Northland regarded the Trolls as either mindless killing machines or merciless marauders intent on the destruction of the other Races. Few people knew that it was actually a brave Troll who had made the Warlock's defeat possible, and that that Troll had given his life so that a valeman might live.

The perception of the evil Troll persisted until the War of the Forbidding, in which Trolls from the Northland joined with Dwarves and Elves to protect the Elven homeland. Led by the Maturen Amantar, the Trolls fought fiercely in the battle for Arborlon. By its end, both Dwarves and Elves had gained new respect for their Northland neighbors.

Unfortunately, the Southland did not share that respect. To most of the Race of Man, Trolls were ignorant savages. That perception remained until the War of the Shadowen, when the Rock Trolls, under the command of Axhind, allied with the Free Born against the Federation, at which point the Trolls were venerated as heroes by everyone—everyone except the Federation.

Part of the reason for the distrust, aside from the Warlock Lord's rampages, is the fact that Trolls are reclusive, preferring to remain in their mountain strongholds in the far reaches of the Northland. They steadfastly maintain their own language and culture, rarely mixing with the other Races.

Trolls

The largest and strongest of the Races, the Trolls thrive in the desolate north. They were bred for it, through brutal natural selection and mutation. Their human ancestors were the few hardy souls who survived the brunt of the apocalypse of the Great Wars. Most had been caught unprepared when the wars broke out, and had scant shelter. Many fled to the mountains, only to die in earthquakes and avalanches. Over time, the unforgiving ravages of radiation and plague shaped their genetics. Their survival skills were forged by the fire and ice of a climate in tumult, and by the desperately hungry predators who considered them prey. Most died, but those who lived gradually evolved into a new Race, a Race bred for survival against all odds—a Race that had learned to fight for the right to live while rejoicing in the glory of that battle.

The rigors of the struggle changed them. Their skin darkened and thickened until it resembled a protective layer of slightly burnt tree bark. They grew large and muscular and, at least among the males, completely hairless. They lost the smallest finger on either hand as well as most of the facial definition common among the other Races.

There are actually several different types of Trolls, but the best known are the fierce Rock Trolls of the Northland. There are a number of lesser Trolls, living far from the Northland. All are smaller than the Rock Trolls; all have been born of mutations caused by the fury of the energies released by the Great Wars. Some, like the Mwellret of the Eastland, have major differences in physical characteristics that set them apart, though most species of Northland Trolls are similar to each other in build and appearance.

Rock Trolls are the largest and most powerful members of any of the Races. The average male stands between six and a half and seven feet in height, taller than even the largest Man, and usually weighs over three hundred pounds. Born into a warrior tradition, they are considered the finest fighters in the known world. No other Race can match them for skill, strength, or ferocity in battle, though they often lack the more sophisticated tactical skills necessary for commanding armies.

The lack is not surprising considering the fact that the Trolls never fought as an army until forced into service by the Warlock Lord. They live in isolated communities centered on a single tribe, which itself has usually formed around a few core families. It was that very isolation that made it possible for Brona to conquer and subjugate most of their Race. Each tribe stood or fell alone. And alone, none of them was a match for the Warlock Lord or his magic.

Each tribe is itself as closely knit as a family unit, with the Maturen, or leader, taking the role of honored father for the tribe. The Maturen is chosen by the members of the tribe in a surprisingly democratic process. He is not necessarily the best fighter or the most powerful, but he is always the most respected and stands at the top of a complicated hierarchy that includes the shaman, lesser captains, and other positions of importance to the community.

The actual day-to-day administration of the tribe is usually handled by the women, with one woman, chosen by the tribe, serving as the tribal mother, or manager. She oversees food management, early training of children, and matters of commerce. Families within the overall "family" of the tribe are nuclear, and very close. The tribe protects its own. Any children who become orphaned are quickly adopted into another family; widowed wives are given the chance to remarry, usually the nearest unmarried male relative to their late husband, or at least taken in by his household. Tribal identity and tribal pride are very important to the Trolls. When going to battle or leaving on a journey, most Trolls wear some token to identify their tribe. This is so that all will know which tribe should be honored by their deeds of glory, and so that an enemy will know which tribe has beaten him and carry that knowledge to the Summerland with his death.

All the men within a tribe are expected to assist in its defense, though those who are skilled in crafts or shamanic arts or those who have lived to be an elder are not expected to participate in the hunt. Women are trained as warriors as well, though they do not usually participate in raids or battles unless the fighting actually reaches their home; then they will fight to the death if necessary to protect the children. It has been said that even a full-grown male Rock Troll cannot stand against the ferocity of a mother protecting her children.

Most of their battles are fought against other tribes of Trolls, or Gnomes and Urdas, and are relatively small skirmishes. To the Trolls, courage and honor are more

The Koden

The Koden, or Northland bear, is the most ferocious predator in the Charnals. Averaging fourteen feet in height when standing upright, and armed with vicious ten-inch claws, the Koden prefers the cold climate of the northern mountains and ranges throughout the Charnals. The Koden is a master of camouflage; its brown or gray coat blends in well with the rocky terrain of the upper ranges, making it easy for the animal to approach its prey. The Trolls consider the Koden a very dangerous and unpredictable animal. Its fur and claws are highly prized as symbols of valor for those Trolls who manage to kill one. Though Trolls are excellent hunters, the Koden often wins.

important than life. Anyone can be born, but to live well with honor requires dedication. Young men reaching maturity often prove their worth in a rite of passage, either by being included in a raiding party or by successfully hunting one of the more dangerous predators, such as the fierce Koden. The only thing more important to a Troll than living well is to die well. For the warriors, especially among the Rock Trolls, that means an honorable death in battle. Those rare individuals who survive into old age are revered as elders and given an honored place within the tribe. When near death, it is not unusual for such elders to deliberately seek out membership in a raiding party in order to achieve their honorable death.

The spiritual health of the tribe falls to the Archeron, or shaman. This person may be man or woman, but is usually someone who has a little touch of the magic. Often the Archeron is a seer, capable of visions of foresight and telling dreams. An Archeron's dreams are always taken very seriously by the rest of the tribe. They are believed in many cases to be communications direct from the gods. Even when the person possesses no magic at all, their

word is deeply respected. The Maturen is expected to always consult the Archeron before making any major decisions that will affect the tribe as a whole.

Though their religion is primarily nature-based, they do believe, very strongly, in an afterlife, and that the actions taken within their life will directly affect their reception in world of the afterlife, or Summerland, as some refer to it. An honorable life will always be followed by a good reception in the Summerland. A dishonorable life, or the breaking of a trust, will culminate in punishment directly related to the deed, for every act has its price, and death is no barrier to the payment of that price.

The burial ritual, so important in many other cultures, is not as important to the Trolls. Among the tribes, the manner of dealing with the dead varies widely. Some are buried, some are cremated, and some are left in the wild in a place of honor. Since it is the manner of the death and the quality of the life preceding it that matter, the handling of the body is secondary.

The greatest rewards in the Summerland go to those warriors who die valiantly in battle. The Trolls believe these are granted a special place in the Great Hall of Valor or Te Ault Naull. Admittance to the Te Ault Naull in the afterlife is more important to the Trolls than life itself. The leaders within the Te Ault Naull are believed to be those accorded the special rank of Res Cru for not only dying in battle, but dying in a noble cause—though the actual definition of a noble cause is somewhat different for Trolls than for the other Races.

Great honor is accorded to those living warriors who have managed to achieve the status of Res Cru and still survive. It is believed that these rare people are already destined for the Te Ault Naull. If they are also the embodiment of all that is noble within the Troll Race, they are even more revered as the chosen of the gods themselves, destined to sit at the right hand of the Maturen of the Te Ault Naull. The Black Irix Award, greatest of the many awards among the Trolls, was created to designate these godlike individuals, so that all who meet them might honor them and gain wisdom from their example.

Trolls also have legends of Res Cru who return from the dead. One of these legends tells of a great hero who will leave the Te Ault Naull to lead the Trolls in glorious battle. Because he will return from the dead, mortals cannot kill him. It is undoubtedly this legend that Brona used to his advantage to convince the Trolls to submit to him. By claiming to have returned from the dead, he was also claiming to have been sent by the gods, as in the

The Black Irix

The Black Irix is the highest honor a Troll can achieve. It is awarded only to those Trolls who epitomize the highest ideals of honor, valor, courage, and integrity. A recipient is considered the chosen of the gods, the living image of everything the Troll Nation cherishes. A large black metal pendant with a cross centered in a circle, the Black Irix is only awarded rarely, as its requirements are so stringent.

The most famous recipient of the Black Irix was the Res Cru Keltset of the Malicos family. Though no one outside the Troll nation knows what he did to earn the award, his actions after receiving it are legendary.

Keltset was one of the few who dared to speak out against the Warlock Lord when he sought to control the Troll city of Norbane. Because of his resistance, the Skull Bearers were obliged to seize the city by force. They killed Keltset's family and blamed their deaths on Dwarf raiders to inflame the populace against the Eastland. Keltset was taken prisoner and had his tongue burned out. He escaped and was rescued and befriended by Panamon Creel. Keltset and Creel aided Shea Ohmsford in his quest for the Sword of Shannara.

Even without his voice, Keltset managed to convince Trolls in the Skull Kingdom to aid the heir to Shannara to gain entrance to Skull Mountain despite the danger. They willingly followed him, enabling Shea to gain access to the sword and to achieve his objective.

The brave Troll gave his life while ensuring Shea's escape from the collapsing mountain. The Trolls believe that Keltset sits at the right hand of the Maturen within the Hall of Valor in the afterlife.

The Black Irix, the Troll Nation's highest award.

legend. The Trolls' natural superstition, though much less extreme than that of the Gnomes, made them targets for the Spirit Lord's manipulation. Of course, not all Trolls were so easily led, especially by the age of the War of the Warlock Lord, but those that did not succumb to his will by virtue of his connection with their gods were forced through more mundane methods. The rest were killed or imprisoned. The Troll nation has never completely recovered from the damage done to their population by the man who claimed to be sent from their gods.

While populations in the rest of the Four Lands have increased, forcing the growth of cities and unification of governments, the Troll population has remained relatively small. Some of the larger tribes have a population of thousands, but the majority have only a few hundred. This is partially due to the warlike nature of the people themselves, but in greater part to the extreme damage done to the male breeding population by the ravages of the Second War of the Races and the War of the Warlock Lord. It is estimated that well over half the men of breeding age were wiped out in the Second War of the Races. The population recovered slowly, reaching almost to prewar levels just in time for the Warlock's next attempt at world domination. The estimates for that war are lower—a little less than half the male breeding population died. These numbers are significant because of the lower fertility rate among Troll women and the fact that Trolls are monogamous and mate for life. Any damage to the breeding population is reflected almost immediately in the reduction of the birth rate. But such hardships are not unknown to the people of the Northland. They pride themselves on their ability to face any obstacle with courage and fortitude.

Most Troll cities and villages are designed to be completely self-sufficient. Trolls are primarily hunter-gatherers, but they do raise some small amount of food within each village. Most tribes maintain at least a small herd of herbivores for providing meat, milk, and hides. This herd is usually sheep or goats, though some of the more nomadic tribes manage herds of Northern Deer.

For the most part, the Trolls are a fixed tribal society, with villages and cities established in permanent locations. Many tribes have winter and summer camps, to follow the migration patterns of their prey, but each of these is itself a fixed settlement. Their settlements consist of homes built of sod and skins, as well as a few stone buildings and tents. The materials used depend on the severity of the weather in that location as well as the availability of raw materials. Most villages are built within an area with natural fortifications of some type, usually within the foothills or mountains.

All communities contain at least one forge, for smelting and casting metal. All metal weapons for the tribe are made by the tribal smiths, including sword blades, spears, axes, and pikes, as well as metal armor pieces. The forge also smelts fine metals for making jewelry. Troll craftsmen are capable of exquisite decorative metalwork, although they do not usually wear much jewelry. The pendants or jewelry they do wear tend to be highly significant of either rank or award, though unmarried women of marriageable age wear adornment to announce their availability, and married women wear theirs to announce their status as wed. Fine metalwork is exported to the Borderlands. Most are traded for manufactured materials, which are considered nonessential luxuries, or for ores from the mines in the South. Fine furs and animal products are also traded, though only when the catch surpasses the needs of the tribe. These items are traded locally first.

A community gathering place, or Moot Hall, is also an essential part of any Troll settlement or camp, though the hall is not always enclosed in a shelter in the more mobile communities. The hall is used as a meeting place for the tribe. It is also the place for ceremonial occasions such as marriages or celebrations as well as official functions such as choosing a new leader or a call for judgment.

Trolls have a fairly refined sense of justice. Within their Race, a demand to face trial or grant justice can never be refused. There are usually at least three judges for any trial, chosen from among the peers of the community. Judgment is usually fair but swift. There are no appeals, and the punishment for any serious transgression is usually death.

Since death is usually considered a constant companion to such a warlike Race, it is small wonder that music, especially the heroic ballad, is a major part of their culture. Each and every warrior is expected to know and be able to perform several of the major heroic ballads. Almost all of them laud a brave warrior and his valiant battles, usually ending in his glorious death. Some of these ballads are of mythical archetypes; others are taken from actual historic events. The best become classics and are shared with other tribes until they eventually become part of the racial culture. Such tales, whether told or sung, are used to teach history, racial and tribal pride, and an understanding of courage and honor within the Troll culture. Chanting and the use of percussion instruments, especially hide drums with wood or ceramic bases, is a common part of all rituals, ceremonies, and bardic per-

The Death Watch

To Trolls, music—or at least the song of horns and drums—is considered important on the battlefield. Troll war horns are used to signal orders and to indicate particular changes in the order of battle. Drums are also used—though not to as great an extent as among the Gnomes—with their percussive beat helping to inflame the warriors' courage before battle and, it is intended, intimidate the enemy.

The most chilling sound to any Troll enemy, however, is the complete silence of the Death Watch. Rarely used, the Death Watch is an announcement to an enemy that no quarter will be given during the battle. There will be no prisoners taken, and every person surviving the initial battle will be put to death.

King Balinor Buckhannah wrote of the Death Watch placed on his city during the battle for Tyrsis: "Suddenly all sound and movement within the enemy lines ceased. The entire Northland army stood at silent attention, their silence more deafening than the sounds of battle. After a long moment, a single armored warrior stepped purposely from the line, bearing a long staff with a single red pennant. He strode to the foot of the wall, then jammed the staff into the ground at the foot of the wall before turning his back on it to walk calmly back to his lines. The unnerving silence continued for a moment more before it was broken by the long, low wail of a Troll war horn. The mournful note sounded twice more, echoing eerily off the battlements before fading again into silence. The moment was broken by the sudden percussion of hundreds of drums signaling the attack."

formance. Almost all heroic ballads are designed to be accompanied by a drum, and almost all have a chorus intended to be chanted or sung by the audience.

Urdas

It was long believed that Gnomes never crossed into the Northland, remaining instead in the more hospitable Eastland. We now know that some species of Gnomes have been within the Northland since the first emergence of the Race. Most of the Gnomes live within the forests at the foothills of the Charnals, though there are probably other undiscovered tribes in more remote locations. There are even a few Gnomes who crossed the passes from the Eastland as traders or trappers and never managed to return home. Some of these Gnomes actually interbred with the Trolls to create a third Race that is neither Gnome nor Troll. They are known as Urdas.

The Urdas are tribal, as are both their founding Races, and are not found anywhere south of the Charnals. Most tribes survive within the forested valleys of the massive mountain range, leaving the heights to the Trolls. More primitive than Trolls, they are small, squat creatures with short, powerful legs and long, gnarled arms. Unlike Trolls, they have a coating of hair over much of their thickly muscled bodies, though they do have the Trolls' blunt-featured faces as well as a Troll-like affinity for weapons. Their culture, however, is reminiscent of the more primitive types of Gnome culture.

Urdas have their own language, though it appears to be a derivation of both Troll and Gnome. Each tribe seems to have its own distinct dialect. They are exclusively hunter-gatherers and do no herding or breeding of animals. Warlike in

the extreme, they constantly raid their neighbors and are known to take captives, especially those believed to have special abilities. They are quite superstitious, like most Gnomes, and recognize magic, though they do not understand it. They have an intense belief in spirits and wraiths as well as in portents and omens.

Fierce fighters, the Urdas use a combination of weapons, including darts, short spears, and their own unusually shaped razor-edged throwing blades, all of which are designed to bring down even the swiftest game. Most tribes are housed within a stockade, usually built of wood with sharpened tips. The average Urda stockade contains a cluster of small huts and open-sided shelters surrounding a central lodge, not unlike the Troll Moot Hall, at least in purpose. The lodge is constructed of notched logs and a shingled roof. Tribes living within the forest often utilize trees living inside the stockade as supports for treeways and lifts. Most stockades are built around wells or springs, and include smokehouses for curing meat from the hunt.

All Urda compounds also have a method of escape for the tribe in case of siege by an enemy. In most cases, this is a series of tunnels leading from key huts down into a main escape tunnel that emerges some distance from the stockade.

Tribal hierarchy is usually broken into several clearly defined groups, with control delegated to a council of men of mixed ages. Warrior males hold the highest level in society, with women, children, and the aged at the lowest levels.

Though the rest of the Races consider both Urdas and Trolls to be warlike barbarians, they are both quite civilized compared to the wild Northland that is home to both of them.

The Eastland: Land of Dwarves and Gnomes

The Dwarves have always had to fight a constant battle against the Gnomes to protect their homeland, but that battle has given them the strength of will that has ensured their survival. —Prince Balinor Buckhannah

The Eastland, more than any other of the Four Lands, is a region of divisions and complexity. Home to three Races as well as numerous creatures born of old magic, the land east of the Rabb is in constant conflict. Dwarves dominate the southern section, Trolls and Gnomes dominate the north, and the central section is constantly disputed. The actual populations and lines of territorial demarcation change with the winds of fortune and time, while the creatures of magic and Faerie, who have lived here longer than any, ignore the struggles of their mortal neighbors.

The Eastland is defined by its great forest, the Anar. Divided into the Lower Anar, the Central Anar, and the Upper Anar, the sections of forest, and their connecting mountains and plains, are each distinct regions. The Lower Anar, a dense old-growth forest bordered by the Battlemound Lowlands on the west and the foothills of the Ravenshorn on the east, is the heartland of the Dwarves. The Central Anar, between the Wolfsktaag Mountains and the Ravenshorn Mountains, is home to both Gnomes and Dwarves. West of the Wolfsktaag, in the forest at the edge of the Rabb Plains, lies Storlock, home to the special breed of Gnome Healers called Stors.

Gnomes, Mountain Gnomes, and the lizard-like Trolls known as Mwellrets populate the Upper Anar, as well as the northern part of the Ravenshorn.

Dwarves

The Dwarf Race, like the other Races, evolved from human ancestors that survived the Great Wars. Their progenitors escaped the holocaust by hiding underground in bunkers, shelters, tunnels, and caves. These people probably expected they would have to hide for only a few years, but their subterranean exile lasted generations. Over time, they adapted to conditions within the caverns and tunnels that made up the whole of their world. They developed an underground civilization and a unique language as their bodies changed. The tunnels favored those with short, stocky frames and powerful muscles adapted for small spaces and hard climbs. Their eyes adapted to darkness as they learned to survive in their dim, rocky prison. Centuries after the end of the Great Wars, it was a new Race that climbed out of the caves to face the blinding light of a changed world. The Men who first found them named them Dwarves, after the mythic creatures they now resembled.

The Dwarves had survived underground, becoming skilled miners and stonemasons, but when they left their cold, dark prison, they vowed that neither they nor their descendants would ever return. To this day, all Dwarves have an abhorrence of closed-in spaces, especially those that are underground. They are happiest in the forest, where the darkness comes from the shade of the thick foliage overhead, and the closeness is only that of tightly interwoven plants.

Emerging from that long darkness, the Dwarves embraced life within the forests, rejoicing in homes built within the open air and ornamented by gardens nurtured by soil and sunlight. All the things they had lost for centuries as the price of survival became extremely precious to them. Yet they retained the traits that had helped them endure their exile. For Dwarves, a willingness to work hard was second only to iron determination and fortitude. Among them, those capable of meticulous planning and a dedication to order were highly regarded. Even today, every Dwarf community is distinctive in its carefully planned design, neat and orderly homes, and well-constructed buildings. And each Dwarf community, no matter how remote, always has a garden, even if the soil and seed must be carried in a handful at a time.

When the lands were partitioned after the First War of the Races, the Dwarves were given the Eastland, along with the Gnomes. The Druids, including the Dwarves within their number, believed the vast forests of the Anar would be more than adequate for both Races. Unfortunately, the decision laid the groundwork for territorial conflicts that have continued throughout the history of the Eastland.

Dwarves have managed to hold the Central and Southern Anar, as well as large portions of the Ravenshorn, for most of their history. It was in the years just prior to the Second War of the Races, during the reign of King Raybur, that the Dwarf nation reached its greatest extension. Before the war, Raybur controlled all the territory from the edge of the Lower Anar forests south of the Silver River to the Rabb River in the north, as well as all but the northernmost sections of the Ravenshorn and all of the High Bens. Only the Wolfsktaag, which belonged solely to the creatures of old magic, remained outside his rule. Unfortunately, King Raybur was also forced to watch his entire kingdom disappear beneath the conquering armies of the Warlock Lord. His people were driven into exile in the forests and deep mountains. All the Dwarf settlements were destroyed, including the capital of Culhaven and the Fortress of Stedden Keep.

Raybur and his people had been overrun, but not defeated. It was not in their nature to give up. Despite their losses, the Dwarves rallied behind Raybur and the Dwarf Druid Risca to go to the aid of the Elves. They arrived in time to trap the Northland army on the Streleheim Plains as the Elves closed from behind. Without the Dwarves, Jerle Shannara would not have been able to defeat the Warlock Lord that day.

The Dwarves never regained all the territory they had lost, but they did rebuild a

Raybur, Warrior King

Honored as the greatest ruler in the history of the Dwarf nation, Raybur was a warrior who was chosen to rule. As a boy, he had fought against the Gnome tribes in the constant battles to drive them back from Dwarf lands. As king, he continued the fight, pushing the Gnomes back and extending the boundaries of his kingdom till it was twice its previous size. During his reign, Dwarves held all of the Central and Lower Anar, all the way to the Rabb River and beyond.

When the Warlock Lord attacked the Eastland, Raybur marshaled the Dwarves in a brilliant series of defensive battles. Aided by the Warrior Druid Risca, Raybur managed to hold off the Northland army while evacuating most of his population to the comparative safety of the deep forests. Even after his son was killed, he still led his forces at the final battle on the Streleheim Plains. The Druid Risca was killed in that final battle of the war.

After the war, Raybur began a massive reconstruction of the Dwarf lands. All the towns and villages had to be rebuilt, but Raybur wanted them improved. He approved the design and construction of the famous Meade Garden in Culhaven, rather than simply rebuilding the existing garden, and had Risca buried there. But his greatest legacy was the dams of Capaal. Determined to protect the lands that the Trolls had destroyed, Raybur spearheaded the plans for the most ambitious project ever undertaken by the Dwarf nation—a series of dams and locks on the Silver River Gorge that would control and regulate the flow of waters into the Anar, protected by a massive fortress that would also serve to protect the Dwarf lands. His fortress of Capaal still stands, and has allowed the lands of the Lower Anar to flourish.

He was buried in the Meade Garden in Culhaven, near his dear friend Risca.

Raybur, warrior king of the Dwarves.

Hendel, a Dwarf hero, nemesis of the Gnomes. He died at the battle for Tyrsis.

thriving nation. Gnome tribes moved into regions conquered by the Northland army, and had to be driven back. Some say the new Dwarf kingdom was made stronger because of being constantly tested by Gnome incursions. For outlying areas, Gnomes were a constant threat. In most cases, the better-prepared Dwarf Hunters were superior fighters to their Gnome counterparts. Raiders caused damage, but rarely managed to take and hold Dwarf lands. The skills of battle, honed while fighting the Raiders, proved invaluable to the other Races in the wars that followed. Dwarf Hunters and Sappers helped hold the line at the battle for Tyrsis during the War of the Warlock Lord. Sixty years later, they fought side by side with the other Races against the Demons of the Forbidding in the Battle for Arborlon.

Fifty years after the War of the Forbidding, however, the Dwarves discovered they had trouble in their own lands. The Gnomes escalated their attacks on the Dwarf outposts, and the Dwarves were no longer able to keep the usually inferior Gnome Raiders at bay. Somehow, the Gnomes actually began to push the Dwarves back toward the Silver River, taking over lands that had belonged to the Dwarves for centuries. At first, no one knew that the Gnomes were controlled by the Mord Wraiths and aided by the dark magic of the Ildatch. By the time the Dwarves realized the extent of their peril, the dark magic was firmly entrenched within the Ravenshorn Mountains, and the Silver River, key to the survival of the Lower Anar, began to turn foul from Mord Wraith poison. Before the war was over, the Gnomes and Wraiths managed to capture all the Dwarf strongholds and settlements within the Ravenshorn and throughout most of the Upper and Central Anar. Even the great fortress at Capaal fell to the Mord Wraiths and their Gnome army.

The Ohmsfords managed to destroy the Ildatch and cleanse the Silver River, bringing an abrupt end to the war, but at the cost of many lives. Once the Gnomes were no longer driven by the Mord Wraiths, the Dwarves were able to regain their lost lands and drive the weakened raiders back toward the Upper Anar.

Peace, or its closest Eastland equivalent, lasted for several generations before it was shattered. This time the threat came not from Gnomes, Trolls, or Demons, but from the very people whose borders the Dwarves had protected—the Race of Man. The Federation claimed the Dwarves were enemies of the Southland that had to be neutralized. The Dwarves found themselves facing the might of a well-trained Southland army, with no allies. The Borderlands had already succumbed, the Elves were gone, and there were no Druids. But Dwarves, being who they were, could not surrender simply because the odds were too great. They were driven from their cities, but they continued to fight. They were harried in the forests and wildlands, but they continued to fight. Their families and any prisoners were rounded up and sent to the mines at Dechtera, there to face the nightmare of the dark, cold earth. Thousands died in the mining tunnels, locked away from the sun. The Dwarves fought on.

For five long years the remnants of the Dwarf army held off the Federation juggernaut, always just managing to deprive the larger force of victory as they drew them deeper into the unforgiving wilderness of the Anar. But after five years, the Federation decided to put a stop to the Dwarves once and for all. They brought in creepers and Seekers. The creepers were unstoppable. The wilderness did not even give them pause as they relentlessly hunted the Dwarves, brutally killing all they caught. The Eastland surrendered soon after the creepers appeared, the only time in the history of the Dwarf nation that they ever surrendered to anyone.

Unfortunately, capitulation did not save the Dwarves. The Federation occupied their cities, destroyed their gardens, and used the citizens as slave labor. Unlike the Borderlands, where there was at least a pretense of a protectorate government, the Federation rulers of the Eastland made little attempt to disguise the fact that they intended to wipe out the Dwarf Race. Most of the major construction projects built in the Southland during those years were built with Dwarf blood.

The few Dwarves who escaped created a resistance movement. It was small and poorly provisioned, capable only of harassing the occupation force. It was not until the Federation Army was defeated in the Westland that new life was instilled in

the Dwarf resistance. With the destruction of the Shadowen and the support of the Free Born resistance in the Borderlands, the Dwarves rallied behind Morgan Leah and eventually expelled the Federation from their lands.

The scars left by the Shadowen-controlled Southland did not heal easily. Everyone knew someone who had died in the mines. Everyone had seen what Federation control could do to a proud people; they had seen the squalor and poverty it brought to their tidy communities. In many ways, it was much worse than the destruction wrought by the Warlock Lord centuries before. Years later, when the Federation once again decided to attempt to control the Borderlands, the Dwarves were among the first to join with the Free Born against the Southlanders, determined to ensure that the holocaust perpetrated on their Race would not happen again.

Land of the Dwarves

Nurtured by the Silver River that tumbles out of the eastern mountains, the vast woodlands of the Lower Anar contain the largest concentration of Dwarf communities. Most of the larger villages and towns, including the capital of Culhaven, are built within easy traveling distance of the river as it flows west through the forest and lowlands to end in the Rainbow Lake.

The Eastland territory controlled by the Dwarves begins at the Battlemound Lowlands, just east of the Mist Marsh. The Battlemound cuts a bleak, uneven swath through the grasslands that stretch between the massive trees of the Black Oaks and the forest of the Lower Anar. Local farmers avoid the area, and even the Dwarves are cautious when crossing it. Things born of old magic reside within the

The Siren Tree of the Battlemound Lowlands, beautiful but deadly.

hills and trenches of the Battlemound. Sirens, wights, and wraiths are known to prey on unwary travelers. Most people wishing to reach the Eastland attempt to avoid the Battlemound, either using the Silver River or passing to the south of the lowlands.

CULHAVEN

The capital of the Dwarf nation, Culhaven, lies east of the Battlemound, within the forest of the Lower Anar. Located just south of the banks of the Silver River, the town is the center of Dwarf culture and commerce. Founded in the early days of the Four Lands as the center of Dwarf government, Culhaven grew to be the largest town within the entire Eastland. In the days of the First and Second Wars of the Races, it was the home of the main garrison of the Dwarf Hunters, an elite unit of warriors that made up the backbone of the Dwarf army. The Northland army burned the original village to the ground during the Second War of the Races. Fortunately, due to King Raybur's foresight, most of its citizens had been evacuated and hidden deep in the Anar. Those families who insisted on remaining in the village were annihilated.

Culhaven was rebuilt after the war, but with improvements in design and materials. As a symbol of the rebirth of the town, the Dwarves planted a garden, now known as the Meade Garden, which is still considered by many to be the most beautiful garden in the Four Lands.

Though Culhaven has changed in size several times over the centuries, it has always served as the center of government for the Dwarves. Near the Meade Garden, across the main street, the Assembly Hall contains all government offices as well as the meeting hall where the council gathers to decide issues of importance to the Dwarf community.

Most matters of day-to-day policy are left up to the individual towns and settlements. Since many Dwarves are trappers, traders, and hunters, they tend to live in far-flung communities that preclude any attempt at truly centralized control. The

Siren Tree

The Siren Tree uses illusion and music to attract its prey. Found only in the lowlands of the Battlemound, it resembles a normal tree except for the long needles upon the tips of its branches. Those who have survived an encounter with the tree tell of being drawn by the sweet sound of a woman's voice, her song bright and irresistibly seductive. The source of the enchanting music usually appears as a young girl, seated beneath the tree, though other illusions may be used to draw animals or other prey. The girl encourages travelers to approach and join her beneath the tree. Gnarled prehensile roots emerge from the loose soil around the tree, immediately snaring those who do. The girl vanishes, and the last sight most victims see are the poison-laden needles on the tips of the tree's branches as the previously immobile plant reaches to drive the needles into its victims. The poison renders the victim unconscious, making it easy for the Siren to feed on the paralyzed prey.

The poison itself is deadly only if left untreated. There are several potions developed by the Dwarves that have proven effective against the Siren's toxin. The carnivorous Siren Tree is not truly a plant, as its nervous system more closely resembles that of an animal. It is not truly an animal, either, but rather a little of both, shaped by the ancient magic that gave birth to it.

The Meade Garden of the Dwarves.

Meade Garden of the Dwarves

After the Second War of the Races, the Dwarves decided to build something special in honor of those who died in that war, especially those who were killed when the first town of Culhaven was burned. Because they were Dwarves, the memorial was not to be a statue or a building of cold stone, but rather something that spoke to the thing they cherished most—life. They decided to build a garden. They chose the rocky slope near Culhaven's town center, where the dead ground was permanently scarred from the ravages of the fire. It did not matter that the soil was barren or that nothing had ever grown there. They were determined to bring life out of death— to make the damaged land bloom as a symbol of their own perseverance in the face of adversity.

Special soils and plants of all varieties were brought from across the lands and placed in a carefully terraced pattern of stones and soil reminiscent of a waterfall. Painstakingly nurtured, the resulting Meade Garden became one of the wonders of the Four Lands. Flowers and plants from many different regions flourished in the garden year round, the varieties changing with the seasons in an ongoing kaleidoscope of color and texture. Everyone passed the gardens while going to and from the interior of the town. It was the pride of Culhaven and the entire Dwarf nation.

In an attempt to permanently demoralize the Dwarves, the Federation destroyed the garden during their occupation. A defeated Race could not be allowed to keep something so closely tied to their pride as a people. The Dwarves were helpless to prevent its destruction, but the daughter of the King of the Silver River was not, and used her magic to restore the garden to its full glory with one touch. Her gift made it even more precious to the Dwarves, who have carefully maintained it ever after—for her as well as for themselves.

council mainly rules on matters of national importance and on grievances that cannot be solved by the local elders.

Culhaven also contains shops and trading centers filled with the products of Dwarf artisans. Fine metalwork and jewelry, carved furniture, and elegant sculptures are interspersed with produce markets, leather workers' shops, and, of course, the workshops of armor makers. There are also furriers, though most furs are traded to outland cities for manufactured goods and specialty foods.

CAPAAL

Four days' march upriver from Culhaven, the Silver River spills from the mountains into the Lower Anar from a massive gorge, known as the Wedge. Spanned by a single bridge, the Wedge marks the beginning of

the rugged Ravenshorn Mountains of the far Eastland. Upstream from the Wedge lies the fortress of Capaal, its dams and locks all that prevent the fury of the raging waters of the Silver River from flooding the lands below.

Capaal was built by edict of King Raybur as part of the massive restoration campaign that followed the end of the Second War of the Races. The intricate series of locks and dams was the most extensive engineering project ever attempted by the Dwarves. Before the dams were built, the lands below the Wedge were subject to seasonal flooding that often wiped out whole villages, including Culhaven, as well as seasonal droughts that left some areas low on water for weeks at a time. The dams of Capaal allowed the Dwarves to control the majority of the water supply for the lands between the Ravenshorn and the Rainbow Lake, thus ensuring an even supply year round. The locks enabled boats to pass through the river in both directions, a feat previously impossible. Trappers and hunters were able to transport their goods by boat instead of having to pack them down through the mountain trails. The lake formed by the dams, called the Cillidellan, became a valuable habitat for fish and waterfowl.

Once the dams were in place, permanent settlements could be constructed in areas of the river valley that previously had been unusable because of flooding. Hunters and trappers could get supplies more often and could get their catch to market much faster. Because of its importance to the survival of the communities it served, Capaal was also designed as a fortress, able to protect its locks and dams from almost any attack.

Built to span the natural canyon between the mountains, Capaal consists of three dams, one below the other, with the main fortress built atop the highest dam and spanning the entire distance between the cliffs, making external access to the lower dams impossible. A forbidding structure of white stone with battlements and watchtowers along its length, Capaal is considered the guardian of the Dwarf lands.

The machinery that regulates the locks and dams is concealed within the lower levels of the dams and the fortress. The Dwarves who work within the lower levels to keep the machinery running do so only because of the supreme importance of the dam to their communities. None can stay in the dark, cramped quarters for very long, so duty shifts for those who must tend the machines are shorter than for those atop the battlements or in the upper

The fortress and triple dams of Capaal.

chambers. It is a tribute to the fortitude of the Eastlanders that they have managed the dams so long and so well despite their natural abhorrence for the confined spaces of the building's cramped interior. To soothe the souls of those who must work within Capaal's cold stone walls, the Dwarves brought a little bit of the Meade Garden with them. Located in an atrium high on the northern watch is a flourishing garden area filled with transplanted plants and trees set beneath glass and open sky.

Behind the High Dam, the Cillidellan is a large lake that reaches well back into the mountains. Below the dam, sheer cliffs flank the lower dams and the two small reservoirs that pool behind them. The only way down from the fortress is across catwalks or through underground passages. There are underground passages throughout the entire area to allow access to or escape for those within Capaal if the citadel falls under siege. Tunnels bore through to the mountains on either side, as well as deep into the North, their covers well hidden and locked, their openings rigged to collapse if forced.

Though it was built to be impregnable, Capaal has fallen into enemy hands twice since it was commissioned. During the Gnome Wars—or the War of the Mord Wraiths, as it was also called—the Mord Wraiths managed to take Capaal by summoning a Kraken. The Dwarves recaptured it only a few weeks later, once the Mord Wraiths had been destroyed.

The second time was during the Shadowen War, when Capaal and all the lands around were claimed by the Federation. The Dwarves who ran the machinery were allowed to stay, but most of them were locked in the lower chambers with the machinery they tended.

DUN FEE ARAN

Above Capaal, the Silver River cuts north into the Ravenshorn Mountains, a contested land of Dwarves, Trolls, and Gnomes, before it enters a valley dividing the High Bens from the Ravenshorn range. It is there, along the cliffs flanking the river, that the Gnome prisons of Dun Fee Aran stand.

Dwarves originally built Dun Fee Aran as a deep mountain fortress on their eastern frontier guarding the Silver River. Over the years, as the boundaries shifted and the Dwarf territories waned, it fell under the control of the Gnomes. Lacking the Dwarf compulsion for order, the Gnomes allowed the keep to gradually fall

into disrepair. In the years after the War of the Forbidding, the Gnomes converted it to a prison. The cells were always available to those who were willing to pay. There were always slaves and prisoners for sale

Kraken

A creature from the deep ocean caused the fall of Capaal. The creature, a Kraken, was summoned by the Mord Wraiths and their Gnome army, and set upon the fortress's defenders. Most Kraken cannot live out of salt water, but this one was mutated by dark magic to enable it to attack the battlements from the waters of the Cillidellan. Measuring over 150 feet in length, the Kraken resembles an ocean squid in shape. It has a barrel-shaped body with four fin-covered legs. Long, grasping tentacles protrude from the front, their surfaces covered with suckers large enough to engulf a man's face. The creature's beak is over four feet across and made of sharpened bone. Prey is grabbed by the tentacles and either smashed or drawn directly into the beak, where it is crushed and devoured. The Kraken at Capaal is the only one ever seen outside of the Blue Divide. It was reported killed by Garet Jax.

there as well. Anyone locked up there stayed locked away until they rotted, or until someone paid a higher price to own them. Dun Fee Aran is one of the few places where Gnomes actually live within a stone building. Most Gnomes are more comfortable in primitive huts. They usually prefer to live in structures made from skins and plants, or in caves.

Gnomes

Unlike most of the other Races, Gnomes have no distinct nation. Tribes of various types of Gnomes can be found scattered throughout the central and northern sections of the Eastland, and even into some parts of the Northland, but their primary habitat is the forests and hill country of the Upper and Central Anar.

Gnomes are the most primitive of the Races. There are several different species,

but all of them are descended from people who survived the Great Wars by hiding in the hills and forests in affected areas. The survivors who emerged from this brutally primitive existence were little more than animals. Almost all Gnomes are small and slight of build, with straight dark hair, yellowish roughened skin, and primitive features. All are tribal in nature, with a deeply rooted belief in the supernatural. The more primitive species, such as the Spider Gnomes, are extremely animalistic, wearing little or no clothing and having only rudimentary language skills. Those living in more settled areas tend to wear more clothing and have a more complex dialect, with most Gnomes sharing versions of what is known as the Gnome Tongue. A few Gnomes have even become fluent in other languages, leading scholars to believe that it may be lack of exposure to knowledge, rather than inability to learn, that has kept most Gnomes in such primi-

A Gnome Sedt, or chief, rules the tribe.

tive circumstances.

Extremely warlike, Gnomes will usually raid anyone within their perceived territory who has something they want or need. Their weapons of choice are slings, bows and arrows, knives, and swords, though they will use anything that comes to hand. The Gnomes can and do use horses when available, though they are poor horsemen compared to Elves or even Men. Their Tracking skills, however, are far superior to most of the other Races. Gnome Trackers are always considered the best of the breed. They are excellent hunters and always know where natural foods grow best.

Most of the time, Gnomes are busy raiding each other at least as often as they raid the other Races. Tribes do not ever band together unless forced by a supernatural entity. Each tribe has its own chief, called a Sedt, and its own gods and ceremonies. Tribes come together only at certain preordained ceremonies designed to appease various major gods such as those within the Wolfsktaag. Each tribe is governed by a council—usually made up of elders and respected war chiefs—who advise the Sedt.

Gnomes are nomadic, moving their camps to follow the game, or the seasons or the whim of the Sedt. Some tribes have a fixed pattern of migration, while others simply follow the path of least resistance, almost literally going wherever they are led. They prefer huts and tents but have no qualms about using houses if they are available, though they seldom know how to care for sophisticated dwellings.

Gnomes have always outnumbered the other Races, but until the Warlock Lord forced them to unite, their greater numbers were not a threat because of their lack of organization. The Warlock Lord used the natural Gnome fear of the supernatural to force them to serve him. They believed the Skull Bearers were gods. The fact that Skull Bearers had the abilities of the dark magic reinforced that belief. The Warlock Lord used the Gnomes primarily to fill his lines, since they had neither the skill nor the dedication of the Trolls. They also had no qualms about wandering away if game that was more interesting was on the horizon.

Religion is extremely important to most Gnomes. Each tribe has a shaman who presides over a complex series of rites and rituals designed to appease the gods

Trackers

All Races have men and women who are Trackers, though Gnome Trackers are considered the best within that elite group. Trackers have the ability to trace the movement of anything that lives by studying the ground and surrounding area. They can recognize the faintest signs and interpret their meaning. Though this often seems like magic, it is actually an almost instinctive skill that comes of being close to nature and understanding the land as few people ever can.

Most Trackers are at home only within the wilderness. They tend to avoid settlements and large towns whenever possible. The only company they truly enjoy is that of other Trackers.

The most famous Gnome Tracker was named Slanter. Often known as the Gnome who was not quite a Gnome, Slanter spoke several languages fluently and lived most of his life away from the Gnome territories. He became a hero during the War of the Ildatch and was the only one of Jair Ohmsford's protectors to survive the quest. He was also one of the few Gnomes ever to win the respect of the Dwarves.

A Gnome warrior.

involved in every phase of tribal life. Some tribes even sacrifice their own kind to appease angry gods. Any power of magic or seeming magic that they do not understand is perceived as a god. Most Gnomes have an instinctive ability to sense magic. It does little to protect them, since they do not understand it or its use. Only the shaman, who is usually a seer, has any use or understanding of magic.

Icon worship is very common among Gnomes. Often the more unusual spoils of a raid or war are treated as holy relics and placed on a wooden platform as part of a ceremony. Unusually crafted swords and knives are more likely to be worshiped or

used in ceremonies than as weapons of war.

Perhaps the most feared sound in the Eastland is the sound of Gnome drums. The Gnomes use drums made of hide and wood in all aspects of their lives. All ceremonies involve chanting accompanied by the drums. Long-distance communication, usually used only in time of war or during large raids, is done with drums. War drums are used to invoke the spirits of war before a battle to ensure a favorable outcome. During the Second War of the Races and the War of the Warlock Lord, thousands of these drums sounded their ominous percussion day and night as the Gnomes summoned their spirits to protect them and destroy their enemies.

Gnome women traditionally manage the village and are keepers of the hearth and children. In most tribes, they are not granted equal status with men unless they do something unusual to gain that status. If a woman proves the gods favor her, she may be granted higher status. Women fight only in the final defense of their children, and then only if they cannot run away.

STORLOCK

Not all Gnomes are primitive and nomadic. Within the Central Anar, near the Rabb Plains, the Gnomes of Storlock have very little in common with the rest of their Race. The Stors are a single tribe of Gnomes, founded by a former Druid named Stor Rualitan, who have dedicated themselves to the healing arts with the same intensity that their cousins have dedicated themselves to raids. Stor was part of the Druid Council, but at some point he and his followers decided that gathering knowledge at Paranor was not enough. They wanted to actually use their knowledge to help people. These few Gnomes left Paranor and established Storlock, a vil-

Jachyra

The beast known as the Jachyra was believed to be little more than a legend until Allanon discovered one loose within the Wolfsktaag Mountains near the Chard Rush. Jachyras were Demon creatures from the time of Faerie that had been locked behind the Forbidding since it was first formed in the age of Faerie. The Mord Wraiths managed to use the magic inherent in the Eastland Mountains to bring two of them from their prison. One mortally wounded Allanon before he could destroy it, and the other was set to guard Heaven's Well, where it killed the Weapons Master.

Almost unstoppable, the huge fire-colored monster resembles a misshapen jackal with huge teeth and rending claws. Both teeth and claws are tipped with a poison that affects the spirit as well as the body. The Jachyra feeds on pain, both its victims' and its own. There is no known defense other than complete annihilation. They will tear themselves apart to see their victim destroyed.

lage dedicated to healing and exploring the healing arts. The Gnomes who serve at Storlock are called Stors in honor of their founder.

The Stors live and work in a village that was built for them by the Dwarves. In direct contrast to all other Gnome tribes, they are a people of quiet concentration and calm determination. The finest Healers in the land, they give of their gift freely. All are welcome, no matter the Race, but only Gnomes chosen by the Stors are allowed to work and study with them as Healers. The only exception ever made was for a gifted and determined young man named Wil Ohmsford.

No one knows whether the current Stors come from a single tribe or from different tribes. Once they are dedicated to the healing arts, they never speak of a life beyond Storlock. They practice their arts with herbs and natural remedies, never magic, believing that magic is too unreliable for healing and that the side effects are too damaging.

All Stors dress in the garb of their order, a white hooded robe and sandals. They all live within the village and rarely travel far from Storlock. The other Races keep them supplied with food and satisfy their other material needs. The Dwarves, and many of the Gnome tribes, believe it is good luck to bring gifts to the Stors, who never ask for payment for their services or refuse anyone in need.

Storlock is built within the edge of the forest around a pond of clear waters that are said to have unusual restorative powers. The wooden village consists of a main Healing Center, a number of cabins for visitors and patients, and a village behind the Healing Center with living quarters for the Stors and those Gnomes and Dwarves who assist in the maintenance of the village. The Healing Center itself is a large building with several wings to accommodate private and group sickrooms, a surgery, examining areas, waiting areas, and a large apothecary where herbs and potions are stored and prepared.

WOLFSKTAAG

Though Gnomes have raided throughout the Eastland, there is a place where Gnomes will not go. The Wolfsktaag Mountains, east of Storlock, are believed to be a place of gods and spirits. Twice a year the Gnomes travel to the Pass of Jade, one of only two commonly known openings into the interior of the range, to make offerings to appease the spirits of the Wolfsktaag Mountains. The Dwarves, who are more pragmatic, simply state that there are creatures of old magic living within the ancient mountains. The Wolfsktaag Mountains cover a large part of the Eastland, running north and south between the Rabb Plains and the Central Anar, and are believed to have existed long before the Old World and the Great Wars.

These mountains are the only ones within the Eastland that contain no human habitations. Skilled Dwarf Trackers will cross through them, but even they sometimes fall prey to the tricks and illusions of the area, becoming lost and disoriented. The Druids believed that the Wolfsktaag was a place where the magic from the Great Wars and that of Faerie have "pooled" to create a region where creatures born of such magic find a strong resonance. The magic within the area is not evil, but it is quite strong and not sympathetic to humans. In these mountains, humans are trespassers.

It is the domain of shape-shifters, born of the magic of Faerie—those creatures that can blend their shape at will and seem to have no certain shape of their own. It is

One of the many creatures that lurks within the Wolfsktaag Mountains.

also the home of great ur'wolves, wraiths, logworms, gnawls, and even a creature from the time of the Great Wars related to the creepers. These beings seldom leave the haven of their mountains. Most will not attack a cautious traveler. But in places where old magic is strong, nothing is ever certain.

Truls Rohk

There is a legend of a Borderman bewitched by a shape-shifter. In the legend, the Borderman leaves his homeland to live forever with the shape-shifter in her kingdom of magic. Unfortunately, part of the story is true. A Borderman and a shape-shifter once crossed the forbidden territory between mortal and immortal. Both eventually paid the price with their lives. Their offspring, the only man living within the edge of the Wolfsktaag, must pay the price anew each day of his life.

Truls Rohk is both mortal and shape-shifter. Orphaned at an early age, he is a man of two worlds, for shape-shifters are creatures of old magic and have no use for mortals, and mortals fear the things of magic that they cannot possibly understand and control.

The Grimpond

Deep within the wilds of Darklin Reach, in the depths of a forgotten lake, lies a creature neither living nor dead known as the Grimpond. Both Avatar and shade, the Grimpond is an oracle that will answer questions, but never quite as the querist wishes. Though the Grimpond will not speak of its own origins, there is no doubt that it has existed since the time of the Old World. Even the Druids do not know what or who the Grimpond was or how its spirit came to be imprisoned within the waters. Though only a spirit, the Grimpond claims to have seen all of mankind's rise and fall and all of the tragedies of human existence before and since, with eyes that are more than eyes and ears that need no sound to hear.

Through the thousand thousand years the Grimpond has lain trapped, it has grown bitter. It claims to know what will be as well as what was, but it seems to take delight in misleading with truth that is shaded in half-truths and deception. The only person who ever managed to gain pure truth from the shade was Brin Ohmsford. She used the wishsong to force the Grimpond into giving her the answers she needed to succeed in her quest. The Grimpond never forgave her. It waited for many years until it was able to take its revenge on her descendant, Walker Boh. The Grimpond's advice led Walker to the Hall of Kings, where he lost his arm and almost his life.

Like other shades, the Grimpond is limited to its domain, but its spectral form can appear to have any face, and usually appears wearing the face of the querist. It will only appear to one person at a time, and always as a cloaked figure rising out of the mist of the lake. Unlike the spirits of the Hadeshorn or those within the well of Paranor, the Grimpond does not require a special summoning or the use of magic. It has the ability to appear when it wishes for as long as it wishes. Such abilities suggest that the Grimpond may once have been a creature of Faerie, though even the Grimpond itself may no longer remember the tragedy that brought it to its eternal prison.

DARKLIN REACH

Northwest of the Wolfsktaag, along the course where the Chard Rush approaches the Rabb, lies Darklin Reach, another haven for creatures of magic and those who wield it. Dominated by the chimney-shaped pinnacle known as Hearthstone at its center, Darklin Reach is a thick wilderness of forest broken by a single quiet valley that contrasts sharply with the wild land surrounding it. The valley was home to Cogline and the Bohs for centuries. It was Walker Boh's birthplace. The neatly kept stone and timber cottage that used to nestle under the trees is long gone, destroyed by the Shadowen many years ago, but the peace that was laid upon the land by the people who loved it still remains.

Not far from Hearthstone is the lake that is home to the Grimpond, a spirit creature believed to have existed since the time of Faerie. Further to the northeast, several miles of savage wilderness and towering forest away, is the ridgeline known as Toffer Ridge, home of the Spider Gnomes.

Spider Gnomes are a different species than most other known Gnome types. More primitive than most, they resemble nonhuman primates more than people. Their bodies are hunched and wiry, their arms and legs are angled and crooked, and they are covered with coarse hair. The spiderlike appearance is enhanced by the fact that they usually avoid clothing and tend to creep along the ground and up trees on all fours. They also burrow in the ground and trap prey in a manner similar to some species of spider. Extremely superstitious, they are prey to the werebeasts living in the moor below the ridges.

To appease the werebeasts, which they perceive as either evil spirits or gods, or perhaps both, each fall the Spider Gnomes make a regular pilgrimage to the edge of the moor below Toffer Ridge, where they spend a month in ritual prayer to the spirits of the moor, calling on the dark spirits to send the winter and protect them from the mists. They often sacrifice their own people to the werebeasts in the mists, though not always by intention. Ironically, the ritual works in that the werebeasts are content to remain within the moor for the winter, but only because they have fed off the Spider Gnomes for the entire month of their ritual. The sated werebeasts have no need to hunt Gnomes on Toffer Ridge because the Gnomes deliver themselves for dinner.

The werebeasts that live within Olden Moor are creatures of old magic, a form of shape-shifter, though much more primi-tive than those living within the Wolfsktaag. Creatures of dreadful shapes and forms, they prey upon mortal beings weaker than they, snaring both body and mind to drain away their lives. Their natural shape is that of a wolfish creature covered with both fur and scales. Few of their victims ever see their true form, as they use the power of illusion to draw their prey close. They pull familiar images from the mind of their prey and use their power and the prey's fear to give them form, waiting for the right opportunity. Once close, they immobilize their prey with poison that slowly weakens the victim and allows the werebeast to feed on its life. The poison is one that afflicts the mind and spirit as well as the body. Even a full-grown moor cat is not always a match for a werebeast.

Mwellrets

East of the wilds of Darklin Reach, the Ravenshorn Mountains rise out of the forests. Within the towering mountains lie the source of the Silver River and the homeland of the Mwellrets.

Moor Cat

Moor cats resemble house cats in shape and color, but unlike house cats, they average between eight and fourteen feet in length and often weigh as much as five hundred pounds. A wild carnivore, moor cats live within moors and at the edges of low-lying forests. They are considered very rare, though part of that rarity may be due to the cat's ability to become nearly invisible at will. Moor cats can change their coloration very quickly to match their surroundings, much like an octopus or a chameleon. This ability allows them to compete with the werebeasts and other predators that share their habitat.

Extremely long-lived, moor cats have been known to bond to people, especially those with an affinity for animals. Once they have bonded, it is a lifelong commitment for the cat. They will defend and protect their person and family, even at risk of death. Cogline was the first human known to have tamed moor cats. His adopted family, the Bohs, always had at least one moor cat within their family.

The Mwellrets are a form of Troll originally native to the swamps and lowlands. Like all Trolls, they were descended from human survivors of the Great Wars who were exposed to the energies unleashed during the cataclysm. The offspring of these survivors mutated to adapt to the fearsome conditions of the postwar planet. The ancestors of the Mwellrets fled to the forests. Unfortunately, the cataclysm raised oceans and flooded much of the land, changing their forest refuge to poisoned swampland filled with diseased plants and mutated animals. The Northland Trolls had grown huge and strong within the harsh environment of the mountains; the Mwellrets also endured drastic changes, but they became reptilian, growing scales where skin had once been and adopting many of the characteristics of lizards. Their arms and legs grew short and developed claws, while their bodies developed a snakelike flexibility.

But Mwellrets also developed the ability to shape change. Though they lack the magic of creatures such as the shape-shifters and the werebeasts and cannot change the basic characteristics of their bodies, they do have the ability to alter the shape of their body at will, to adapt to the demands of any environment. They can mold their shape like putty, lengthening or shortening bones and muscle. This ability enabled them to progress back up the scale toward civilization much faster than other types of Trolls or Gnomes. The Gnomes claim that the Mwellrets also have command of dark magic, which they use to "twist" their victims, forcing them to do their will. The more pragmatic Dwarves insist that it is some form of hypnotism, but by either name it is still a powerful tool, especially when combined with the Mwellrets' other talents.

Sometime after the First Council at Paranor, the Mwellrets migrated out of the swamps and broken forest of the moors into the Ravenshorn Mountains. The Gnome tribes they encountered were terrified of these creatures that could change shape at will and seemed to command dark magic. The Mwellrets initially ignored the Gnomes but eventually used their superstition against them. They asserted their authority over the frightened Gnomes and insinuated themselves into their culture as their chiefs and eventually their masters. The Mountain Gnomes became slaves to the Mwellrets, their culture lost to the needs of their Troll masters. The Gnomes who resisted were brutally reminded of the superiority of the Mwellrets.

The Mwellrets were content to rule their mountain home, far from the swamps that had birthed them. They never officially joined in the Second War of the Races. Nor did they participate in the War of the Warlock Lord; instead they struck a deal with the Dark Lord and agreed to supply him with Gnome slaves for his army, so long as he supported their rule of the Ravenshorn. They were to get all of the Ravenshorn Mountains, while the Warlock Lord would rule the rest of the Four Lands. Throughout two wars, the Mwellrets sent thousands of Mountain Gnomes to die in the front lines of the Northland army, acting as living shields for the Rock Trolls and Skull Bearers, while the Mwellrets remained safe in their kingdom, reigning as lords over all the mountains.

GRAYMARK

To help cement their rule over the region, the Mwellrets built a fortress high above the surrounding lands, near the pinnacle that was the source of the Silver River. Graymark, as it was called, was built atop the rim of a wall of peaks surrounding a deep valley near the edge of the

Graymark, citadel of the Mord Wraiths.

Ravenshorn range. Gnome slaves labored and died for several years to complete the structure. When done, Graymark was a nearly impregnable fortress that over-looked the whole of the lands around it, including the Ravenshorn and the Silver River. Only a few years after Graymark was finished, the Mwellrets controlled all of the Ravenshorn Mountains as far as the

dams of Capaal. The Dwarves stopped going into the mountains, and the Mwellrets never came out.

There are only a few entrances into Graymark, and all pass within clear view of the battlements. The citadel was designed to house large numbers of Mwellrets within the upper chamber, as well as an entire army of Gnomes within

Graymark
Level 8 - 10

To Heaven's Well

High Tower

10th

Open

9th

Open

North Keep Tower
8th level has door to landing

South Keep Tower

9th

Open

Tower Tops as labeled

Any levels between 7 and top are like 7

Stairwells have roofs

Gnome Army Tower

8th

Open

N
W — E
S

Graymark
Level 6-7 same

North Keep Tower

High Tower

8th level has door to landing

South Keep Tower

Graymark Front

Graymark is on a ledge so ground level is constant throughout, but not beyond

Croagh

High

South

North

Army Tower

Behind castle

Keep

	Level 10
	Level 9
	Level 8
	Level 7
	Level 6
	Level 5
	Level 4
	Level 3
	Level 2
	Level 1 Ground
	Cellar 1
	Cellar 2
	Tunnels
	Tunnels
	Tunnels

Croagh circles Maelmord Pit, descending to meet keep again below ground

Road switchbacks, winds down

the barracks and battlements. Beyond Graymark, a pinnacle of rock lifted high above the top of Graymark's battlements. Within a cavern atop the peak was Heaven's Well, the source of the Silver River. The waters bubbled up from the depths of the earth to spill into a broad basin before cascading out of the cavern through a crevice to fall to the riverbed below. When Graymark was built, a long winding spiral of stone called the Croagh was constructed, reaching from the top of Heaven's Well along the edge of Graymark's battlements and down into the depths of the valley below. The original purpose of the winding ribbon of stone has been lost in history. Some Gnomes claim it was a sluice, designed to transport diverted water from the well to various levels of the keep as well as to the valley below. The Gnomes often used the Croagh to gain access to Heaven's Well, which was believed to be a sacred place. The

Graymark Cellar 2

Mwellrets allowed the Gnomes to worship as they wished, so long as they also worshiped their masters.

The Croagh was not the only sophisticated structure within Graymark. The keep also contained an elaborate system of sewers that made use of natural crevices and tunnels to dispose of waste from the keep. The Mwellrets were born in the swamps, but they preferred a dry and clean environment. The sewers allowed wastewater to flow along these tunnels to empty into a deep crevasse within the cliffs. Walkways were carved along the edges of the flow channels to allow slaves to clear debris and maintain the tunnels. Iron grilles closed off the sewers to prevent unauthorized entrances.

Gnomes who had outlived their usefulness were disposed of through the Caves of Night, a series of caves running through the mountain to Graymark's lower levels. Formed during the cataclysm of the Great Wars, the caves would not support torches or flame of any kind. Within the caves, the floors were covered with Procks, mouths hidden in the rock of the floors. Gnomes were driven into the darkness of the caves, and those who stepped on a Prock fell into its open maw and were crushed. The caves could only be navigated safely with the aid of the Fire Wake, a colony of tiny glowing creatures who could be summoned to form a concentrated light within the caves. Mwellrets knew the secrets to controlling

Procks

Procks are believed to be a by-product of Old World technology gone mad. Though they are not actually alive, they appear to be living creatures embedded in the rock floor of the cavern known as the Cave of Night. The jagged, gaping fissures of the Procks' "mouths" open and close randomly. As they close, the stone walls of the Procks' interior grind together. Sensitive to pressure, the fissures open immediately beneath anything that lands upon the "mouth." The victim usually falls into the resulting opening and is crushed when the Prock closes again. The Cave of Night is thick with the stench of the Procks' victims and reverberates with the continuous grinding sound made by the many fissures as they open and close.

The Ildatch

In the age of Faerie, near the time when all life was created, the Demons are said to have compiled a book of spells that contained all the knowledge of their dark magic. The book was called the Ildatch, and the power of its dark lore inspired fear in even the most powerful of the Elven magicians. The Elves seized the book, but even they were not immune to its lure. Even though they knew the danger and the extent of its power, some of the Elven magicians tried to use the book's magic. They did not survive. The rest attempted to destroy the book, but the Ildatch disappeared.

Rumors and legends were all that existed until the First Druid Council was convened. As the Druids gathered in the remnants of old knowledge, an ancient book appeared within the collection. The Druid Brona was the first to discover it. The dark secrets within its pages enabled him to build an empire as the Warlock Lord and to overcome death. Only the Sword of Shannara stopped his rampage.

The Ildatch, ancient living book of dark magic.

The Ildatch survived, buried in the rubble of the Skull Kingdom. Allanon attempted to find it, but the book managed to remain hidden until a sect of Brona's mortal followers discovered it. They may have been called by the power of the book, for it was a living creation of the Demon world.

The humans carried the book into the Eastland, to the valley protected by Graymark. The Mwellrets that ruled there allowed them to place the book within the valley, where they used the book's dark magic to build a living swamp-forest to protect it. They paid homage to the book, learning its magic as it transformed them into its willing disciples. When they emerged from the valley years later, they had been transformed into the Black Walkers, or Mord Wraiths. Their souls and their mortal lives had been traded for the power of the dark magic. The Gnome Tracker Slanter wrote of the Mord Wraiths: "They're like something stolen from the dark—as if each were a bit of night broken off. When they pass, you never see them. You never hear them. You just sense them—you feel their coming."

Brin Ohmsford and the wishsong finally destroyed the Ildatch, which had survived for untold millennia. With its destruction, the Mord Wraiths died and the Maelmord collapsed.

the Fire Wake, but even they did not know its origins or that of the Procks.

After the Warlock Lord was destroyed, several of his mortal followers came to Graymark bearing a talisman from his reign. The Mwellrets allowed them access to the valley behind Graymark, where they and the book disappeared. Almost immediately, the sparse woodlands below began to change, growing into a rotting jungle that consumed the valley. Called the Maelmord, or "living wood" in the language of Faerie, the swamp-forest moved and breathed. It was alive.

For almost a half century after the Maelmord began to form, the Mwellrets ignored the jungles beneath them—until black creatures crawled from its depths to the fortress above. Claiming to be the rightful heirs of the dark power of the Warlock

Lord, these Black Walkers, or Mord Wraiths, demanded the fealty of the Mwellrets and demanded that the keep and all the lands of the Ravenshorn be ceded to them. When the Mwellrets refused, they were driven from Graymark by force, their small magics no match for the dark magic wielded by the Mord Wraiths. They still fought back, but their Race began to sicken and die. No young were born to them. They realized that the Mord Wraiths were punishing their disobedience with the quiet extermination of their Race.

The Mord Wraiths took over Graymark, turning it into a place of death where the only things that lived were the Gnomes who served their new masters. Mutens and new creatures of dark magic guarded its halls and battlements even as the Maelmord guarded its chief treasure, the ancient book of dark magic called the Ildatch.

Ten brave people and a moor cat braved the dangers of Graymark to put an end to the Mord Wraiths and their poison. In two separate groups, each with an Ohmsford, they attempted to destroy the Ildatch and cleanse the Silver River. Though their missions were separate, it took the combined skills of Brin and Jair Ohmsford, and all who aided them, to put an end to the Ildatch and the poison of the Mord Wraith.

During the battle, the Croagh was destroyed, Graymark was damaged, and the valley of the Maelmord collapsed into the ground, leaving a deep chasm where the valley once existed.

The Mwellrets have never recovered from the damage done to their Race by the Mord Wraith's curse, though they are attempting to regain the affluence they enjoyed before the Ildatch came to the Eastland.

The Westland: Land of the Elves

Elves are the Healers of the land and her creatures, the caretakers needed to keep the magic safe and secure. —Walker Boh

The Westland is a land of lush forests, wide grasslands, and ancient mountains. It is a land with Rovers, Drifters, and Old World magic. But above all else, it is the homeland of the Elves.

History of the Elves

Unlike the other known Races, the Elves are not a descendant of Man but rather his predecessor. Each of the other mutated Races, Gnomes, Trolls, and Dwarves, is a survivor of the Race of Man, named for mythical creatures from the legends of

Man. For many centuries Man believed that the Elves were also mutations, and they named the Elves for the legend they resembled. In fact, the Elves are the survivors of that legend. In the early years after the Great Wars, it served their purpose to let the other Races believe them to be as Man said they were—especially since one of the prices they had paid for the survival of their Race was their immortality.

The Elven Race was born in the age of Faerie, at a time when the world itself was young and new to life. Magic was strong and primal, and the creatures of that age lived and breathed the magic as their lifeblood. The Elves of that age shared the world with Dwarves, Gnomes, and Trolls as well as Unicorns, Sprites, and all manner of others now lost to legend.

They also shared the world with Demons, Ogres, and other creatures of darkness and nightmare. The Demons wanted only to feed off the land and take from it without care for the world or its survival. The Races, such as the Elves, that wanted to preserve and nurture the world were in constant conflict with those who sought only their own gratification. After centuries of this, those who wanted to preserve the world joined together, as did those who wanted to destroy it. The entire world was polarized into two opposing forces. War erupted, furious and unrelenting, each side seeking a final resolution to the conflict. The Faerie folk were determined to banish the Demons, who in turn were determined to annihilate the folk of Faerie. As the conflagration raged, the fate of the earth hung in the balance.

In the end, the Elves and other Faerie folk triumphed, banishing the Demons into an otherworldly isolation behind a magic wall of Forbidding. That wall of Forbidding was anchored within this world and maintained by the Ellcrys. The Elves, who had sacrificed much to create the Forbidding, were given the charge of nurturing and protecting the Ellcrys for all of time as it, in turn, protected the world.

Once the Demons were banished, the world, and those within, thrived—including the then-infant Race of Man. The creatures of Faerie paid little more attention to Man than to the other animals and wild creatures that lived within the land. He was simply part of the world and her life.

But Man became a very resourceful and competitive species, soon dominating large sections of the planet. Most of the creatures of Faerie, including the Elves, simply avoided him, retreating deeper into

the wild lands and forests as his numbers increased. The creatures of Faerie did not reproduce quickly, if at all, and soon found themselves outnumbered.

As Man expanded his domain and began to emerge as a force in the world, the Elves decided to remain hidden. Had they chosen otherwise, it is possible that the history of the world, and the fate of the lost creatures of Faerie, would have been far different. But the Elves thought it best to keep to themselves, avoiding this barbaric young Race—though they did not avoid him completely. Man knew of the creatures of Faerie, but they were regarded with fear or distrust because they hid in shadows and played mischievous games at Man's expense. It was a dangerous world, and anything that preferred to hide was considered a threat by the fledgling Race.

Man grew to dominate the world, destroying entire habitats to create room for his growing civilization and causing the extinction of many of the creatures of Faerie who were tied to those habitats. His focus was on the comfort and advancement of his Race, with little or no care to the protection of the world he lived within. The Elves viewed the destruction of the land with growing alarm, but by the time they realized the extent of the danger, they were too few against mankind's growing millions. They had few defenses. Their once-powerful mastery of magic had been allowed to fade, for they had thought the need for powerful magic at an end when the Demons were banished. Without constant use, the knowledge and skill were lost. The Elves were left with only small magics—grounded primarily in nature and healing—to counter Man's invasive behavior. Outnumbered and overpowered, they adapted by fading into the wildlands, until the memory of their existence faded into myth.

One of the Elves' greatest skills has always been the ability to blend into any natural surrounding, becoming invisible to any who are not trained to see. This ability served them well in the years Man dominated the world, for as Man's technological civilization grew, the wild places diminished, forcing the Elves to become more and more reclusive, even as their sacred task of caring for the earth became more and more difficult. They hid within parklands and wilderness preserves, often in plain sight of vast cities—but always undiscovered.

Their isolation kept them from realizing the growing instability within Man's world. Had they looked, they would have seen the increasing unrest as the factions of Man used the great might of their technology to seek domination over each other. As it was, the holocaust of the Great Wars caught the Faerie folk completely unprepared. Most of the Races that had survived Man's rise were wiped out, along with the lands they protected.

By the time the Wars erupted, most of the Elves had retreated to the farthest corners of the world. They lived in small groups. Many of the larger villages were nestled within the few wild areas still untouched by Man—the heart of the deepest forests, the most remote valleys, and the wildest jungles. This reclusion saved the Elven Race, but only barely. Their numbers were decimated. Most of their remaining magic was lost in those terrible years as they expended it trying to keep the tortured world alive. When the final shudders of the violated planet subsided, the Elves still lived, but, like the humans, they too had been changed by their ordeal. By the time the vestiges of the human Race began to emerge, the Elves had changed to resemble them.

Originally, the Elves were a nearly immortal species, living for hundreds, even thousands of years or more. The changes wrought throughout their struggles shortened their lifespan even as it gradually compensated to make them more fertile. They were still connected to the earth magic but had lost most of the knowledge and skill required to wield it. Most of the great Elven scholars and wizards were lost. Most of the tools of magic, including most of the Elfstones, had also been lost. The few talismans that remained were jealously guarded.

Man and the cataclysm of the Great Wars had nearly destroyed the planet. But the Elves realized they had a share of the blame for the destruction because of their isolationist policies. They were determined that it would not happen again. As a Race, they joined together and decided that this time they would not hide in the shadows. When the survivors of the changed Races emerged, the Elves met them as equals and were assumed to be one of them.

It was the Elves, led by Galaphile, who convened the First Druid Council. They realized that, as the oldest of the surviving Races, they had a responsibility to guide the other Races toward an understanding of the balance needed for the world's survival. To do this, they had to minimize the use of science as a developmental tool, lest Man simply re-create the path that had led him to disaster.

The Elves of this period were a fragmented Race, living in separate and extended family groups spread out across the land. Galaphile was the first strong leader within the Elves. After he established the First Council at Paranor, the Elves began to unite as a people. They began to form a nation and eventually, inspired by Galaphile's example at

The Elven Army

After the Great Wars, the Elves were forced to rediscover warfare, a skill they had not used since the Demon Wars. Elves were always natural archers and Trackers as well as skilled horsemen, but other military disciplines had to be learned.

Elven military strategy centers on the Elves' natural strengths. They lack the brute strength or hand-to-hand fighting ability of the Rock Trolls, so the Elves rely instead on their speed and skill and, most of all, their tactical expertise. All of the great captains have learned to make use of the terrain—and to improve it wherever possible with traps and snares. "If the enemy cannot reach you, he cannot kill you" is a common adage among the Elves.

Most Elven commanders prefer to fight a defensive battle, forcing the enemy to attack a fortified location. When this tactic is not possible, quick strikes and feints are usually employed, capitalizing on the Elves' speed and ability to disappear into the surrounding terrain. Elves will never stand toe to toe with an enemy on level ground unless there is no other option. Most Elves wear only light armor with chain-mail vests and leather guards to ensure that their mobility and speed will not be impaired. Communications always play a major role. The Elves' ability to communicate quickly and efficiently with the units in the field has often made the difference between victory and defeat. To those unfamiliar with the Elves who watch them perform on the field of battle, it often appears as if the Elves can read minds, because they respond so quickly to a change in the order of battle.

The army is under the direct command of the king, though he can appoint someone to command for him, as Ander Elessedil appointed Stee Jans during the War of the Forbidding. The Elven army usually consists of pikemen, archers, lancers, foot soldiers, and cavalry as well as Hunters and Trackers. Elven Hunters and Elven Trackers are both elite units within the main army with specialized skills.

Paranor, to choose a leader who would guide them in this new age. They named that leader as their king and selected a council of elders to guide his rule. Arborlon became the capital of the new nation.

During the First War of the Races, the Elves joined with the Dwarves and Trolls under the leadership of the Druids to defeat the Race of Man. When the Four Lands were partitioned, the Westland became the Elven homeland. The war marked the first time the warriors of the Elves had ever been gathered together under one banner. From that time forward, the Elves have always maintained a standing army.

The Elven Army had proven so effective during the First War of the Races that Brona focused his attention on neutralizing them before his own army marched again. He knew that they depended on their king for leadership and guidance, so he sent a special force of Gnomes and Skull Bearers to assassinate King Cortann Ballindarroch and his family in their beds. The resulting upheaval delayed the entry of the Elves into the Second War of the Races, allowing the Warlock Lord time to conquer most of the Eastland and overrun the Borderlands. By the time the Elves had crowned Jerle Shannara as their new king and rallied behind him, the Northland army was at their doorstep.

The Elves would have fallen but for the aid of the few surviving Druids, the courage of their king and queen, and the sword infused with Druid magic. The Northland army was far larger and contained Rock Trolls, but the Elven army had superior tactics, greater speed, and the advantage of terrain. With the sword and Druid magic to aid them, as well as the skill of the Elven generals, the Elven army managed to turn the Northlanders before they reached Arborlon. Timely intervention by the remains of the Dwarf army further enabled them to trap the Warlock Lord and defeat him on the Streleheim Plains.

Victory allowed the Elven nation to prosper and grow, populating the Sarandanon and the surrounding area. The Shannara heirs mysteriously died out and were replaced by the Elessedils. By the time the Four Lands faced the Warlock Lord again, a young king named Eventine Elessedil led the Elves. Unfortunately, the council was so dependent on their king that it very nearly cost them the war.

To keep the Elves and Dwarves from joining against him, as they had done to great effect twice before, the Warlock Lord struck straight into the Borderlands in order to capture the Southland and separate the two great armies. In a battle near Paranor, a Gnome regiment captured Eventine Elessedil. So long as the king was missing, the Elven Council would not ride to the aid of the Borderlands.

Eventine escaped, aided by Flick Ohmsford. His return galvanized the Elves to action. By the time the Elves arrived to assist the besieged city of Tyrsis, the Northlanders had breached the outer walls. If Shea Ohmsford had not succeeded in destroying the Warlock Lord with Jerle Shannara's sword, the Elves' arrival might have availed little. As it was, the Elves arrived in time to drive the Trolls and Gnomes from Tyrsis after the Northlanders were demoralized by the sudden destruction of their Skull Bearer commanders and the storm and earth tremors that followed.

Approximately fifty years later, it was the Elven nation that was forced to call on the Borderlands for aid, as well as all the other Races, when the primordial evil banished by their ancestors threatened the homeland.

Jerle Shannara

The most famous of the Elven kings, Jerle Shannara had never intended to become any more than the commander of the Home Guard. A distant cousin of the reigning king, Courtann Ballindarroch, Jerle was chosen to succeed Courtann when the Ballindarroch family was assassinated on the eve of the Second War of the Races. A skilled warrior, Jerle led his people to victory against the Northland army, defeating the Warlock Lord in single combat with the magic of the sword of truth the Druid Bremen had given him, the sword known forever after as the Sword of Shannara.

Jerle married Preia Starle, a skilled Tracker. Together they adopted the survivors of the Ballindarroch family, a son and a grandson, and had three daughters of their own. They ruled well for many years, as did their heirs, until the dark years when the Warlock Lord's minions assassinated all the Elven descendants of Shannara.

The Shannara name has been eradicated from the Elves, but the Shannara blood lives on within the Ohmsfords and the Elessedils, as Jerle's name lives on in the songs and stories of the land.

Eventine Elessedil, King of the Elves

Eventine Elessedil is considered to be the greatest of the Elven kings. His reign spanned almost sixty years and saw the Elven nation through the War of the Warlock Lord and the War of the Forbidding.

While still a boy, Eventine was Chosen by the Ellcrys. He ascended the throne as a young man at the untimely death of his father. The Elves expected a brash youth but discovered their king to be a shrewd administrator and a brave warrior who believed that a leader must ride in the vanguard to inspire his people. He was known for his uncanny ability to see all sides of even a complex issue and chart a course that would best serve his people.

He died at the age of eighty-two but did not go easily. After sustaining numerous battle injuries during the War of the Forbidding, he was attacked by the Demon known as the Changeling. He defeated the Changeling despite his injuries but was mortally wounded. With his typical determination, he refused to die until he received word that his lands were safe and the Forbidding had been restored.

Eventine Elessedil, greatest of the Elven kings.

It had been three thousand years since the Great Wars, and thousands more since the Demon War in the time of Faerie. In all that time, the Elves had carefully protected and maintained the Ellcrys, but the true purpose of the tree had faded into legend. When the Ellcrys began to fail, Demons began to appear. The Elves were suddenly faced with the fact that they knew almost nothing about the Ellcrys or the Forbidding she imposed. To make matters worse, they no longer had use of the magic that had enabled their ancestors to defeat the Demons all those eons ago, and only imprecise instructions from the Elven Histories to tell them how to restore the Ellcrys. Their only hope for survival lay in young Amberle Elessedil, her protector, Wil Ohmsford, and their quest to find the Bloodfire and restore the Ellcrys. For the Demons could not be defeated by strength of arms, merely delayed. Only the restoration of the Ellcrys would banish the Demons.

Eventine and his army found themselves defending the Westland from the Demon Horde with little more than courage and iron. The only magic they had was from the Druid Allanon and a staff made from the living wood of the Ellcrys. The might of the Elven army was insignificant compared to the multitudes from the void of the Forbidding. If not for the brilliant tactical leadership of Stee Jans and the Bordermen of the Free Corps, the Elves would have lost Arborlon to the Demons. Dwarf Sappers, Wing Riders, and even a regiment of Rock Trolls aided them in their desperate struggle. It was the first time since the First War of the Races that Trolls, Elves, and Dwarves all fought on the same side.

Wil and Amberle did succeed in locating the Bloodfire, deep within the caves of Spires Reach, in the wilderness of the Wilderun. They left with the Captain of the Home Guard and an escort of trained Elven Hunters. They returned with only a Rover girl and a young Wing Rider, just in time for Amberle to sacrifice herself to restore the Forbidding before the Gardens of Life were overrun.

Eventine Elessedil and his eldest son, Arion, were killed during the course of the battle. Arion fell at Halys Cut, early in the fighting. Eventine died of his wounds shortly after the last battle. Ander Elessedil became the new king of the Elves.

Ander lost his own son, Edain, twenty years later, when the Prince died repaying his people's debt to both the Dwarves and the Ohmsfords. He fell at Graymark while defending Jair Ohmsford from the Mord Wraiths. But his death did not affect the Elven people as greatly as the death of the Druid Allanon weeks earlier.

With Allanon's passing, the last of the Druids was gone from the land. The Druids had

The Ellcrys Staff, a gift of living wood.

been founded by the Elves. Their magic had protected the Elves even as it safeguarded the lands. Many of the Elves felt that magic was essential for the security of their people. It had been magic that had turned the tide in the First and Second Wars of the Races. Without Allanon's magic, the War of the Forbidding would have been lost before Amberle's return. They began to explore ways to recover the ancient Elven magic wielded by their ancestors.

The Elves were no longer the people of Faerie their ancestors had been. The magic was no longer an integral part of their being, but something vast and wild that would not be easily tamed. In trying to restore the old magic, some of them changed. They succeeded in becoming creatures of magic, but they were twisted by it and began to hunger for magic for its own sake. They became creatures known as the Shadowen and began to feed off the magic of the land, forsaking the Elven oath to nurture and protect it in favor of their hunger.

When the rest of the Elves realized what was happening, they tried to help, but the Shadowen rejected all aid and refused to give up the magic. The Shadowen were banished from the Westland. The banished Elves moved to the Southland, where they used their abilities to gain power, creating the Seekers and gaining control of the Coalition Council. They used the Southlanders' distrust of magic and outsiders against them, manipulating them until they had control of the Federation itself. The

Ander Elessedil, Elven King.

Seekers hunted down those with the use of magic so that the Shadowen could turn them into other Shadowen, or feed off their magic and discard them into the Pit at Tyrsis. The lands of the South began to sicken and die. The Federation blamed the Elves and made plans to move against them.

Appalled at what their countrymen had become, and terrified of the ultimate outcome of their rampage and the Federation's mobilization, the Elves decided to leave the Four Lands. Almost exactly two hundred years after the Elves had restored the Forbidding, they gathered their people into Arborlon and disappeared from the Westland.

They used an Elfstone called the Loden, which had been kept hidden away since before the Great Wars, to move their entire city to a new location. Assisted by the Sky Elves and their Rocs, they chose a location away from the Four Lands, where they would be safe. It was an idyllic island far

out in the Blue Divide called Morrowindl.

For many years, Morrowindl was a paradise. But the Elves could not forget the danger they had left behind. Some of the Elves used the old magic to create living creatures that were improvements on existing creatures, but born to serve and be self-sufficient. These experiments were so successful that they decided to create creatures that were more sophisticated. Using spirit and blood and bits of themselves, they built an army of men. These men were Elves but less than Elves. They formed an army designed to defend the Elves while living outside the walls of Arborlon. They were hunters, soldiers, and guardians of the realm, totally dedicated and self-sufficient, with no desire but to serve.

The Elves sent them out to their posts and forgot about them. But they had overreached their abilities. The creatures slowly

Shadowen

The Shadowen were so named because of their uncanny ability to separate their essence from their body and absorb another being. The first Shadowen were Elves who dared to believe they could harness the immense power of earth magic. The sought to use the magic in ways that were never intended, coming to rely on it so heavily that it subverted them. They became addicted to it, becoming parasites that fed on living things to consume the earth magic within. The magic changed them until they needed to feed to survive. They used up the humans around them as well as the earth that sustained them. While the magic was strong, the lure to steal it and feed off it was stronger still. They began to siphon the magic of the earth itself, trapping it for their use while the land sickened.

They were destroyed when the trapped earth magic was set free.

began to change. They left their posts and began to roam the forests, hunting and killing. They became Demons and began to feed off anything that lived. By the time the Elves realized what was happening, it was too late. The damage could not be undone.

The King ordered a wall of stone built around the Arborlon. Once it was in place, he powered it with the magic of the Loden, creating a protective barrier of magic to keep the Demons out. It was called the Keel. The Demons grew stronger and began to feed off the life force of the island, draining its magic until the entire island grew sick and the once dormant volcano began to rumble ominously.

Queen Ellenroh Elessedil inherited the besieged kingdom when her brother Asheron was killed by the Demons. As the magic of the island drained away, the Demons were drawn to the magic that protected the city, and she was faced with a nation trapped within walls of failing magic as the island turned to a world of horrors around them. They would have perished there but for the arrival of Wren Ohmsford and her mentor, Garth of the Rovers. Wren had come to Morrowindl in answer to a charge from Allanon's shade, not knowing that she was Ellenroh's granddaughter or that her true name was Wren Elessedil.

The Elves decided to return to the Westland and face the Federation. The Queen asked Wren to assist her in transporting Arborlon and her people safely away from the island. Nine people (the Elven number for luck) made up the Queen's party. Arborlon was returned to the Loden's protection and carried across the island. By the time the Wing Riders rescued them from the beach, only Wren and the Captain of the Home Guard still lived.

Wren continued her grandmother's quest and returned Arborlon to the Westland. She ascended to the throne and

The Loden

The Loden was an Elfstone that had been hidden and preserved by the Elves for use in time of need. Unlike most Elfstones, it was designed to be used for a specific purpose; it could be used only for that purpose and for defense, and only a limited number of times. The Loden enabled the Elves to transport the entire city of Arborlon and its people to Morrowindl and back. Its defensive properties were used to power the magic of the Keel that kept the city safe on the island.

Elven lore states that the city was actually removed to the inside of the stone, but many scholars believe that the stone simply created a doorway to the same dimension that had once held Paranor, then replaced the city on the chosen site once that door was reopened.

The Loden was affixed to a polished black walnut staff known as the Ruhk Staff, itself imbued with Elven magic. The staff channeled the earth magic within the stone.

Queen Wren Elessedil destroyed both the Loden and the Ruhk Staff after she returned the Elves to the Westland.

The Loden and the Ruhk Staff, magic enough to save a nation.

Wren Elessedil, greatest of the Elven rulers, and her mentor, the Rover Garth.

Wren Elessedil

The greatest of the Elven rulers, Wren Elessedil grew to womanhood believing she was the daughter of an Ohmsford and a Rover. Raised by the Ohmsfords until she was five, she was trained by the Rovers in the arts of survival. Her mentor and constant companion was a deaf Rover named Garth.

She discovered her true lineage only while fulfilling a charge given her by Allanon's shade. She was the granddaughter of Queen Ellenroh Elessedil, the child of an Elven princess and a Wing Rider, destined to fulfill a prophecy.

Wren returned the Elves to the Westland and became both the Warrior Queen and the engineer of a new age of Elven outreach and peace. Under her guidance, the Elves reaffirmed their vows to be caretakers of the land and expanded them to include the whole of the land, rather than limiting it to Elven territories.

led the Elves against the Federation and the Shadowen, who immediately moved to destroy them. Her army held the Federation long enough for her cousins to release the magic the Shadowen had imprisoned. The resulting backlash destroyed the Shadowen, allowing the Elven army to defeat the remains of Federation forces and drive them from the Westland.

Once the Federation threat was ended, Queen Wren restored the ancient Elven healing tradition and sent Elves from among the Chosen out into the Four Lands as Healers to be caretakers of all the earth. She also established a long-term alliance, a contract, with the Elves of the Wing Hove to serve as scouts and messengers for the Land Elves.

But the Elves were still a cautious people. Years later, when Walker Boh approached Wren's great-granddaughter Aine to rebuild the Druid Council at Paranor, she refused to support an autonomous council. She feared the power of the Druid Council and the magic they might wield, as her ancestors had feared the Federation and the Shadowen. A few years later Aine sent her son and heir Kael on a voyage to recover a great treasure of magic that had been reported to survive the Great Wars. Kael and the Elfstones he carried were lost. Queen Aine died with a broken heart. Kael was found thirty years later, ruined and drifting in the waters of the Blue Divide. He died a few days later.

Aine's surviving son, Allardon, finally agreed to support Walker's new Druid Council, but only if the Druid would undertake a quest to discover the truth of what Kael had found. Allardon was killed the day he made the agreement. The expedition he commissioned set sail aboard the airship *Jerle Shannara*, carrying with it the hopes of the Elven people and the future of the Druids.

Arborlon

The homeland of the Elves spans the area from the Valley of Rhenn in the east to the Hoare Flats and the Great Divide in the west. To the south, the Westland extends to the Myriam Lake at the edge of the Irrybis Mountains, and north to the Breakline. The capital city of Arborlon sits nestled within a wood atop the heights of the Carolan, a towering wall of rock that rises abruptly from the east bank of the Rill Song River and protects the western approach to the city. Access to the top of the Carolan is provided by the Elfitch, a hooked, spiral stone-block rampway that drops along the forested cliffs through seven walled gates, one for each level of the rampway. For pro-

Amberle Elessedil and the Ellcrys.

The Ellcrys

During the Demon Wars in the Age of Faerie, the Elves were faced with a terrible dilemma: they needed to defeat the Demons to save the earth, but their existence was based on the preservation of life. They could not destroy the Demons outright and be true to their own sacred purpose—despite the fact that the Demons intended to annihilate all of them. They decided to banish the Demons. The magic required to create such a powerful banishment had to be something that would last for thousands of years, and that could be renewed at need. The Elven Wizards managed to create a magic that would bind the Demons forever outside the world, but to work it had to be powered by the greatest sacrifice of all, the willing gift of a life. They bonded an Elven life with the Bloodfire to create the Ellcrys, a living tree whose inherent magic would forbid the Demons access to the world. The Ellcrys had to be a woman, so that she could produce a seed to insure the continuation of the magic. The silver bark and bloodred leaves of the resulting tree became the symbol of Elven dedication to the land. Her formation was the culmination of the Elven belief that one must give back to the land for the life that has been taken.

Unlike a normal tree, the Ellcrys has the power to remove living parts of herself. During the War of the Forbidding, the Ellcrys stripped a living limb from herself to serve as a staff—a magic talisman—to help protect her people as they battled the Demons. While the Ellcrys lived, the staff was warm as if lifeblood flowed within it. It was her right hand, with her magic, carried forth to support her defenders.

The Ellcrys has always been tended by the Order of the Chosen in a tradition as old as the Ellcrys herself. Candidates for the Chosen are selected from the young Elves who have crossed into maturity the year before. At dawn of the New Year, the candidates are brought to the tree. One by one, they pass beneath her limbs, pausing momentarily. The tree chooses her caretakers by touching them upon the shoulders with her branches and whispering their names within their minds. Most years, only young men are chosen, but if the Ellcrys fears a decline in her health, or believes that death approaches, she will select a girl to follow her as the next Ellcrys. If death is certain, the Ellcrys will call the girl to her and give her the Seed, to be taken and immersed within the Bloodfire. During the year of the Second War of the Races, the Ellcrys selected a woman as a member of the Chosen, possibly because she could feel the earth's magic being subverted in the North and feared her demise. The Ellcrys did not fail, however, and the girl simply served her year and returned to her life.

The Chosen spend their year of service living within the Compound of the Chosen near the Gardens of Life. They spend most of each day in service to the tree. Designated by traditional white robes, they are her companions and caretakers. They speak to her and nurture her, though she rarely speaks to them after their Choosing. Once they have served, they are exempt from the traditional Elven duty of service to the land, and are honored as former Chosen.

The name of the first Ellcrys has been lost in the shrouds of time, as was the exact manner of the rebirth, but the current Ellcrys' former incarnation is well known. She was Amberle Elessedil, granddaughter of the famed king Eventine, who was himself a member of the Chosen. Amberle, driven by fear, was the only Chosen one to leave the Order. Her leaving brought disgrace on herself and her family, but it saved her life. All the remaining Chosen were slaughtered by an escaped Demon. Amberle's return and her harrowing journey to find her destiny are now legendary. She gave up her life and the love of young Wil Ohmsford to save her people. Today her name is honored even as the Ellcrys she has become is honored.

tection, battlements ring each gate to close off passage to the gates and ramps above. The turns of the Elfitch are set back and measured to allow each gate and ramp to be defended from the one above. In peacetime, the gates stand open and the ancient stone is thick with flowering vines. The Elfitch was destroyed during the War of the Forbidding and was not rebuilt until late in Queen Wren's reign.

Though the Elfitch is the primary access route, there is a series of smaller stairways winding upward through wooded sections of the cliff further south. In time of war, these stairways are destroyed.

The plateau of the Carolan runs back to the deep forest in a broad, rolling plain spotted with woods, isolated cottages, and the solitary closure of the Gardens of Life. Arborlon lies within the fringe of trees to the east, and beyond Arborlon is the Valley of Rhenn. The Rhenn provided the Elves with a natural defensive position to the east. Thick forests and mountainous terrain prevent access from anywhere outside the valley, which begins as a gentle stretch of grassland spread between clusters of low foothills and quickly narrows and rises until it is a slender vise flanked by steep bluffs. The valley has always been guarded. In the entire history of the Westland, no enemy has ever successfully reached Arborlon from the Rhenn.

The city is centered on the compound of the Gardens of Life, the home of the Ellcrys. Tending the Ellcrys is the most sacred post within the Elven culture, and is done by the Order of the Chosen, young people who are selected by the tree herself to serve as her caretakers for a year. The Ellcrys sits in silver and crimson splendor in the center of the gardens, symbolic of the central role the tree plays in the hearts of the Elven People. Beyond her role as the

source of the Forbidding, the Ellcrys and the Gardens of Life are the symbols of the land and her sacred magic—the magic of life. The Elves' entire existence is focused on reverence for that life. Their duty has always included the nurturing and sustenance of every living thing that grows within or walks upon the earth.

The Gardens are walled with ivy-covered stone and guarded by the Black Watch, a traditional unit of Elven Hunters uniformed in black and crimson and armed with pikes. The sole purpose of the Black Watch is to protect the gardens and their sacred tree. Within, special gardeners assist the Chosen in caring for the Ellcrys and the lush plants and flowers that adorn her resting place. Both the Ellcrys and the Gardens of Life have existed since the War of the Demons in the age of Faerie, though their locations have been changed from time to time through the ages to keep them safe.

The Gardens of Life are flanked on one side by the home of the Chosen, a walled compound surrounded by evergreens and adorned by flower gardens and vegetable patches. On the other side stands the Palace of the Elven Rulers, a three-story manor house of wood and stone connected to outbuildings and surrounded by a stone wall. The area is under the watchful eyes of the Home Guard, the elite corps assigned to the protection of the ruler and the royal family. The Home Guard are usually impossible to spot unless they wish to be seen, blending into their surroundings as only Elves can.

Beyond the palace are the administration buildings of the High Council. Within the largest of these is the Council Chamber, the heart of the Elven government. Built of oak and stone, the cavernous chamber is hexagonal in shape, with a high ceiling arched with wooden crossbeams that form a star at their joining. The front of the chamber is dominated by the royal throne, a great hand-carved oaken chair set atop a riser of steps and flanked by the banners of the houses of the Elven kings. The Shannara arms are among them. The Elessedil crest, the spreading boughs of the sacred Ellcrys surrounded by a ring of Bloodfire, hangs above the throne.

Large wooden entry doors lead into the chamber. Gallery seats, a dozen rows deep and fronted by a low iron railing, border the surrounding walls. In the center of the chamber is a large oval table of carved wood with twenty-one chairs for the members of the High Council. The King rules the Elves, but the council must approve all major decisions. The Elves were the first people within the Four Lands to crown a king, and they are the last to still use a monarchy as their preferred form of government. It has worked well for the Elves; they have rarely had a poor or weak leader, and the strongest of them has been tempered by the advice of the council. It is here that the Elven rulers receive the traditional pledge of loyalty, the right hand

Cyan Elessedil, first Elven Queen.

over the heart.

Outside the government compound, the rest of Arborlon consists of homes and shops built to blend in with the natural lay of the forest and plain. Treeways thread

Elven Women

In the early years of the Elven nation, women did not participate in war or government. Their skills were usually focused on the primary duty of all Elves—that of nurturing and healing the land and people. Some few women were Trackers, scouts, and trainers of the war horses, but women did not fight in battle until Queen Preia Starle, the finest Elven Tracker of her day, joined her king in the front lines during the battle for the Rhenn. She fought at his side right up to his confrontation with the Warlock Lord, despite being severely wounded. During Jerle's reign, Preia encouraged Elven women to become active in every aspect of Elven life and government, and sponsored several to the Home Guard. Since that time, women have had an increasingly strong role in defending, and eventually ruling, the Elves.

The first queen of the Elven nation was Cyan Elessedil, who ascended to the throne approximately 130 years after the War of the Forbidding. Since her time, many of the greatest rulers of the Elves have been women, including Ellenroh, Aine, and the great Wren Elessedil. Though the majority of the Elven army is still male, the women who do choose to serve within its ranks are highly skilled and valued.

through the upper boughs of the largest trees, and cottages nestle into their trunks. Gardens and bright colors abound, with stone walkways and bright flowers guiding the path to even the lowest dwelling. South of the city, the woods open onto the bluff that holds the airfield for the Elven airships. There are usually at least a half dozen airships moored at the field at any given time.

Arborlon's main road passes across the Carolan in front of the Gardens of Life and the palace. It leads to the Valley of the Rhenn in the east and the Elfitch to the west. Many visitors who have seen only the cities of the Southland marvel at the fact that such a large city can coexist so harmoniously and unobtrusively with the land around it. But it is that reverence for the land that sets the Elves apart from the other Races.

Below the Carolan, a solitary bridge spans the Rill Song. The main road passes through miles of forest before opening into the wide sweep of the Sarandanon Valley, the breadbasket for the Elves.

The Sarandanon is a fertile stretch of level farmland dotted with small clumps of trees and pockets of spring water. Sandwiched between woodlands on the south and east, the Kensrowe Mountains on the north, and the broad expanse of the Innisbore Lake on the west, the valley is filled with farms growing corn, wheat, barley, and other seed crops. It has served for generation as the principal source of food for the Elven people.

At the far end of the Sarandanon, the Rill Song River ends in the Innisbore Lake. Beyond the lake, the jagged ridges of the Breakline Mountains stand tall against the horizon, curving north above the Kensrowe into the wilderness of the Kershalt Territory. Between the Innisbore and the Kensrowe, Baen Draw leads to the rugged hill country below the Breakline.

Only two passes split the Breakline to tie the land of the Elves to the Hoare Flats beyond. South lies Halys Cut. North lies Worl Run. During the War of the Forbidding, the Demons came into the world at Hoare Flats. The Elven Army fought bravely to hold the passes. The defile at Halys Cut is still partially blocked by the avalanche triggered by Allanon's magic during that battle.

The Fortress of the Chew Magna

North of the Kensrowe is the range of mountains believed to be the oldest in the land. One of the few ranges to remain untouched by the cataclysms of the Great Wars, the Breakline Mountains are still largely unexplored. Within these ancient peaks lies the ruined crater that once held the Fortress of the Chew Magna. It was hidden from human eyes for untold millennia.

Built in the age of Faerie, the Fortress and the mountains that surround it survived the age of Man and the Great Wars, though most of the people who built it passed to dust long before. The Fortress was constructed within a protective ring of peaks at the edge of an ancient crater, a focal point for the powerful lines of earth magic found within the mountain region. It is the only known fortress to have survived from the age of Faerie, its survival made possible for so long only because of the dark treasure hidden within its midst. For though the Fortress appeared to be abandoned, its discoverers found that the last of its inhabitants still lived within its innermost courtyard. They had been transformed from living Elves and Faerie creatures into an immortal barrier of trees and

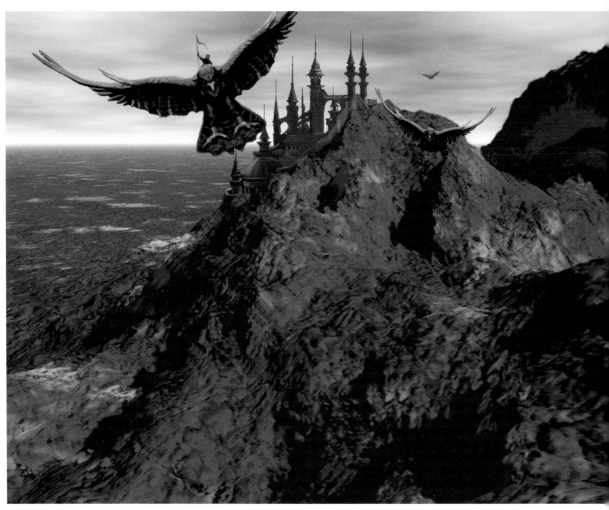

The lost Fortress of the Chew Magna.

plants, protecting the talisman responsible for their transformation, the Black Elfstone. All of their humanity had been stripped away, leaving only their hunger and need and the darkest essence of their being. They survived to feed on the power of the Elfstone, and it in turn kept the castle and the garden alive throughout the ages in a twisted symbiosis.

The Elfstone was discovered and removed in the time of the Second War of the Races. With its removal, the magic, which was all that had maintained the ancient structure, dissipated. The fortress that had survived since before the dawn of Man collapsed into dust and rubble in only moments.

The Matted Brakes

To the south the Rill Song crosses the Drey Wood, a dense forest running eastward from the river to high, craggy bluffs. Immediately below Drey Wood, the Rill Song swings westward at the edge of the Matted Brakes, a lowland marsh choked with vegetation. The Brakes split apart the vast Westland forests from the banks of the river, their stagnant lakes and thickets inhabited by creatures that are both

The Black Elfstone

One of only three Elfstones known to have survived the ages, the Black Elfstone is a gem as black as ink, with magic more powerful than any other known Elven talisman. Created by the Elves during the time of Faerie, when their magic was at its height, it, like all Elfstones, was designed to join the necessary properties of heart, mind, and body. But the Black Elfstone was the only one to combine these properties within a single stone.

The Elfstone's magic is to subvert other magic, no matter its form or strength. Its power is the power of absorption; just as black is the combination of all colors and absorbs all light, so does the Black Elfstone combine all the properties of the user to absorb all magics. This power of the void has no known limits, but the magic it absorbs is transferred into the one who wields the stone. If that person is not capable of containing the absorbed magic, he or she becomes corrupted by it or destroyed. No one can use the Black Elfstone and remain unchanged by that use. There is evidence that even the ancient Faerie creatures that protected it were not immune. Many were corrupted by the magic they absorbed.

No one knows for certain what purpose the stone was originally intended to serve. It was discovered within the ancient ruins of the Fortress of the Chew Magna, hidden within a gathering of sentient trees and vines. The dark garden was all that was left of the Elven and Faerie creatures who had been corrupted and transformed by the use of the stone's power. The Elven Druid Tay Trefenwyd retrieved the stone and was the first since the age of Faerie to use its power. He defended his party against a small army of Skull Bearers and Gnomes, using the Elfstone to destroy them. They were instantly annihilated, but the absorption of their dark magic destroyed Tay as well. He succeeded in keeping its power from the Warlock Lord, but at the cost of his life.

The Druids found a safer purpose for the Elfstone, using it to absorb the magic that hid Paranor away when it left the realm of the living. To protect the stone, the Druids hid it inside the Hall of Kings, within a covered niche in the floor of the Assembly. It remained there for many years, until the Faerie creature Uhl Belk located its hiding place and took it for his own. He replaced the Elfstone with an Asphinx so that anyone who discovered the loss would not survive to report it. Walker Boh was the one unlucky enough to discover the Asphinx. With the aid of another creature of Faerie, he not only survived, but also managed to regain the Black Elfstone from the Stone King and use it to restore Paranor. The Elfstone's power enabled him to absorb the magic and legacy of the Druids as well, becoming the newest of their order, as Allanon had intended—though there is no doubt that even Walker would have been destroyed had he had not been strong enough and determined enough to withstand the torrent of magic that transformed him.

The Black Elfstone is currently locked within a secret vault in Paranor, protected by Druid magic.

vicious and cunning, capable of destroying even something as powerful as a Shadowen creeper. Only experienced Elven Trackers cross the Brakes.

South of the Matted Brakes, the twin towers of the Pykon straddle the broad channel of the Mermidon River as it passes toward Callahorn. The Pykon forms a natural gateway into the Rock Spur Mountains, which is guarded by the empty halls of an abandoned Elven fortress. Built in the early years of the new

175

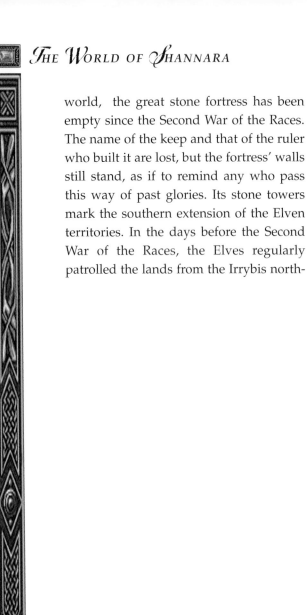

world, the great stone fortress has been empty since the Second War of the Races. The name of the keep and that of the ruler who built it are lost, but the fortress' walls still stand, as if to remind any who pass this way of past glories. Its stone towers mark the southern extension of the Elven territories. In the days before the Second War of the Races, the Elves regularly patrolled the lands from the Irrybis north-ward. But in the aftermath of the Second War of the Races, outposts on the far edges of the realm were abandoned. The Elves pulled back into the northern forests and valleys nearer to Arborlon.

Within the keep, passages wind through the stone of the mountain down to a hidden cove on the river. The expanse of the Rock Spur beyond the Pykon marks the end of the Elves' influence.

The Westland: Guardians of the Air

Both Rovers and Wing Riders share a fierce independence that holds them apart from the rest of the world. It is fitting that both should end up as masters of the sky. —Walker Boh

Sky Elves

The Elessedils control the land north of the Pykon, but they are not the only people within the Westland. They are not even the only Elves. In the early years of the Ballindarroch dynasty, a small group of Elven families left Arborlon to begin a settlement south of the kingdom's borders, though no one remembers the exact incident that led to the migration. The families were among the contingent of Elves who had opposed the consolidation of Elven communities into a kingdom. By the time Jerle Shannara was born, most of the Elves within the kingdom had forgotten that those families had ever existed.

The Elven expatriates established their settlement below the Irrybis Mountains, still within the Westland but beyond the influence of the Elven rulers. They built their village on a series of shoreline cliffs on the edge of a rugged, uncharted stretch of mountainous forest bordering the Great Divide and called it Sea Hove. Surviving as hunters and fishermen, the Elves established a community run by a Council of Elders that were voted on by their peers and ratified by the population at large. Theirs was the first representational government within the Four Lands.

The settlers soon discovered that they

Wing Rider battles War Shrikes.

had neighbors. A hunter stumbled on a rookery of giant birds in the cliffs a few miles from the settlement. The birds nested in caves that overlooked the waters of the Blue Divide. They named the birds after the Rocs of ancient legend.

At first the Elves were careful to avoid the rookery, but the size of the birds led some among them to dream of flight. They set out to communicate with the great birds and finally to train them to carry riders. The first attempts to harness and train the birds met with failure. The powerful animals were quite willing to accept the Elves within their rookery and to allow themselves to be touched, but they reacted violently to being controlled or ridden. A number of men lost their lives in falls from angry mounts as the great birds pitched and rolled several hundred feet off the ground. Refusing to give up, the Elves decided to begin working with the fledglings.

Unlike the mature Rocs, the babies did not object to having harness straps on their bodies. The Elves discovered that the adults were perfectly willing to allow access to the babies, so long as the Elves brought food to the nest. Further, each fledgling developed a bond with the Elf who worked with it. By the time the fledglings were able to fly, they had already developed a rapport with "their" Elf and were willing to trust him. It then became a simple matter to train the birds to the commands of their rider. The Rocs allowed the Elves to greatly expand their hunting and fishing territory. In exchange, the elves defended the rookery from the many predators that considered Roc eggs and chicks a delicacy. They also cared for any Rocs affected by illness or injury.

In honor of their new alliance, the men who had bonded with the Rocs were given the title of Wing Riders, and the Elves renamed their village and its adjoining rookery Wing Hove. After a few generations, the older wild Rocs died out, leaving only the generations that were bonded with the Elves. The birds became members of their Wing Riders' families, with a Roc often being passed from father to son. The Wing Riders became the chief providers

Rocs

Rocs are the largest bird in the known world. With a wingspan often in excess of thirty feet and the ability to carry several grown men, the birds have become the heart and soul of the community now called Wing Hove. Rocs come in a variety of colors, from a light golden color to blue-black, usually sporting bright red plumage around the crest, head, and neck. Though far from the fastest of the large birds, they are the most powerful. They can fly for up to three days without stopping for food or rest.

The Rocs nest in caves, usually high up in coastal cliffs. They prefer to roost on high plateaus, though they will also roost in large trees or on a stone outcropping if nothing else is available. Rocs mate for life and often mourn bitterly at the death of their mate, though they can occasionally be convinced to take another. Their chicks mature quickly at first, but it takes two years before they are strong enough to carry a rider safely. Their average life span has increased since the Elves began to care for and protect them. A healthy adult often lives for over a hundred years, serving several Wing Riders during the course of its life.

The birds' favorite food is fish, though they are omnivorous and feed on vegetation, especially wild grains, and small mammals as well. Their main predator is the Shrike.

The Training of a Wing Rider

A Wing Rider candidate begins training at a young age. Once nominated, he must train until adulthood, and must bond with a Roc. The oldest birds are used to train the youngest riders. At first, the candidates simply ride with a Wing Rider until they get used to flying. A root used to alleviate motion sickness is given to the boys until they no longer need its assistance. Once they are comfortable with flying, they are given more and more control until they are finally ready to fly alone. At the same time they are taught how to care for the birds, for without the Roc, there can be no Wing Rider. The care, feeding, grooming, and comfort of the Roc are paramount. The boys must care for the Rocs assigned to them before they are allowed to see to their own needs. The bird must be fed before they eat, and must be groomed and bedded before they sleep. Even the harness must be cleaned regularly to keep it strong and soft.

The ability to fly a Roc is not enough to grant Wing Rider status, but only apprenticeship under the guidance of a Mentor who himself follows the requirements of the Master of Flight. The Master oversees the training of all young riders until they are granted Wing Rider status, at which point they are under the command of the Senior Wing Rider.

Once an apprentice is ready to fly alone, he begins a series of training missions designed to teach him how to survive in the wild and how to perform the tasks a Wing Rider might be asked to perform. These missions grow in complexity and duration through the years until the boy reaches manhood. Because Wing Riders must be independent thinkers and often work alone, survival skills are emphasized. The only hard rules are that no apprentices may land within the Wilderun or travel to known War Shrike roosts. The boys must also learn fighting skills, both on land and from the air, as well as tracking, hunting, and fishing.

When a boy reaches manhood, he must bond with a Roc. Sometimes Rocs are passed from father to son, or grandfather to grandson. In such cases the boy is often already well acquainted with the bird and they bond easily. Birds who are mourning for lost riders often find it more difficult to establish their next bond. It may take time for those Rocs to accept their new riders and bond as tightly as they did with the old.

Young birds of training age are bonded with the oldest unpaired apprentices. These apprentices have the hardest path, for they must assist in the training of their young charges before they can become Wing Riders. The Master of Flight will guide them, but it is their hands and legs and their voice that must teach the commands and reassure the young birds when they are frightened. These apprentices take their birds out paired with their Mentors on his more experienced bird until the young Roc is comfortable with the requirements of a Wing Rider. The apprentice bonded to a young bird must often wait longer before gaining full Wing Rider status, for such status will not be given until their bird is ready to join the flight and perform its duties, but they have the additional prestige of having formed and guided that Roc for those who will follow after. Many of those who bond to maiden birds become Mentors or even Masters of Flight themselves.

Once the apprentice has fulfilled the requirements of the Master of Flight and has bonded with and performed well on a fully trained Roc, he is granted full Wing Rider status. In the ceremony the Master of Flight presents the young Wing Rider with his own shiny calling whistle to replace the worn training whistle he has used previously. The boy can then not only call himself a man, but a Wing Rider—one of the elite who live in the freedom of the skies.

Shrikes and War Shrikes

Natives of coastal cliffs along the Blue Divide and the Tiderace, Shrikes are a fierce predatory hunting bird. Shrikes measure up to three feet in height and have occasionally been used for hunting, though they are difficult to train and impossible to truly tame. Ferocious fighters, they were rumored to have been used to hunt men in the barbaric days of the old kingdoms. They are a Roc's chief enemy. Though far smaller than a Roc, Shrikes have been known to gang up on the larger bird and bring it down by sheer force of numbers. The only bird more dangerous than a Shrike is their larger cousin, the War Shrike.

Unrivaled as a fighting bird, War Shrikes also live in colonies along the cliffs lining coastal plains, and have their nesting grounds on an island well out in the Blue Divide. Rarer than their cousin, they are only slightly smaller than a Roc but much faster over a short distance, leaner, and much meaner. All Shrikes are fiercely territorial, but War Shrikes will use their cruelly hooked beaks and razor-edged talons to fight to the death, with little thought for their own survival. When possible, a number of War Shrikes will also gang up on a Roc, whose only defense is to gain altitude and attempt to outdistance them. War Shrikes are fast short-range fliers but often will not follow a Roc beyond a certain distance.

They cannot be trained or tamed, though there are rumors that the Ilse Witch has managed to capture and tame one with her magic and uses it to haunt the skies of the Four Lands—though even she must leave it hooded and hobbled when she is gone.

for the community, for they were able to hunt game from the air and fly over the Blue Divide and spot schools of fish for the fishermen. The birds were capable of carrying several people, or one person and a large game animal.

After an attack by creatures that had wandered too far from the Wilderun, the Elves realized that the Rocs could also be trained to fight. Elves and Rocs began to experiment with different fighting styles on the ground and in the air. Together they managed to drive most of the predatory Shrikes from the area around Wing Hove and defeat the enemies of the Elves as well. The Wing Riders and their Rocs became the protectors of Wing Hove the way the Elven Hunters had always protected Arborlon. The Wing Riders became the most honored and trusted members of Wing Hove, the symbol of their way of life. Soon most of the Council of Elders consisted of Wing Riders.

The Sky Elves, as they now called themselves, did not reestablish contact with the Elves in Arborlon, whom they called the Land Elves, until the War of the Forbidding, at which point the Druid Allanon convinced them that the need was greater than their ancestral distrust of the monarchy. Only six members of the Hove flew to Arborlon at the Druid's request, but those six helped turn the tide of battle, while their youngest apprentice managed to save the day by bringing Amberle Elessedil and the Ellcrys Seed back to Arborlon in time to end the war.

The Wing Hove maintained sporadic contact with the Land Elves after the battle. When the Land Elves decided to seek a new homeland, the Wing Riders helped them to find an island suitable for relocation. They transported the Elven King and the Ruhk Staff to Morrowindl, never knowing that the Loden on the Staff held the entire city of Arborlon and her people.

Once the Land Elves were gone, the Sky Elves realized that they were now the main targets for the Federation's anti-Elven sentiment. The Federation would not care that they were a separate people; to the Federation, Elves were Elves, and the Irrybis Mountains were scant protection against the growing might of the Federation army. They moved Wing Hove to a series of islands offshore, where they could still access their hunting grounds but would be safe from discovery or attack. They told their few friends remaining on the mainland to light a signal fire if they were needed. After a century, they faded into legend.

The Wing Hove thrived in its new home. Unlike the Land Elves, the Sky Elves felt no need to rediscover the old magic. They had magic enough in their bond with the Rocs and with their island home. Because they were a small community, with only about five thousand people, they needed only a small island to be comfortable.

They maintained contact with the Land Elves on Morrowindl for many years. One of their own even married into the royal family. But in time, the changes wreaked by the magic on Morrowindl made it more and more difficult to reach the Elves living there. When several experienced Riders who tried were lost, they Sky Elves stopped trying.

It was Wren Elessedil, then known as Wren Ohmsford, who rediscovered the Sky Elves. Though she did not know she was the daughter of a Wing Rider, she used knowledge given her by the Addershag, a seer in Grimpen Ward, to light the watch fire and summon the Wing Rider who patrolled the shoreline. A Wing Rider called Tiger Ty answered the call and transported Wren and her Rover companion to Morrowindl. He returned to carry

her and the Loden that contained her people back to the Westland, where she reestablished Arborlon.

Tiger Ty and the Sky Elves joined Queen Wren's battle against the Federation. During the war, they provided aerial reconnaissance, aerial bombardment, and even limited transport for a covert strike. It was the first time since the Great Wars that a force of arms in the air was used in battle.

After the victory against the Federation, the Sky Elves also returned to the original Wing Hove, though they maintained a small outpost on their island. Inspired by the young Elven Queen, they decided that they too should return to the lands and make a stand.

The joint victory against a common enemy laid the groundwork for Queen Wren's alliance with the Sky Elves. The fact that she carried the blood of both within her veins and had won their respect was also a major factor in the alliance. The Sky Elves were still fiercely independent and still did not believe in monarchical government, but they respected Queen Wren and considered her almost one of their own.

The alliance has survived to this day, despite the fact that Wren's descendants have often fallen short of her example. Wren never tried to force the Wing Riders to submit to her rule, and so long as that tradition continues, the Wing Riders will continue to assist the Land Elves.

Wing Hove has grown into a thriving community of ten thousand, including around a thousand Wing Riders, depending on the number of mature Rocs available. They have expanded their holdings to include outposts on islands as far to the west as Mesca Rho, allowing them to patrol the full extent of the Elven territorial waters and beyond.

Rovers

The Elven Wing Riders are no longer the only people in the sky. The Rovers, outcasts of all nations, have become the leaders in the conquest of the sky with their creation of the airship. But long before the airship was born, the Rovers roamed the whole of the Westland. From the Kershalt to the Irrybis, from the Valley of Rhenn to the Blue Divide, even into the Wilderun, the Rovers were at home everywhere.

No one—including the Rovers—knows the origins of the Rovers, other than that they are of the Race of Man. They have always lived free, tied to no single place or people other than their own wagons and families. In the years before the Federation War, they lived as traders and thieves, traveling in caravans of brightly colored wagons and dressing in brightly colored silks. The wagons were their homes and carried all their worldly goods. Some claimed their music and their clothes were purposely bright in defiance of all the

Rovers travel the lands in brightly colored wagons.

A Rover's Life

Rover wagons were once a symbol of freedom across the plains of the land. By day the Rovers worked at a variety of trades, for they would do anything that would gain them coin or goods. Trading and stealing were the most common occupations—usually together. It was not unusual for a Rover band to steal something of value and then insist on selling it back to the one who lost it. By night, the wagons were circled, and the Family gathered together for song, stories, and dancing. No one in the Four Lands could rival the Rovers for revelry, and no one but a Rover could hold Rover ale.

darkness rising around them. Like the Elves, Rovers believed the land should be nurtured and protected, and that it belonged to everyone, especially to those who traveled it.

The only loyalty a Rover had was to the Family. Most people within the Four Lands distrusted them. Only the Elves allowed them free run of their territory, and only because they both honored the land. Elsewhere the Rovers were tolerated only for the goods and services they brought. It was said of them that any good deal made with a Rover was a better deal for the Rover. Their horses were highly prized, for they were the finest breeders and trainers in the lands. They were also the finest horse thieves.

Rovers traveled in Families, tribes of people brought together under one Leader who was the father figure for all. Though they behaved as if related, not all of the members of the Family were actually connected by blood. In the years before the Federation, the Rovers followed the Way, in which women were considered subservient to men and could be bought and sold. They believed it was the natural order of things for women to serve and obey the men who protected and provided for them. It was also common practice to sell or trade wives and children to other camps. Those entering their camp were expected, by tradition, to demonstrate that they understood and followed the Way. Ironically, one of the strongest Rover women of all time, Eretria Ohmsford, overcame the dictates of the Way to become one of the heroes of the quest for the Bloodfire. Without her aid, it is unlikely Wil and Amberle could have succeeded in their quest. Eretria married Wil and was mother to the famous siblings Brin and Jair Ohmsford.

In later years the emphasis on the Way diminished, until by the time of the rise of Federation, women within the Rovers were at least equal to men. The growth of the Federation pushed the Rovers into the Westland, for the Southland became an inhospitable place to anyone who was an outsider, even when they only wanted to trade. Once the Elves left, the Rovers had the Westland to themselves. No one knew the art of survival better than the Rovers, an art they taught to their children at an early age. They remained free spirits, primarily hunters and Trackers, since there were now few beyond their own people with whom they were able to trade.

It was the Rovers' survival skills that prompted Alleyene Elessedil to give her daughter to be trained by the people everyone else despised. She knew Wren would need to be stronger and have better survival skills than any Elf before her. She chose Garth of the Rovers to give that gift to her daughter. A deaf and dumb Rover, he was the best there was at staying alive. It was his training that enabled Queen Wren to survive her ordeal on Morrowindl and return the Elves to the Westland.

The Federation tolerated some Rover traders, but only just. And if anything was amiss, the Rovers were the first blamed for it, as well as the first to be punished. The Federation believed that any people who lacked a homeland, central government, and army lacked power—though it must be said that the lack of a homeland also kept the Rovers from being important enough to attract the attention of the Federation army.

In the years of the Federation expansion, more Rovers began to take to the sea. Rovers had always been sailors, but now more of them turned to the sailing life. It was a natural expansion of their

Eretria, the bold Rover girl who married an Ohmsford.

nomadic lifestyle, and many discovered that they were happier on the water than on land. They alone of all the people were not tied to the land, for their homeland was wherever they happened to be. Whether they found themselves on the swells of the sea or on the open plains made no difference. The fact that the ocean was free of Federation control was a compelling incentive. Rovers became pirates as well as sea traders, eventually taking control of the trade along the western seacoast. They improved upon the existing ship designs and discovered that they had a flair for shipbuilding. Before the Rovers took to the sea, speed and efficiency were not considered important. Boats were primarily used for fishing. Rovers introduced frigates, capable of running at higher speeds than the slower brigs previously in use. The Rovers were the first to use seagoing vessels for trade, and the first to build ships fast enough to compete with land-based trade routes. The ports of Bracken Clell and March Brume became second homes to these seafaring Rovers—the first being the decks of their ships—and the bright colors the Rovers wore became synonymous with the sea trade.

March Brume

The advent of ocean-borne trade caused a massive increase in demand for high-quality ships of all types and sizes. The port of March Brume turned its attention from fishing to producing vessels of all types, and within a decade the tiny village had tripled in size and become the shipbuilding capital of the West. Predominantly a Southland community, it was home port to many of the Rovers who sailed or built the tall ships. March Brume became the nearest thing the Rovers had to a homeland. Rover shipwrights and craftsmen established homes near the shipyards and created a community—though, being Rovers, they came and went as their mood dictated.

Shipwrights from all over the Four Lands plied their trade within March Brume. Elves, Men, and Dwarves, Free Born and Federation—all conducted business within the city. Everyone who was not involved in buying ships was involved in building ships or feeding and housing those who built the ships.

Among all the shipwrights, there was none better than the Rovers, for only the Rovers truly loved and understood the sea and the manner of craft that could best sail her surface. They also understood the importance of keeping a bargain or protecting a confidence. And there was none better to sail the ships than the Rovers. It was well known that only a Rover captain had a chance against a pirate, for the pirates who sought to lighten the loads of the trading vessels were also Rovers—a fact that did little to redeem the Rovers' reputation with the other Races. Ironically, it was one of these pirates, a man named Ezael Sterret, who revolutionized travel and changed the nature of shipbuilding forever.

Airships

Ezael Sterret had a notorious reputation as a brigand, but he was also an inventor. He wanted to find a way to improve his odds by building a faster ship that would not be subject to the whims of the wind and tides—one that could easily outrun all others. Even the fastest schooner was limited to the power of the wind, which was changeable at best. He began to experiment with the idea of a sail powered by light. Working with different materials, he developed a material that

Airships

The modern airship resembles a sailing vessel, but one that sails on air rather than water, and is powered by light. Airships are usually twin hulled with two or three masts set into cross-braced decking between the hulls. Since they may have to settle on water if their crystals fail, all airships have a seaworthy hull. Warships, the largest of the ships, average 100 feet in length and 30 in width. They can manage speeds of over twenty knots while flying comfortably at altitudes over a thousand feet. Airships vary widely depending on their intended function.

Collector sails called light sheaths absorb the light that powers airships. The sheaths are sensitive enough to gather any light, either direct or ambient, from any source, day or night, for conversion to energy. Direct light is best, but is not always available, so the ships are designed to survive on ambient light. A tiny amount of starlight is enough to lift the ship into the air. Once a ship is functional, it must be tethered to an anchor pin when not underway to prevent it from floating off. The sheaths are broad and straight at their lower end where they fasten to the booms, but curved where the spars draw them high above to a triangle's point. They are designed to make use of the wind for additional thrust, as well as to limit drag.

Light gathered by the sheaths is relayed by radian draws, lines that take the heat down through the decking to the diapson crystals within the parse tubes. The crystals receive the light and convert it to energy to propel and steer the ship. The parse tubes direct the energy they create. The crystals are protected by metal hoods which control the amount of light energy they draw through the radian draws from the light sheaths. Hooding and unhooding the crystals determines the amount of thrust and the direction of travel. The rudders control the direction of the thrust by controlling the direction of the energy released through the parse tubes.

Diapson crystals, the heart of the engines, are made from a crystallized mineral that is common within the Four Lands. These crystals can only convert light energy to thrust after they have been precisely shaped by a master craftsman. A crystal that is flawed or poorly shaped will either fail to adequately convert the light, or shatter under the strain of the conversion. Even well made crystals will explode if allowed to draw too much power without venting it through the parse tubes. Most warships have at least two sets of crystals.

The pilot box in front of the bridge contains the controls for the parse tubes, hoods, rudders, and main draws. The radian draws are raised and lowered by the crew, but most ships are designed to allow the pilot to control everything, including the draws, if needed. It takes years to become a skilled pilot able to fully understand the nuances of hooding and unhooding the crystals and setting the draws. A momentary mistake can send the ship plummeting to the earth.

The warships are fitted with metal-sheathed horns on the ends of their pontoons, which serve as battering rams. Their decks and pontoons are covered with metal armor, and they have metal-shielded fighting ports along the rail to protect fighters in an engagement. Most have catapults attached permanently to their fore and aft deck which are used to launch buckets of metal shards or burning balls of pitch at the enemy.

Each warship can carry a compliment of at least two dozen soldiers in addition to the crew. The soldiers travel below decks, but position themselves on the deck to fight, using safety lines to avoid a fall. Bows arrows, slings, and javelins are used during long-range engagements while spears and blades are used in close combat. Long jagged-edged pikes, ropes, and grappling hooks are used to draw an enemy ship close so that the soldiers can tear apart her sails or sever her radian draws. The crew of an airship is not expected to fight unless their ship is being boarded.

could absorb and transfer light, even ambient light. That same year diapson crystals were discovered. The crystals, if shaped correctly, were capable of transforming light into a new type of energy that provided lift. Ezael combined the two in a radical new type of ship that used light energy to fly.

His first ship was awkward and unreliable. Its maiden voyage lasted only a few minutes, flying only a hundred yards before crashing to the ground. But it flew. Soon others began to experiment with the new technology, refining the design, working with different ways of controlling the crystals and directing the energy until, several years later, the prototype for the modern airship was born. Two decades after Ezael's first flight, airships had replaced sailing ships within many of the shipyards of March Brume. Travel was revolutionized as airships proved they could replace sailing ships and horse-drawn wagons while exceeding both in speed.

The Rovers, who had proved so capable on the high sea, proved equally at home in the air. Their ships were sleek and fast, their captains skilled and courageous. Only the Elves came close to matching the craftsmanship of the Rover shipwrights or the skill of their captains and crews. But the Federation and the Free Born, locked in the beginnings of their war, also realized the enormous potential of the airship. They immediately set out to build and commission ships of their own. They realized that the side who controlled the skies controlled the ground below as well. The war was in its sixth year when the combatants watched hopefully as the first warships lifted off to do battle for the skies. Unfortunately, the early ships fell far short of that hope, often lumbering out of the skies and into each other before ever

engaging with the enemy. March Brume doubled in size as its shipyards struggled to keep up with the constant orders for new craft. With the airship technology still in its infancy, there were only a handful of shipwrights who understood the mechanics involved well enough to build airships that would actually fly.

As the war escalated, so did the need for better ships and more-skilled pilots. The Rovers had both but refused both sides when approached to fight for their cause. So far as the Rovers were concerned, the war was a territorial and trade dispute and had nothing to do with them. If either side wanted Rover ships, they could pay for them. If either wanted Rover captains and crews, they could pay for those as well.

After watching their awkward airships fall to the ground while the more graceful Elven airships sailed away unscathed, the Federation grudgingly realized they needed the Rovers. They began to commission Rover-built ships and hire Rover

The Jerle Shannara

The prototype for a new design of long-range warships, the Jerle Shannara was built by famed Rover shipwright Spanner Frew. Spanner was rumored to have once been the notorious pirate Black Beard. The ship was commissioned by the Elves for a voyage of discovery in search of an ancient treasure of magic. Captained by the infamous Redden Alt Mer, believed by most to be the greatest of captains, the Jerle Shannara is sleek and fast, with much more cargo room than a traditional warship. Her living quarters are set into the decking and, unlike in most airships, extend almost to the waterline. Though she lacks the size and weapons capability of a ship of the line, her speed and agility are far superior to that of any other warship.

The airship Jerle Shannara.

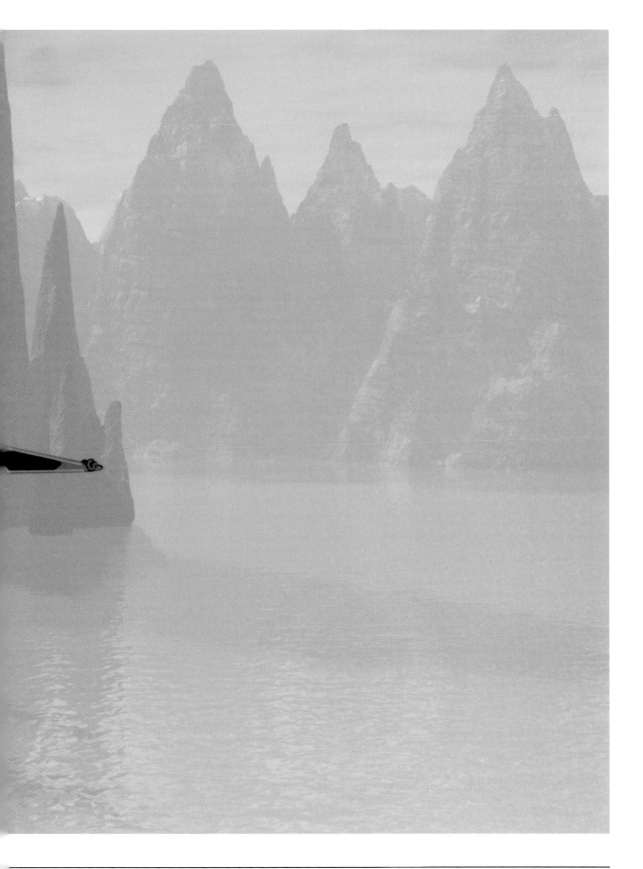

crews to man them. The Free Born also hired Rover mercenaries, but their pockets were not nearly as deep.

The Rovers were perfectly willing to accept work from either side and honor their contracts. They also understood the importance of keeping a confidence once given. In March Brume, both Federation and Free Born often struck deals with the same shipwrights and traveled the same streets, as if they were not locked in mortal combat miles away on the Prekkendorran.

Unfortunately, there were many who resented the Rovers' willingness to treat equally with Federation and Free Born, and still others who wished their commissions handled with the utmost secrecy. For those special clients, and for their own peace of mind, the Rovers established a secret shipyard, away from the crowds and prying eyes of March Brume. The yard never remains in one location for more than two years running, but it is always located within a sheltered cove unknown to any but the Rovers and the discreet Wing Riders. The traveling shipyard has dozens of coves from which to choose, and the Rovers who work within it value the old Rover traditions. They prefer to be isolated and constantly moving, even when there is no known threat.

The Rovers who live and work within the hidden yard usually bring their families. Children old enough to assist are trained in shipbuilding or related crafts. Everyone contributes to the community, and the settlement provides food and housing for all its

members. It is set up in the manner of the old Rover tribes in that all within the community are as family to one another. No Rover would dare reveal the location or purpose of the settlement to an outsider, though all within the larger Rover community know of its existence.

It was within this secret shipyard that the *Jerle Shannara* was built and the famed shipwright Spanner Frew created his finest designs.

The Wilderun

Though the Rovers share most of the Westland with the Elves, there is one section of the Westland that the Elves have completely abandoned to the Rovers as well as any others desperate enough to travel or live there. It is the tangled mass of wilderness to the west of March Brume known as the Wilderun, a place of desperate souls and old magic.

The valley of the Wilderun lies within the curve of the Irrybis Mountains and is ringed by the Rock Spur and the shroudslip. The Wilderun is a jumble of depressions, bogs, and ridges, broken only by a few solitary peaks that lift above the forest canopy. The most distinctive of these is Spires Reach, lifting out of the Hollows in the center of the Wilderun like a beacon.

It is beneath the pillar of Spires Reach that Amberle Elessedil found the Bloodfire, the magic that allowed her to be re-created as the Ellcrys. An ancient magic dating from the birth of the world, the fountain of Bloodfire

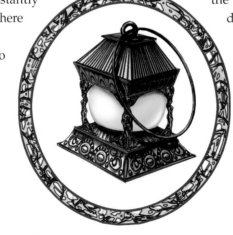

A Glow Globe, used to light the tunnels beneath Spires Reach.

lies hidden within the deepest reaches of the tunnels below Spires Reach, in a cavern behind a waterfall. It was within this cavern that Wil Ohmsford faced and killed the Demon known as the Reaper, saving Amberle and changing himself and the Ohmsford legacy to follow.

There is only one village within the Wilderun, the village of Grimpen Ward. It was originally established centuries past as an outpost for hunters and trappers and the few families who settled within its forests. There was game within the Wilderun, but hunting was never easy and the catch never plentiful. It did not help that there were dark creatures born of the old magic within the valley who seemed to enjoy hunting the hunters.

There was little money in such difficult prey, but the hunters who were weary of the forest were often willing to spend all they had gained on entertainment that would help them forget the things they had seen. Grimpen Ward's entrepreneurs discovered there was more profit to be had from providing such entertainment than from trading, especially in such a remote location. There was no authority within the Wilderun, and therefore no limit to the diversions an ambitious merchant could supply. Eventually the town gained a reputation as a center for gambling and drugs, a place beyond the laws of the land. The Elves shunned it, but Rovers discovered that there was always money to be made if one was careful. Grimpen Ward became a gathering place for the lost souls of the lands, as well as the cutthroats and thieves who fed upon them. Those seeking to escape their past, or those who had nothing left to lose, came to the town and remade it in their image.

Grimpen Ward has existed for centuries, but it still has the look of a temporary shantytown. It has become a place where only the strongest and fastest survive, where the dregs of the Southland come to escape and forget. Those who are not victims are predators, and some of the predators often pretend to be victims.

The seer known as the Addershag was one such predator. She was secretive and mysterious but was known to allow her victims to believe her a prisoner, giving visions at will for scraps of food. When she tired of them, her "captors" discovered that her powers went beyond the gift of sight and that her magic rivaled that of the Druids. No one knows why she chose to feed off the desperate souls of Grimpen Ward, save that she, like all seers, was haunted by her gift and may have needed escape and oblivion as much as they. She finally found her peace after having lived over 150 years.

The citizens of Grimpen Ward are careful to avoid venturing far from their town. Everyone knows that witches and warlocks haunt the forests of the Wilderun,

Seers

There are people born within all the Races who have a special gift of the magic that allows them to "see" glimpses of the future. These seers become shamans and religious leaders in the more primitive Races, and advisors in the rest. Most seers have no control over their gift. All are haunted by the dreams and visions that tell them of what must be. Though most believe they cannot change the future they see, they are usually willing to share their vision, despite the fact that the future cannot be changed. Some, like the Addershag, use their visions to help bring about the future they see. All seers usually spend their lives searching for a peace that only death will grant.

with magic that has its basis deep within the Hollows that lie in the center of the valley.

The Hollows were once home to the witch sisters Morag and Mallenroh, creatures from the age of Faerie. Though the sisters destroyed each other in the time of the quest for the Bloodfire, a warlock rumored to be their brother still lives within the caves of the Hollows. Called the Morgawr, he is reported to have scales and reptilian features similar to the Mwellrets, but with a powerful man's body. In recent years he has brought a witch to live there as well, a witch who can kill with her voice. The people of Grimpen Ward are loath even to speak her name, but others know her as the Ilse Witch. Unknown to most, the formidable witch is an Ohmsford. Even the Rovers dare not cross the witch and warlock.

The Lands Beyond

There's a lot of luck in being a sailor. Flying airships is tricky business, even with an experienced captain. —Rue Meridian

For centuries, the Four Lands have existed without exploration or contact with distant lands. In over two thousand years, the immigration of the Elves to and from the doomed island of Morrowindl was the only serious attempt to explore and colonize distant lands. The one major expedition sent out by the Elves to explore the lands beyond the Great Divide never returned. The sole survivor from that expedition lived long enough to bring a map, which, coupled with notes from the Druids, has created a new understanding of the lands beyond.

Flay Creech

Flay Creech is a small island located west of the coast. Ten days' journey by air, the island is small enough that it can be easily missed by any not seriously looking for it. The island measures approximately a half mile across its widest part and is distinguished by a rocky outcropping shaped like a lizard's head just off the southern coast. The island is gray and barren, its only vegetation a few clusters of scrub trees and weeds. The most unusual features of the island are the distinctive gullies that crisscross its barren surface. The gullies and channels are broken only by shallow ponds of seawater. Initial

The Giant Eels of Flay Creech

The eels of Flay Creech may use the island as a spawning and feeding ground. Larger than any other known eel, their bodies resemble the sleek, speckled bodies of an ocean eel. Unlike the ocean eel, they average between eight and thirty feet in length and will attack anything that enters their domain. Though they are not poisonous, their sharp teeth can easily tear and shred larger prey. They remain hidden beneath the waters of the Blue Divide until an intruder lands on the island; they then boil out of the water to converge on the hapless victim. When in an attack frenzy, they will often attack each other, and will feed on their own dead or wounded. Susceptible to magic, they are not afraid of it. A deadly predator, the eels are capable of launching themselves from the ground and striking like a snake. The eels have somehow been conditioned to protect the island.

observers were at a loss to understand what caused the channels. Those who made landfall on the island quickly discovered the cause. They are tracks worn in the earth over the years by the bodies of the island's hidden protectors, the deadly giant eels. The eels defend the island from anything that seeks to set foot on its surface.

Shatterstone

Northwest of Flay Creech, the next large island is Shatterstone. Named for its forbidding mountains and rugged cliffs, Shatterstone is approximately thirty miles across at its widest point. Three small islands arrayed in a row lead to the southeastern edge of the island. Made from the rugged tips of a huge mountain range thrusting up from the depths of the ocean floor, the island consists of jungle-covered peaks and deep canyons. As lush and green as Flay Creech is barren, Shatterstone's surface is covered with impenetrable jungle, broken only by small lakes and the bare edges of the windswept peaks and cliff edges. Silver waterfalls leap from the high mountain streams to fall thousands of feet into the green valleys below.

Even the waters around the island abound with life. Pods of whales and dolphins skim the surface of the Blue Divide, while seabirds feed on the smaller fish. On the island, birds, mammals, and insects thrive throughout most of the island.

All the creatures of the island seem to avoid one valley. Even insects avoid it. It is the valley of the living jungle. A power believed to have been created in the time of Faerie guards the valley. Rooted in the soil of the valley and manifested in the jungle itself, the power it wields is greater than that of the Druids. Like the eels, the jungle has been conditioned to protect the treasure hidden in its valley. It can sense anything that moves upon the soil that nurtures it. Its only known weakness is its inability to penetrate rock. Unfortunately, there are very few bare rocks in the valley. It kills with vines that rip its victims to shreds, or with poison brambles that carry a deadly toxin.

Shrike Island

Though it has long been known that the Shrikes had a nesting place apart from the Westland cliffs, the location of such a nesting ground was only recently discovered. Shrike Island is a rugged island of cliffs and rocky peaks surrounding a lush tropical jungle and inland lakes. Hundreds of Shrikes and War Shrikes make their homes on its cliffs and ridges. Extremely territorial, Shrikes will attack anything that approaches their island.

Mephitic

Far north of Shatterstone, where the wind grows cold, lies an island that is much larger still. Low and broad, Mephitic lacks the high cliffs of Shatterstone or the rocky shoals of Flay Creech. Its rolling hills, wide grasslands, and thick forests resemble parts of the Westland more than an island in the middle of the Blue Divide.

Though the island is now deserted, there is evidence that it was inhabited long ago. All that is left of those inhabitants is a massive keep, ancient and crumbling. Built atop a low bluff, the castle's blind windows look out across the plains to the west. As large as Paranor, the keep's walls and outbuildings extend out across the grasslands for a mile in all directions.

The people who conceived of and built the fortress are gone, but the castle itself lives. A spirit, from an unknown age, infuses the very walls of the keep, protecting all the treasures within with the magic of deception. Anyone entering the keep finds himself disoriented and lost in a puzzling warren of courtyards, halls, and battlements. Though the foundations of the keep are real, as are some of the stone ruins, the castle itself is not as it appears, but rather a vast labyrinth of mirages and illusions integrated into the stone and designed to deceive. Though the protection is largely passive, the spirit can be brought to life by the theft of one of its treasures. The keep then becomes a deadly trap intent on snaring its victim. Pits open up out of solid ground; traps and portcullises appear from out of walls; the very walls move to trap a thief.

Fortunately, the range of the spirit's abilities is limited. The spirit's magic does not extend beyond the walls to the plains beyond.

No one knows what happened to the people who initially built the keep or how the spirit came to inhabit its lonely outpost, though it is likely the spirit has survived since the age of Faerie.

Ice Henge

Beyond Mephitic, the next large landfall is the continent of Parkasia. Its southeastern tip juts into the Blue Divide in a large peninsula. The outer edge of the peninsula is surrounded by small atolls, most of which are barren, and protected by an impenetrable wall of icy cliffs towering over a thousand feet above the waterline into the clouds above. The steep cliffs are broken by caverns carved out of the rock and narrow fissures covered in mist. The land is called Ice Henge. Shrikes inhabit the cliffs, feeding on the fish and other sea birds. A breach in the cliff wall of the peninsula opens into a large bay. The bay is rimmed by a towering range of snow-capped mountains and glaciers that reach down to the water's edge through gaps in the rocky peaks. Floes broken off from the glaciers float within the waters of the bay like small snow-covered islands, some rising several hundred feet above the waterline.

The bay feeds into a channel that narrows before opening onto an inner bay. The inner bay, also littered with floes, opens into a narrow channel that leads inland to the towering deadly series of ice pillars called the Squirm.

The Squirm is named for the movement of the pillars, which twist and thrust together in a grinding motion like giant sets of teeth. They guard the only passage inland from the bay. Any unsuspecting sailor who attempts to pass through the Squirm is usually ground into pulp and splinters. The seabirds follow anyone who sails into the channel in anticipation of a meal. No one is certain whether the pillars of the Squirm are a product of magic or of science and technology, though both may affect them.

Beyond the Squirm, the channel broadens, twisting through a bleak landscape of barren cliff walls and dotted with small rocky islands. Trees cling to the ridgeline in small clusters. The waters are curiously warmer here, with no glaciers or floating ice. As the channel progresses inland, the sharp-edged cliffs retreat and soften into gentle slopes covered with greenery and lush forests. Farther inland, the gentle slopes give way to rolling hills as the river splits into numerous tributaries that form lakes, smaller rivers, and streams. The main channel narrows, and the trees on its banks thicken until the river is hemmed in by old-growth spruce and cedar. The river ends inland in a large bay surrounded by forest. Numerous waterfalls feed into the bay from dozens of rivers and streams.

Several miles beyond the bay lay the ruins of an Old World city. Occupying the entirety of a broad valley ten miles long and five miles wide, the ruins gleam in the sunlight. Unlike Eldwist, which also dated from the Old World, before the Great Wars, the buildings in this city are low and flat, with high windows and broad spaces. Believed to be a haven for storing machinery, and possibly for construction, the entire city is made of sheets and struts of metal. Even the streets and passageways are paved with metal, though the grass has managed to break through in places, buckling the rusted metal as nature attempts to reclaim the ground. Holes in the walls of some of the buildings reveal burned-out interiors, testament to the fact that this place did not survive the Great Wars unscathed. There are rumors that a safehold called Castledown may lie somewhere in the city.

Morrowindl

Over a century ago, there was another island in the waters of the Blue Divide—a paradise with high mountains and beautiful beaches topped by the lofty crown of an extinct volcano called Killeshan. The Land Elves settled it in an attempt to escape the Federation and the Shadowen. The Elves experimented with old magic while living there, eventually using it to make creatures that were never intended. The creatures were subverted by the magic and eventually transformed into Demons, who consumed the earth magic of the island. The Elves escaped, but the island itself did not. Turned into a place of horrors by the Demons, it exploded as the loss of earth magic caused Killeshan to erupt violently. It was said the Sky Elves could see the island burning from the shores of Wing Hove.

A Legacy of Magic, Darkness, and Light

Within my own land, I am the way and the life. I am the bearer of the light of the Word now and always. —The King of the Silver River

Many changes have affected the lands since the Great Wars. Technology and knowledge have been lost, and Men have mutated to survive. But the single greatest difference between the new age and the Old World is magic. Though very few understand magic, and fewer still have the use of it—whether through talismans or innate ability—the existence of magic has affected our view of the world at large. In the Old World, magic was a myth. In this one, there is no doubt—even for those who have never seen it—that it exists. But where did it come from?

In actuality, the magic has always been here. It is the miracle of life. It is the land and all things within it. Though access to magic's more dramatic functions has varied through the ages, the magic and its power has not. What has changed is our ability to see and accept it, brought about largely by the integration of those who can wield it into a society dominated by those who cannot. The integration has created a general understanding that magic is real, for both good and ill. That knowledge has changed us, making us more aware of the extremes of light and dark—an awareness that may have been lacking in the last age, when technology was usually gray.

Magic first appeared at the dawn of time, when the Word made the creatures of Faerie. These first Faeries were given gardens to tend, gardens that covered the whole of the land, along with a charge to protect and preserve the land of the world and all the things that lived upon it, crawled within it, or flew above it. The world was a sacred Eden, and magic was within all the land as well as the creatures of Faerie that guarded and nurtured it. They had dominion over the land; their magic was second only to the might of the Word. These first Faeries had no names, for there was no need of names in that age.

But the world changed. Other creatures of Faerie were born. These were also creatures of magic, but they were different from the first Faeries—their power was not as great, their ties to the land not as strong. Some of these creatures were the forebears of the Elves, others the ancestors of the shape-shifters, still others children of first Faeries, such as Morag and Mallenroh. They too were given the land in trust, that they would preserve and protect all that lived, though their charge was a voluntary one.

Unfortunately, some among them became selfish; they forsook their charge from the Word and began to take from the land and its life for their own gain. Others discovered the darkness that balanced the light of the Word, and became one with it. The Faerie folk, still honoring their trust from the Word, fought against those who are now known as Demons. Constant battles between Demons and Faerie folk tore at the world, upsetting its balance. The struggle continued, unresolved, pulling at the balance of the world, until eventually the sides polarized into the army of light and the army of darkness. Their battle became a desperate war between good and evil. The Ildatch was born of this time, created by the Demons, who strove to harness all of the magic to their cause.

The beings of good were victorious, their use of the magic strengthened by the willing sacrifice of one of their own, something the Demons could not understand, much less re-create. The Demons were locked away behind the Forbidding. But the conflict had brought darkness into the world and proven that the creatures of Faerie had a choice. Darkness was as much part of the magic as was light.

The creatures of Faerie continued to protect and preserve the land, but the world aged and the Faerie people began to fade with the rise of Man. The evolution of the world took away almost everything that had existed in the beginning, including the first Faerie creatures. One by one they died away, lost in the passing of the years and the changes of the world.

Some few managed to survive the age of Man, hidden within their gardens, lost to myth and legend. They secretly wielded the magic and held to the trust given by the Word. The Great Wars destroyed many of them. The Wars of the Races destroyed more. The younger creatures of Faerie were also affected, but they were more numerous and had a higher survival rate. Finally, of the first Faeries, there remained only two: the being Man has named the King of the Silver River, and the being who named himself Uhl Belk, the Stone King.

The King of the Silver River

All of the first Faeries drew their magic from the elements of the land, and each was tied to that element. The King of the Silver River derived his strength from lakes and rivers. He was attuned to all the waters that fed the earth, and he was grounded in the fluid waters of change. He survived the Great Wars much as he survived the age of Man, because of his ability to accept change, even catastrophic change. He watched, safe within his garden, filled with sadness at the loss of what had been and hope for what might be.

At the birth of the new age, he emerged. There was magic in the land again. The first Faerie greeted it with his own magic, the magic of life. The myth of his existence gained acceptance as truth as he made himself known as protector to those deserving travelers in his land who were in need. He had no name, but the people gave him one. They named him the King of the Silver River, for his garden was placed near the Silver River and the waters of the Rainbow Lake. He built his garden near the river to nourish it, to give it life and draw life back again.

Like all of the first Faeries, the King of the Silver River possessed magic that was almost invincible in his limited domain near the river. Beyond its limits, his magic faded. He made use of its strength within the Silver River region. Appearing predominantly as an old man or a young boy, always carrying the light of the Word before him, the King of the Silver River became a legend. No one knows his true form, for it is not one that mortals could understand, but one of wind and water and quicksilver life. No one can find or enter his garden without his permission or escort, for it lies beyond human senses.

In this age, he has been generous with his attention. Many of the Ohmsfords have seen and spoken with him. Some were even privileged enough to visit his garden. Each was given rest and aid on his or her journey. Jair Ohmsford actually returned aid to the King of the Silver River, and in so doing helped save the lands. He was

The King of the Silver River.

given the charge of cleansing the poison of dark magic from the Silver River. The young Ohmsford was the first mortal known to receive magic talismans from the Faerie king. He was given Silver Dust to cleanse the river and a Vision Crystal to aid in locating and assisting his sister. Bek Ohmsford was the only other human known to have received such a gift. Bek was given the phoenix stone by the same being.

Despite the limitations imposed through the waning of the ages, the King of the Silver River has proven that he is still dedicated to the land. Though he is the last of his kind to serve the Word, he has continued to keep the trust.

The Stone King

The King of the Silver River was one of two of his kind to survive into the new age. The other was the creature known as the Stone King.

Whereas the King of the Silver River took his magic from the waters, Uhl Belk, his brother, took his magic from the earth's stone. His strength came from constancy and immutability. The King of the Silver River was named by those he aided; Uhl Belk named himself, for he believed that a name would anchor his being and give him permanence.

The Stone King was disturbed by the changes that racked the land. He survived by hiding from the chaos that reigned during the Great Wars, but he was shaken by the changes wrought with the birth of the new age. Everything he thought to be permanent had changed. Uhl Belk hid himself in the age of the past, making his home within the ruins of a city that had survived the Great Wars. Its structures were doubtless comforting to him in an age when all else was new.

He could not accept the change that had become the only constant within the world. He became obsessed with creating permanence and ending all change. Embedding himself in the ways that sustained him, he became so focused on his own need to survive that he forgot his charge from the Word. He lost all connection with the living land and burrowed deeper into the ageless stone of the past. Life itself and the changes that were a natural and necessary part of that life became his enemy. He schemed to re-create the world as a place devoid of change—devoid of any life but his own.

The wars and the changes they

The Vision Crystal, given to Jair Ohmsford by the King of the Silver River.

wrought had diminished his realm until he had only a tiny bit of land on the peninsula of Eldwist. He turned the entire peninsula to cold stone and made the city of Eldwist into a frozen monument to the age that was. It was not enough. He could still sense the changes throughout the living land, and they caused his fear to intensify. He began to hoard magic to make himself strong enough to extend his domain to the world of men.

But he could not do it alone. He, like all the first Faeries, was tied to his home. His attempt to render himself more permanent had also tied him permanently to the transformed city. In order to continue the expansion of his domain he created a child to act in his place. That child was the Maw Grint.

Maw Grint

An elemental, formed of the rocks and soil rather than flesh, the Maw Grint was given the power to turn the land to stone, to feed on the land and all that grew upon it. Like most elementals, he was originally given human form. The Maw Grint set out to transform the world for his father. He succeeded, slowly expanding the stone until it consumed the isthmus and the edge of the lands it connected. But the Stone King's fear made him impatient. To speed the process, he infused his child with greater and greater amounts of his own magic. The magic changed the Maw Grint. Over a period of only a few years, he was transformed from a man into a massive burrowing creature that was both slug and worm, though many thousand times larger than either. Not surprisingly, the Maw Grint went mad from the onslaught of too much power absorbed too quickly. Uhl Belk lost control of his child. The creature turned on his father, eager to usurp the power he now hungered for, hunting him when he was not feeding.

Uhl Belk relied on the power of the Black Elfstone, stolen from the Hall of Kings, to control his creature. He could have killed his child, but preferred to control it and allow it to continue to feed.

The King of the Silver River felt the changes in the land and learned about his brother. He learned of the fact that he not only had forsworn his oath to protect and preserve the land, but was actively destroying the life upon it. His was the only magic strong enough to stop the Stone King, but he could not leave his land.

Quickening

The King of the Silver River created a child of his own. He created a daughter from the things within his garden: a tree for bone, soil for form, metal ores for muscle, flower petals for skin, a unicorn's mane for hair, and a living dove for her heart. The King gifted her with a part of his own magic and breathed life into her. Called Quickening, she was sent into the world to gather her champions and do battle with the Stone King.

Aided by Walker Boh (who was not yet a Druid), Morgan Leah, the Tracker Horner Dees, and the assassin Pe Ell, she journeyed to Eldwist to face the Stone King. The allies managed to retrieve the Black Elfstone from the Faerie lord. Once he no longer had the stone to protect himself, Quickening let the assassin kill her, sacrificing herself to allow her magic to heal the land and end the Stone King's reign. Because Quickening was an elemental, she could not kill herself, nor could she be killed by conventional means. The assassin was included in her party because he alone possessed a weapon that could kill a Faerie creature—the stiehl. The magic released at her death reduced the Maw Grint to the elements of which it was spawned, and returned the land to life. The stone city of Eldwist was absorbed into the renewed land, leaving the central

Silver Dust

When Mord Wraiths poisoned Heaven's Well and the Silver River, the King of the Silver River created a magic that would cleanse his river of the pollutant if used at its source. This magic was given the form of river sand and placed within a leather pouch. The Faerie king could not leave his domain to travel to the source, but he could send his magic with Jair Ohmsford. The dust cleansed the river, eradicating the dark magic and its poison from the waters along the entire length of the Silver River.

Silver Dust, Faerie magic.

dome as the only remnant of the lost city. Many believe that the Stone King still lives, imprisoned within the dome by Quickening's eternal magic.

In the age of Faerie, there were more Faerie creatures and Races than there are humans today. Though most of them did not have the power of the first Faeries, they were all creatures of magic. Only a small number of these beings managed to survive the ages, usually by hiding in wilderness lands and places of power. After the Great Wars, the magic of the land pooled within these places of power. Some of the magic was somehow changed and strengthened in the aftermath of the wars. A number of the surviving creatures of Faerie emerged into the world from their hiding places, while others remain in their wild sanctuaries. Many of them, such as the Elves, still protect and preserve life, but most simply survive. The Elves evolved and changed until they were no longer recognizable as creatures of Faerie. Other creatures also changed but kept their nature and their affinity for the earth magic. Many still survive within the places of wild magic, such as the Wolfsktaag, Darklin Reach, and the Wilderun.

The Stiehl

In the age of Faerie, a weapon was forged that was the soul of death given form. A silver-bladed knife with its name engraved in the handle, the stiehl is the ultimate weapon. It can cut through any substance, breach any defense, and kill even creatures of Faerie. It was first discovered in a cave deep within the Battlemound Lowlands, amid a pile of human bones. Its magic has the ability to call to it those with the will to wield it. The stiehl is currently locked away in the depths of the Druid's Keep.

Morag and Mallenroh

Deep within the Wilderun, within the depression known as the Hollows, lived two of these creatures of Faerie. Known by the names they gave themselves, Morag and Mallenroh, these sisters were two of the more powerful creatures to survive from the age of Faerie. They were daughters of one of the first Faeries, an Old One said to have long since departed the land. These witch sisters claimed to be the last of their coven from a Faerie Race of witches and warlocks, though that claim has since come into question. They lived in the protected land of the Wilderun, deep in the Hollows, watching from their hideaway as the world they had known was slowly destroyed and transformed.

Those who saw them and survived reported that they were identical sisters, each possessed of stunning physical beauty beyond that of any mortal woman, and each twisted by a terrible ugliness of spirit. One legend says that they took their original form as humans in the early age of Man. At that time, they were still tied to the land and its needs, and interacted with humans when necessary for that purpose. Their beauty often swayed mortals to aid them in their task. As the world changed around them, they became reclusive, trapped in their land as the magic left the outside world. As the centuries passed, they became bitter, spiteful, and petty toward each other. They forgot their purpose. The charge to preserve and protect life was corrupted into the need to control it.

Within the Hollows, they wielded the power of life and death. Those who pleased them were granted life, though they became living playthings. Those that did not found their deaths. Mallenroh's favorite servant was an elf who had stum-

Morag and Mallenroh, the witch sisters.

bled into the Hollows as a young man. He was transformed into a wizened Gnome-like creature of sticks and fur. Though he was given immortality, he paid the price with his sanity.

As was the case with most of the more powerful creatures of Faerie, they were tied to their land and its magic. They ruled the Hollows with iron control but rarely ventured away from the source of their power. There are legends of one or the other of them occasionally visiting human men who wandered too close to their domain. If the man was lucky, he lost a portion of his life to the witch and spent the rest of it dreaming of her beauty. If not, he was killed.

It was a mortal man who is believed to have caused the feud between the sisters that consumed their lives and eventually led to their deaths. Mallenroh claimed that she had found a handsome mortal to love and that Morag had killed him. Morag claimed the same. It is probable that the hapless mortal was literally torn apart in a struggle between the two greedy witches, each of whom was focused more on besting the other than on the well-being of any mortal.

Evenly matched, their war lasted for centuries. Morag controlled the east of the Hollows and Mallenroh the west. They lived in separate stone towers at each end of the Hollows, each trying to destroy the other and take her sister's land and power

for her own. Spires Reach, in the center of the Hollows, marked the dividing line of their domain.

The balance of power shifted when Wil Ohmsford brought Elfstones into the Hollow. Both sisters sensed the magic, and both knew that such magic would tip the balance of their eternal war. Though neither could use the Stones unless they were freely given, both wanted them. Mallenroh tried to force Wil to gift them to her, but Morag confronted her before she had succeeded. They battled, using all the might of their magic against each other. In the end, they destroyed each other and reduced Mallenroh's keep to ashes.

The Morgawr

Despite the deaths of the witch sisters, magic is still strong in the Wilderun. A warlock calling himself the Morgawr, which means "wraith" in one of the lost languages of Faerie, has claimed to be the heir to their magic. He has claimed he is their brother and also descended from a creature of Faerie.

Unlike the witch sisters, the Morgawr has no innate magic of his own. His magic is nevertheless quite formidable for all that it has been leached from the land and built up over his lifetime. He can travel at will, though he prefers the Wilderun and the dark magic that thrives there. Those who have seen him report that he was once human in appearance but has become more reptilian over time, until he resembles a larger, more powerful Mwellret. With his magic to aid him, the Morgawr has mastered and surpassed the Mwellrets' shape-shifting ability, though he relies primarily on deception and trickery to achieve his goals.

The Dagda Mor

As the age changed and the Faerie creatures died out, so too did time affect the Ellcrys and the Forbidding. Though it took far longer, the Ellcrys aged and failed and the Forbidding weakened. Ironically, the Demons of the age of Faerie survived and multiplied within their prison, while most of the Faeries who imprisoned them became extinct. When the Forbidding failed, there was none left to face them but the mortals who had inherited their land. Most of those had lost the magic long before. If the Forbidding had not been restored with the rebirth of a new Ellcrys, the Demons would have easily overrun the land.

The most powerful of the Demons was the creature who called himself the Dagda Mor. A creature born of the integral darkness of creation, he was made of the darkness intended to balance the light of the world. It was gathered to extreme within his being, creating a Demon who parodied Man but shared nothing of his life. The darkness within him shaped his body so that his resemblance to a man was slight. The dark magic had warped his back into a massive hump. Greenish hair protruded

Staff of Power

The Dagda Mor's Staff of Power channeled the Demon's magic. He was one of the only Demons known to use magic in the manner of the Druids. Most Demons were themselves magic and did not make separate use of it. The Staff of Power allowed the Dagda Mor to direct his magic into red Demon fire. When in use, the staff glowed red. Unlike Druids, the Dagda Mor could not direct Demon fire without the staff.

The staff also served to call creatures that could be bent to the Demon's will, such as the great Northland bat brought down to serve as a mount during the Demon War.

The Dagda Mor was aided in his dark magic by his Staff of Power.

from his body in large tufts, and reptilian scales covered his forearms and lower legs. Both his hands and feet ended in claws. In his time, he was a brilliant warlock, but his affinity for the darkness twisted his body and corrupted his brilliance. He was not the most powerful of the Demons, though his power was far greater than most, but he was the smartest. He ruled the others, having broken in grisly fashion those who opposed him.

Imprisoned within the Forbidding, the Dagda Mor's hatred of those who had imprisoned him became madness. When the Forbidding weakened, he was the first to exploit that weakness and return to the world, hungry for vengeance. His Staff of Power channeled his dark magic and allowed him to pull from the earth's own magic to enhance his own. He believed that the world rightfully belonged to the Demons and that all who lived upon it were trespassers.

The Changeling

One of the Reaper's favored minions, the Changeling was a creature of Faerie who could take on any form and become anything, alive or dead. Unlike shape-shifters or Mwellrets, his transformation was undetectable. Though he lacked the raw power of the Dagda Mor, his intelligence and ability to deceive made him one of the most feared of Demons. His natural form is reported to be that of a sleek, spidery primate with a misshapen head and fierce jaws.

The Reaper

Cloaked in robes the color of damp ashes, the Reaper was the most powerful of all the Demons. It was a killer, all the dark impulses of predation concentrated into

A Fury, one of the Demons of the Forbidding.

one being and given life. Killing was the sole function of its existence. In the age of Faerie, it was the most feared of all the Demons. In the new age, it was almost invincible. Wil Ohmsford is the only man to have looked upon the Reaper's face and lived.

The Reaper served the Dagda Mor only out of whim. In the dark void of the Forbidding, it killed other Demons, kept in check only by the promise of an entire world filled with victims.

Protected by the eternal prison of the Forbidding, the Demons did not change and die out, as did their earthbound counterparts. All the legends of demonic creatures that have survived as tales were based upon the ancient memories of the dark creatures, burned into racial consciousness. The Demon War allowed those who fought it a chance to see firsthand the Furies and Ogres, Dragons and Demon Wolves that had previously been relegated

The Furies

One of the few Demons with a definite sex, Furies were always female. A Demon from the age of Faerie, they wore the faces of beautiful women, but had jaws and voices of monstrous cats. Their bodies were a sinuous combination of human and feline, with razor-tipped claws on hands and feet. Though they were usually small, no larger than a large dog or a child, they were very deadly. Born of madness and bloodlust, Furies lived on human flesh and hunted in packs. Their numbers and ferocity compensated easily for their small size. They usually walked on all fours, but in battle could stand on their hind limbs and attack with jaws and tearing forelimbs.

A distinctive mewling sound usually heralded their presence, though few victims survived to tell of it. Their favored tactic was to overwhelm a victim with the sheer weight of their numbers, dragging it down to be shredded and devoured.

to those stories. Fortunately, the Dagda Mor, Reaper, and Changeling were destroyed, and the Demons that survived the war were imprisoned anew behind the Forbidding.

The existence of such Demons is proof of the duality of the world and its magic. Throughout the history of the land, the magic has promised great power. It is both a power for good and a power for evil. The magic can be safely used only by those creatures born to its use and mindful of their own limits. Originally, only those born of Faerie could touch the magic. In this age, innate magic has been interwoven into certain humans even as it has left the Elves. But for all, whether they are born to the magic or simply learn to use it as the Druids do, there is always danger. The magic is power. It creates its own addic-

tion. If misused, even by those born to it, it can change and corrupt the user.

The history of the Four Lands is defined by the misuse of magic and the resulting corruption, even as it is salvaged by those who embraced the magic, and its dangers, to combat that darkness. The difference between the heroes and the villains is often defined by the difference in their character as well as their ability to remain focused on the good of the land. The heroes are those intrinsically bonded to the charge given by the Word long before they were even born—the same trust that was given to the first of the Faeries at the dawn of time. Though many do not even know of the formal charge, these heroes have often paid with their lives to protect and preserve the world and those who live within it.

Parkasia: Voyage to a New World

In a far distant land of Old World science and primitive cultures, the most amazing thing I discovered was my own truth. —Bek Ohmsford

Far to the west of the Four Lands, over the expanse of the Blue Divide, lies a mostly unexplored land of ancient ruins, shape-shifters, and primitive hunter-gatherers. What little we know of this land came from Walker Boh's expedition across the Blue Divide aboard the airship *Jerle Shannara*. The Druid led a group of Men, Elves, a Dwarf, and a shape-shifter in search of a treasure of unimaginable value—a treasure of ancient magic. The survivors returned, after enduring great loss and hardship, with a different treasure: the discovery of a new land and new people.

They called the land Parkasia, the name the natives had given it.

Walker's company was not the first to attempt the crossing. Thirty years before the *Jerle Shannara* sailed, Prince Kael Elessedil, heir to the Elven throne, had convinced his mother, Queen Aine, to allow him to lead an Elven expedition of three ships along the same course. None of those ships ever returned.

Thirty years later, Kael Elessedil was discovered adrift in the Blue Divide. Barely alive, he had been blinded and his tongue cut out. Only a bracelet bearing the Elessedil crest—the spreading boughs of the sacred Ellcrys surrounded by a ring

The Great Rover captain Redden Alt Mer, known as Big Red.

of Bloodfire—gave any clue to his identity. His single other possession was a map, written in his own hand in an indecipherable language. The last of his doomed expedition, Kael did not survive long enough to return to Arborlon.

Kael's map spurred a renewed interest in the mysterious land across the ocean. Kael's brother Allardon was determined to discover the truth about the fate of his sibling's expedition as well as the treasure he had set out to find. King Allardon was forced to turn for answers to the Druid named Walker Boh, the only one who could decipher the ancient language of the map. That map became the guide for Walker Boh's expedition. Authorized by King Allardon just before he died and reluctantly supported by his son, Kylen, the second expedition's official charge was to search for the remains of the first while attempting to find the treasure described on Kael's map.

Kylen sent his younger brother Ahren along, as well as Ard Patrinell, the captain of the guard who had failed to save his father. It was well known that Kylen had

no faith in the success of the expedition, and that he supported it only because he had no choice but to honor his father's agreement. Many believed he was deliberately sending Ard Patrinell and Ahren to their deaths.

After months of difficult travel and narrow escapes from the islands of Flay Creech, Shatterstone, Shrike, and Mephitic, the *Jerle Shannara* reached Ice Henge on the southern tip of Parkasia. Three of the islands held keys described in the map as being essential to the quest. On each of those islands, only the Druid's magic allowed the company to collect the necessary keys and escape. They also discovered they were not alone. The Ilse Witch hounded them in a ship called *Black Moclips* with a crew of mercenary Rovers and Mwellrets. Unknown to both, her mentor the Morgawr followed close behind with an entire fleet of ships crewed by Mwellrets and dead men. The Ilse Witch and the Morgawr each intended to have the treasure for themselves.

Upon reaching the mainland, Walker's expedition discovered a land warded by miles of impenetrable cliffs of ice-covered rock. This was Ice Henge. Shrikes roosted in caverns and on ledges along the cliffs watching for prey, while the unpredictable winds and icy mists made flight over the tops impossible. The cliffs formed a frozen barrier around the entire southern tip of the peninsula. After several more days of sailing, the voyagers followed the map, finally discovering a break in the wall on the northeastern edge of the peninsula.

There, the cliffs receded, opening into a large protected bay backed by a towering range of snowcapped peaks. Glaciers ran through the mountains down into the water. Small mountains of ice that had broken off the glaciers floated in the bay

The Crew of the Jerle Shannara

The first expedition to Parkasia sailed with three ships. The second, under the Druid Walker Boh, had only one: the Jerle Shannara, with thirty-five men and women aboard her. But while the first, failed expedition had been completely manned by Elves, the Druid's company was extremely diverse. He chose Rovers to crew and handle the ship. The great Rover captain Redden Alt Mer, known as Big Red, was put in command of the ship. His sister, Rue Meridian or Little Red, served as navigator. The shipwright Spanner Frew, who had overseen the design and building of the Jerle Shannara, was charged with handling repairs along the way. Furl Hawken and ten other Rovers filled out the crew.

The Elven King sent his younger brother Ahren Elessedil as the representative of the Elven crown; the former Captain of the Home Guard, Ard Patrinell; the Healer Joad Rish; the Tracker Tamis; and a company of Elven Hunters.

But the Druid wanted more than strong arms and willing fighters. He needed magic that could back up his own. He selected young Bek Ohmsford, heir to the Ohmsford magic and the magic of the Sword of Shannara; Quentin Leah, holder of the famed Sword of Leah; the seer Ryer Ord Star; and the halfling shape-shifter Truls Rohk.

To aid with hunting and reconnaissance, Walker enlisted the aid of Hunter Predd and two other Wing Riders. He also recruited the Dwarf Panax, a skilled warrior.

Of this number, only a few returned. Included among the survivors were Bek Ohmsford, Quentin Leah, Ahren Elessedil, the Rovers Redden Alt Mer, Rue Meridian, and Spanner Frew, and the Wing Riders Hunter Predd and Po Kelles. But added to their number was their former enemy Grianne Ohmsford, Bek's sister and the woman who would one day rebuild the Druid order.

Bek Ohmsford and Rue Meridian married shortly after their return, giving birth to a son, Penderrin Ohmsford. Quentin Leah became a respected leader in Leah, but he never fully recovered from injuries sustained during the voyage, and eventually died from their complications.

like huge islands. Within the protection of the bay, the winds stilled. The first bay led to a channel through the mountains, a second bay, and a narrower channel. Spurred by a mass of warm moist air from the peninsula's interior, the mists grew heavier as the expedition sailed upriver, reducing visibility to dangerously low levels.

But the channel was blocked. Huge pillars of ice stood side by side like floating sentries guarding the interior. At first the pillars floated calmly, seeming much the same as the glacier ice in the bay. There was enough room between them to allow a ship tight passage. But then they suddenly came to life, crashing against each other as if they were caught up in some furious quest to destroy each other. Any hapless sailors foolish enough to attempt passage during the deceptive calm would be crushed by these pillars. Called the Squirm, they warded the single sure way into the interior. Only magic could guarantee safe passage. Kael had used the Elfstones to secure passage for the first expedition; Bek Ohmsford used the magic of the Sword of Shannara to secure safety for the second.

Bek Ohmsford wields the Sword of Shannara at the Squirm.

Castledown

Beyond the Squirm, the land changed. Ice and bitter winds gave way to temperate breezes and calm waters. Greenery and forests replaced the barren rocks of Ice Henge. The voyagers marveled at the sudden change. They did not realize the temperate weather was caused by the machine-mind Antrax, hidden deep within the bowels of the earth.

After anchoring in a large bay, Walker led all but the Rovers inland seeking the place called Castledown and the safehold it protected. Several miles inland, Walker's party discovered the ruins of a city built during the time of the Old World. Made entirely of metal, the city covered the whole valley floor, ten miles wide and five long. The buildings were low and flat. Some appeared to be large raised platforms rather than buildings, and none looked as if it had ever been a dwelling, at least not for humans. Even some of the streets were made of metal. Machinery with cables and dials filled many of the structures. It was a city of warehouses and

factories. A city that had once been made for machines.

The whole city bore the scars of an ancient conflict. Much of the metal was twisted and burned out. Many of the structures had gaping holes in their thick metal walls, and debris littered the streets. The ruins of Castledown were a mute memorial to the ferocity of the Great Wars and the technology that had spawned them.

Deep inside the city, the expedition discovered a broad metal-carpeted clearing, surprisingly free of any debris or scarring. The area was roughly square in shape, studded here and there with oddly shaped walls and partitions of various heights. In the center, an obelisk more than a hundred feet tall towered over the square, with a single door recessed into its front panel. Depressions set into the door's surface matched the keys taken from the islands. A red light blinked steadily above a single door in the obelisk, the only sign of life in ruins that appeared otherwise dead and deserted.

Realizing that the obelisk marked the entrance to Castledown, Walker attempted to reach the door, triggering a defense grid that reacted instantly to his intrusion. Laser ports set into the walls and partitions throughout the square released beams of fire that raked the trespassers. Creepers appeared from unseen hatches and rushed to attack the company. Partitions rose and fell to create traps for those caught out on the square. The people who had created Castledown were long dead, but the machine they'd built to ward it, the thing called Antrax, was still functional—and very deadly.

Most scholars believe that the machine-mind, Antrax, was not intended to be harmful. Built during the decade before the Great Wars broke out, Antrax was originally designed as a receptacle to protect human knowledge. Its creators wanted to be certain that the knowledge built up over the ages could be preserved, even if humans themselves could not.

The city may once have been an industrial complex. Those who built the machine-mind used the complex both as a place to work and as a decoy to pull unwanted attention away from the true nature of their project. They appeared to be designing machinery—possibly for military use—while they were actually constructing the underground storage complex.

It took many years, and many lives, to complete the project. The complex, once finished, extended a mile beneath the surface and more than five miles in every direction. All the corridors contained surveillance eyes and sensors to ensure complete security. The machine-mind itself was formed of many separate components linked together over the vast site. The information was stored as recorded energy, possibly within crystals, and was cycled constantly.

When the builders' worst fears were realized and the Great Wars ravaged the world, the machine-mind remained safe, unaware in its subterranean domain, keeping its treasure in trust for those who would one day come to claim it. At this time, it knew nothing of the weapons that had been secretly installed in the complex. It did not yet have control over them or any reason to use such things.

There are indications that, shortly after the Great Wars ended, one of the creators, a lone survivor, returned to the complex. He had the codes and used them to change the directives governing the machine-mind. He told it of the war and of the end of the world. Then he told it of the weapons and directed it to use any means necessary to survive and protect

the data within its banks—to kill anyone or anything that trespassed without the proper codes. The machine was directed to expand and develop in whatever way was needed to guarantee the safety of itself and its data. It is probable that any previous instructions for the method and time of releasing the data to the heirs of humanity were lost when the new directives were installed. So far as the machine-mind knew, no one could be allowed access to the protected knowledge. Ever.

While the machine-mind was created by Men, it used technology we no longer understand. It could think and plan. It learned how to fight and how to grow, expanding itself into new areas and building new weapons to fulfill its directive. It had access to all the knowledge Men had amassed, and could use that knowledge to build whatever it needed. When creatures and humans appeared again and started exploring the ruins, it first fought them with the weapons it had been given, then used its store of knowledge to create better weapons.

The people continued to come, sometimes even finding ways underground. So it continued to kill. The people, a primitive tribe that called themselves the Rindge, named it Antrax or, in their language, Demon Machine. It adopted the name, never knowing the meaning. Despite the defenses, the Rindge continued to explore the city, learning to avoid the defenses. Antrax searched for a new weapon that would stop the trespassers. It discovered possibilities from among the legends stored within its banks of knowledge and combined them with technology to create weapons that worked against the intruders.

They called the weapons Wronks. The Wronks drove the intruders away, and they stayed away. But Antrax discovered

Wronks

A grisly combination of living flesh and machinery, Wronks were created by the machine-mind Antrax to defend its domain from human intruders. Antrax made Wronks by capturing living humans and grafting their heads and some of their living tissue onto mechanical components. Many of those captured and made into Wronks were still alive and conscious after the process, trapped within the machinery and under Antrax's complete control. This allowed Wronks to utilize the physical and mental skills of their unwilling living components while enhancing those skills with the durability and strength of hardened steel alloys and built-in weapons.

Wronks were extremely difficult to kill. Those with living heads were protected by an impenetrable transparent shield. Sensor devices and built-in weapons systems made them more than a match for more primitive weapons. Since they were almost impossible to kill in a direct confrontation, the Rindge developed a system of pitfalls in which they trapped and either buried or dismantled the Wronks. Once buried deep enough, the machinery often lost contact with Antrax and ceased to function. Without support from the machinery, the human components eventually died.

The most terrible of these Wronks was also the last. Built from Ard Patrinell, former Captain of the Home Guard, the Wronk had all the Elf's battle skill and tactical knowledge. He destroyed an entire Rindge village before he was finally brought to bay and killed. It took the combined skills of Quentin Leah and the Elven Tracker Tamis to finally bring him down. Tamis, once Ard Patrinell's love, sacrificed her life to end his threat—and his torment.

that Wronks were valuable tools—more versatile than any made out of machinery alone. It wanted more. It began to hunt the people to make more Wronks.

Over the centuries, Antrax's solar power cells started to fail. To fulfill its directive, then, it had to find a new source of power. It created probes and sent them out into the vastness of the world. Through the messages relayed back from these probes, Antrax discovered a faraway source of energy: magic, and the people who wielded it as if it was a part of them.

Antrax had become far more than a mere machine. Probes and sensors extended its domain by feeding back data from anywhere in the world. It could even send out energy that was interpreted as a seer's dream to lure the magic users to its lair.

To ensure that only those it needed would find it, the machine-mind used its probes to set up a testing ground on the islands between itself and its prey, making use of the natural dangers that inhabited the islands. Any who had the use of the new power could pass the tests.

Kael Elessedil used the Elfstones to prevail over the dangers and horrors of the islands on his voyage to Parkasia, only to see his men killed and himself captured upon arrival at Castledown. Antrax found a way to use its living captive and his stones as a power source. For thirty years the Elven Prince lived a nightmare as his mind was manipulated and his body drained. For thirty years Antrax grew larger and stronger on the magic of the Elfstones.

But such hard use took a heavy toll.

The Phoenix Stone

Gifted to Bek Ohmsford by the King of the Silver River, the Phoenix Stone contained Faerie magic that could be used but once. In the hands of the King of the Silver River, the Phoenix Stone appeared as a strange silver-colored stone on a chain. It had a translucent surface that revealed a swirling liquid center. Once Bek touched the stone, the movement stopped and the surface became opaque. The only indication that the stone was other than ordinary was the slight warmth it radiated.

The King of the Silver River told Bek, "When you are most lost, it will help you find your way. Not just from what you cannot see with your eyes, but from what you cannot find with your heart as well. It will show you the way back from dark places into which you have strayed and the way forward through dark places into which you must go. In your body, heart, and mind—all will be revealed with this."

But Bek gifted the stone to Ahren Elessedil, who took his words to heart. In a time of great need, the Elven Prince cast the stone on the ground and shattered it. He discovered that the stone not only guided its holders where they needed to go, but also provided a magic fog that hid them from their pursuers.

The stone, dead after one use, was named for its ability to help users find what they needed to become whole or "reborn."

Kael began to fail. To survive, Antrax had to find someone else to release the magic. It sent the broken Elf back home—with a map as bait to snare another who could wield the stones.

When Walker's expedition arrived, it contained much more potential than the machine expected. Not only did Walker bring with him one who could wield the stones—Ahren Elessedil—but he brought his own Druid magic as well as that of others: Quentin Leah and the Sword of Leah, and Bek Ohmsford and the wishsong.

Antrax captured the Druid, invading his mind and siphoning the magic from him much as it had from the Elven Prince. But the machine-mind sensed additional magic: enough to fuel itself for hundreds of years.

Yet the courage and strength of the party thwarted the machine. They joined with the indigenous people to fight its Wronks and creepers. Two of them, the Elven Prince Ahren Elessedil and the seer Ryer Ord Star, even found a way to invade Antrax's inner complexes undetected, by using the Phoenix Stone to guide them and mask their passage.

Ahren and Ryer found Walker and helped him get free of the machine. Ahren managed to use the failing remnants of the Phoenix Stone to help him find and retrieve the Elfstones, barely avoiding being trapped as Kael had been years before. Ahren and Walker used their magic to wreak havoc on the heart of the machine, engaging in a pitched battle with the creepers and fire lances that protected Antrax, but the defenses of the ancient machine were too strong. Walker was forced to use his magic to overload its interior power intake, frying the machine-mind and all access to the knowledge it protected. The backlash from that attack fatally wounded Walker. The dying Druid was found by his friends Bek and Truls

Doors to the Netherworld

Walker Boh died in the land of Parkasia from wounds sustained battling the machine-mind called Antrax. Traditionally, when Druids die or lie near death, they are taken to the Hadeshorn so that they may be carried into the netherworld. But such portals are not limited to the waters of the Hadeshorn. Many Druids believe that most of the waters of the world form a channeling medium to the netherworld. Still lakes and hidden waters are the most powerful channels, with the magical water of the Hadeshorn strongest of all, but all water will channel to a certain degree. Any quiet lake or still pond can serve as a conduit between the living and the dead.

When their time is near, Druids can feel a connection to the nearest portal to the afterlife. They are drawn to the water, where they will be greeted by the Druids who have gone before them. Once they have gone into the waters, Druids have been known to reappear from other waters to those they knew in life, but such visitations are limited to a short march of days following death. After that, only the Hadeshorn itself remains open to the shades that have passed, and even then they can appear only if properly summoned.

Rohk, who carried him to a special lake, hidden in an ancient cavern far underground. There he was embraced by the shade of Allanon and carried into the lake to the afterlife. Walker's shade has since appeared many times at the Hadeshorn.

Soon after Antrax was destroyed, the weather began to change. Storms racked the entire region as the climate seesawed after being artificially controlled for centuries by the machine-mind. Those storms raged on and off for several months, lashing the southern peninsula of Parkasia until the climate found balance again. As it must have been thousands of years ago before Man used technology to alter it, the unforgiving climate of Ice Henge gathered the lands south of the mountains into its frigid embrace.

Now the ruins of the metal city are blanketed in frost. With Antrax dead, the portals to the underground heart of the city lie blasted open. The battle-scarred corridors of Castledown are empty, save for the shattered ruins of creepers and debris of its lost glory. In the central power

Ryer Ord Star, seer and empath.

Ryer Ord Star

Born with the combined ability to be both seer and empath, Ryer Ord Star was desperate to understand the gifts that haunted her. She became apprentice to the Addershag, the renowned seer of Grimpen Ward, in an attempt to learn how to use her gifts: the sight, which showed her the future, and empathy, which allowed her to ease pain. The Addershag had no use for anything but the sight, and eventually threw Ryer out because she could not rid herself of her empathic nature.

She was soon recruited by the Ilse Witch to be her spy on the Jerle Shannara. Ryer agreed, but found herself drawn to Walker Boh and his company. After using her empathy to save the Druid once, Ryer was linked to him, a link that allowed him to see her heart and her betrayal. But he accepted her nevertheless.

The relationship changed Ryer. She openly shared her visions with the Druid and tried to save him when he faced Antrax, even braving the depths of Castledown with Ahren Elessedil to reach the Druid and free him from the Antrax machinery. Without her help, Walker could not have destroyed the monster machine. But Ryer could not save him from his wounds.

Later, Ryer and the Elven Prince were captured by the Morgawr. In an attempt to buy time for Grianne and Bek's escape and to keep the Prince alive, Ryer continued to play the part of the dutiful seer and spy, misleading the Morgawr with her visions and hiding the Elfstones. Once the time was right, the young seer helped Ahren escape his captivity, even though she knew it would cost her her life.

The Morgawr tortured her brutally for her betrayal, but before he could feast on her soul, she found release, dying as a hero.

chamber, the vast twin pillars that were the heart of Antrax stand cracked and burned. The storage units no longer hum their song of ancient knowledge, the extraction chambers are empty save for slagged metal, and the extraction ports throughout the chamber are burned. All the lights have gone out save the strange flameless lamps. The secrets of the Old World, the prize for two intrepid teams of explorers, lie forever beyond reach, either destroyed in the final overload or frozen into the machinery itself.

Land of the Rindge

The *Jerle Shannara* expedition discovered a Race of primitive humans living on the Parkasian peninsula. Calling themselves the Rindge, they, too, are descendants of humans mutated during the aftermath of the Great Wars—though for them the beginning of time dates from the Great Wars, as if there had never been an Old World. Any history or memories of who they might have been before are lost.

Mutations generated during the wars have given the Rindge distinctive reddish copper skin, curly red hair, cinnamon-colored eyes, and burnished teeth. They speak an ancient dialect that most closely resembles a variation on the Dwarfish tongue.

An aboriginal hunter-gatherer society, the Rindge are tribal in nature and have developed a hierarchy of high chiefs and sub-chiefs to oversee their villages and tribes. Though they tend to live in relatively small village groupings of less than a thousand, their numbers are spread throughout Parkasia and the continent beyond. Each village is part of a larger tribal group, usually made up of two to five villages. Each tribe is fairly self-sufficient, though different tribal groups specialize in different skills. Some tribes are primarily hunters, while others specialize in farming. Craftsmen of various types are scattered throughout the tribes. Each tribe has its own territory and trades with others only when necessary for goods and services they cannot produce.

Quentin Leah wields the magic Sword of Leah.

Most Rindge villages are constructed of easily available materials such as wood, mud, and bark, with the buildings—often open-air huts—spread out to make use of the natural contours of the terrain. Rooms are divided with hanging blankets or reed screens. Most villages have no defensive walls or moats; the natives prefer to use an elaborate warning system and a network of hidden traps and snares. If danger threatens, rather than fight an enemy that cannot be easily stopped, the whole village escapes to protective terrain while their warriors defend the escape route.

Each village has a medicine man or woman who makes use of local plants and roots as rudimentary cures. These people are rarely gifted healers. Serious wounds sustained on the hunt or in battle are usually fatal, which probably accounts for the natives' low population density.

Rindge tend to prefer temperate climates, usually wearing sleeveless tunics, short pants, and sandals strapped on with long laces that tie up to the knee. Hunters wear leather wrist guards and carry a variety of weapons, including spears, javelins, six-foot-long blowguns, and knives. The blowguns are their favorite weapon. Most warriors and hunters have the ability to blend almost completely into their surroundings, allowing them to get close to their prey or evade a predator. Occasionally, tribes war against each other, but before Walker destroyed Antrax, it and its creeper and Wronk minions were their greatest enemy.

While Antrax still functioned, it sent out creepers to prey on the Rindge, capturing them to use as spare parts for Wronks. The Rindge are a very superstitious people, and the power of the machine led many tribes to believe that it was a god. According to some of the Rindge legends, Antrax created humans. Many viewed its continued attacks as a sign that their god was taking them back because he was disappointed in them. These tribes often paid tribute to win the god's favor; some even delivered human sacrifices to the Wronks that had once been part of their tribe. The storms that followed the destruction of Antrax were seen as proof of their god's anger, driving them from their homes.

Other tribes believed Antrax was a demon. They hunted down its creepers and Wronks, trapping them in deep pits with sharp rocks embedded in the bottom. If they managed to trap a creeper or Wronk, they destroyed it using razor-tipped arrows to pierce the metal while prying its joints apart with spear hafts.

Perhaps as a result of their battles with the creepers and Wronks, the Rindge developed unusually sophisticated fighting techniques, especially for a tribal people. They fought in units designated by weaponry, with heavy spears usually at the fore and javelins and blowguns to the rear. This arrangement was maintained even during travel, with each small group kept intact as a unit, prepared to face ambush or an unexpected encounter. Scouts were used to patrol both front and rear.

But such battle formations could not always protect the Rindge from Wronks. The last of the Wronks destroyed an entire village and most of its defenders before it was hunted down and killed by Quentin Leah and the Elven Tracker Tamis.

The storms that followed the destruction of Antrax forced the southern tribes to migrate north, finding a new home on the other side of the Aleuthra Ark range.

The Aleuthra Ark Mountain Range

The Parkasian peninsula is divided by a towering mountain range, the Aleuthra Ark, which extends down the interior from northwest to southeast like a jagged spine. This rugged series of towering peaks, deep canyons, and wide valleys extends for several hundred square miles across the heart of the peninsula before smoothing out into broad grasslands in the northeast. The tallest of these peaks rise more than six thousand feet above sea level. While conifers, mostly cedar and spruce, grow on the lower reaches of the mountains, the peaks are bare. Most stand shrouded in snow, their rocky heights swept clean by the vicious northern winds. Shrikes and hawks make their nests on ledges along the steep cliff walls, but little else can survive the wind and cold.

The lower forested elevations are more hospitable, providing a habitat for all manner of forest creatures such as the Parkasian wolf and several varieties of rabbit and deer. But there are areas within the forests of the southern mountains where, as in the Wolfsktaag, ancient magic and residuals of the Great Wars have pooled. These areas are home to shape-shifters and other creatures more of spirit and old magic than of flesh. The Rindge tribesmen avoid these areas of wilderness, for they have learned that the shape-shifters value their solitude and do not appreciate trespassers in their domain.

The entire range is cut by numerous valleys, carved out over thousands of years by rivers wearing through the rock on their way from the heights down to the sea. Many of these valleys are so deep and wide that rain forests have grown up in their humid depths. The largest and old-

Shape-Shifters

Shape-shifters are as much creatures of spirit as they are of flesh and bone. Born of Faerie magic, they can shape themselves to appear as anything—or as nothing at all. Some believe that their magic allows them to live on a plane slightly outside that of mortal senses. They are creatures of spirit energy and seem to be able to form that energy into any mold needed.

Preferring isolated wilderness areas, shape-shifters live in communal groups. There are strong indications that they can communicate with one another almost mind-to-mind, using a natural connection that binds all shape-shifters within a region. Those few who have chosen to show themselves to humans appeared either as large, powerful creatures only vaguely human in shape, or as formless specters resembling shades of the dead more than anything alive. If a shape-shifter decides to hide, nothing living can find it.

est of these valleys, nestled between the northern edge of the range and its heart, is called the Crake. Formed from the action of several large, slow streams, the Crake contains a dense, steamy rain forest cut off from the rest of the world by the mountains that encircle it. A thick canopy of jungle trees and vines covers most of the valley, obscuring the sunlight and limiting the plant growth on the valley floor.

Unlike the barren mountains above, life within the Crake is abundant. Ferns of all types, sizes, and colors grow in thick profusion. All manner of insects from foot-long slugs to brilliantly colored butterflies feed on the plants, while brightly plumed birds feed on the insects and various animals feed on both.

Perhaps because of the relative isolation, within valleys like the Crake live creatures that exist nowhere else on the peninsula. The largest and most dangerous of these is the lizard-like creature natives call the Graak, which can grow to a height of over fifteen feet at the shoulder. Resembling a cross between a dragon and a lizard, the Graak is carnivorous and dominates the food chain of the jungle. Equipped with huge jaws of needle-sharp teeth, thick, crusted skin, and clusters of

horns on its head and spine, it is a formidable predator. Its slick, mottled skin provides perfect camouflage for the shadowed depths of the rain forest, allowing it to blend seamlessly into its surroundings.

Despite relatively short, stubby legs, the quadruped Graak is capable of speeds in excess of that of a fast horse, even through dense jungle terrain. Once prey is cornered, powerful leg muscles and huge talons allow the Graak to lift onto its hind legs while slashing its prey with its forelimbs, though it usually prefers to grab smaller prey in its jaws, crushing them until it can suck the meat and fluids from their bones.

Graaks usually mate for life, but lay eggs only once or twice a decade, raising their young until they are old enough to fend for themselves. Once they reach adulthood, younger Graak usually leave to find their own mates and territories.

These great dragons were once the most feared predator in the region, but a new danger was unleashed by the Morgawr. Determined to capture Grianne Ohmsford and gain the magic of Antrax, the Morgawr used his dark magic to create cauls to hunt his human prey.

Cauls are natural creatures that have

The Morgawr, Dark Power of Deceit

Mentor to the Ilse Witch, the Morgawr was a power-hungry warlock who used his dark magic for control and manipulation. Claiming to be related to the witch sisters of the Wilderun, the Morgawr more closely resembled a Mwellret and was most comfortable with them. While he had the ability to shape-change at will, his natural appearance was that of a large, scaled, reptilian humanoid.

The Morgawr, hungry for power, preferred to work in secret. He was responsible for kidnapping and subverting young Grianne Ohmsford, turning her into the Ilse Witch and manipulating her magic for his own purposes. He also arranged the rise of Sen Dunsidan to the position of Federation Prime Minister by murdering his rivals. He was the first magic user known to create cauls, an abomination of nature and magic, though he taught that skill to the Ilse Witch. Mwellrets served him willingly, but he controlled his human slaves by devouring their minds and souls, creating a force of mindless, walking dead.

The Morgawr was killed by the spirit of the keep on the island of Mephitic after a pitched battle with his former student, Grianne Ohmsford.

The Morgawr.

been forcibly transformed by magic into ferocious, magic-enhanced predators. The first caul in Parkasia was created by the Ilse Witch, who transformed a wolf into a Jachyra. Once she was no longer in a position to control it, it continued to mutate until it became much larger and developed poisonous venom. That caul went mad and tried to turn on its creator, only to be killed by Truls Rohk. While predatory animals are usually preferred as the basis for cauls because of their sharp natural instincts, the Morgawr used human prisoners, creating fearsome killers with monstrous wolf-like bodies and human cunning.

Once transformed, a caul retains the memory of its past life as well as the horrendous pain of the transformation. They are forever linked to their creator, but can be controlled only so long as that creator maintains the binding magic. Released from control, the caul will usually attempt to turn on its creator. Left on their own, cauls often continue to mutate, slowly going mad from the pain and the horror.

Some cauls remained when the Morgawr left Parkasia. Only time will show what damage they will do as they mutate and lose their minds.

The *Jerle Shannara* never penetrated beyond the Aleuthra Ark range, though its crew made tantalizing discoveries that hint of a broad new land beyond those so far discovered. One of the brave voyagers, the Dwarf Panax, remained behind to travel with the Rindge into the northern grasslands, choosing a life in the unknown wilds of Parkasia over the one he left behind. Perhaps in time, others may follow in his footsteps.

The Druids of the New Order

If the Four Lands are to find peace, we as Druids must help them find the way. —Walker Boh

ruids have always been a part of the Four Lands, but the Druid order disappeared almost entirely during the years of the Second Druid Order. After the Shadowen Wars, the Druids became more myth and legend than reality. Once the Shadowen were defeated, Walker Boh, the last of the Druids and sole living representative of the order, retired to Paranor and disappeared within the great keep's imposing walls. For many years, Paranor remained silent. Walker and the Druids faded into myth. Paranor and its treasures were all but forgotten until Walker suddenly emerged, decades after he had withdrawn, with no sign that time had touched him. He had been born well over one hundred years before, but appeared to be only half that age. To most of the people of the Four Lands, his return was a miracle wrought by Druid sorcery. Those aware of the Druid arts knew that he had emerged from the Druid Sleep.

The Rise and Fall of the Third Druid Order

Walker spent the next thirty years in desperate pursuit of his lifelong goal: rebuilding the Druid Council. But he had no interest in simply re-creating councils of the past. Walker envisioned the new Druid Council as a body made up of members of each Race but completely independent of all nations. A council of adepts would work to unlock the secrets of life's most difficult and challenging problems, while striving to improve the lives of all the peoples of the Four Lands. Unfortunately, the governments of the lands were caught in a precarious balance of power, and none of them was willing to relinquish power or autonomy to Druids. Walker's long absence from the lands meant that people had forgotten all he had done. The fear and distrust of the era had, in turn, given them reason to fear anything they did not understand, especially the magic commanded by a Druid. Even the Elves, traditional friends of the Druids, feared a strong and independent Druid Council. Queen Aine Elessedil fervently opposed the formation of Walker's council. Her successor, Allardon Elessedil, though more sympathetic to Walker, supported his mother's choices.

Faced with failure at every turn, Walker became desperate. He wrote in his journal, "If the Four Lands are to be united in peace, the magic must be controlled by a Druid Council that is answerable to no single government or people, but rather to all. If I cannot find a way to convince at least one of the nations to back my Druid Council, I will be the last of the Druids for all time."

The tide suddenly appeared to turn when a Wing Rider found the lost Elven Prince, Kael, and a map, which the Elf King Allardon was forced to ask the Druid to decipher. Walker used his skills to translate it, recognizing his chance to trade his services for the backing of the Elven King. He knew the Elves would be hungry for the magic promised by the ancient parchment.

He was not disappointed. In a private meeting held in the Gardens of Life, in the Elven capital of Arborlon, Allardon renounced his opposition to the Druid Council and promised the support and blessing of the Elves. Walker agreed to spearhead an expedition to seek out the answers promised by the mysterious map. The agreement was predicated on Walker's return from the expedition with the promised magic and the lost Elf-stones. All spoils were to be shared fully between Elves and Druids, but Walker insisted that the Elves would share only in magics they were able to use and understand. Anything beyond their understanding would be controlled by the Druids. Since all known magic had originated with the Elves in the time of Faerie, Allardon agreed.

Moments after the conclusion of that historic agreement, assassins attacked the Elven King and the Druid. Walker was able to deflect and neutralize the assassins, but was unable to save Allardon from his own guards. An arrow fired at the assassins by a member of the Home Guard caught the King in the chest. He lived only long enough to ensure that the agreement was properly inscribed and witnessed. Walker was to lead the expedition. If and when it returned, the Elves were bound to support the formation of a new Druid Council.

Walker Boh did not survive to see this become reality. After living more than 150 years, he died an ocean away from his home in Paranor without fulfilling his dream. But before his death, he managed to pass along the Druid legacy. In much the same way that Allanon had passed it to Brin Ohmsford, Walker used his last moments to pass his calling to Grianne

Grianne Ohmsford, From Villain to Hero

Born with the Ohmsford wishsong and raised with dark magic, Grianne Ohmsford spent most of her life in a battle between good and evil. The daughter of Araden and Biornlief Ohmsford, she was orphaned at an early age and taken in by the Morgawr. This dark creature encouraged her to believe that the Druid Walker Boh was responsible for her family's murder, and used her thirst for vengeance to shape her for his purpose.

Under the Morgawr's training, Grianne became one of the most feared creatures in the Four Lands, and was known as the Ilse Witch or "Singing Witch." All compassion died in her when her family died, killed in part by her self-loathing at her failure to save even her young brother, Bek. As the Ilse Witch, she manipulated and killed to further the Morgawr's plans for domination of the Four Lands. Many believe the Ilse Witch was responsible for the attack on the Elf King Allardon Elessedil. Her own magic, enhanced by the sorcery she learned from the Morgawr, made her almost invincible. Many officials throughout the land owed their positions of power to her dark gifts.

As she approached adulthood, she became determined to free herself of the Morgawr. Now that she was no longer a willing tool, he, in turn, plotted against her. In an effort to rid herself of him and gain power, she followed the Druid Walker on his quest across the Blue Divide, determined to gain the treasure for herself.

But she returned from that voyage a different person. During the expedition, Grianne was forced to face her brother, Bek, and a powerful truth through the magic of the Sword of Shannara. The exposure to the combination of Walker's last charge and the magic of the sword of truth drove Grianne into catatonia as she struggled to accept the horrors of her life. Only the love of her brother brought her back.

When she finally returned to herself, she had changed, desperate to atone for her dark deeds. Her first act of contrition was also an act of revenge. She helped destroy the Morgawr—the creature responsible for her seduction to the dark.

On her return to the Four Lands, she took up the mantle of the Druids, as Walker Boh had demanded, becoming Ard Rhys of the Third Druid Council. During her tenure she rebuilt the Druid order, became the first human to set foot in the Forbidding, and eventually managed to negotiate an end to the Federation–Free-born war.

She was shaped by the Morgawr's darkness into the Ilse Witch, and by Walker Boh's need into the Ard Rhys, but in the end she shaped herself to make her own destiny.

The Rightful Ard Rhys, Grianne Ohmsford, returns home to face her enemies.

Ohmsford. Such a choice would have seemed quite appropriate, given her wish-song magic, except for the fact that she had spent her youth as one of the most feared creatures of the Four Lands: the Ilse Witch.

Grianne Ohmsford was a powerful sorceress, heir to the Ohmsford magic and trained by the Morgawr. With the magic of the Sword of Shannara and the support of her brother, Bek, Grianne managed to overcome the darker part of herself during the long, arduous voyage back to Arborlon. After her return, Grianne visited the Hadeshorn, where she was reported to have consulted with Walker Boh's spirit. Days later, she took her place as Walker's chosen heir.

The Druid calling must be taken up voluntarily. Walker may have chosen Grianne, but she did not have to answer that call. Most believe that she chose her path in search of redemption for her life as the Ilse Witch. She had been one of the most notorious forces for evil, and Walker had offered her a chance to become an equally powerful force for good.

But Walker's goal, and now Grianne's, was the creation of a new Druid order, which could not be formed without support from the Elves. Since the original treaty authorizing the expedition specified Walker's safe return, Ahren Elessedil, one of the survivors of the expedition, neglected to inform his brother, King Kylen, of Walker's death. By reporting only on the successful events, Ahren used Walker's treaty with the Elves to force Kylen to support the formation of a new Druid Council. King Kylen grudgingly sent twenty candidates with Ahren to join the Druids. Later, when Kylen discovered the deceit, he banished Ahren from Arborlon.

As Walker had known, where the Elves led, the other Races followed. With the Elves as examples, Grianne soon had talented candidates from throughout the lands at her doorstep. She gathered them together to form the Third Druid Council, and was named Ard Rhys, High Druid, over them. Walker's dream of a multinational, multiracial council had come to pass. Grianne's stated goals for the Third Druid Council were to help the Races become strong, independent, and peaceful neighbors, put an end to the war between the Free-born and the Federation, and reintroduce a mix of science and magic into the world for the betterment of all men and women.

Unfortunately, Grianne was not Walker. She led the Council for twenty years but never really managed to attain lasting success with any of its goals. She brought Paranor back to life and filled its halls with Druids, but was constantly thwarted in her attempts to bring peace or prosperity to the Four Lands. Few could forget or forgive her past life as the Ilse Witch. Many of the governments did not trust an order of Druids that was led by the Ilse Witch.

Kylen, discovering that he had been tricked, tried to recall the Elves he had sent, then, failing that, turned the Elves against the Druid order. Sen Dunsidan of the Federation remembered Grianne's years as the Ilse Witch, whom he had betrayed, and refused to trust her change. With both men determined to rebuff Grianne's attempts to broker peace, the war on the Prekkendorran continued to rage. The Ard Rhys refused to give up, working for years to convince both men to accept compromise and consider peace. Just when it seemed she had finally convinced Kylen to consider a truce, he was killed on the Prekkendorran and the blame for his death was laid at Grianne's feet. His son and heir, Kellen Elessedil, blamed

Tagwen the Dwarf

The Third Druid Council brought life to Paranor, filling the ancient keep with Druids, apprentices, and scholars once again. But a fortress the size of Paranor required a large staff to serve all those within its walls. Chief among the mass of unsung workers was the Dwarf Tagwen, assistant to the Ard Rhys. Though he had no interest in Druid lore or magic, Tagwen knew most of the secrets of Paranor. Grianne Ohmsford chose the officious Dwarf to serve as her personal assistant soon after her return from Parkasia. He stood by her side and helped her rebuild the Druid order from nothing. He often wrote of his job that he wanted nothing more in life than to make the Ard Rhys comfortable, taking over whatever menial tasks might allow her to do her work more comfortably. He was her invisible right hand, content to be ignored by most as long as he could remain close to Grianne. Friends believe that he loved her but was content to do so in silence, not wishing to inflict his true feelings on her.

But the administrator Dwarf was forced to become a hero, despite his lack of ambition or magic. In order to save the Ard Rhys and the Druid order he served, he had to abandon both and go out into the world to find help.

On his quest, Tagwen fought battles, suffered wounds, met the mystical King of the Silver River, and saw more of the world than he had ever intended. He was instrumental in returning Grianne Ohmsford to her position in Paranor, and he stood by her side until she left that post.

Tagwen continued to serve the Fourth Druid Order for many years. Though he insisted he was only an administrator, the leaders of the order relied on him for his invaluable knowledge and wisdom.

Tagwen the Dwarf, reluctant hero.

Grianne and the Druids for his father's death, and therefore refused to consider any negotiations involving the Ard Rhys or the Druids.

Over time, the distrust seeped into the heart of Paranor itself. Many within the order sought to have Grianne removed, though it is doubtful that all had the well-being of the order at heart. Kylen's death may have been the catalyst that brought matters to a head. Young Kellen's rebuff marked one more major failure of Druid leadership in the minds of many within the order. It is almost certain that Grianne was aware of the internal discontent. There were rumors that she was being counseled to disband the order in an attempt to start over.

The conflict came to a head one dark night when a renegade band of Druids led

Liquid Night

Spells and potions have always been a part of Druid lore. One of the most dangerous potions ever used by a Druid originated not from Druid Histories but from the demonic dimension of the Forbidding. The potion was named for its appearance, that of an indeterminate black substance with a texture similar to chalk. Appearing to be the essence of a pitch-dark night caught in a small glass bottle, it had a nonreflective surface that absorbed even the brightest lights. It was effective against the most powerful or adept victim.

Despite its potency, liquid night did not kill its victim outright. Instead, the victim's body, as well as all traces of any magic, was transported through a portal to the Forbidding. Once liquid night came in contact with living victims, it wrapped them in its impenetrable darkness and sucked them out of existence in this world. Grianne Ohmsford, the only known survivor, wrote of the experience:

"I felt as if the room was moving—or that I was moving in it. An unnamable blackness consumed me. I tried to get free, but I could not move or even cry out. The clinging blackness enveloped me like a shroud, slowly tightening. Then I felt it inside my mouth, my nose, and my ears. It penetrated my body and mind until there was nothing left but its black nothingness. And then there was nothing at all as I lost consciousness."

Of course, banishment to the Forbidding was considered a death sentence to any but a demon. When first used, it was believed that the portal created by the potion was a one-way, onetime creation. In fact, the portal worked both ways, replacing the victim with a demon from the Forbidding. While it was initially believed that the portal dissolved completely after the spell was completed, it was later discovered that it remained in place, though closed. The darkwand, an equally strong magical talisman from this world, could reopen it and allow one person passage in and out. The darkwand was the only known antidote for the banishment of liquid night.

The potion was most effective when supplemented with common support spells. Until it was used, it was as dangerous to its handler as to the intended victim. Even a single drop could cause serious harm. Once used, the glass bottle had to be destroyed on the chance that some tiny dregs might remain. Because of this volatility, it was necessary to use spells to create a magic funnel to convey liquid night to the victim while standing behind a closed, locked, and warded door. The potion, once loosed, spread out and was even seen creeping out from cracks under the doors as if searching for another victim.

The only known sample of liquid night was created by demons within the Forbidding. It worked perfectly, leaving no body, no evidence of foul play, and no remnants.

by Shadea a'Ru managed to eliminate the Ard Rhys by using a potion, known only as "liquid night," to send her into the Forbidding. To all outside the group, it appeared that Grianne had simply disappeared from her bed sometime in the night. In the confusion that followed Grianne's disappearance, Shadea a'Ru became a bulwark of strength to the order. She immediately cast suspicion upon the Rock Trolls charged with guarding the Ard Rhys, feeding existing fears and doubts that had lain dormant, but not dead, since the Warlock Wars. Grianne's choice of Rock Trolls instead of Elves as sentries had gone against the tradition set back in the time of Galaphile and the First Druid Council. Before Shadea could use that fact to fan suspicions into a flame of hatred, the Rock Trolls left Paranor. Shadea was named as acting Ard Rhys by a majority of the Druid Council and took over its leadership.

Shadea immediately embraced her new position, making it clear that only the highest standards of performance would be tolerated under her administration. Within days of her appointment, she brought in Gnome Hunters to replace the missing Troll sentries and dismissed two of the younger Druids without any explanation of their failings. Even Grianne Ohmsford had never dismissed anyone without giving him or her both a rationale and a chance for redemption. She also pressured the Council to break with its former position of neutrality to form an alliance with the Federation. The Council resisted, due largely to Gerand Cera, an influential Druid who opposed any action that would bring the Council into opposition with the Elves. Secretly, Shadea also sent out an expedition to capture or kill Grianne's surviving family.

With such tactics, it was not long before the new Ard Rhys found herself facing the same problems of distrust from within and lack of respect from without that had plagued her predecessor. The only external ally willing to stand with her was Sen Dunsidan, Prime Minister of the Federation. But he would support Shadea only so long as she could deliver Druid backing for the Coalition against the Free-born in the Prekkendorran war, or at least guarantee that the Druids would take no action against any move the Federation might make. As Shadea continued to press for consensus from the Council, more Druids were dismissed and several disappeared outright, creating a climate of unease and distrust among the Druids.

Facing the erosion of her support, Shadea surprised the Council by taking Gerand Cera, her chief opposition, as her consort. Their union soon gave her control over his followers and assured her dominance in the Council. The union, while effective, was short-lived. Gerand Cera was discovered dead in Shadea's bed less than a week later. There were no obvious signs of foul play, and no formal accusations were ever made, but most within the order believed that Shadea disposed of him just before leaving to solidify her alliance with the Coalition.

The veiled threat of Shadea's power and the promise of the formal alliance with the Federation solidified most of the council behind Shadea's leadership, though for many it was a loyalty founded more on fear than on respect.

A small group of Druids opposed Shadea and what they viewed as her usurpation of the Druid order. When Shadea's minions managed to capture Grianne's brother, Bek, and his family, these few Druids, led by Trefen Morys and Bellizen, worked to free them. Before they could act, Penderrin Ohmsford, Bek's son, disappeared from the room in which he had been imprisoned. Khyber Elessedil, a young Druid and a member of the Elven royal family, had been captured along with Penderrin. When Penderrin disappeared, leaving only the young woman behind, Shadea tortured the young Elf before ordering her execution. Khyber managed to escape the Gnomes sent to kill her and join with the Ohmsfords and their rescuers. Together they hoped to find a way to aid Grianne and Pen, who had gone to retrieve her, if they managed to return from the Forbidding.

Triagenel, the Net of Magic

Creation of a triagenel, or "Druid net," is considered the ultimate test of Druid skill and teamwork. A triagenel requires the perfect combination of three magics from separate sources. Once these threads of power are interwoven and anchored in place, they create a green, glowing net of pure magic capable of containing and neutralizing even the most powerful magic wielder.

The triagenel is triggered by the flesh and blood of a living presence. Once a living being enters an area protected by a triagenel, its presence triggers the collapse of the net onto the intruder, rendering him or her incapable of movement. Triagenels are not usually triggered by magic, resulting in at least one case in which magic was used to weaken the triagenel before it went off to allow its victims a chance at escape. But the merest brush of a fingertip by a living person will release the inescapable trap.

Once caught in it, no one has ever escaped an undamaged triagenel. Only its creators can undo it or release its prey. But despite its strength, a triagenel has only a limited life span. The same high-energy magics that give it its strength and sensitivity will cause it to become unstable and collapse in only a few days, depending on the strength and skill of the builders.

While every student of magic learns about triagenels, there are few with the skill necessary to build one. The difficulty is compounded by the fact that the formation requires not just one skilled adept but three, each of equally advanced abilities, able to work together to form a balanced construct. No one outside of the Druids has ever succeeded in constructing a triagenel. According to the Druid law of the Third Druid Order, even Druids were forbidden from attempting to construct a triagenel without the authorization and supervision of the Ard Rhys. Such attempts were allowed only to prove that a Druid had managed to reach a high level of proficiency and was capable of combining talents with others of similar skills and aspirations.

Shadea and her allies, fearing that the banished Ard Rhys might find a way back from her prison, used Druid magic to create a great construct, known as a triagenel, and set it in place in the High Druid's sleeping chambers to capture Grianne. But within the walls of Paranor, cracks began to show in Shadea's order. Bek Ohmsford used his wishsong magic to sabotage the triagenel while Rue, Khyber, and the Druids loyal to Grianne hid in the secret passages and worked with the Troll Kermadec to undo Shadea's plans.

Shadea's short reign as Ard Rhys ended in spectacular fashion on a bright afternoon less than two months after it began. The Rock Trolls, who had left Paranor under suspicion, returned in an army a thousand strong and surrounded the great keep. Before they could attack, an explosion rocked the High Druid's tower. Grianne had returned from the Forbidding.

In moments battle raged within Paranor as Grianne faced Shadea in the High Tower while the Troll army stormed the keep. Though fierce, the battle lasted less than an hour. Shadea died, felled not by magic but by a Troll spear.

Grianne resumed her role as Ard Rhys and took back control of the troubled Druid Council. Days after her return, Sen

Clipps, a Druid Intruder Alert System

Since the years of the First Druid Council, Paranor has been rife with intrigue and plots. Every Druid had secrets to protect, making security a critical issue. But living sentries were inadequate for the task, especially when faced with all the tunnels and secret passageways that honeycomb the keep. To protect themselves, the Druids instead devised security systems using bits of reactive magic that would warn of intruders.

These little bits of reactive magic, called clipps, were especially popular during the years of the Third Druid Council. Once constructed, the clipps were usually embedded in the walls, floor, and ceiling of a passageway or room. If anyone or anything passed into their field of sensitivity, they reacted to the presence, alerting their creator immediately. While they are not nearly as powerful or as difficult to defeat as magic webbing or a triagenel, they are quite effective. It is very difficult to remove, destroy, or disable clipps without setting them off, but it is sometimes possible for a skilled practitioner to mask them, effectively blindfolding them so that they do not sense the presence of an intruder.

Dunsidan died, and a new Prime Minister took over the Coalition Council. Grianne used this change of power as an opportunity to broker peace between the Federation and the Free-born, achieving at last one of the goals that had eluded the Druids for fifty years.

Before the ink dried on the new treaty, Grianne dissolved the Third Druid Order and dismissed those still in service. Officially stepping down as Ard Rhys, she chose three young Druids from among her defenders to succeed her, charging them with the formation of a new order that would be composed of candidates of their choosing.

As Grianne wished, the Fourth Druid Council has no single Ard Rhys, but rather a council of three: Khyber Elessedil, Trefen Morys, and Bellizen.

Shadea a'Ru, Usurper of the Druid order.

Shadea a'Ru and the Renegade Druids of the Third Druid Council

Shadea a'Ru, also known as the Usurper Druid, is best known for having led a coup that deposed the Ard Rhys of the Third Druid Council in a bid for Druid-led domination of the Races. She ruled as acting Ard Rhys for only a few months.

A striking, physically imposing South-lander, Shadea was an orphan. Her mother died giving birth, and her father was killed on the Prekkendorran when she was only eight. Sent to live with relatives, she ran away at the age of ten to live on her own amid the streets and alleys of Dechtera. By the age of fifteen, unusually tall and strong for her age, she survived by doing odd jobs for the soldiers at the Federation barracks. Toughened by her life in the streets, she proved she could protect herself if needed, and in turn earned the respect of the men. Some of them trained her in weaponscraft. By the time she reached twenty-two, she was a skilled fighter, outperforming her instructors and earning a place on the front lines of the war. By twenty-four, she was a highly respected fighter.

But Shadea wanted more. In the Federation–Free-born war, the only certain end for a soldier was death. The following year, she met a crippled man who offered her a chance to explore new horizons. A practitioner of magic, he offered to teach her how to weave spells and mix potions in exchange for companionship. She eagerly took the bargain, proving to be a good student, easily able to grasp the subtle nuances of magic and the skills required to wield it.

A year later, the man died in Shadea's arms. But he had given her a hunger for sorcery and the power it promised. She continued her studies alone, taking breaks only to visit occasionally with her Federation friends. During these visits, she made no attempt to hide her growing dissatisfaction with the Federation and its restrictions. Her outspoken attitude drew unwanted attention from some patriotic toughs, who drugged and attacked her, keeping her for days. She survived using the willpower she had developed while living on the streets, then hunted down her attackers one by one and executed them. Fearing repercussions, she fled the Federation, leaving behind the ashes of her past life to seek a new one. Over time, Shadea's body healed, but her soul never recovered.

She heard about the Third Druid Council, but wanted to be certain of acceptance, so she traveled to Grimpen Ward in the Wilderun. Isolated among the fugitives and castoffs, Shadea worked to perfect her skills and expand her knowledge. Already adept with potions and spells, she expanded her studies to include earth power and the elements. She was particularly fascinated with shades and dead things—especially those that could be made to serve her. Her skills grew stronger and darker as she discovered the power of blood rituals.

Shadea had never been squeamish about killing for survival, the necessities of war, or revenge, but now she discovered and embraced a different sort of killing: ritual sacrifice to unlock magic power. The compassionate part of her soul withered and died as the power seduced her. She knew there were other, safer ways to achieve her goals. But they were too slow and granted too little power. She stopped caring whether her victims were human or animal; all that mattered was the power that was the end result. And she wanted more.

When the beautiful Elven sorceress Iridia Eleri wandered into Grimpen Ward, the two immediately realized they were kindred spirits. Iridia was an outcast herself, half mad with unrequited love for Ahren Elessedil, a man she could never win. She had a burning desire for vengeance. The two women, realizing they were stronger together, formed a friendship based on mutual cravings.

Together they made the journey to Paranor and applied for admission to the Druid order. Grianne, the Ard Rhys, saw only their skill and dedication, never recognizing the madness burning behind their eyes in her own desperation to find suitable candidates. They were accepted into the order and rose quickly in the ranks.

After three years of service, Shadea realized that the Ard Rhys no longer embodied the ruthless strength of the Ilse Witch. She believed the order was doomed to failure so long as the Ard Rhys was unwilling to sacrifice lives to force control over the other Races. Never willing to accept failure, Shadea was maddened to see the order foundering when the solution seemed so simple. She understood what had to be done to force the Races to bow to the Druid order, but the Ard Rhys either couldn't see it or refused to do what was necessary. Either way, she was an unworthy leader. It was clear that Iridia felt the same way. To Shadea, the obvious solution was to eliminate Grianne and take up the mantle of the Ard Rhys herself.

She and Iridia spent the next five years scheming and gathering allies. They were soon joined by three others who had

Scrye Basin

High up in one of the towers of Paranor, in a room called only "the cold room," rests one of the most powerful tools of Druid magic, the scrye basin. Deceptively simple in appearance when not in use, the scrye basin seems nothing more than a raised stone basin filled with deep green waters. The bottom of the basin is etched with a map of the Four Lands, overlaid by a glowing gridwork. But nothing in Paranor is simple. On closer examination, even a casual observer will see that the lines in the grid pulse gently, as if alive.

The gridwork mirrors the lines of power that crisscross the Four Lands and bind the earth. Insulated by the thick stone walls and high tower around it, the arcane waters within the basin sense and react to any magic used within the land. When powerful magic is released, the waters respond by swirling and the grid glows and pulses, allowing an observer to pinpoint the location and sometimes the relative strength of the magic being used. The vibrations and ripples from a magical event can outlast the event itself by several hours if the magic was powerful enough.

Originally used to find talented individuals for recruitment into the order and to warn of possible danger, the basin is one of the reasons Druids have always appeared all-knowing. It can also be used to spy on the magical activities of other Druids when they are away from Paranor.

Whenever possible, at least one Druid or apprentice is posted in the cold room to monitor the basin. All apprentices are trained to read the scrye waters, and some adepts can use magic to enhance readings that are days old.

Druid scrye basin.

reasons of their own to despise the Ard Rhys. The Dwarf Terek Molt, though stolid, was hungry for power and chafed at the restrictions Grianne imposed—restrictions that he felt prevented him from achieving his destiny. Pyson Wence was a Gnome who bore no resemblance to the superstitious pagans so typical of his Race and wielded his magic with treacherous precision. The third was Traunt Rowan, a Borderman warrior who sought to right the wrong that had allowed the Ilse Witch to become leader of the Druids.

The coup was initially successful. Grianne disappeared, and Shadea a'Ru was appointed acting Ard Rhys. But Shadea soon found that power is more easily gained than held. Her web began to un-ravel as soon as she had completed it. Her own hunger for power blinded her to the fact that she had become a pawn in a demon's game, and had underestimated her opponent. One by one the conspirators fell until only Shadea and Pyson Wence faced the fury of the Ard Rhys when she returned from her otherworldly prison. The Gnome fell to Grianne's deadly wishsong, leaving Shadea alone against Grianne and her defenders the same way she had left Grianne alone in the Forbidding. Shadea a'Ru died that day in the High Tower of Paranor, never knowing she had been used by the dark forces she sought to control, never knowing that her bid for power had almost plunged the world into darkness.

Changing Life in the Four Lands

If the Races are ever to be brought together again, if we ever hope to better the lives of the people of the Four Lands, this war must first be ended. —Grianne Ohmsford, Ard Rhys of the Third Druid Order

*I*n the years since the Federation–Free-born war began, the world known as the Four Lands has expanded into new areas. Explorers have made new discoveries far to the north, while engineers have made new strides in science and technology. Existing cultures have grown and changed. Most of the discoveries and changes were driven by the needs of the war on the Prekkendorran, each side constantly pushing for new weapons and better airships. Most of the battles were confined to the Prekkendorran, but the effects and demands of the war involved the whole of the Four Lands and beyond.

The seeds of the Federation–Free-born war were sown in the previous conflict, during the time of the Shadowen. The ambition of the Federation and the Coalition Council to control all of the Four Lands began with their dark influence. But even after the Shadowen were destroyed, the Federation sustained its determination to regain the lands it had lost.

The Federation– Free-born War

While it began as a simple desire to annex Callahorn to the Southland, the Federation–Free-born conflict became a war pitting unification against independence, and eventually pitted the Elves—as the most powerful and influential members of the Free-born alliance—against the Federation's Coalition Council.

The Elven rulers would accept no less than victory, for a defeat would put the territory-hungry Federation at their doorstep. The war began under the rule of Allardon Elessedil. Allardon wanted an end to the conflict, but saw himself as a bulwark against the Federation tide.

Pied Sanderling, hero of Elven Rock.

When he was killed, his son Kylen took over, determined to smash the Federation. After decades of fighting, the Druid Ard Rhys managed to convince Kylen to consider negotiation, but before this could begin Kylen was killed on the Prekkendorran. His son, the young Kellen Elessedil, blamed the Ard Rhys for his father's death and refused to consider negotiation.

For Kellen, the war became a lifelong obsession to avenge his father. In his last battle, he insisted on taking his sons Kiris and Wencling—fifteen and thirteen—with him, unaware that the Federation had a new and deadly weapon and was luring him into a trap. Believing he had a tactical advantage, Kellen notified his allies of his plans only after his fleet was in the air. He took most of the Elven airfleet into an ambush, and it was decimated by the Federation's new fire launcher.

The war would have ended in bloody defeat for the Free-born at that moment except that Pied Sanderling, former Captain of the Home Guard, managed to cripple the *Dechtera,* the flagship that carried the fire launcher. But the loss of the Elven fleet and much of the Elven royal line forced a retreat. It would have been a rout save for the leadership and courage of Pied Sanderling, who formed up the remains of the Elven line, making a stand in a draw between the twin plateaus of the Prekkendorran. He named the place Elven Rock and announced that there the Elven force would take a stand, becoming a rock against which all enemies would be smashed.

Using a combination of archers and the famed Elven triangle formation, Pied Sanderling's plan worked. The approaching Federation army came through the defile to be ambushed first by archers, then by the battle triangles; finally it was

The Red Cloaks of Callahorn

Often considered the finest single cavalry unit in the Free-born coalition, the Red Cloaks of Callahorn, pride of the Borderlands, are named for their distinctive crimson battle dress. The heavily armored unit is famed for its ability to mow down opponents with lance and sword during a charge. The red of the warriors' cloaks has become an icon that strikes terror into the hearts of any who stand against them.

Built on the heroic tradition of the fabled Border Legion, the Red Cloaks of Callahorn were formed after Callahorn declared its independence from the Federation. The Border Legion was disbanded when the Federation forced the dissolution of the monarchy, but its traditions inspired a new generation. The onset of the Federation–Free-born war provided the incentive to re-create the Legion's old glory. Throughout the years, the Red Cloaks of Callahorn have proven themselves its worthy successor.

trapped by a flanking movement of Pied's reserve forces. The name Sanderling gave to the barren draw became synonymous with Elven perseverance in the face of adversity.

Despite the heavy losses, the Federation regrouped and moved to the west in an attempt to trap the remnants of the Elves while sending the main army to pin the Dwarves and Bordermen still holding the heights. Pied led his Elves to the east through rough and boggy terrain. He managed to reach the rear of the Federation lines and attempted to break through to rejoin the Dwarves and Bordermen. The timely arrival of the Red Cloaks, the horse units of Callahorn, tipped the balance and allowed the Elves to gain the heights, reuniting the Free-born forces once more.

But the combined forces could stand against the Federation only as long as the fire launcher was permanently disabled. Pied Sanderling's last official act was to lead a contingent of his Home Guard behind enemy lines to attack the launcher while it was still grounded. They used tiny one-man flits to attack the shipyard. The attack was successful, if costly, ending

the threat of the fire launcher and evening the balance of power on the battlefield once more.

While the Elves were unable to end the war, handing it off from generation to generation, it was the Federation that pushed to keep it going. During the last decades of fighting, the impetus to continue came largely from one man, Sen Dunsidan, and a series of mysterious allies who sought to control and use him.

A proponent of the war from his youth, Sen Dunsidan was an ambitious man, though he attempted to hide his desires. He rose to become Minister of Defense, a position he held for fifteen years, overseeing the war for the Coalition Council. His first secret alliance was formed with the Ilse Witch. His opponents often died of mysterious causes, though their deaths could never be linked to him. For many years he seemed content to await his chance to rise within the council, even giving the Ilse Witch his finest ship and Rover crew in exchange for her aid.

A short time later, Sen's fortunes suddenly changed. Soon after the death of Allardon Elessedil, the Elf King, the Federation Prime Minister and his chosen

Personal Aircraft, Single-Wings, and Flits

The increased use of airships during the war created a need for smaller personal aircraft. The first of these, a nonpowered folding glider called a single-wing, was designed as a lifeboat for airships. Resembling a large kite, the single-wing makes use of air currents, allowing the pilot to steer and adjust elevation through the use of a steering bar. The wings never saw wide usage because of the impracticality of storing enough for all aboard. The first wing-equipped ships discovered that their crews were usually too preoccupied trying to save the ship to make use of the wings.

Since they can be launched only from elevation, off either an airship or a cliff, they never caught on as pleasure craft, either, though some captains routinely keep a few single-wings folded in compartments in their pontoons—especially if they have family aboard.

A more popular personal craft is the flit, a powered, single-man airship. Unlike the single-wing, flits can be launched from the ground. Fast and maneuverable, they can reach speeds of up to sixty miles per hour, much faster than the fleetest airship. Flits are powered by a single diapson crystal fed by a short mast and one small square sail that can be partially reefed or let out to change direction and thrust. The crystal provides enough power for two hours of flight without the sail. Originally favored by Gnome raiders, they became popular with both sides during the Federation—Free-born war for quick personal transport and surprise raids on enemy installations.

Because of their weight limitations, the tiny ships have very little armor and no attached weaponry, but they're sturdy enough to withstand minor weapons fire. In airborne flit attacks against airships, Gnome raiders used long, edged weapons to damage their target by slicing lines and draws. Though it is not as fragile as a single-wing, the flit's small size and reliance on its wings for additional lift and control make it susceptible to high winds and air currents.

The flit, a one-man airship.

successor also died. These events catapulted Sen Dunsidan into the office of Prime Minister.

The night after the tragic deaths, two hundred men disappeared from Federation prisons and twenty-four ships were stolen from Rovers working for the Feder-

ation. Sen Dunsidan was never quite the same. He became a haunted, ruthless man. He had betrayed the Ilse Witch to make a deal with her mentor, the Morgawr, and had seen that creature's dark magic firsthand.

For the next year, Sen Dunsidan ruled

The Fire Launcher

Desperate to gain a tactical advantage, Federation engineers focused their attention on finding ways to get more power from the diapson crystals that converted light to energy. One engineer, Etan Orek, discovered that a group of carefully balanced diapson crystals could be placed in a series, small to large, in a shielded box. If the balance was perfect, using a pyramid-shaped crystal as the initiating power supply, each group of crystals multiplied the power of the ones before it. The final result, when focused through a tight aperture, was a powerful beam of energy. The greater the light source, the more destructive the beam. Orek mounted the box on a swivel platform that allowed it to swing left and right ninety degrees, and equipped it with a sighting system and recoil springs. After fine-tuning a set of controls that allowed the operator to vary the amount of energy the fire launcher released, it was ready for use on a warship. Instead of finding a way to enhance airship speed, Orek had created a devastating weapon that could shoot a beam of fire over long distances.

Because of the individuality of diapson crystals, each weapon had to be separately crafted by hand. The container had to be built so that each crystal rested in its own shielded chamber. When in use, the shields between the crystals were lifted to allow energy to flow.

The fire launcher promised a quick end to the Federation–Free-born war. But the weapon was never mass-produced. The first prototype was destroyed in an Elven raid; the second, by the Druids. Etan Orek died in a mysterious fire in his lab, which also destroyed the remaining weapons and all his notes. Because of the secrecy of the project, no other engineers knew the secrets that made Orek's fire launcher work.

After the war, the Druids outlawed the use of diapson crystals in weapons systems.

The fire launcher, lightning from the sky.

the Coalition with an iron hand, pressing the engineers for new designs and the Rover shipwrights for better airships. He arranged to have only the best weapons brought down from the Troll forges in the north. But none of these things changed the stalemate on the Prekkendorran.

A little more than a year later, the Ilse Witch returned, claiming to be only Grianne Ohmsford. She sought out Sen—but not to punish him for his betrayal. She was Ard Rhys of the Druids, and she wanted his aid in ending the war. He no longer trusted anyone who held power, however. He was willing to talk, but he wanted her dead.

The means arrived in the hands of two more dangerous allies. The Druid

Iridia Eleri offered him a way to remove the Ilse Witch, now Ard Rhys, for good. He soon allied with Shadea a'Ru, who promised him Druid support against the Free-born.

The Ard Rhys disappeared and Shadea took power, but the promised Druid support did not materialize. Before Sen could press the matter further, the engineer Etan Orek created a new weapon that rendered Druid support unnecessary. For the first time in many years, Sen Dunsidan saw the possibility for victory at hand. With several of Orek's fire launchers, he could not only win the war for the Federation but also dominate the entirety of the Four Lands.

Yet Sen was not done with alliances. Iridia returned, to become his own personal Druid adviser. She was changed, but Sen was too blinded by his own ambition to pay close attention. He never realized that Iridia was dead, and that his alliance was in fact with the Moric, a demon in her skin.

Sen used the new weapon to decimate the Elven fleet. For the first time in more than thirty years, the Federation scored a major victory. The new weapon gave the Federation the ability to decisively burn airships out of the sky without coming within striking range of their weapons.

Unfortunately, Sen's flagship was damaged in the battle, and his weapon was grounded. Iridia pressured him to forget the Prekkendorran and take the battle directly to Arborlon. But he tasted victory.

The day after his ship was repaired, a lightning raid by a dozen Elves on flits left the airfield, and his ship and weapon, a smoldering ruin. Sen immediately ordered replacements for the weapon and a better ship. Iridia pressed again for an attack on the Elven capital, but Sen was

determined to win on the field. The Free-born forces were advancing, and his position on the Council was in jeopardy.

He traveled to Arishaig the next day to meet with his engineer, but while Sen Dunsidan entered the workshop, something else came out wearing a human skin. A few days later the Free-born army managed to overrun the Federation defensive lines, sending the once-invincible Federation army on a retreat deep into the Southland. The Coalition Council recalled the Prime Minister, but Sen Dunsidan was no longer in the Southland to answer.

The war finally ended, not through battle, but through negotiation. The Druid Ard Rhys negotiated an end to the war with the new Prime Minister.

The Expanding Frontier

The expanded use of airships over the last several decades has created unprecedented access to remote areas. Air travel has resulted in new exploration and expanded trade among formerly isolated groups and the rest of the Four Lands. This change has brought increased prosperity to Races such as the Trolls, who can now trade more easily with the Southland, while creating new work for Rovers.

Many Rovers, disillusioned with the war on the Prekkendorran, left it to use their ships to transport passengers and goods. The newest ships, now capable of both air and water travel, allow their captains to take passengers on expeditions into rugged terrain in much the same way that sea captains once took passengers on ocean excursions. While this work is somewhat safer than fighting in the war, these Rovers still face danger from Gnome raiders, dangerous weather, and creatures that lurk in the remote wilderness.

Some, like Bek and Rue Ohmsford,

Rue Meridian Ohmsford, Little Red.

specialize in transporting expeditions into the Eastland. Others choose a more dangerous path, smuggling contraband and secretive passengers for the high fees such runs demand. Those who make these secret runs prefer a new breed of ship, called sloops, which are designed for speed rather than carrying cargo. These sloops make use of a design that is ancient among sailing vessels, but very new for airships.

Unlike most airships, sloops have no pontoons and a very low, flat profile. Carrying only a single mast and spars rigged for a mainsail, foresail, and flying jib, the sail configuration allows the billowing jib to catch a wider swath of ambient light for conversion by the diapson crystals.

One of the fastest of these new sloops, the *Skatelow*, was owned and operated by the Rover captain Gar Hatch. The *Skatelow* had been modified even beyond the basic sloop design, with everything including the pilot box trimmed or recessed into the hull to cut back on drag. Though she was only seventy-two feet long, she was powered by eight diapson crystals, instead of the usual six or seven. The combination of the lack of stabilizing pontoons and the extreme thrust from so many crystals made her difficult for any but an expert pilot to handle.

Based out of Syioned on the banks of

Bek and Rue Ohmsford

After surviving the expedition to Parkasia, Bek Ohmsford and Rue Meridian married and opened an airship business based in Patch Run. With a fleet of two expedition-size airships, Swift Sure and Steady Right, they specialized in transporting expeditions throughout the Eastland. Rue Meridian, also known as Little Red, received much of her training while flying with her older brother, Redden Alt Mer, as a mercenary in the Federation–Free-born war. Those skills were further honed during their expedition to Parkasia. Rue and Redden trained Bek Ohmsford to sail. Together Bek and Rue were responsible for helping to overthrow the renegades within the Druid order and end the threat of the demon invasion.

But it was their son, Penderrin, who used his fledgling sailing skills and magic to journey deep into the wilderness. His skills helped him save his aunt and, ultimately, the world.

Cinnaminson

Though blind from birth, the Rover girl Cinnaminson could see things mortal eyes could not. Her gift allowed her to see beyond the horizon and through deepest darkness, as well as to sense things that could not be seen. As the secret navigator aboard her father's airship, the Skatelow, Cinnaminson used her gift to guide the ship through fog banks, darkness, and storms, enabling him to make runs that no other captain would dare. Her father intended that she serve with him for the rest of her life, but she fell in love with Penderrin Ohmsford during his voyage to the Charnals.

Her ship was attacked by the assassin Aphasia Wye. Cinnaminson alone survived, kept alive and forced to use her gift against her love. Despite Wye's abuse, she found the courage to lead the assassin astray. She was willing to sacrifice herself for Penderrin's safety.

Pen and his band managed to rescue her. She joined Pen's expedition into the Inkrim, using her gift to guide him to the island of the tanequil, where she sacrificed herself once again to assure that Pen would gain the darkwand he needed.

Her sacrifice took her from a life with Pen, but she gained the true sight and freedom she had never known as one of the aeriads that served Mother Tanequil.

the Innisbore, Gar Hatch made his reputation by catering to passengers who needed to travel very fast and very quietly. He was famous for his ability to sail through places no one else dared go, and trusted because he understood how to keep secrets—for the right price. His own secret weapon was his daughter, Cinnaminson, who served as his navigator.

Cinnaminson, blind Rover girl.

The girl was blind from birth, but had the ability to see more clearly with her mind than any sighted person.

This advantage gave Gar Hatch the confidence to accept a contract to fly Ahren and Khyber Elessedil, Tagwen, and Penderrin Ohmsford to the Lazareen, a lake at the foot of the Charnal Mountains. He realized there was something odd about them, but he was never told that they were also attempting to evade a party of Druids and Gnomes. Under the best circumstances it was a long and difficult voyage, but for Hatch, it was also his last.

The city of Anatcherae is the last bastion of civilization against the northern wilderness. Built by Trolls and Bordermen after the Second War of the Races, it began as a ramshackle outpost for trappers. With the advent of airships, however, it grew quickly into a sprawling city of twenty thousand people. While the city still maintains much of its rough-and-tumble frontier character, it has grown into a bustling trade port, servicing all traffic passing along the corridor formed by the Charnal Mountains on the east and the Knife Edge Mountains to the west.

Anatcherae sits perched on the western edge of the legendary Lazareen, a huge inland sea nestled at the foot of the Charnals. Second only to the Rainbow Lake in size, the Lazareen is a dead sea, its slate-gray expanse rarely affected by wind or weather.

Fed by snowmelt from the peaks through dozens of rivers, the Lazareen is as much as three thousand feet deep in places. Sailors who travel the lake insist its waters reach all the way to the nether-world. Swirling mists created by the confluence of cold winds off the mountains and warm air from the water add to the mystery, sometimes reaching for ships like grasping fingers from another plane. Many travelers report that they have seen wraiths in the mist, and that the lake itself is alive.

The Druids say the Lazareen is connected to the netherworld, but unlike smaller bodies of water, its vast expanse becomes a prison for those spirits who cannot find their way through. They are doomed to haunt its surface, punishing sailors with their howls of unearthly pain—howls that drive men mad. Sailors who hear their cries become catatonic, leaving their ships to the mercy of the wind. Many affected ships have crashed, losing all aboard to join the dead trapped in the lake.

Mountains frame the edge of the great lake on the east and south, but the entire northeastern shore is a floodplain comprising miles and miles of wetlands. The Slags, as they are called, are a tangled maze of swamp and quicksand, filled with old-growth cypress and cedar and populated by creatures best left to night-

Ahren Elessedil, Druid and Elven Prince.

mares. Throughout their misty reaches, swamp grass hides pools of quicksand large enough to swallow an entire ship.

Smugglers have been known to use the murky depths as a hiding place, though only those who know the area well dare to risk the dangers of the swamp. Among the vines and trees live creatures whose tentacles mimic those vines, but who prey on anything living that comes within their reach.

It was within the Slags that Ahren Elessedil made his stand against the renegade Druid Terek Molt in an attempt to save Khyber, Penderrin, and Tagwen from capture and death. Ahren tricked Molt so that Khyber could use the Elfstones against him. The renegade and his ship were destroyed in a great conflagration that left scars on the trees still visible years later, but Ahren Elessedil paid with his life. He died to buy time for Penderrin and his company to reach the island of the tanequil. The Elven Prince was cremated on a funeral pyre to assure that his body would not become food for scavengers.

Beyond the Slags, the land lifts into scrub and then forest as it rises into the foothills of the Charnal Mountains. Miles to the north of the hills through the edge of the Charnals is the land of the Rock Trolls.

Once primitive and nomadic, the Rock Trolls of the Charnals have changed over the years. The Ard Rhys of the Druids, Grianne Ohmsford, hastened that change by bringing the Troll people back into the Four Lands as the protectors of Paranor.

Trolls have given up their sod-and-skin buildings for more permanent dwellings of stone. This new permanence has done nothing to alter their nomadic lifestyle, however. Each tribe maintains several different villages, migrating among them as needed. The timing for migrations is decided by the Maturen and the Elders. Some villages may have better forage and hunting areas while others have superior fortifications.

All Troll villages contain concealed forges. While they may travel from one village or city to another, the forges ensure that their trade travels with them. Since the war on the Prekkendorran began, Troll-manufactured weaponry has dominated the field while fine metalware from their smiths dominates the marketplaces. Unlike past wars, the Trolls have not joined either side, preferring to profit from others' madness. Some choose to become mercenaries, but they are usually young and only serve long enough to prove themselves in battle.

While the Trolls have chosen not to join the war, they have not lost their willingness to fight at need, or to defend themselves. Taupo Rough is one of the Troll villages built for defense. Seated on a low bluff against the cliffs on the lower edge of the Charnals, the village is ringed with a defensive wall of stone and protected to the rear by the natural barrier of the cliff wall. Catapults line the inner edge of the defensive wall.

The ever-present forges are built within the mountain to protect and hide them. Ventilation shafts direct the smoke and ash well away from the village area, keeping the air clean and preventing enemies from spotting the forges. The mountain is riddled with tunnels, some natural and some Troll-made, to provide access to the forges and mining areas. The tunnels also provide a well-defended escape route for the entire village in the event of an attack. All tunnels are riddled with traps and falls, and many lead into endless mazes. Provisions enough to feed the entire village for months are stored within the mountain in case of a siege, and several of the tunnels lead to passages through the mountains.

Within the village, each dwelling is warded by heavy ironbound wooden doors and shutters. Most walls have weapons ports cut into them. The approach to the village is protected by hidden channels full of flammable oil that can be set alight with a fire arrow. The streets are designed to confuse anyone unfamiliar with the path.

In each home, Trolls live with their extended family, often with three or more generations. Within the village, existing houses are allocated based on need. Larger families make use of the larger homes, while smaller families use smaller dwellings. If a family grows too large for their dwelling, they trade with another that has lost a member until each one has the house that comes closest to fitting their needs. All homes belong to the tribe as a whole, not to the individuals.

Despite their neutrality, renegade Druids and their Gnome warriors attacked Taupo Rough during the reign of the Usurper Druid. The Druids even brought

Troll Pledge

Whenever Trolls travel into dangerous, unknown territory or prepare for battle, they perform a ritual in which they first kneel in a circle and touch the earth to seek protection from the land they pass through, especially if it is land they might have to fight upon. Then they walk the circle, one by one, touching each member to pledge their lives in support of one another. The pledge includes a promise that they will stand together as brothers if the spirits bless them with protection and guidance.

the Trolls' worst enemy—Mutens. The village was burned and sacked. The Troll defenses held long enough for most of the villagers to escape into the mountains and from there to another safehold. The unprovoked attack, coupled with the earlier dismissal from their service at Paranor, convinced the Trolls to attack Paranor.

Unlike years past, when a Troll army would have been forced to travel by land, Trolls now use airships configured as large, flat transport barges. These barges can reach altitudes of only a few hundred feet and are comparatively slow, but they enable a large force to move much more easily and quickly than ever before.

Beyond Taupo Rough, across the peaks of the Charnals, lies the Klu, the most rugged and barren range within the northern Charnals. Created by a cataclysmic shift in the earth's crust, they jut skyward in jagged broken pinnacles of treacherous, barren rock.

East of the Klu lies the Inkrim, a huge, dark valley more than a hundred miles across. The depths of the valley are choked with old-growth forests and tangled undergrowth. Believed to be older than the Races, the Inkrim probably existed before the Great Wars. The wildlife, protected and unchanged since before the Great Wars ravaged the rest of the world, bears only slight resemblance to counterparts outside the valley.

The Inkrim is also the ancestral home of the Urdas, who have lived within its shadowed reaches since the destruction of the Old World. Their primitive tribal culture thrives within the great forest, hunting the lesser beasts and worshiping those more powerful. For them the depths of the valley are sacred, for they know it is home to spirits and beings as old as Faerie. Some of those spirits sign to those who have the ability to hear.

Stridegate

Toward the center of the valley, where trees old before the Races were born crowd out all else, stand the ruins of a lost city. It was Stridegate, a city grown old before the first Council of Druids was formed. Stridegate's ruins spread for miles over the valley floor. In most places, the outer wall has deteriorated to nothing but a ragged pile of stones. Inside the wall, the remains of palisades, broken façades, and shattered towers give tantalizing hints of the lost glory that was once a thriving city.

To the Urdas, the ruined city is sacred. They guard it against intrusion, attacking any who try to pass within its boundaries. But they will not cross into the ruins themselves, even to pursue intruders. Instead, they gather to form a living barrier beyond the wall, chanting to the spirits of the city as they hold a vigil against the escape of the intruders.

But the Urdas are not superstitious fools. They know the city is not truly dead. Deep within its rubble, hidden be-

The ruined city of Stridegate.

yond a wall that has somehow survived, lies a wondrous garden, untouched by the ravages of time and neglect that have taken their toll on the rest of Stridegate. Flowers of all types and colors spill in riotous brilliance from unbroken rock walls. Water spills from sparkling fountains while streams shimmer past shining marble benches and flowering hedges. Walkways of crushed stone and tile meander among well-tended lawns and flower beds, leading to shrines bright with sculptures and elaborate designs, some inset with precious metals that glimmer in the light.

More than a mile wide, the gardens extend to a broad stone stairway that rises over a hundred feet to end on a grassy knoll. Beyond the knoll, a ravine drops away between the grassy area and a forested pinnacle of rock that forms an island in the air. The pinnacle appears to be about a quarter mile across, completely surrounded by the deep barrier of the ravine. Vines and trees choke the ravine, obscuring the depths in shadow. The only access is via a stone archway connecting the garden to the pinnacle. A bare span of fifty yards in length, the bridge is narrow, only eight feet wide, with no railings on either side to prevent a fall.

The archway is constructed of massive, wedge-shaped stone blocks, each weighing more than two thousand pounds, cut and fitted with the narrow end down in such a precise manner that the weight of the bridge holds the blocks in place with no pins or supports. The seams marking the edges of each block are almost invisible due to the perfection of

Aphasia Wye, Assassin

Born in Dechtera and orphaned at a young age, Aphasia Wye was horribly disfigured in his youth. The scars never faded, leaving his limbs twisted like that of a misshapen spider, and his face and body equally marred. But his mind and soul bore even deeper scars than those on his body.

Aphasia found solace only one way—by killing. For him, killing provided a ritual cleansing. The only time he felt alive and whole was when he was dispensing death, mutilating and eviscerating his victims. Killing became an art form. Alone and friendless, he turned himself into a master assassin. He never failed in making his kill. Those who saw him move, sometimes skittering on all fours across rooftops, compared him to a spider, though never to his face.

Aphasia met Shadea a'Ru when they were both looking for the same deserter. Aphasia got to him first, and there was little left for Shadea. But it was the beginning of a strange friendship that eventually led Aphasia to live with Shadea in Grimpen Ward, then later to become Shadea's assassin once she ascended to the leadership of the Druids. Armed with the legendary stiehl dagger, Aphasia went after Penderrin Ohmsford. An easy task, to kill a young boy. Unfortunately, the boy had protectors: Druids, Rovers, and Trolls. A wild moor cat thwarted one attack, badly injuring the assassin before it died.

When Pen proved a difficult target, Aphasia became obsessed with him, following him to the island of the tanequil, where he found the boy alone and unarmed. But Aphasia forgot the boy's talent for finding protectors. The boy was not truly alone. In the midst of his attack, Khyber Elessedil used her magic to knock the assassin over the edge of a ravine, into the chasm where Mother Tanequil waited. Aphasia Wye died as horribly as he had lived, crushed to death in the embrace of Mother Tanequil's powerful roots.

the placement; stone abutments at each end keep the remaining stones tightly pressed together. Such construction is impossible without the use of great technology or great magic. But the bridge shows none of the age and wear of the city, indicating that it was constructed long after the city was already dead—yet there was no one to build it.

But something guards it. A flat-topped boulder on the garden side warns against crossing the span. Carved with ancient symbols in the Gnomes' language, the boulder's message warns that the place is forbidden. Those who dare cross over will die. The carvings are so worn with age that they are almost obscured, but their meaning is still clear.

The pinnacle island is home to the tanequil, ancient creatures of Faerie. The tanequil send their welcome to a select few via the air spirits known as aeriads. Penderrin and Cinnaminson were allowed to cross over to secure a darkwand from the tanequil, welcomed by the song of the aeriads. The assassin Aphasia Wye was also allowed passage, hunting for Penderrin Ohmsford who had gone before, but the invitation was an illusion that led to his death.

Beyond the bridge, old-growth trees hundreds of feet tall cover the island, their branches intertwined so tightly they shut out the sunlight. Scattered outcroppings of rock jut from between the tree trunks on the pinnacle, while ravines split the forest

The gardens of Stridegate and the island of the tanequil.

floor. Down in the darkness of the ravine, something huge and ancient moves within the shadows. Anyone daring to cross the bridge uninvited ends up in the ravine, crushed and devoured by massive living roots.

The forested pinnacle is a place of magic. Though it appears to be only a quarter mile wide, the distance is an illusion. Those allowed entrance may walk for miles without ever reaching the edge, and the path is ever changing. But deep within the center of the forest, a single ancient tree stands illuminated by the sun, its grandeur dwarfing that of the forest around it as the surrounding trees pull back their branches. Unlike the other trees, its bark is a strange mottled black and gray, its deep green foliage edged in bril-

liant orange. It is the tanequil. Not a tree at all, it is a living, intelligent creature of Faerie. But the thing that moves in the depths of the ravine is also the tanequil.

The entire pinnacle and the massive root system buried below are all part of the same dualistic Faerie creature. The branches above in the light are Father Tanequil, while the roots hidden below are Mother Tanequil. Together they are two entities forming one creature, he of the light, and she of the darkness. Father Tanequil gathers the light with his leaves while Mother Tanequil feeds in the dark. Her roots, ever changing and flexible, extend throughout the ravine and into the garden beyond. It is the magic of the tanequil that tends the garden, keeping it forever beautiful.

Aeriads, Spirits of the Air

Aeriads are immortal spirits of the air with the voice and manner of young women. The tanequil is father and mother to these spirits, who serve as the eyes and ears and sometimes voice of the great Faerie creature. But the aeriads were once human. Each spirit is that of a young woman, lured to the tanequil by the song of the others and convinced to join their dance. Each girl's body now lies in the embrace of Mother Tanequil's nurturing roots, protected and preserved for all time, while her spirit is free to roam the immensity of the Inkrim and its gardens.

It is believed that Mother Tanequil feeds on the spirit energy of her aeriads, her only companions in the darkness, but in exchange they gain freedom from human pain and infirmities, immortality, and the companionship and joy of their sisters.

A branch from Father Tanequil formed the basis for the darkwand that enabled Penderrin Ohmsford to rescue his aunt from the Forbidding. The tanequil formed a special branch from its heartwood for Pen, but required a sacrifice of both body and heart in exchange. Pen paid the price, losing two of his fingers as well as his beloved Cinnaminson.

But Cinnaminson did not die. She joined the aeriads, giving her body into the keeping of Mother Tanequil while gaining immortality, freedom, and the sight she had never known.

The Darkwand

The darkwand was a magic talisman of shining black-and-gray wood, carved with ancient symbols of power that glowed red when activated. Formed from the heartwood of Father Tanequil and carved by Penderrin Ohmsford, the staff was designed for a single purpose—to restore the balance between the world and the Forbidding. That balance was undone when Grianne Ohmsford was exiled and a demon released in her place. Only ancient magic, such as that of the tanequil, could breach the Forbidding and restore the balance.

A darkwand could only be formed as a result of a willing sacrifice from the tanequil, which could only be given as a result of the supplicant's fear for the safety of another. The tanequil formed the wand from its heartwood, deep within, bringing it to the surface and forcibly severing the resulting branch. In exchange, Pen was forced to sacrifice two fingers, blood for sap, flesh for bark, and bones for wood. But for the magic to work, Pen had to understand the true nature of sacrifice, giving up something of his heart as well. He had to lose his true love, Cinnaminson. The tanequil took her as a gift and companion for Mother Tanequil.

Once the staff had been given to him, Pen had to carve the symbols into the wood while blindfolded, activating the magic and binding the darkwand to himself. Only Pen could use the darkwand to travel to the Forbidding and bring Grianne back. Only he could use it to send the demon back into its prison and seal the breach.

The darkwand was alive with the life of the tanequil until its purpose was served, but it was never sentient. Warm to Pen's touch, it was impervious to fire violence and magic; it could respond to his selfless need to save another, reacting in a limited way to protect and guide him.

The Land of the Forbidding

Everything within the Forbidding whispers of death. And yet this world of demons has survived for thousands of years. —Grianne Ohmsford

he Jarka Ruus
Before the dawn of Mankind, the Faerie waged a terrible war that pitted the creatures of the light against those of the darkness, with the fate of the world caught in the balance. The forces of light eventually triumphed over the dark things, banishing them from the world for all eternity beyond an impenetrable barrier known only as the Forbidding, which was warded by the magic-born tree, the Ellcrys. In the Elven tongue, the demons were named the Jarka Ruus, banished people.

The Elves, one of many Races of the Faerie, were charged with maintaining the Forbidding and protecting the Ellcrys. But over time, even the descendants of the Elves forgot about the Jarka Ruus. Five hundred years passed, and the world was given a brutal reminder when the Ellcrys started to fail and the creatures of darkness began to break through the weakened barrier, prompting the War of the Forbidding. The forces of darkness were defeated when the Ellcrys was reborn, reinstating the integrity of the barrier and returning the Jarka Ruus to their prison.

That war gave the world a taste of the dark creatures locked within the Forbidding, but even then no one really knew or

248

The Forbidden Hadeshorn

The world of the Jarka Ruus was based on the world the Faerie inhabited, and the Forbidding remained attached to that world after its creation, as a mirror image of it. As the age of Faerie passed to the age of Men, our world's geography changed and its identical twin in the Forbidding altered alongside it, two worlds being irrevocably linked. Entire civilizations of Men rose and fell until the holocaust of the Great Wars, but within the Forbidding the exiled demons were safe from the unleashed destructive power of Mankind, even while the continental upheaval and shifting the Great Wars produced in our world affected the land's shape in the world of the Jarka Ruus.

understood what the Elves had actually created all those millennia ago. Not even the descendants of the Elves who built it knew what really existed beyond the barrier. Many believed it was simply a kind of limbo world built with Elven magic. Of course, most preferred not to think on it at all.

But the Forbidding is not another world. Because of the records of Grianne and Penderrin Ohmsford, the only two humans ever known to have traveled within it, we now know the Forbidding to be the same world but on another plane of existence. The magical might of the entire ancient Elven nation, which was quite prodigious in that time, combined to open a doorway to a separate plane of existence only half a step removed from our world. The result was an identical, but permanently separate, world. Demonkind had fought for control of the world, so the Elves, in effect, gave them the world, or at least a version of it, while forever sealing them away.

Grianne Ohmsford wrote, "My world has seen Races created out of myth, out of a time when they were real, made new again by the changes wrought in the survivors of the Great Wars. The world of Jarka Ruus has seen its denizens frozen in time, unchanged by the tumultuous wars

that destroyed the Old World, until the myth is reality born of nightmare."

At the time Grianne saw it, the only similarity between the worlds that remained was the basic topography of the land. All the major mountain ranges, plains, and valleys share the same placement as in the world of Men, though they have different names. Everything else was altered. There were no major cities, only occasional villages and fortresses. The land itself appeared sickly and decaying, infected over the millennia by the dark magic leaching into it from the exiled demons. Most plants appeared blighted or twisted as if the soil itself sickened them, the flora as dangerous as the demons themselves at times. Most water sources were fetid and algae-choked. The earth and the sky above were gray and colorless. There was no sunlight, only a heavy, unbroken ceiling of clouds. Night brought only a deepening gloom. The weather rarely changed. It was either overcast or raining. No one knows if the lack of sunlight is a result of the altered plane or of contamination by demonkind's wicked magic.

Grianne wrote, "Nothing of that world suggested that living things were welcome or encouraged."

The inhabitants of the Forbidding still call themselves by the ancient Elven name

Jarka Ruus, but they have changed its meaning from "banished peoples" to "free peoples." They insist that the language they speak has nothing of the hated Elves within it, and that the Jarka Ruus chose to come to the Forbidding to be free from oppression and escape their enemies.

Despite that assertion, the Jarka Ruus enjoy very little freedom, save that granted by the savage anarchy of survival of the fittest. Those within the Forbidding were banished because they were unrepentant and unable to overcome their instincts for killing long enough to function in a civi-

Labels on map: orthland, The Lazareen, Taupo Rough, The Slags, Anatcherae, Stridegate, Tiderace, Eldwist, Razor Mtns., esert, Skull Kingdom, ull Mtn., Malg Swamp, Charnal Mtns., Upper Anar, Ravenshorn Mtns., Malmont, Edge Mtns., Lethe R., Grimpond Toffer Ridge, Graymark, Streleheim Plain, ion, Hearthstone, Olden Moor, Rabb R., Darklin Reach, Silver River, Tennison Pass, Pass of Jade, lley of, henn, Storlock, High Bens, Dun Fee Aran, Paranor, Chard Rush, Kennon, Dragons Teeth, Rabb Plains, Wolfsktaag Mtns., Pass of Noose, Valley of, ermidon R., Shale, yrsis, Varfleet, South Watch, Silver River, Capaal, ake, Rurine Mtns., Culhaven, Cillidellan, Mist Marsh, Leah, Rainbow Lake, Battlemound Lowlands, Wedge, Lower Anar, Lowlands of Clete, dren, Black Oaks Forest, Prekkendorran Heights, Elven Rock, Dechtera, THE WORLD OF SHANNARA, Stern, Wayford

lized manner. That has never changed. Their inability to form civilized, supportive societies guarantees that the Jarka Ruus will remain forever trapped in their primitive way of life. They have never known great civilizations, or great wars. They have never known peace. But whereas the Elves lost most of their magic due to misuse, the Jarka Ruus retained all of their magic in all of its forms, its use necessary to survive the brutality and evil nature of their own kind.

Most of the land is divided into territories, each ruled by the most powerful

Strakens

The most powerful demons within the Forbidding are the witches and warlocks known as Strakens. These creatures not only have the use of magic but are adept shape-shifters as well. The most powerful of the Strakens can appear in whatever shape they wish. Their most common appearance is that of a black-skinned humanoid covered in spiky growths. Taller than a tall human, they can appear even larger when their spikes are raised. The spikes react to emotion, rising or falling to indicate displeasure or interest. When using this appearance, their faces are usually flat and devoid of expression, save for cold blue eyes.

Most Straken do not wear clothing, but they always have an assortment of wicked, edged weapons strapped to their bodies. While they are skilled in the use of weapons, they usually prefer to use intimidation or magic. One of their favorite tools of control is a conjure collar.

While some of the demons in the Forbidding live in villages or colonies, only the Strakens build castles and fortresses. Only the Strakens make servants of lesser demons. Among themselves it is believed that the Strakens are ranked according to their power and the strength of their magic. Powerful Strakens even make servants of other Strakens, sometimes choosing from the strongest members of the opposite sex for breeding purposes to continue their line and expand their territory.

Tael Riverine, Straken Lord of Kraal Reach.

demons, usually witches and warlocks known as Strakens. All who live within a warlock's territory, including any lesser Strakens, owe fealty to the Lord of that territory. While there are no cities, massive fortresses dominate the land, marking the seat of power for the area. Most of the intelligent beings live in small villages or colonies outside the fortresses, but within its realm of influence.

Weaker beings serve the Straken Lord to gain access to its protection. Within the keep it is not unusual to find lesser demons such as Goblins serving as servants, or demonwolves serving as guard dogs and hunting animals, but the most valued servant is usually the "Catcher." It is the Catcher's job to track, locate, and capture any prey the Straken requires. A rank of honor, each Straken Lord has only one Catcher, though he or she can be of any Race. Skilled Trackers are highly valued. Only the best Tracker can be elevated to Catcher. Once elevated, the Catcher lives in the keep and answers only to the Straken Lord.

Ulk Bogs, one of the more intelligent Races of demon, occasionally serve Strakens as Catchers. Like the Gnomes of the world of Man, Ulk Bogs have a primitive tribal culture, living in homes burrowed into the ground. They resemble Spider Gnomes in appearance, small in stature, with monkey-like spindly limbs and hairy, gnarled bodies, but are more advanced culturally. Usually growing to a

Weka Dart, the Ulk Bog

Thrown out of his tribe for eating another tribe's young, Weka Dart faced certain death in the unforgiving land of the Forbidding. The Straken Lord of Kraal Reach, Tael Riverine, recognized Weka's talent as a Tracker and offered him the position of Catcher. Knowing this to be a position of honor, the Ulk Bog took it, aware that the alternative was death in the wild. There were only two ways for an Ulk Bog to survive—within the safety of a large tribe or under the protection of a Straken.

Weka Dart often bragged that he could track and trap almost anything that lived. But he could not always please his master, and found himself replaced by another, a creature named Hobstull.

Once again reduced to surviving on his own, he wandered the land, plotting a way to get his job back. He knew his master was waiting for something, and he was determined to get to it first. He found Grianne Ohmsford shortly after her arrival in his world, and used his skill at lying to convince her that he would aid her, while plotting to deliver her to his former Lord.

When she disrupted his plan but was captured anyway, he decided instead to help her escape. Impressed by Grianne's magic and fueled by his anger with his former Lord, he led Grianne out of her prison on the condition that she must try to help him escape the Forbidding. Using his woodscraft and mimicry to keep them both alive, he delivered her to her nephew and the way home.

Before Grianne could make the attempt to take him out, he disappeared. No one knows if in his loneliness for his own people, Weka Dart decided it was better to live in exile in the land he knew than attempt to reach a land with no other Ulk Bogs in it, or if he really believed he could survive on his own.

The Conjure Collar

One of the tools that has allowed the Strakens to be so successful in their domination of the Jarka Ruus is the conjure collar. Designed to be used on beings with magical abilities, the collar effectively neutralizes a captive's magic. When activated, the collar inflicts blinding, debilitating pain on the wearer at the first hint of magic use. Once locked in place, the conjure collar can only be removed with a special key. Any serious attempt to remove it results in the same punishment.

Strakens primarily use conjure collars to control prisoners and to train pets, though they have been known to use them on one another.

The conjure collar.

maximum height of four feet, Ulk Bogs have elongated limbs and bony protrusions on their bodies. Their skin is dark and leathery beneath a wiry hair-coat, and their teeth are long and sharp.

While they are humanoid and can walk and stand upright, Ulk Bogs prefer to move in a crab-like scurry using all four limbs. They rarely travel in a straight line, scuttling aimlessly back and forth over a given route instead. Gifted with a high metabolism, they do not seem to tire from their inefficient movement. It is possible the wandering motion allows them to detect more scents or food sources.

Most Ulk Bogs eat roots, mushrooms, eggs, and small rodents, but some have been known to go cannibalistic and eat their young. Those that do are usually expelled from the tribe. This is a terrible punishment. Members of the tribe separated from the group's protection do not usually survive long.

Some Ulk Bogs are skilled at weaving and beadwork, while others excel as trackers. They have their own language and can adapt to situations quickly. Some can even mimic the calls of other creatures perfectly. All Ulk Bogs are natural-born

liars. Such an adaptation is not surprising in a small, comparatively weak being. Speaking whatever they believe will help them the most, with no regard for truth, may be a necessary survival trait in a species that shares its world with Strakens.

The most powerful of the Straken Lords is Tael Riverine, Lord of Kraal Reach. His domain, the largest of all the territories, stretches from the Dragon Line in the north to the Quince in the south, and from Huka Flats in the west to Brockenthrog Weir in the east. His fortress stands on the same plateau that the city of Tyrsis occupies in the world of Man. But the Fortress of Kraal Reach is nothing like the city of Tyrsis.

A dark and forbidding structure hewn of stone, the fortress bristles with spikes, firepots, and demons. Multiple walls, magical wards, and murder holes line every path. Demonwolves guard the outer walls, ensuring that any who attempt to enter or leave without permission will not survive to reach their goal. Unlike Tyrsis, there is no mountain behind the plateau. It has worn away over the ages, leaving the keep to stand like a rugged, hard-edged crown above the desolate lands that surround it. But there are tunnels under the plateau, though they are not as numerous as those running under Tyrsis, lacking the extensive sewers and human-made passages that enlarged that network.

It is believed that most of the other Straken Lords deferred to or avoided Tael Riverine, hoping that he would not take their territories in his thirst for dominion. But the Lord of Kraal Reach wanted more. He wanted to conquer the world of Man and become Lord of all.

The separate plane guaranteed an unbreachable barrier between the two worlds—unbreachable except for the gateway guarded by the Ellcrys and her magic. Nothing, it was believed, could break through the dimensional barrier so long as the Ellcrys remained strong. Tael Riverine found a way to alter that equation.

The Straken Lord discovered that, while it was true that none of the beings imprisoned in the Forbidding could cross the barrier back into our world so long as the Ellcrys lived, it was possible to breach the barrier in small ways. Some scholars theorize that he may have used the residue of evil remaining in the Dark Lord's domain to exploit a weakness left over from the time of the War of the Forbidding. Such a weakness would have created an impossibly tiny breach in the barrier, forcing the demon to spend centuries working to enlarge it enough to get information and, eventually, a small vial of demonic magic through the breach. Such a tiny flaw would never be large enough for a being to cross without an immediate response from the Ellcrys, but Tael realized that the magic of the barrier would allow a being to cross over without disturbing the Ellcrys as long as that being was simultaneously exchanged for someone from the

The Moric, Demon Changeling

When the demon Lord Tael Riverine discovered he could send one being into the world of Man, he chose the demon who called himself the Moric. Unlike the Changeling who had breached the Forbidding five hundred years earlier, the Moric was not a shape-shifter. It actually absorbed the essence of its victims, feeding on them and donning their skin. That essence gave the Moric access to their minds. So long as it wore a victim's skin—like clothing—it had access to his or her knowledge and memories. The Moric usually removed the skin when it was not needed, storing it in a bag like old clothes. When it discarded a skin, it lost all the knowledge and memories of that victim, but it had to discard one victim before it could fully feed on another. It was possible for the Moric to eat food, and thereby gain limited sustenance while in a skin, but it rarely chose to do so, preferring the satisfaction of a complete feeding.

A feral creature native to the swamplands within the Forbidding, the Moric preferred to live in swamps and sewers whenever possible, even while in the world of Man. To survive, it had to consume the essence of other living things, but it could go for weeks between feedings. As it absorbed its victim, the Moric's body mass changed to fill out the victim's skin. It often acquired a sallow, slightly emaciated look after a few days. Naturally appearing as an amorphous combination of amphibian and human, it had smooth skin, a sinuous body, and large claws and teeth. Much stronger than a human, the Moric proved almost impervious to physical attack, but it was susceptible to magic.

other side—thus maintaining the balance on each side. He then further reasoned that, once one select demon made it outside the Forbidding, it would be possible for that demon to destroy the Ellcrys and open the barrier for all.

Toward that end, Tael worked for many years to concoct and perfect a dark magic potion that would open a portal and allow the exchange. He also used his tiny peephole into the world of Man to entice and subvert a willing pawn. Had his plan worked, the demons would have been able to cross over and invade the Four Lands and the world beyond. The conquest would probably have been terrible and short. The magic of Faerie, which has all but died out in our world over the millennia, is still strong among the creatures of the Forbidding. The Races of Man would have been hopelessly overmatched.

Creatures of the Dark World

In the Forbidding, magic is simply another weapon, like teeth and claws. Most of the beings within the land are creatures spawned of magic. Power is all that matters, for the law of the land dictates that the strong or cunning survive, while the weak become prey. Almost everything that lives within the land is prey for something else. As in the world of Man, there are levels of intelligence, from humanoid creatures that can think and form societies, such as the warlocks, to the most basic and instinctual killing machines, like the Asphinx. In between are all the creatures humans once believed lived only in myths and legends. Dragons of all types and sizes, Harpies, ogres, Furies, Giants, Goblins, Ulk Bogs, Gormies, kobolds, and

demonwolves roam the land while nightmares such as Graumths and Asphinx slither under it in tunnels and burrows.

Of these, the Furies are arguably the most dangerous, despite the fact that they are not large or strong and have no magical powers of their own. Armed with razor-sharp teeth and claws, these woman–cat hybrids always attack in numbers and will continue the fight until their prey is worn down by their sheer ferocity and numbers.

Graumths, also called cave wyrms, while less numerous than Furies, are equally deadly to any who dare to travel underground. Making its home in caves and tunnels deep underground, the Graumth has been known to travel through shallow tunnels when hungry. A huge, powerful, insect-like worm, the Graumth has a narrow, reticulated body protected with a covering of bony plates and armed with vicious mandibles. It can move with surprising speed on short, spiky legs, using its clawed feet to grab and tear its prey. While Graumths can measure up to fifteen feet tall and twenty feet long, they have the ability to dramatically reduce their size, squeezing themselves through openings a quarter of their normal height and width.

The cave wyrm senses its prey through scent and through vibrations in the earth. Once prey has been located, the creature uses its speed to run it down. A single Graumth has been known to obliterate and consume an entire company of Goblins, leaving only their indigestible armor behind. When on the hunt, they sound like a cross between a huge, huffing steam kettle and an angry bull.

The Graumth's eyes are very sensitive, allowing it to see clearly in the dark. But it can be temporarily blinded if subjected to bright light. Unfortunately, such

Grianne fights to regain her own form after she has turned into a Fury.

tactics usually only make the creature very angry. A blinded Graumth is still very deadly to any within range, and the creature recovers quickly.

Though most are less deadly than the Graumth, dragons are much more numerous and therefore inflict a much higher overall death toll. There are at least fifty different varieties of dragon within the Forbidding, from the smallest Drachas, measuring six to ten feet in length when full grown, to the huge stone dragons, which often resemble small mountains when at rest. The larger ones, such as the stone dragon, have only rudimentary intelligence but can be extremely vicious. The smaller Drachas tend to be more intelligent. The largest of these reach only about twenty feet in length, but it is a mistake to consider a Dracha less dangerous than a dragon because of its diminutive size. While dragons are relentless, and will not break off an attack until they are

either successful or disabled, Drachas often back off when they realize they are overmatched. Known to hunt in packs, they also employ stealth and appear to plan their attacks. Dragons are almost always solitary hunters except when mating. Very few creatures can stand against a pack of Drachas.

The largest population of dragons and Drachas live within the Dragon Line mountain range. Rarer species such as the snow dragon and the fire dragon live in more remote areas with more extreme climates.

While dragons are not magical creatures, they are extremely dangerous. Larger dragons' defenses include not only a formidable arsenal of claws and teeth but also scaly armor over most of their bodies and the ability to breathe fire. Drachas do not breathe fire, but they can spit venom. Most varieties of dragon have wings and the ability to fly, making it easy

Wincies

Although no plants were exiled to the Forbidding, the dark magic leaching off the demons has altered the normal development of all flora. Those that have not sickened have changed and mutated. There are large numbers of carnivorous plants, and many that bear poisoned fruit, as well as those that have protective spines and thorns. The few grasses that survived have become tough and sharp-edged. Algae thrive.

One species—the wincie, a tall, spidery hardwood—developed a thick screen of tightly interlocking branches and emits a strong scent, which repels snakes and other crawling reptiles. This tree's long, thin branches interlock, knotting together so tightly that flying creatures cannot penetrate them. This has made the wincie a preferred refuge for many of the smaller creatures of the land: The tree's adaptation for its own protection now protects others as well.

for them to locate and attack prey on the ground. Some have razor-edged plates along their spines.

All dragons are carnivores, preferring to feed on fresh-killed meat, and all have tough, leathery hides covered by plates of armor-like scales. No being is immune from dragon attack. Even Strakens fall prey to these large killing machines. Dragons make no distinction among prey, though they seem to be especially fond of Harpies.

Dragons are one of the few creatures that can easily kill a Harpy. Looking like a cross between a severe-faced woman and a very large vulture, the Harpy has the face of a woman and the body of a bird. Its face is usually more sharply featured than that of a real woman, with hard bird-like eyes and a jutting, pinched mouth that suggests a beak. Despite the human-like face, Harpies lack the ability to speak, communicating instead in shrieks, calls, and coos. Unlike a human woman, they have venom sacs in their mouths. Their bodies are man-size and covered with dark feathers. Huge hooked talons allow them to grab and slash their prey. A full-grown Harpy may have a wingspan of twenty feet or more.

More intelligent than dragons, they

also use their wings to gain advantage, often working together as a coordinated group to trap and kill their prey. They also squabble among themselves, clawing and spitting venom at one another.

Nesting near regularly traveled pathways, they turn them into feeding grounds, descending upon unwary creatures, blinding them with their venom, and killing them with their sharp talons. When focused on prey, however, they are single-minded to the point that they often become prey themselves. While they can out-think and outfly most dragons, they are easy prey if one catches them on the ground. Too large to escape quickly, they are no match for a dragon's strength.

Much quieter killers, Asphinx prefer to live in almost invisible colonies within rocky soil. The snake-like creatures only react when disturbed, but their reaction is lightning-quick. Anything that blunders into an Asphinx colony is assured a quick if painful death—the bites turn them to stone in minutes.

Asphinx do not seem to feed on anything, though it's been theorized that they may gain sustenance from something in the stone around them. Unlike most other creatures within this dark land, Asphinx

Penderrin Ohmsford uses the darkwand to mesmerize a rock dragon in the Forbidding.

don't actually search for prey. Once something has stumbled into their colony and been turned to stone, they usually relocate the colony to another site. Travelers must be alert for burrows within any large rocky areas. These tiny burrows are the only sign of the deadly snake.

Though this list of creatures comprises some of the deadliest and most interesting, the Forbidding contains too many others to list. There are as many creatures within the land of the Jarka Ruus as ever filled a nightmare, all of them born of dark magic, all of them fighting for survival or dominance. That is their nature.

Rediscovering the Old World

One day it will end and the Word will be destroyed, because the magic of the Void has always been the stronger of the two. The frailties and weaknesses of Mankind are insurmountable. Those same weaknesses are the strengths the Void will exploit to ensure that destruction. —Findo Gask

Until recently, we knew very little about the actual events that occurred during the last centuries of the Old World. But our attempts to gather and catalog knowledge from obscure sources have resulted in the discovery of a number of previously unknown manuscripts, both Elven and human. These documents contain new information about the darkest and least known period of human history: the collapse and destruction of the Old World. These fragile pages are all the more surprising because some of them actually date from the time of the Great Wars and the collapse of the Old World civilization. They make up the only surviving written record of a time when the world was in complete chaos, when almost every living creature was more intent on survival than on preserving information for an uncertain future. Yet these unknown authors somehow found a way to preserve their knowledge in the hope that a future generation might discover it. Though incomplete, the manuscripts provide new insights into the mystery of human survival during those dark times and may give scholars a clearer understanding of the forces that led to the collapse. What follows is an attempt to create a tapestry of the final era of a world that is long since lost to us, a world where the Void fought and won ascendance over the Word, and where human- and Elvenkind alike struggled to survive as the world they knew turned to ruin.

—Khyber Elessedil

The Seeds of Destruction

The struggle between the Word and the Void, good and evil, order and destruction began at the dawn of time and will almost certainly go on until the final end of all things. The Word is the force for life, order, and balance, while the Void is death, chaos, and imbalance. Both seek to control the magic that is the lifeblood of the world. The Word seeks to maintain balance and harmony, the Void to usurp the magic and use it for dominance and destruction.

Throughout most of known history the war has raged, with neither Word nor Void able to gain a clear victory. In the time of Faerie, the Word rose to ascendancy upon the banishment of the demons into the Forbidding. In that time, Elves and creatures of magic joined in the struggle to keep the magic in balance and hold the Void at bay. But humans changed all that. As humans grew in number and began to take over the earth from the creatures of Faerie, the Void saw an opportunity to turn the tide. Unlike the Elves and Faerie creatures, humans were largely blind to the magic around them and unaware of the precarious balance of their world. The Word relied on the strengths of the human heart and will to protect the world, while the Void relied on human frailties, greed, and ignorance to destroy it.

Khyber Elessedil, Elven Princess and Druid.

During the last centuries before the collapse of civilization, only a special few among humankind even knew that magic existed and understood the need to protect the balance. Most believed the world was simply theirs to exploit, an attitude that made them willing pawns for the Void. Those who could have provided guidance, such as the Elves, withdrew into their own hidden enclaves, becoming little more than myth.

Demons of the Void

The Void used this fertile ground to sow the seeds of destruction, seducing souls already twisted with greed and hatred with promises of unlimited power. The Void nurtured their inner darkness until they rotted within, eventually shedding their humanity entirely to become servants of the Void. These disciples of darkness became demons, front-line generals for the Void.

Though not the same as the dark creatures of Faerie locked within the Forbidding, these demons were all the more dangerous because they came from human stock. They still carried the withered husks of their humanity within them, the better to recognize and corrupt others. They were particularly dangerous because they could use their lost humanity to masquerade as Men and walk un-

detected among the population. These demons used their understanding of human weaknesses to spread their poison among willing hosts, gradually growing in number over the years as humanity lost faith with itself and compassion for its world.

The promise of unlimited power and the potential of eternal life proved a powerful inducement. But it was a dangerous promise. To gain such power, demons had to sacrifice everything that made

Findo Gask

Findo Gask may have been the longest-lived demon in human history. Even Gask himself once admitted that he could not remember the century of his turning, much less of his birth. What cannot be disputed is the fact that Findo Gask sowed death, pain, and destruction throughout his life. It was Gask who planned and created slave camps and demon breeding programs during the final days of the Old World. It is speculated that he may have also played a part in inspiring the Spanish Inquisition and the Nazi experimental labs and death camps in previous centuries.

Best known for his "preacher" guise, Gask liked to look frail. As an old man, wearing a wide-brimmed hat dressed all in black and carrying a large black leather book, looking much like a preacher from earlier times, he easily gained access to his victims. In the time before the Great Wars, he was never seen without that special book. Most who saw him believed he clutched a revered religious book. But Gask's only religion was that of the Void. And the large black leather-bound tome was the Book of Names, a talisman of death that magically recorded the names of his victims as they died, allowing him to savor the memory of their deaths.

Unlike most who embraced the Void, Gask did not become a demon for reasons of passion, but because of a driving curiosity. Wickedly brilliant, he liked to experiment—preferably on live subjects. He wanted the unlimited time and power that service to the Void would give him so that he could indulge his curiosity. His cool, calculating mind and his immunity to the passions that drove others were probably responsible for both his success and his lengthy survival. He wanted to know how things worked, what drove humans to the edge, and how they died. Eventually, he wanted to know how to make demons out of children. After years of experimentation and untold thousands of victims, his breeding program proved horrifically successful.

Gask was more than a scientist. As a tactician, he led the armies of once-men and demons that eventually overran the American continent.

Findo Gask was also a ruthless opponent of the Word, earning a reputation for hunting down and killing Knights of the Word.

them human to embrace the Void. Once pledged, they began to shed their human trappings, rotting from within even as their bodies changed around them. Their baser instincts and darkest desires took over, causing their souls to wither and shrink as all that was good within them died. Eventually, their humanity became nothing but a memory, their withered souls reduced to blackened, dried husks. Any passion for life usually turned to a hatred of those still human.

Once its servants were transformed, the Void required only that they survive while following their dark nature. For most, that nature included working toward the complete destruction and eradication of the human race—satisfying their own base desires along the way. Thus would the Void triumph over the Word and demonkind inherit the earth.

Demons are able to take on any form they desire, but they often remain surprisingly connected to their human origins, choosing to appear human. In most cases, demons choose a human form that will allow them to blend in with their intended prey. But some choose that form simply because they cannot totally forsake the very humanity they despise. Some have claimed that they find themselves inexplicably longing for human companionship while being driven at the same time to destroy those humans. This dichotomy, when paired with the demonic inclination to indulge in excess, may be responsible for the tendency of many demons to self-destruct early in their "careers."

For most demons, time is required to build the new body, or shell, that will contain their blackened essence. The process usually begins as the original body starts to rot away. Unlike that original body, the shell is simply a container and disguise; it can be damaged or destroyed without

killing the demon inside. So long as the central essence remains intact, the demon simply discards the ruined shell, goes into hiding for a time—sometimes months—and creates a new one. Such destruction probably causes pain for the demon—though many demons enjoy pain—and certainly creates a hardship by forcing the creature to go to ground while it grows the new body. But the process does not kill. The only way to kill a demon is to destroy the vile blackened husk encased within the body. Too many so-called demon hunters failed to kill their foe because they succeeded in destroying the demon's body but did not notice the winged essence escaping.

For some demons, however, the loss of a shell is simply a minor irritation.

The Ur'droch

The ur'droch was a type of rare demon that lacked a solid form. While most demons adopted human bodies or the forms of fearsome predators, the ur'droch chose to avoid any particular form at all. Existing as an indefinable shadow that could climb or hang on any surface, it could become part of the darkness, waiting to attack unsuspecting prey. A shadow creature shunned even by other demons, the ur'droch preferred a solitary existence, lurking in dark corners or hidden crevices. It never spoke, avoiding contact with others, even other demons. Yet with the ability to sprout teeth or claws at need, the ur'droch was particularly deadly. Its amorphous nature helped to make it virtually indestructible. Since most demons chose their forms based on their human desires or lives, it is difficult to imagine what forces could have driven the human beneath the ur'droch to sink so far from its origins.

These rare shape-shifting demons have the ability to grow a body within moments instead of days or months. They can change form almost at will, becoming anyone or anything. Many of these shape-shifters use this ability to infiltrate sensitive areas without causing suspicion. They simply kill someone who has access and take his or her place. Some of them have been known to remain undiscovered for years. Some may never have been discovered. Shape-shifters often use a separate, more bestial, form when they hunt. The speed of their transformation allows them to explore their desires, often turning themselves into fearsome killing machines dredged from the darkest part of their warped imaginations.

The demonic transformation also brings power and, for most, access to magic. Each demon has different abilities, often dependent on the person each once was. Most develop the ability to warp perceptions and cloud the minds of their victims. Many can kill or wound with a touch. Some can do it with a look. In the centuries immediately preceding the Great Wars, demons focused their efforts on manipulating humanity's own baser instincts, sometimes subtly swaying those already susceptible to suggestion to make damaging choices. After the wars, all attempts at subtlety were abandoned in favor of blatant destruction.

Knights of the Word

The Word, too, chose champions, recruiting warriors strong of heart and soul who were willing to pledge their lives to protect the world and defeat the forces of the Void. These men and women, Knights of the Word, were always fewer in number than the demons. But they made up for this in dedication and valor, each willing to make any sacrifice to protect the balance and keep the demons at bay. Usually chosen from the best and bravest warriors of their day, these Knights were given only one weapon, a magic staff that served as both talisman and weapon. That staff and their own courage were all that stood between them and their enemies.

Unlike demons, who could evolve from once-men or be recruited by other demons, Knights could only be created by the Word at the hands of the Lady who was its voice. Once Knights embraced the

To Become a Knight

Before the Great Wars, the Word summoned its chosen Knights by calling them to Betwys-y-Coed in Wales, to a place called the Fairy Glen. There, those deemed worthy often came upon strange sights. John Ross met a fisherman enjoying the waters of the glen, only to find that this angler was much more than he seemed. A former Knight of the Word, he was Owain Glyndwr, a Welsh Knight dead several hundred years at the time—and John's remote ancestor.

The ceremony always took place at night, the only time the fairies come out. The Lady, always ageless, ethereal, and beautiful beyond human imagining, personally met her Knights, told them of the need, and accepted their service with an embrace.

In later years when the Void held sway, the Lady met her Knights solely in dreams, though she was still accompanied by her trusted fisherman warrior.

The Rune Staff of the Knights of the Word

Knights of the Word are charged with great responsibility and given great magic to accomplish their tasks. The rune staff they carry is both the symbol of their office and the source of their great magic. Appearing at rest to be nothing more than a highly polished black walnut walking stick, the staff is unique to each Knight, answering only the touch of its owner. Once the magic is summoned, the silver runes etched into the staff pulse and glow with power.

Lady, they were bound forever to their charge. Only she could grant release.

Most Knights lived a solitary, nomadic existence, fighting demons by day and haunted by their dreams at night. The dreams were a part of Knighthood. In the centuries before the Fall, Knights lived and fought in two worlds: the present when awake, and the future while they slept. In both, the Knights fought a never-ending battle against the forces of the Void, but in the dreams they were forced to face the future world of their failures. The devastation of that future was both a horrific reminder of the price of failure, and a source of vital information for their

Honor Roll of the Knights of the Word

Throughout history, many Knights have proven themselves in battle for the Word. While all have been worthy, a few have earned a reputation and honor beyond those of their peers.

Owain Glyndwr forsook the needs of his countrymen to serve the Lady, and now has the honor of serving at her right hand for eternity.

John Ross, once crippled for trying to reject the staff, went on to save Nest Freemark from falling prey to demonic influences. He gave his life protecting the gypsy morph from Findo Gask.

Angel Perez overcame her childhood in the broken barrio of Los Angeles to rescue thousands of children and serve as protector to the Elves of Cintra.

Logan Tom saved thousands from imprisonment in slave camps and became the protector of Hawk, the gypsy morph, and his chosen family.

Logan Tom, Knight of the Word.

success in the present. The events they were forced to endure in the future could always be avoided or postponed by actions in the present. Both present and future were real, though the future followed no set time line and could change as events in the present unfolded. Knights often died in their dreams, sometimes more than once.

Unfortunately, there was a price to pay for living in both present and future at once. The magic of the staff worked in Knights' dreams only if it had not been exhausted in the present. If Knights were forced to summon their magic in the present, they'd have to spend an entire night of dreaming in the future without any means of defense. This tended to make Knights very careful about expending magic, as the suffering they endured in the future felt very real, for all that it left no lasting physical effects.

Some faltered under the intense pressure of battling demons night and day. These Knights became potential prizes for the servants of the Void, who immediately sought to turn them to the Void through treachery and deceit. Once turned, Knights

O'olish Amaneh

Shaman, warrior, and prophet, O'olish Amaneh was the last known survivor of the Sinnissippi Indians. Known as Two Bears, Amaneh was born in Springfield, Illinois. One of three children born to the last of the pure-blood Sinnissippi descendants, Two Bears lost his father to drink when he was a young man. His mother died of a broken heart soon after. His brother was killed in a fall from a construction site in New York City, and his sister died from a drug overdose alone on the streets of Chicago, leaving him the last of a forgotten tribe.

Two Bears fought during the Vietnam War as a LURP, serving on long-range reconnaissance patrols deep into enemy territory. A ruthless and skilled fighter, he was credited with many verified enemy kills, and even more rumored. Some say he killed so often that for him the line between life and death became blurred, leaving him able to move back and forth between the worlds of the living and the dead. Some say he died in the jungles of Southeast Asia and that it was his ghost that returned home. What is known is that he returned from the war changed: unafraid of death, but forever altered by its close embrace. After the war, he almost never removed his military jacket and unit patches.

Two Bears became a shaman while serving in Vietnam, claiming that his powers were revealed to him during the war's madness. He used his shamanic powers to connect with the spirits of his people and to help others in need of guidance or knowledge. But his connection to magic extended far beyond his shamanic skills, for O'olish Amaneh also became a servant of the Word. Something more than a Knight, he never bore a staff of his own, though he handled many. Serving as the Lady's emissary and enforcer, O'olish Amaneh placed each new staff in the hands of its Knight, and recovered each staff once its time was done. He also prevented Knights of the Word from giving up their charge or falling to the Void, using deadly force if necessary.

There is no record of Two Bears's death. He was last seen just before the final destruction of the Old World, during the collapse more than 150 years after his birth, still wearing his Vietnam jacket.

of the Word are dangerous opponents, for their magic is just as powerful working for the demons as against them. Only a few Knights have fallen to the lure of the dark, and most of those lived only long enough to regret it.

Most Knights, however, did not falter. They found ways to use what they had gleaned from their dreams of the future to push that future back. For hundreds of years, the Knights succeeded in keeping the demons from taking control of the world, though they never managed to defeat them completely. Then, in the time known as the twentieth century by Old World reckoning, things began to change. Pollution from human factories and machines began to damage the earth. Conflicts that had previously been limited to a single region took on global proportions. And humans, almost certainly aided by demonic machinations, created weapons capable of destroying the planet. The Void slowly gained power as more and more people gave in to their baser natures, becoming fodder for demons.

Of course most people knew nothing of the battle that raged around them, even those drawn into the conflict as victims or pawns. Blind to magic in all but its most extreme applications, they simply went about their lives completely unaware of either demons or Knights. But there were exceptions: people who were born with magic or who came from a culture that had embraced the magic with the old ways.

Certain tribal cultures, like those of American Indians and Tibetan monks, recognized magic and understood the need to protect the world and its wild places. Some individuals even fought for the Word either as or alongside its paladins.

One such tribe, the Sinnissippi Indians, protected a large swath of the land known as Illinois along the Rock River Valley. Their territory included one of the oldest forests in that region, also one of the old sources of earth magic. For centuries, they lived as one with the land and the forest creatures. But in time they, too, lost focus and began to turn away. Despite their dedication to the land and its magic, they fell prey to the ravages of their own flaws, eventually dispersing until nothing was left of the tribe but their name and their dead. The name was reduced to a sign on a city park.

The last surviving member of this lost tribe, O'olish Amaneh, became a servant of the Word. It is only through his words, passed down from those who knew him, that his people are remembered.

Nest Freemark

There were also rare cases of individuals born into magic. This talent was usually hereditary, as in the case of the Freemarks of Hopewell, Illinois. In this family, the ability was passed through the women, though not always in a direct line. The first of the women known to have had the use of magic was Gwendolyn

The Sylvans

Sylvans were a Race of forest creature whose origins date to the time of Faerie. Born in pods, they were usually only six inches tall and looked like animated dolls made of leaves and sticks. Each sylvan spent its life protecting the magical balance of the woodland or wild area into which it was born, usually with the help of an owl assistant. In rare cases, as with the sylvan known as Pick—who protected Sinnissippi Park of Hopewell, Illinois—they had assistance from people or Elves who were also aware of the magic.

Sylvans became extinct during the Great Wars when so many creatures died with the destruction of the world.

The Maentwrog

An old Indian legend tells of the year madness and sorrow found the Sinnissippi. It was the year the maentwrog chose to feed in the Rock River Valley. The creature, a huge mass of powerful sinew and wicked claws, was one of only a handful that had originated thousands of years earlier in the time of Faerie. No one knows why the maentwrog came to the river valley, though some say it must have been sleeping deep in the forest, possibly for hundreds of years, until the smell of the Sinnissippi people awakened it and drew it forth to feed. The creature had an appetite not for flesh and blood, but for souls. It rampaged through the forest and into the villages, preying on humans and animals alike. It did not kill them, though. Rather, it tore their souls out of their bodies while they still lived. It feasted on those souls, leaving their bodies hollow and their minds consumed by madness.

Tribe members sent their best warriors against the beast, knowing it had to be stopped, but they could not kill it. The maentwrog was a ruthless raver, a berserker bent on destruction, but it was not a mindless beast. It hunted with skill and cunning, outwitting and defeating the bravest and strongest warriors. The shamans of the Sinnissippi realized the creature could be stopped only with magic. They also knew they lacked the power to kill it. They would have to find another way.

On a bright moonlit night when the magic was strong, all the medicine men and women gathered their might together in the depth of the ancient forest and wove a trap for the maentwrog. To bring out the creature, one of their own offered it the soul of a shaman. The maentwrog came forth, unable to resist the temptation of such a soul. But before it could devour him, the shaman sacrificed himself to close the trap, sealing the creature inside the living wood of an oak born of earth and blood magic.

For hundreds of years the legend of the white oak passed down through the medicine men and women to their children, and through the sylvans of the forest to one another. But eventually the Sinnissippi and the legend passed from the memory of Man. Only the tree and the monster it held remained, mute testament to the forgotten shaman who gave his life to keep the maentwrog locked away. For many years, only the sylvan guardian and the ghosts of the Sinnissippi knew the truth.

The great white oak died when a demon released the maentwrog with its own blood magic. But the maentwrog did not survive long, falling to the stronger magic of John Ross, Knight of the Word.

Wills, followed by her daughter Caroline Glynn, then Caroline's grandniece Opal Anders, then her niece Evelyn Freemark, Evelyn's daughter Caitlin Freemark, and her daughter Nest Freemark. The gifted Freemark women joined with the local sylvan to protect the ancient forest nearby and keep stable the balance of the magic. It was one of the few cases in the last centuries of the Old World in which humans and forest creatures joined forces to work for the good of the world.

But such talent also tended to bring unwanted attention from the servants of the Void. Some of the Freemark women discovered themselves interacting with demons as the Void sought either to control their magic or to render them ineffective.

The most famous of these women was Nest Freemark, who joined forces with both a sylvan and a Knight of the Word to fight demons. She is credited with giving life and permanent form to the legendary gypsy morph. Named for the wife and mother of Welsh and English kings, Nest was the sixth and last of the talented Freemark women, heir to a tradition of magic and responsibility. But she was also unique in that she carried not only her mother's magic but also that of her father, who was a demon of the Void. Her mother, Caitlin Freemark, died as a result of that demon's treachery. Nest's unusual heritage made her a valuable asset to either Word or Void. She had to choose her path and learn to fight for that choice at the age of fourteen. She was aided in her battle by John Ross, and by Wraith, her guardian demon-hound. But Wraith, though born of demon magic, had been changed by Eve-

The Gypsy Morph

Gypsy morphs are extremely rare magical beings formed of shards of loose, wild magic that come together in the ether. A morph had the potential of becoming a weapon of incredible power. But a morph's wild magic is rare and unstable and can only hold together for a short time—a month at most—before breaking apart again. If the morph can find a form that suits it, it can last longer, taking on at least the life span of the thing or person it becomes. Each morph is unique, its magic like no other. Wild magic, such as morphs are made of, is unpredictable, with the potential to become either good or evil. Unlike most creatures, morphs are not created by the Word, but are a consequence of other creations and energies. A morph comes into being because the world is the way it is, full of various magics and the consequences of using them.

A morph first materializes in a shimmer of lights, a collection of glowing motes. It can be caught only with a magical, gossamer light net designed to be attracted to the morph and close about it on its own, sealing it in. Morphs begin to change immediately after their appearance. Unfortunately, such changes attract demons by affecting power lines in the earth. At first morphs change very rapidly from one thing to the next. After a time, the number and frequency of changes diminish. During this process morphs are self-sustaining, needing no external food or drink.

While demons are drawn to morphs, they can recognize them only when they are actively using their magic. There have been only a handful of occasions in the course of history in which the servants of either the Word or the Void managed to find a way to both capture and unlock the magic of a morph. Stories of gypsy morphs are the stuff of legends whispered in awe.

The last known morph appeared approximately eighty years before the Great Wars. It was captured and protected by John Ross, and eventually unlocked by Nest Freemark. It used its last transformation to become her unborn child. Sometime in adolescence the boy disappeared, only to return decades later as the street child known as Hawk, carrying both the wild magic of the morph and the combined demon–human magic that was Nest Freemark's legacy.

Hawk, unaware that he was either gypsy morph or Nest Freemark's son, became the leader of the Ghosts, a tribe of street children, and shared with them his dream of leading them all to a safe future.

Tatterdemalions

Tatterdemalions are magical creatures having the appearance of waif-like children with unusually large eyes. Largely insubstantial, they are made of air and the coalescing memories and dreams of dead children. They are born fully grown and do not age, but live only a short time. Most tatterdemalions take on the aspects of the children who formed them, becoming something of those youngsters themselves, but they can never achieve real substance. They can access some of the memories of which they are made, but they have no memories of their own.

Tatterdemalions come together mostly by chance, wander about like ghosts, and then fade. It is magic that shapes and binds them for the short time they exist, and when the magic can no longer hold them together, the memories and dreams simply scatter into the wind and the child-like creature dissipates to nothing.

Despite their incredibly fragile and short-lived nature, they are among the few Faerie creatures to survive the unbalancing of magic by the demons. Tatterdemalions usually serve as messengers for the Word, able to travel anywhere in the world on the back of the wind.

Demons cannot hide from a tatterdemalion, who can sense demon-stink, or demon presence, as well as recognize those the demon has touched or claimed. While this is an invaluable ability, it also makes tatterdemalions prime targets for demons. This, combined with their very short life spans and extreme vulnerability, leaves them in a constant state of fear. Yet most are amazingly courageous, often giving their all-too-brief lives to protect others.

lyn Freemark's human magic into something much greater. His dual nature gave him the ability to save Nest from her demon-father once she made her choice to stand on the side of the Word.

Following in her grandmother's footsteps, Nest used her gift to assist the local sylvan in caring for the old-growth forest, one of the last ancient places of magic in the land of America. She was also a gifted athlete, an Olympic champion runner in middle-distance events, setting records that stood for many years. It is not known whether her great talent was simply a natural gift or whether it was related to her inborn magic.

Her greatest accomplishment, however, was in unlocking the secret of the gypsy morph, the being that was the key to salvation for both human and Elven Races. The gypsy morph became her un-born child in its final transformation. She gave birth to the boy it became, creating a legacy of human, demon, and wild magic never previously known to exist.

Even years after her death, Nest's magic continued to protect those she loved. The bones of her left hand became the magic talisman that guided and protected her son in his new incarnation as Hawk.

Unfortunately, people like Nest and her family, who understood the importance of the precarious balance of the world, were too few and the demons in the world too many. Global warming and pollution caused by human carelessness began to change the planet. Animosities among races, religions, and political bodies grew into bitter hatred and finally into open conflict. Eventually, as the world grew more and more hostile, order began to break down and the countries of the world turned against one another in the greatest holocaust since the demons of the Forbidding ran free. Nuclear weapons, biological weapons, poison gas, and all manner of explosives devastated entire continents. Governments failed; famine and disease spread. Technologies of all kinds became useless with the loss of power grids and communications arrays. Satellite systems broke down as the complexes designed to monitor them were destroyed, and the world slid into barbarism and chaos. Eventually the balance tipped in favor of the Void, leaving most of humanity struggling to stay alive as demons led once-men in a bloody rampage across the planet.

The Fall of the Old World

Though I was the last of my people, I was made strong by the fire that tested me, and I was given purpose. —O'olish Amaneh

In the aftermath of the Great Wars, governments collapsed. People either banded together in enclaves or broke into subsistence colonies, militia groups, and tribes of nomadic stragglers. Most of the survivors within the cities gathered in walled compounds, usually inside sports arenas. Left with no official government, each compound developed its own internal rule of law.

The largest, best-fortified of these included the Chicago compound, the Seattle Safeco compound, the many compounds of Los Angeles, and the Tacoma com-pound. Each had its own military and raised its own food in the open areas. All looked with suspicion on anyone or anything from the outside.

Freaks and Mutants

There was good reason for their fear, as the radiation and ecological disasters that had devastated the world did not always kill those who were exposed. Instead of dying, many people simply changed, becoming something different from what they had been. The compound dwellers called these beings Freaks, lumping everyone who appeared different under one damning label. They were also known as Lizards, Croaks, Spiders, and Moles. Once human, they had become the monsters of the time.

The Croaks were the most dangerous. They were zombie-like remnants of human beings who had ingested too much of the poisons and chemicals used in the terrorist attacks and reprisals that followed. Racked by the change in their bodies and shut out of the compounds, the Croaks roamed the streets and waited to die. Unfortunately, they usually didn't. Their pain and near insanity, coupled with their mutations, made them dangerous. The toxins that changed them also meant that even their smallest bite or scratch was poisonous. Of all the so-called Freaks, only Croaks were predatory enough to hunt others while they slept. The mutation damaged their throats, leaving them with deep guttural voices. They were slow and not particularly smart, but enormously strong.

The Moles and Spiders were so named because they tended to live deep underground. The Moles, who lived far below

Hawk, leader of the Ghosts.

the surface, suffered massive changes in bone structure that left them small, squat, and heavy. The Spiders had gone to ground when the bombs fell, surviving by burrowing. They lived on earth, air, and water that should have killed them, but

Street Kids

The devastation of the world led inevitably to orphans who had no adult to speak for them. Since most compounds would not take orphans, these children usually banded together in tribes for survival. It was not unusual for a city to host five to ten different tribes of feral children in its streets, usually surviving off whatever they could scavenge from abandoned warehouses.

One of the most famous tribes was that of the Ghosts, a group of ten children who made their home in underground Seattle. Their motto: "We haunt the ruins of the world our parents destroyed." Their leader, Hawk, was the mortal form of the legendary gypsy morph, though he did not realize this for many years. Unlike many tribal groups, the Ghosts were more than just a tribe. They prided themselves on being a family. The mother figure, Owl, was a cripple bound to a wheelchair. Yet the Ghosts accepted her and valued her when no others would.

The other members of the Ghosts were Fixit, Panther, Bear, Candle, River, Chalk, Sparrow, and Squirrel.

Feeders

Unseen by most except for a flicker in the corner of an eye, feeders are the Void's creation, an enigmatic part of the equation that defines the balance in all things. Feeders are not animal, mineral, or vegetable, but all of them. Neither alive nor dead, they literally feed on people. No one is exempt, no one spared. When madness prevails over reason, when what is darkest and most terrible surfaces, feeders are there. Seen as dark, shadowy shapes by those few who can see them at all, they come out of the shadows to feed on human emotions. The madness of anger, fear, and hate will draw them to feed. Killing is the most powerful form of madness, and provides their best food source. Feeders are only interested in the living, though the passing from life into death offers them the most exquisite and rare banquet of human emotions. They increase and decrease in number and grow stronger or weaker depending on the emotions and behaviors around them. When they feed, they tend to drive their victims to madness. The ancient writers who spoke of the Furies may have been among the few who could see feeders.

Knights of the Word all gain the ability to see feeders when they are given their staff. Those born to the magic, too, usually find feeders visible. Most others cannot see them until the final moments of a particularly bad death.

instead caused mutations that left them small and quick, with bulbous bodies and long limbs. Most suffered mental decay as well, losing the capacity for highly complex thought or expression. They became primitive in nature. The Spiders usually lived in otherwise abandoned buildings, preferring basements or underground tunnels with a dozen entrances and exits. They were able to climb easily, moving smoothly over even rough terrain.

Once the changes began, they were ostracized by everyone, so most banded together in tiny tribal splinter groups. Shy and reclusive, some lived in communities away from other habitation. Since they lacked the teeth and claws of the more dangerous mutants as well as the mental dexterity to use sophisticated weapons, they defended themselves with more archaic implements such as clubs and staffs.

Lizards got their name from the scaly covering that eventually replaced their human skin. The mutation also blunted or erased their human features while giving them increased strength and size. Most Lizards lived out in the open, often hunting in groups. They became very strong and dangerous, though, unlike Croaks, they were not known for being arbitrarily aggressive.

The Once-Men

Demons used the collapse of civilization with its resulting chaos to establish a solid hold on the world. Led by Findo Gask, they began the systematic extermination of the remnants of humanity. But they needed an army to do it. Before the Great Wars, demons were only able to recruit others to their cause in relatively small numbers; most humans were still resistant to their lies. But the devastation of the world made their job much easier. With resources dwindling, the strong began attacking the weak. Many living outside the compounds believed that those inside

The Lightning S-150 Armored Assault Vehicle

The Lightning S-150 AV was designed and constructed during the military buildup preceding the fall of the North American governments. Designed to be completely self-contained, the Lightning provided protection and defense for a crew of one to four people. Michael Poole, leader of one of the most infamous freeman militias, modified the Lightning S-150 to turn it into a formidable support vehicle used during his assaults on slave camps.

The modified Lightning featured state-of-the-art lightweight construction with reinforced composite armor plating that could resist armor-piercing rounds. Front and side windows were composed of bulletproof, heat-resistant, high-temper glass. Large tubeless solid tires set onto a high chassis gave the vehicle superior ground clearance and maneuverability, enabling it to negotiate even difficult terrain.

Designed to hold a maximum of four people, the rear seat doubled as a sleeping area with food storage and preparation compartments set off to the rear. A complete water collection, storage, and purification system—one of the later modifications—provided self-contained survival for its crew for up to one month, though lack of rainfall in later years made this system almost obsolete.

Boasting a top speed of sixty kilometers per hour, the high-efficiency Mercedes engine and standard-transmission power train combined speed with power. Modified to run completely on solar power, the original version of the Lightning was a hybrid, designed to run on a combined variety of fuels. The climate changes that occurred in that last century, with reduced rainfall and cloud cover, made solar the best choice, with almost unlimited sunlight available most of the year.

Defensive systems included a state-of-the-art code-keyed security lock to prevent unauthorized entrance and an electromagnetic grid defense shield. Weapons systems were also equipped with individual security lockouts so that access to the operations console did not ensure access to weaponry. Perimeter alarm sensors effective for up to fifty yards protected the vehicle from stealthy intruders.

The Lightning also carried an impressive arsenal of offensive weaponry. Long-barreled cannons armed with flechette rounds lay recessed within the wide fender housings and could be elevated into firing position in seconds. Four external dart missile launchers could lock on and destroy mobile targets while two cannons fired high-impact BRom charges capable of punching through concrete. Spools of torch wire packed in airtight compartments could be released and unraveled for a precise air-activated, high-intensity burn that could cut through steel and high-grade alloys.

A roof rack provided additional storage and cargo capacity, though, since the rack was a late modification, anything on it was outside the armored protection of the vehicle.

were inherently inferior. Demons found rich ground for recruitment among desperate people who wanted to believe that the strong had a right to destroy the weak. Those willing to give up anything to be among the strong were easily corrupted by demon lies. The demon-led armies of these corrupted people, who were once human, began to swell.

The once-men came from angry, violent people, those most easily swayed into believing the lies. They came from the

Old World Weapons

While most technologies failed or fell into disuse early in the collapse of civilization, weapons technologies of all kinds remained in high demand. Where once only sportsmen, hobbyists, and collectors owned weapons, the breakdown of order made personal weaponry a necessity for survival. These included all manner of projectile weapons as well as more archaic but equally deadly hand-to hand weapons.

Firearms remained the most popular form of protection, though the older jacketed lead or steel bullets fell out of favor as flechette rounds replaced them. Flechettes were razor-edged darts made of steel or other high-grade alloys, usually equipped with fins for stability in flight. Lighter than bullets, they produced less recoil with greater muzzle velocity and, even at smaller calibers, could pierce most of the lightweight Kevlar body armor then used to deflect bullets. Larger flechettes, such as the Armor-Piercing Fin-Stabilized Discarding Sabot round used in 120mm anti-tank guns, were even capable of penetrating reinforced armor and were often more effective than a high-explosive round.

Flechettes could be fired individually, as in the anti-tank round, or packed in mass charges, much like an Old World shotgun cartridge filled with needles. The preferred mass-packed charge was much less accurate, especially at long range, than an Old World rifle or even a single flechette, but the dispersal pattern from massed charges usually created a much larger kill zone at close range. This increased zone gave some flechette weapons, such as the Tyson 33, the capability of neutralizing multiple targets with a single shot. It also required little or no marksmanship skills to operate effectively.

Handheld firearms designed to fire flechette charges became the predominant weapon for urban combat. The most powerful of these was the Tyson 33. Capable of firing several rounds in sequence from an eight-round magazine, it fired a .33-caliber multi-flechette round with enough force to tear a hole through a foot-thick stone wall. The round was filled with multiple razor-edged carbon steel flechettes and, when fired, had a three-meter dispersal pattern capable of taking out several targets simultaneously. This weapon, 990 millimeters in length, had a single thick black alloy-metal barrel and a shoulder stock; it was usually equipped with a leather-wrapped pistol grip.

The Ronin, a smaller, more easily handled flechette, lacked the brute force of the Tyson. It had a lower muzzle velocity and slightly smaller cartridges, but its ten-round magazine and faster rate of fire made it effective in a firefight. The most effective single-shot flechette was the .60-caliber, nicknamed the scattershot. Though it was capable of firing only a single round at a time, that one densely packed razor-edged flechette round could cut a swath up to seven meters wide.

Perhaps the most flexible of the high-powered handheld firearms was the Parkhan Spray. A fully automatic machine gun, capable of firing flechettes, incendiaries, balls, or armor-piercing rounds, the Spray had a firing rate of up to 550 rounds per minute. It was gas-operated, and ammunition could be belt-fed or fed from a magazine.

There were also several handgun versions of the flechette manufactured for personal protection. They varied from the very small precision shot-stealth pistol, with only a single flechette in each round, to the .45-caliber semi-automatic firing massed flechettes at a muzzle velocity of 252 meters per second. Each was easily hidden but wickedly deadly at close range.

But the most stealthy of the personal defense weapons were those using poison. Among these, the most easily concealed was the viper-prick, a poison-packed dart filled with deadly toxins; it came in a protective package that could be easily hidden until needed. Death was not always immediate, but it was certain. For those who did not want to get that close to their target, stinger dart guns provided a particularly deadly alternative. Packed with a virulent neurotoxin, the darts fired from stingers had an effective range of up to ten meters, but most victims were dead long before they could cover that much ground.

A less lethal close-contact weapon was the prod. Particularly popular for crowd control, the prod was a solar-charged electrical staff that could shock even a Lizard unconscious with a touch. Consisting of a 1.5-meter metal bar with electrical contacts at one end and an insulated handle and trigger mechanism at the other, the prod could be set for variable levels of intensity and duration, giving the user the choice of stunning or killing the target. Effective until the charge depleted, the prod could be fired in several short bursts, or the trigger could be locked down for a sustained release. A sustained release at full power was usually lethal, especially if the point of contact was in a vulnerable area. Since it had few moving parts and needed only a few hours' exposure to the sun to recharge, the prod was an invaluable weapon at a time when resources were limited but danger commonplace. A projectile version of the prod, a stun gun, provided lower power but similar protection, and could be fired from a distance of up to fifteen feet. The stun gun's electrodes were connected to the control trigger by wires, requiring both shooter and target to remain connected. For distance without wires, the charged weapon of choice was the less common arrow stunner. Arrow stunners carried a self-contained charge that dissipated into the target on contact.

Of course many low-tech weapons were just as deadly as firearms, poisons, or electrical prods, and most were easier to acquire. Knives such as the classic K-Bar or bowie were essential survival tools.

Some low-tech weapons, like the adzl and the shuriken, were effective only in the hands of a skilled fighter. The adzl was a staff with barbed tips at both ends and a cord-wound grip at the center. It could be thrown like a javelin, wielded like a staff, or used as a stabbing weapon like a pike. Adzls were rare and usually found only among Elves or tribal cultures from remote locations.

The shuriken, or throwing star, originated on the continent of Asia, but proved a valuable and stealthy weapon in the hands of an experienced warrior. Most effective when tipped with poison, throwing stars came in a variety of shapes and sizes. All shuriken had razor-sharp cutting edges, and all were easily concealed.

remnants of broken armies and scattered law enforcement bodies, from failed militias and paramilitary organizations, from a culture of weapons and battle, and from a mind-set of hate and suspicion. But the result was the same for all: Once they embraced the demon propaganda, they quickly succumbed to madness.

Just as with demons, the once-men changed emotionally and psychologically first, then mentally and physically. Layer by layer they shed their human skin, taking on the look and feel of monsters until their humanity was gone. On the outside most still appeared human, though with blank eyes and empty expressions. The change also gave them the ability to survive where humans could not. They no longer needed clean air to breathe or clean water to drink. They did not need good food and were immune to plagues or poisons. Indeed, as once-men they were now part of the poison. And for the most cor-

rupt, the change continued until they became full-fledged demons.

Eventually, the once-men outnumbered the humans. The once-men and the demons systematically began rounding up those who had survived the ecological and military attacks, placing them in slave camps, and exterminating those who did not join.

Initially, the demons and their once-men faced opposition from individual militias and military groups. But over time, they gradually destroyed and defeated most of them. The compounds increased their militias and fortified their arenas, but in the end none could stand against a sustained attack. This left only the few Knights of the Word, who were finally relegated to saving survivors rather than trying to stop what had become an unwinnable war.

Two of the Knights caught in the final struggle to save humanity were Logan Tom and Angel Perez. Logan Tom, a child of the compounds, had been raised as a member of a militia that fought to free captives from the demon slave camps. When the militia was destroyed during an ill-planned attack on the Midline Slave Camp, he eventually became a Knight of the Word. During his service to the Lady, he was given his most important task: to find and protect the boy who had become the Gypsy Morph.

Angel Perez was a daughter of the Los Angeles barrio. As a Knight of the Word, she became legendary for her battles with demons and once-men. A fierce and savvy fighter, she also had the ability to make others see the horrors of the war by looking into her eyes.

When the demon army came to Los Angeles, she realized that the war was lost and the compounds would fall. She set herself the task of saving as many children

Angel Perez, Knight of the Word.

Pancea Rolt Gotrin Cruer

Pancea Rolt Gotrin, Cruer by marriage, was a powerful Elven Queen from a powerful family. Known as a Witch Queen, she commanded powerful magic at a time when the Elves still had the use of their magic. She outlived her husband, succeeding him on the throne and reigning for many years. Even before she took the throne, Pancea witnessed the increasing encroachment of humans on the world as they moved into the wild places and took them for their own. She saw their blindness to the magic and their fear. She decided that Elven magic was too dangerous in a world where superstitious, brutal humans outnumbered Elves. During her lifetime, she hid some of the most powerful Elven magic talismans in remote locations so that they would not be easily discovered. She created the dragon of the ice caves on the summit of Syrring Rise to protect the Loden Elfstone. She decided to protect her people further by ensuring that they would never be able to find these treasures by taking the three blue seeking stones with her to her grave. Her magic stayed within her, even after death.

as possible. She created a special guerrilla force from outcasts, survivalists, and drifters skilled in staying alive to help her protect the children and take them to safety. She rescued well over a thousand children from the Los Angeles area before their compounds fell, placing them in the hands of her people and sending them to safety.

But the Lady had plans for her, and sent her to save the Elves as well.

The Elves

While the humans fell, the Elves remained hidden away in their enclaves, where they had retreated centuries earlier with the rise of humankind. Their main enclave, Arborlon, was hidden deep in the Willamette National Forest, a place the Elves called the Cintra. There, in homes cleverly built into the deep forest amid trails invisible to any but Elven eyes, the Elves fought to keep their lands free from the damage and pollution the humans had created, though many knew it to be a losing battle. They had given up their magic with the advent of Man and had

only their skills with the land and healing abilities with which to hold back the coming danger. Yet most refused to believe the danger could reach them.

The demons planned to let them remain hidden away until they had exterminated all humans. There was even a plan

Kirisin Belloruus.

279

The Dragon of Syrring Rise

At the summit of the mountain humans once called Mount Rainier, and the Elves have always known as Syrring Rise, ice caves hid a secret Elven talisman. Within the deepest of these caves, an ice-covered stone dragon sits in mute splendor. But while his stone cannot move, the magic that constructed him protects his treasure from any but the most worthy. Within the heart of the dragon, at the end of magically enhanced winding tunnels, the Loden Elfstone was protected in a setting of fire for centuries until Kirisin Belloruus braved the dangers to win it free of its hiding place.

to help Elves hide further by using the Loden to lock themselves away from the world. Some among the Elves, led by Kirisin Belloruus—cousin to the reigning King—thought to save their people by searching for the lost blue Elfstones and the Loden Elfstone. They wanted to enable the Elves to seek safety by enclosing the Ellcrys in the Loden. Angel Perez, who didn't even believe in Elves, found them in time to become Kirisin's protector on his quest to save his people.

They were unaware that enclosing the Ellcrys and the Elves in the Loden had the potential to trap them, leaving the world to the ravages of the Void.

Kirisin and his sister, Simralin, under the protection of Angel Perez, became both heroic adventurers and pawns in this game of survival. Their quest from the crypts of the Elven dead to the top of Syrring Rise and the ice caves had the potential to either save or damn the Elven people.

Index

ABOUT THE AUTHORS

TERRY BROOKS is the *New York Times* bestselling author of more than twenty-five books, including the Genesis of Shannara novels *Armageddon's Children, The Elves of Cintra,* and *The Gypsy Morph; The Sword of Shannara;* the Voyage of the Jerle Shannara trilogy: *Ilse Witch, Antrax,* and *Morgawr;* the High Druid of Shannara trilogy: *Jarka Ruus, Tanequil, and Straken;* the nonfiction book *Sometimes the Magic Works: Lessons from a Writing Life;* and the novel based upon the screenplay and story by George Lucas, *Star Wars® Episode I The Phantom Menace.*™ His novels *Running with the Demon* and *A Knight of the Word* were selected by the Rocky Mountain News as two of the best science fiction/fantasy novels of the twentieth century. He lives with his wife, Judine, in the Pacific Northwest.

TERESA PATTERSON is the author (with Robert Jordan) of *The World of Robert Jordan's The Wheel of Time,* as well as various fantasy stories and nonfiction articles. Before becoming a writer she produced science fiction conventions and received her Master Class rating as a fantasy costumer. She lives in Texas.

ABOUT THE ARTISTS

An artist specializing in science fiction/fantasy illustration for more than twenty years, DAVID CHERRY has received many awards and honors and is a past president of the Association of Science Fiction and Fantasy Artists. Cherry is currently a computer graphics artist for Microsoft and lives in Dallas, Texas.

ROB ALEXANDER has spent the past sixteen years working primarily in the publishing and gaming industries. He has published two books: *Welcome to My Worlds*, a collection of his work, and *Drawing and Painting Fantasy Landscapes and Cityscapes*. His work has appeared on numerous book and magazine covers, and he has been an artist for the popular trading-card game Magic: the Gathering since its inception. He lives in Oregon.